MAGE KNIGHT™

Dark
Debts

Dark
Debts

DORANNA DURGIN

BALLANTINE BOOKS • NEW YORK

Mage Knight 2: Dark Debts is a work of fiction. Names, places, and incidents either are products of the author's imagination or are used fictitiously.

A Del Rey® Book
Published by The Random House Ballantine Publishing Group
Copyright © 2003 by WizKids, LLC. All rights reserved.

All rights reserved under International and Pan-American Copyright Conventions. Published in the United States by The Random House Ballantine Publishing Group, a division of Random House, Inc., New York, and simultaneously in Canada by Random House of Canada Limited, Toronto.

Del Rey is a registered trademark and the Del Rey colophon is a trademark of Random House, Inc.

www.delreydigital.com
www.wizkidsgames.com

ISBN 0-345-45969-5

Maps by WizKids, LLC

Manufactured in the United States of America

First Edition: May 2003

OPM 10 9 8 7 6 5 4 3 2 1

For Aunt Barb, who understands the dream,
and Uncle Dick, whom I suspect will appreciate
Kerraii

ACKNOWLEDGMENTS

With thanks to the Usual Suspects at SFF Net for keeping me company and cheering my snippets, Jennifer for alpha reading, Tom for the work space, Lucienne for staying on top of it all, and Janna and Scott for the crash course in the Land. Most of all, thanks to WizKids and Janna for letting me play not only in their universe but for giving me Kerraii to start with.

Friz is for Betsy!

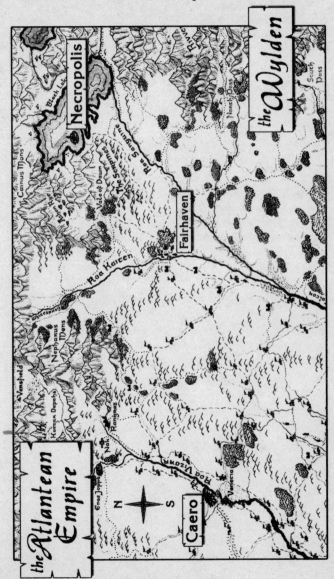

PROLOGUE

412 Tz, SPRING

KERRAII should have known it was coming.

It was too quiet that morning. Not peaceful, just . . . quiet. An eerie quiet that slowly pervaded her senses, persistent and subtle.

No thrushes in the forest undergrowth, rustling in last year's fallen leaves. No kinglets flittering in the lower branches, scolding each other with their tiny voices. No kingbirds in the sky above, swooping after the little hawks that dared to invade their territory.

None of that in the spring Wylden woods, where young Kerraii went in search of early goldenseal. Just a wrongness, with the bright sky full of scudding white clouds and the silence around her as she licked her fingers clean of the honey flake-layer comfit she'd brought with her.

Maybe if she'd realized it sooner, she could have done something to change what came next. But she was young and absorbed in her task, her thoughts lost in anticipation of the evening's impending courtship fete for her sister Willeta. Kerraii had yet to complete the door tabard she'd woven, using wool carefully plucked from the bushes, courtesy of the free-roaming, village-tended sheep: gift of the heart and hand, collected from the land, dyed with herbs chosen not only for their color but for their symbolism and attributes.

A goldenseal infusion sprinkled over the completed tabard would be the finishing touch. Kerraii knelt in the thick, spongy duff of the forest floor, the spicy smell of disturbed ground cover a pleasant tingle in her nose. *One of three* plants she would harvest, leaving the others to flourish and replenish. Later this year she'd be back for the prophet's bell.

Warning came in a rustle of leaf brushing leaf, the kind of noise thrushes should have been making except it came from too high off the ground to have been made by any thrush.

Kerraii froze, drawn from her quiet thoughts. Her keen ears, having failed to attend the not-noise, picked up the wrongness of this one. She froze, long black hair spilling over her shoulder—suddenly, finally, just as alert as she should have been.

The silence held. Kerraii eased to her feet, trying to reconcile her wariness with the fact that within these woods—*safe, home*—she had little to fear. Around her were the generously spaced, high-branched trees of a mature forest, with bushes scattered between and sunlight barely filtering through to dapple the leaf-littered ground. For twenty years she'd run in these woods, knowing every path, spotting every twitch of a whisker beside her. Surely there was nothing.

She caught a sudden glimpse of black and silver, the merest flash of yellow. A new whisper of unfamiliar sound reached her ears. She frowned, feeling the first trickle of real fear before she even understood what she heard.

Suddenly she knew . . . and, just as suddenly, it was too late.

Screaming.

Screaming in the distance, from her village.

For an instant, she only stood there, goldenseal crushed in her clenched hand. And then she ran. Long of leg, sure of foot, she sprinted for the village, thinking *fire* but not smelling it, thinking *tree fall* but knowing the wind was calm. *Raiders,* said a little voice in her head, one with truth in it as she leapt over a cluster of tree roots, whirling to pull a lock of her trailing hair from the grasp of a hazel bush.

Raiders. Oh yes, she ran.

Raiders. She came to a gasping stop at the edge of her village, and saw it was so. The screaming, the running, the bloodshed—strangers stirred chaos and death in her village, Elves dressed as she'd never seen before. Bright armor covered their sweeping black tunics; weapons flashed in their hands. And worse. One warrior, lightly armored over his black tunic and pants, bent strangely over a villager. The villager was no more than an unidentifiable pair of legs and lower torso from Kerraii's vantage point; he kicked and struggled, then went limp. The Elf turned and straightened with a manic gleam in his eye and blood dripping from his mouth and off his chin, looking oddly refreshed and invigorated. The other raiders wreaked havoc among her people, herding them, prodding them . . . killing them.

Kerraii clung to a tree, too stunned to move and helpless to stop the attack. The village spread before her, its main longhouse built among the trees in a sweeping curve of combined households. Living trees provided its form and guided its design; each generation had improved it, adding touches of subtle beauty, integrating the longhouse more completely with its surroundings. It was meant to last forever.

With the screech of wood torn asunder, the end of the longhouse crumbled before her eyes.

Kerraii's fingers clenched the smooth bark of the ironwood tree beside her; horror gripped her so hard it turned to disbelief. *It isn't happening. It* can't *be.* Elves in black and silver harrying her people, hulking green creatures in brown leather armor charging out from behind the collapsing longhouse. *It can't be.*

The black-clad Elves shoved her people toward the center of the village, trampling the carefully tended plantings.

Kerraii saw her mother and cried out, a protest lost in the noise of the assault. Black-clad Elves . . . dark Elves, she realized suddenly. Necropolis Elves.

Another dark Elf flung her younger brother Oaklen into the knot of people forming before the longhouse; Oaklen fetched up against the shins of one of the hulking green creatures. *A Zombie.* It showed him no mercy for all that he was only ten years old. Instead it slapped him away, leaving a trail of blood down her Oaklen's face.

She began to understand. The villagers were being rounded up, snatched from their daily tasks and their peaceful lives. Shoved and sorted into groups. Elders apart from younglings, those in their prime apart from them all—confirming her worst fears, the ones she hadn't even yet allowed herself to consider, the ones about which no one ever talked yet about which everyone knew.

Slave raid.

And with that she finally began to think again, to consider her options. She was swift and graceful; even strong. But she was not trained for other than her husbandry of the land. Certainly she was not trained to the defense of her people. She had only a small harvesting knife at her belt.

Yet she could not run.

As she hesitated, her body taut with the promise of action, Oaklen broke away from the growing huddle of battered villagers. Always a rowdy child, always a gleam of interest or intent or even mischief in his eye—the villagers likened him to Kerraii when she'd been young and untamed—he now betrayed them both simply by being the one person among them all, enemy or friend, to spot Kerraii. He broke away and ran for her, taking no notice of the sickly green hulk behind him.

But the bare-fisted Zombie saw her brother well enough. Graceless and lurching, it nonetheless quickly gained ground on him, coming in from an angle.

Kerraii grabbed her little knife and poised to throw herself at the creature.

Hands clamped down on her arms, crushing them against her body in a cruel and painful grip. Her knife fell from numbed fingers; from her other hand, finally, fell the crushed goldenseal.

"Now that," a sinister voice hissed in her ear, "would be a waste of good material."

Kerraii jerked against the grip, more terrified for Oaklen than for herself; just in those few words, in the possessive tone of her assailant's voice, in the way he crushed her arms to her body to restrain her without badly damaging her, she understood that she was his prize, not his victim.

But the abhorrent Zombie behind her brother had no cunning in its expression, no ability to discern value. It wanted only to stop him and as it latched on to his arm, Kerraii broke her silence with a full-throated scream, struggling futilely in the painful grip of her captor. She succeeded only in bruising her elbows against the high relief of the man's metal chest armor—and in drawing the attention of her huddled friends and family. Until now they'd seen neither her brother's escape nor her own presence, but now they reacted in horror, crying out to her, making aborted attempts to reach Oaklen. Another Zombie slapped down her sister's intended lifemate even as the Zombie holding Oaklen dealt him a few harsh, crunching blows from a meaty fist.

Oaklen's head snapped back; his body went limp. The Zombie shook him a few times for good measure and tossed him carelessly back toward the group. Oaklen bounced a few times and came to a sprawling stop, his neck at such an unnatural angle that Kerraii instantly realized he was dead.

Willeta had just enough freedom to throw herself down on him, to extend a hand out to Kerraii, tears coursing down her cheeks. And Kerraii reached back with everything that was in her. By the Land, she reached out, throwing her heart, throwing her love and grief, but not moving an inch within her captor's grip.

"Kerraii!" Willeta cried.

And Kerraii hung trembling in the man's grip, her muscles and mind untrained for fighting, her will battered by the sights and sounds of the raid, waiting for a better moment.

"You'll not be with them anymore. Not ever," the man said—still behind her, still unseen other than the glimpses she'd gotten of black and silver and even a little yellow, just like those glimpses in the woods by the goldenseal. This one was more than just a soldier. He was quieter, swifter, stronger. For all he spoke to her in the Wylden tongue, he was no Wylden Elf. *Dark Elf.* One hand released her, instantly twining into the long black hair at the back of her neck, pulling hard, but with significance. "Black hair, black eyes . . . You'll earn me favor with Sarnen." Then he gave her a little shake. "Unless you cause too much trouble. Then he'll never have the chance to admire your beauty. I'll kill you myself and leave you by the side of the road for the 'spawn to nibble in our wake. Do you understand that?" His voice came like thick, clotted cream, far too close to her ear.

For a moment, Kerraii's mind raced. She thought of escape and she thought desperately of returning to her family, to share their fate.

He gave her another little shake. "Do you understand?"

Kerraii hesitated. Then she said, at first whispering but then with growing strength, "Yes. I'll do as you say." *For now.*

But as he shoved her away from her sister, her family, her village, she had a sudden dire fear that it might take a very long time for *now* to become *no more.*

CHAPTER 1

420 Tz

THE dank odor of damp stone and old straw filled the room, familiar and stinging. Like all of Necropolis, this room held the stink of untold years of death magic, of power bought by the suffering of innocent and tortured souls, of blood spilled, life debased, and foul treachery revered and rewarded.

Kerraii stared impassively at the sorry collection of Elves and humans before her; they stared back with no apparent understanding of her control over their fates.

This lower room was one of many carved out of the rocky island that held Necropolis. It resided in Sarnen's tower, a building identical to the eleven others ringing the more impressive Prophet's tower. Twelve towers for the Death-speaker Orders and another for the Dark Prophet, the bone avatar that contained the essence of the Grand Magus Tezla, father of them all. Thirteen towers, connected by complex tunnels—some of them public and some of them most decidedly not. Above ground, sky bridges connected the twelve Order buildings to one another and to the other major buildings of Necropolis; the rest of the city was a vast maze of edifices, streets, and secretive, walled courtyards that stank of blood and corruption. But here in the lower levels of Sarnen's

Order, Kerraii faced this tightly packed chamber of used up slaves and contemplated their fate.

It was a fate already decided. These slaves were old, or simply too weak to be of any further use. From child to elder, they no longer served her Lord Sarnen as they should. And they offended her nose with their rank fear and unwashed bodies.

Not for much longer.

Those still showing a spark of intelligence and life regarded her with wary understanding. They knew what she was—a Nightblade, blooded and trained and battle proven, bearing blade and specialized strap harness, her sleek black hair pulled back into a tight, stern ponytail that merely served to emphasize her stunning, refined Elvish features. Nightblades. Assassins. The ultimate in cold death and beauty combined. If the Nightblade style also provided a subtle visual reminder of the stern and unquestioning loyalty expected of her and her sister Nightblades, such thoughts remained unspoken among those who served Sarnen.

As Kerraii served him. Kerraii, Deathspeaker Sarnen's own. His mistress, his most trusted Nightblade, an ex-Wylden Elf who'd moved on to new ways.

Those who resented her position and the relative security it lent her often looked for ways to annoy her, to debase her—like the Death Merchant Skulk, who'd found a way to assign her this menial duty. Skulk's vindictive hatred had been a part of Kerraii's life since her arrival in the dark city, when she'd supplanted him at Sarnen's side. Skulk had never been anything more than a momentary pet project to the Deathspeaker, a human in Dark Sect ranks . . . and he'd never been able to accept the temporary nature of that role. Instead he turned his hatred and revenge on Kerraii. She'd long ago learned to expect it.

Now she forced a bored note into her voice; her gaze skipped over the miserable slaves, never settling long in one place, or on one face. "You have served what purpose you can in your present state," she told them, using the Atlantean tongue she'd learned upon coming to this place eight years earlier. They all knew it; the humans had come here knowing it and the Elves learned it to survive, as had she. Even after all this time of interacting with humans on a daily basis, they still looked short to her—short and stout, though some much more than others. Now no one here carried enough flesh to be called *stout*.

Not anymore.

"It is time to move on. In this you have no choice, but you do have the ability to affect the nature of your continuing service."

They exchanged fearful glances at that. They understood perfectly that such choices were never between anything but the lesser of two evils. But they voiced no question or protest. That, too, they had learned. On this day, Zombie guards stood by both of the chamber's exits, filling the doorways with their bulk and their faint, pervasive odor. Their simple-minded efficiency and unquestioning loyalty made them frighteningly effective guards; in this case Kerraii used them mostly for show. Should this entire chamber full of pathetic slaves choose to revolt, she could easily handle them on her own. Geared up in her battle harness of strategically aligned leather strapping, she was ready for it.

She was Sarnen's chosen.

"From here," she told them, standing as lightly poised for action as she ever was, "you will go to the pits. And in the pits you will die." She paused to let it sink in, if there were any left who could even comprehend or care.

In the middle of them all, an Elvish head lifted. Dark brown hair, lank and dirty as was the norm. Eye color hidden by the shadows of the torch- and candle-lit room. Perhaps there was an unusual spark of awareness behind the old claw wounds scarring her face. She reminded Kerraii of . . .

something. Of things she might once have known but had discarded along the way.

Kerraii met the Elf's gaze with a cold, black-eyed look and judged she'd given them all long enough. "It is your fate to serve as baiting partners for blood-pit trainees and champion warm-up exercises." Kerraii knew those pits. The blood, the screams, the stench of horrible, agonizing death. In those pits, the Dark Sect Elves earned their notoriety and clawed their way up the ranks of Necropolis. The pits held no mercy, no quarter, and the promise of gruesome demise for any who were not quick enough, clever enough . . . or cruel enough.

The slaves knew those pits as well. Many of them had hauled away the horribly mangled bodies it produced.

Kerraii watched her words sink through to them and added, "The choice you make is this. Fight well and provide a challenge for your opponent, and a Necromancer will immediately return you to life, essentially intact—including your spirit. Provide a poor showing, and several hours will pass before your body is brought back to be inhabited by a random spirit, turning your body into a dumb shell, a Zombie. Your existence will be an endless tragedy."

Kerraii paused then, glancing meaningfully over her shoulder where a shuffling female Zombie entered the room to attend her one and only chore: trimming candlewicks. She was one of several Zombies who made the endless rounds of Sarnen's tower rooms, snuffing out candles, pinching off the wicks so the candles would burn clean and long, and relighting them. Layers of wax covered her fingers, dripping down her hands and along her ragged sleeves; soot marked her hands and shift. Her bare feet walked cold stone floors, picking up stains and dirt. Her feet had gone unwashed for so long that the filth crept up her ankles and shins. This mindless chore would be hers until some accident befell her, or until she shuffled in front of the wrong person at the wrong time and earned a final death.

Her presence here was hardly a coincidence. Where Kerraii's words meant little to a wrung out batch of slaves accustomed to misery and threats, the sight of the Zombie woman caught their attention. They were used to Zombie guards, big and hulking and barely human; they barely truly looked at them anymore. But they could easily see what Kerraii saw in this Zombie woman—that she had been young and pretty and had a mouth meant for smiling. Kerraii gave her own little smile, but it had a dry and bitter edge.

She turned back to the slaves and found that same scarred Elvish woman watching her. While the others reacted with moans of fear and despair and useless expressions of determination—all things Kerraii was used to seeing, and all of which would do them no good whatsoever—this woman's face remained calm. Calm, and touched by . . .

Was that pity?

Startled, Kerraii looked back long enough to be sure. *Yes. Pity.* In an instant fury flashed through her. She was Kerraii of the Sect Elves, and she'd risen to her status in record time. She was favored of Sarnen, superbly trained and tutored, and had as much security as anyone in this city—enough to raise the envy that had spurred Skulk to maneuver her into this job. She needed no one's pity.

But through her fury—a fury she allowed to show nowhere but in her black eyes—she understood. The pity was for the very thing she was now forced to do, to send these miserable people from their sorry lot to a fate literally worse than death.

Her thoughts were interrupted by a scuff of sound in the corridor. The Elf woman heard it too; Kerraii saw it in her eyes as they broke contact, impressed despite herself that the woman was so alert. The others were as expected, far too immersed in their own fate to heed such subtle clues.

Kerraii turned an annoyed look toward the entrance as the Zombie guard moved aside. Not much to her surprise at all, Skulk came into view at the door, cloaked and cowled and shadowed to hide his features, as if his short stature weren't enough to reveal his human nature. Here within the Ring of Towers, he usually kept a modest pose—but as one of very few humans to have advanced so far in the Necropolis meritocracy, in the city and countryside he did not fail to present himself in the hard-earned bone helm and armor he'd earned.

Unless he was trying to bully Kerraii.

"Why are these slaves not processed yet?" he demanded, gesturing forward the Seething Knight who had escorted him here. The knight eyed Kerraii, assessing her. Skulk said, "Is there a reason for the delay?"

Kerraii was more interested in the third figure lurking behind him, the one attired in simpler robes and a respectful posture. She did not rise to Skulk's verbal prod. "Merely assuring they are properly motivated before they go to the pits," she said, using the language of the Sect Elves for privacy . . . and because she knew he preferred Atlantean.

"A waste of time," he said. "The important thing is not how they perform, but what use we can make of them. The pits await sparring partners, and I have eager students prepared to practice necromantic arts. You waste their time."

Kerraii gave the lurking figure a sharp glance, suddenly understanding. A Sect Elf Grave Digger, just now learning his skills. Clever of Skulk, indeed . . . the chance to display dominance over her, and the opportunity to deal with these slaves outside the usual pattern, leaving himself as the only one who knew of their scheduling, and therefore with the opportunity to turn his favored sycophants loose to practice on the pit-killed slaves.

And also ensuring that no matter how much spirit the slaves showed against their pit partners, they had no chance of becoming anything but the basest of Zombies. These apprentices could not work quickly or skillfully enough to restore anyone's spirit to their own body. Not in time.

Kerraii told herself that she cared not about the fate of the slaves. But she was not pleased to be used by this human Death Merchant for such a cleanly pierced ruse. It showed no respect for her master. If she allowed it to happen, Sarnen would lose status in the meritocracy. Sarnen—one of the original founders of the Dark Sect, one of the few remaining who had been in Atlantis when Tezla lived—would be made a joke by this human pretending to be a Necromancer.

He would rightly blame Kerraii.

"I understand," she told Skulk, inclining her head slightly. In fact, she understood perfectly. With deliberate obscurity, she added, "I will hasten the processing."

"Enough time has been wasted. This knight will escort them to the pits immediately."

"What makes you think so?" she asked, cocking her head as if in genuine curiosity. The knight stiffened. Where Kerraii wore a simple harness of leather strapping tailored to fit her elegant body and spelled to repel blades, the knight wore an armor chestplate over his black tunic, greaves on his legs and vambraces over his arms. Her attire allowed her to move swiftly, silently and decisively; his merely protected him from poorly aimed blows. Her sword was light and keen and nimble; his was a chunk of metal meant for hacking. She'd witnessed just that when the company of Necropolis Seething Knights had taken her village.

At first glance, it might seem as though the knight had the advantage. But Kerraii knew better.

Skulk reacted to her question almost eagerly. *He planned this. He hoped for this.* Kerraii saw it on his face, the way his eyes widened as any human's in the Vurgra Divide would when catching a glimpse of a Deathspeaker. Delight. In this case, meant to be secret, but not. Skulk said, "These are my orders. If you see fit to resist them, I am not responsible for the consequences."

Kerraii smiled inside. She gave him her most black velvet tones in reply. "My own orders came from my Lord Sarnen, that I should assist you in this fashion. Those are the orders I follow, as they were given."

Skulk shrugged in the most insincere way and flicked negligent fingers at the slaves. They cowered, well aware they were under discussion, and of the hostility hidden beneath the casual tones of a conversation they couldn't understand. Skulk said to the knight, "Take them. Eliminate any resistance you encounter. I trust that is clear enough."

"Perfectly clear," said the knight, his voice gravely and entirely lacking in subtlety of tone. He disregarded the Zombies, knowing they had been set to guard the chamber and would not take the initiative to respond to the changing situation. He drew his sword and in loud, poor Atlantean demanded of the slaves, "You will come with me!"

They immediately glanced at Kerraii, as if she represented their safety as opposed to their fate—when in fact she represented nothing other than Sarnen. She did not yet draw her blade; she allowed faint amusement to show as she asked the knight, "Was your most recent meal good enough to be your last?"

He puzzled out the threat, scowled at her, and moved in toward the slaves, causing a rippled reaction of retreat toward the second doorway.

Kerraii drew her sword, placing herself between the slaves and the knight. She pricked him in half a dozen places while he was still jerking his sword into a sloppy initial guard: his inner elbow, his stomach, his thigh, his neck. Small blood spots bloomed in quick succession, and then she'd moved back and out of his range. "Were you never warned about letting a Nightblade make the first close strike?" She arched an eyebrow at Skulk. "You chose the wrong tool, Death Merchant Skulk. I can wait here while you go choose another—although it does seem like the delay would simply *waste time.*"

Skulk hesitated, quite clearly on the verge of commanding the shocked knight to pursue the fight. But as his gaze flicked between the knight's bloodstained and shaken appearance to Kerraii's composed demeanor, his expression turned hard. He drew himself up and turned away with a dramatic swishing of robe and cowl, his sycophant close at heel, the somewhat befuddled knight hastily bringing up the rear.

Kerraii looked back over the huddled slaves. Most of them could not possibly have understood the conversation or the confrontation, but all of them knew it boded ill for them. The Elf woman's disfigured face showed alarm, as well as the remaining traces of pity and gratitude.

Kerraii didn't need the woman's pity; she didn't intend to be used as Skulk's pawn, not when the ploy showed such disrespect for Sarnen, and when the ramifications would affect her own security. She turned to the Zombies and said shortly, "Take them behind the lakeshore pit rings and kill them all." She ignored the gasps from the slaves, the sounds of exhausted weeping. "Make sure they won't be found for several hours. If you are asked, you will reply only that you took them to the pits."

Too long dead to be returned to life at all. And too late for Skulk to interfere.

Also the very kindest thing she could do for this miserable lot.

The Zombies, loyal to their current orders, not creative or clever enough to consider the contradictions in what they'd heard here, nodded understanding and immediately moved to do her bidding. Such was the slaves' revulsion that even in their final despair, long-ingrained reactions spurred them to shuffle out of the room ahead of the Zombies.

The drab and tattered Wylden Elf made up their center, their strength, her arms around two of them, her hands clutched by others. As Kerraii watched—arms crossed against the cool, slick leather straps of her harness, her stance poised and unaffected—the Wylden Elf looked back over her shoulder, found Kerraii's hard gaze. Unintimidated by it, she spoke the Wylden words for thank you, clearly understanding that they had been spared a worse fate with Skulk's fumbling, unskilled Necromancers.

Kerraii hesitated, then offered the merest lift of her refined chin. Let the woman believe that mercy had something to do with her decision, if it comforted her.

Kerraii knew no such thing as mercy lived on in her soul.

CHAPTER 2

420 Tz

KERRAII left the lower chamber of Sarnen's tower, climbing a series of twisting steps while she turned her attention back to the orders Sarnen had given her as she'd left his most private room to deal with the disposal of the slaves. "Return immediately," he'd told her. "We have things to discuss, and I am in the mood to savor them." *Things to discuss. The Dark Crusade?*

The Vampire Lords exchanged whispered guesses about the meaning of the recently intensified training and war games among the Orders, but as Sarnen's chosen, Kerraii knew the truth behind it all. She knew that Necropolis prepared for the launch of the Dark Crusade. Directed by Tezla himself through the Dark Prophet, the Landwide campaign would remind Atlantis and the Elementalists that the Sect Elves were a force to be feared.

The Dark Crusade. Kerraii's heart gave a few extra thumps at the thought. She took the fast route to Sarnen's quarters, the unlit stairs that by their very nature limited their use to those favored Elves who had earned enhancement of their vision: *Dark Elves,* not because they were chosen for their sleek, dark beauty or because they worked with what many called the dark arts, but simply because so many of them could see without light.

Sarnen's chambers filled the top of the tower; several floors were given over to his personal and administrative use. The top floor itself had been especially designed to his specifications, with a centrally sunken minipit that echoed the structure of a blood pit. Circling the sand-strewn pit were two tiers of seating, constructed of polished blackstone—an outrageously expensive import from the Scythrian mountains made of swirling shades of black and gray and shot through with astonishing silver veins—and left bare of other adornment. Evenly spaced incense braziers climbed the tiers to divide the seating into personal areas just big enough for two.

Kerraii found Sarnen there, seemingly engrossed in the spectacle he'd arranged for his diversion. She knew better than to assume he remained unaware of her presence, even though she'd soundlessly entered through the curtained doorway, passing between plush velvet drapes of the deepest red with the assurance only a few could claim.

Sarnen sat at the pit, watching the action within the low walls; a Feral Bloodsucker played with an unfortunate whom Sarnen had plucked from the ranks of those who displeased him. Brazier smoke twined toward the ceiling, collecting there in a faint haze. Sarnen himself was robed and cowled; unlike many Necromancers, he'd gained immortality late in his lifetime . . . and long before the technique was perfected.

Kerraii waited.

The Bloodsucker stalked its victim with evident pleasure. Manlike from this distance and angle, it was in truth anything but. It carried a misshapen head atop its muscular body, one elongated by bony protrusions. It peered at the world from beady black eyes, and sprang from spot to spot on goatlike lower legs with huge, three-toed hooves that could disembowel almost anything with one sweeping attack. All the same it moved with a peculiar grace, and when it lifted or stretched its wings to intimidate or block the human scrabbling around the pit, it displayed an odd elegance that Kerraii allowed herself to admire, losing herself for that moment in its efficiency and skill.

This was one of Sarnen's favorite Bloodsuckers, one that knew how to draw out the kill, to inspire the most fear and create the best display for Sarnen's entertainment.

And dark entertainment, to one of the most powerful immortal beings in Necropolis—indeed, in all of the Land—had become a priority.

"Kerraii," Sarnen said, his deeply husky voice reaching her with its perpetual impression of a whisper. Of course he'd somehow sensed the moment her attention wandered to the Bloodsucker, that very instant she had relaxed ever so slightly.

"My lord," Kerraii responded immediately.

"Did you handle the situation with Skulk?" he inquired, not bothering to turn away from what might charitably be called a battle in the sand. The human, battered, bruised, and leaking blood, slammed into the stone at his feet. Sarnen didn't so much as flinch.

You knew, Kerraii realized, only just stopping herself from saying it out loud. He'd known about Skulk's machinations, as minor as they'd been. He'd counted on her to discern them and thwart the Death Merchant on her own. The realization both pleased and annoyed her.

"I handled it," she said, her voice its own kind of velvet. "I expect Skulk will play his games closer to home in the future."

"Excellent." His cloak and cowl shifted slightly from the back as he reached for a glass of red wine turned darker with a tinge of blood. Not only the vampiric in Necropolis had a taste for that life fluid. "In reward, I give you control of this pitiful one's fate." Before him, the human crawled feebly across the sand, too broken for speed. "Shall his death be swift? Or shall we let the Bloodsucker play?"

Once, Kerraii would have demurred, attempting to leave

the choice to Sarnen. Once, long ago, she would have made every attempt to avoid responsibility when each choice led to pain and death. Once she would have given the slave's fate over to the Necromancer Rangle, the man who'd overseen her training, rather than speak the order that had them killed. Once—only once—she had actually refused to make the choice at all.

Once was all it had taken.

412 Tz. ONE MONTH AFTER CAPTURE

The Necromancer Rangle prodded Kerraii forward, escorting her into Sarnen's appalling den of entertainment. She'd only been here once before—on that day of her arrival in Necropolis, while she still reeled from the journey and from the twisting route through the underground tunnel system she'd been sure was deliberately meant to confuse her. She knew some of the tunnels and sky bridges now, she knew paths to the towers for the other Orders, but she'd never been back to this dark, smoky room at the apex of Sarnen's Tower.

Until now, when once again she came in the custody of another, this time Rangle, who had been overseeing her indoctrination and training. Only moments earlier he'd yanked her out of a skills assessment session, where she'd been subtly sabotaging her own efforts to sneak up upon human and Dwarvish slaves, always giving them some slight clue—just enough warning to jump aside and avoid her knife. She'd thought herself safe enough, given that the other candidates in her group—earnest, glory-hungry young Sect Elves—performed not nearly as well as she though they tried with all their determination. She'd looked good while still allowing the assigned victims their chance to escape. She'd considered herself clever and safe, right up to the moment

Rangle had clamped his bruising grip on her arm and dragged her away.

Sarnen waved away the scantily clad servant in black veils who bent over his incense braziers, murmuring a command Kerraii, even with her keen hearing, couldn't discern. The servant gave a hasty bow and hurried away, and Kerraii envied her the escape.

Sarnen turned to them, giving Kerraii her second glimpse of his craggy, aged-without-aging features since her arrival here. Skin set tightly over bone in sharp relief, with eyes so shadowed it was impossible to tell their color.

Rangle gave a practiced twist to the hair at Kerraii's neck, forcing her to her knees.

"You have delayed a performance in which I'm particularly interested and for which I have guests arriving," Sarnen said, and Kerraii gave an inward shudder at the sepulchral quality of his voice. "What is your excuse?"

Rangle gave Kerraii a little shake. "She feigns compliance," he said, words that struck an immediate dread within Kerraii, and went on to elaborate. She ceased to listen, thinking again of her family, of her woods, of the comforting, enduring presence of the longhouse as it had been before the raid. Rangle, in the midst of describing the ploy she had thought so subtle in the assessment exercise, sensed her emotional distance. He gave her another little jerk and added dryly, "Even as we speak, she feigns her acquiescence."

No! That wasn't right! She did what she was told, she behaved as she was expected to. She'd seen far too quickly that it was the only way to survive, that even Sarnen's unusual interest in her wouldn't protect her from the consequences of so much as the merest resistance. How could they expect more of her? How could she manage if she couldn't retreat to precious memories . . .

Sarnen gave the merest of smiles, lips stretched over

stained ivory teeth. "So I see," he said. "But perhaps this one is worth a little extra effort."

"So you have said, my lord." Rangle inclined his head, no trace of sarcasm in his voice.

"However," Sarnen said. The single word made Kerraii's heart thud with fear as his eyes wandered up and down her form. She had not yet earned the scant, form-fitting Nightblade's harness for which she had just barely started her unwilling training, but her crude shift seemed so little protection that she suddenly longed for that harness. She'd been told it offered supreme freedom of movement, that the wise Nightblade acquired spells to enhance its attributes . . .

"However," Sarnen repeated, "we are in agreement. She feigns her loyalty, and that cannot be tolerated." He raised a languid hand, and from the darkness of a shadowed area, a Grave Robber came forward. Muscled, crudely attired in roughly woven clothing, the Sect Elf gave the impression he would throw himself to the ground and literally lick Sarnen's boots. Kerraii had seen him lurking around the ground levels of the towers and the training pits—gathering information, spreading information, looking entirely too gleeful about the whole process. As well he might be. He was a man of small talents who had found a way to make himself indispensable. Now Sarnen murmured into the man's ear, sending him out to the circular hallway wrapped around this level. Footsteps rang on the stairs as he descended into the tower.

"My guests will wait," Sarnen said. "Perhaps it will help to keep them humble. We will take this moment to see if this lovely young woman can be salvaged."

"Better to make that decision now than waste more time on her," Rangle said. "There are more where she came from."

"Ah, I think not," Sarnen said. He rose to his feet, placing a proprietary hand on Kerraii's head to smooth back the unruly tendrils of her long black hair. "She would not be so easy to replace, not with such beauty, such potential. Did you know she eluded a Nightstalker outside her village with no particular effort to do so?"

That much was true. Kerraii had seen the flash of silver and black, glimpsed the yellow, but she had not understood the significance. And the Nightstalker had not seen her—at least, not until she panicked, running for home; it was he who had captured and held her as she watched her brother die. It was he who had brought Sarnen's attention to her, anticipating the Deathspeaker's needs and preferences. Now Sarnen gave her a look of such possessive determination that Kerraii quailed inside. "No, we won't toss you out to be pit bait just yet, my wild little Wylden Elf. You may not know it yet, but your untrained little will is no match for mine. We will yet civilize you."

Exactly what she feared. She closed her eyes as his black-gloved fingers traced the line of her delicate pointed ear, the fox-sharp line of her jaw. *Possessive.* If she let him, he would take everything of her and leave behind a Kerraii she couldn't recognize.

The Grave Robber returned, prodding two figures into the room before him. One short, squat, with a face that was mostly taken up by a bushy beard badly in need of a trim. A Dwarf. The other was taller, graced with a patchier, shorter beard and wild, light brown eyes. Human.

Kerraii instantly recognized both of them from the assessment exercise. She gave Rangle a wary look, but wiped it from her face when she glanced at Sarnen. Rangle gave an *ah* of understanding, though Kerraii did not understand at all, and did not want to.

Sarnen looked at her and said quite pleasantly, "Which of them shall die?"

Mutely, she shook her head, not quite able to believe what

she'd heard. The room's incense thickened, cloying and so strong she could hardly think.

"This is not a decision you can decline," Sarnen said. On the other side of the miniature pit, a hidden door slid aside; two figures stood within it. One was a woman dressed in drab witch's skirts hung with bones and knives and other tools of her trade. The other . . .

Kerraii looked, and then looked again, her eyes wide with astonishment and horror. It was nothing more than a skeleton. Lightly armed in studded leather and an old chipped sword, it stood tall, as though it were more than mere bone propped on bone. Its naked skull swiveled first toward Sarnen, and then toward the two men who stood chained before the Grave Robber. There it rested, as though it had found what it wanted.

"Mage Spawn," Sarnen explained, almost kindly. "A Skeleton from the Blasted Lands. They hate everything still alive, just on principle. You need not worry, my dear. The witch has control over it. It was expecting something a little more challenging, but I'm afraid your behavior has altered our plans. Now, which of them shall I give to the creature?"

He asked the question as if he were querying her about the weather . . . another subject Kerraii was unable to address, locked in the shadows of the tunnels and underground rooms as she'd been this past month while her introduction to Necropolis accelerated into training. She looked at him aghast, but quickly put on the expression she'd learned brought her the least unpleasant consequences, a face she had once learned in innocent bluffing games on the Wylden Plateau.

The two prisoners regarded her with dull eyes and little hope. Behind her bluffing face, Kerraii recoiled inside. To condemn either man to death would be anathema, a corruption so far from her upbringing that she found it literally incomprehensible. Respect for the environment and its life grounded her every move, her every thought. These men had done nothing to her, had done nothing to threaten the Wylden Plateau she was sworn to nurture. She gave another barely perceptible shake of her head, a reflection of her confusion.

Sarnen raised one dark, painted eyebrow and Kerraii immediately realized her mistake, but knew of no way to rectify it. One did not defy or refuse those of power in Necropolis.

Regardless, she heard herself say, "I cannot. I will not."

"You see," Rangle said. "The defiance I sensed lurking. She has proven me true."

Sarnen cast an unyielding gaze upon Kerraii—not one full of helpless anger, but one with deep power brewing. The power of his unparalleled skill with Necromancy . . . and the more personal power he wore like a second cloak. "This is a lesson you will learn," he said, hard and cold. "Or, indeed, you will die. You will find we admire spirit here in the towers, but only to a certain extent."

Rangle seemed to know what was coming; his expression held satisfaction. But Kerraii, suddenly deeply afraid for her own fate, did not. While she stumbled over mental images of what Sarnen might do to her, he said calmly, "If you refuse to make a choice, I shall make it for you—the one choice I'm certain you would never consider." She looked at him aghast, forgetting to hide it, as he added, "They will both die, then. And they will suffer for your cowardice."

The prisoners were not so dull of thought and hope as to miss the implications of the moment; they turned to Kerraii, their eyes accusing and bitter, but had no chance to say anything as the Grave Robber shoved them forward, then down the steps so quickly that they stumbled. Hands manacled before them, they had no chance to catch their balance; both went sprawling in the shallow sand.

The Skeleton leaped in after them, silent but for the faintest

sandpaper noise of bone moving against bone. Kerraii stiffened, certain the . . . *creature* . . . would dispatch them in
moments.

It did nothing so merciful. As Sarnen tossed the manacle
key into the pit after them and they scrabbled in the sand to
find it, the Skeleton carved little pieces from their flesh.
With one smashing blow it sliced the fingers from the
Dwarf's hand; the human, bellowing defiance, flung those
fingers at Sarnen, pelting him with them.

Sarnen laughed.

Kerraii closed her eyes, hoping no one would notice, but
Rangle immediately touched her on the arm with a small
wand made of finger bones, causing a terrible prickling of
her flesh. When he removed the wand, the skin under it
looked withered and infected.

Kerraii kept her eyes open after that, trying desperately
not to see as the Skeleton dispatched its victims, giving a
huge sigh of relief when the two finally lay facedown in the
bloody sand. It was over.

Except it wasn't. With no sign of effort, Sarnen brought
the men back to life, so expertly reincarnated so soon on the
heels of death that they lost nothing of themselves.

And they died again. And again. And again.

And finally, when there was nothing left of them to put
back together, and when Kerraii had broken down in sobs
of guilt, it stopped. A slave came with several baskets and
gathered what was left of the prisoners while the witch re-
asserted control over the Skeleton, forcing it back through
the door from whence they had come. Another slave swept
the floor clean and laid fresh sand as Sarnen surveyed the results of his little lesson with satisfaction. He said to Kerraii,
"I see in you great potential, but you will have to earn your
way to the privileges that await you with me. You may be
hard to replace, but you are indeed replaceable. Never forget
this fact."

Kerraii nodded blindly, staring at the floor. Whatever spirit she'd clung to until now had fled her. She'd rebuild herself to survive, but as with the Zombies, she would not be quite the same as the original . . . or even *nearly* the same.

Sarnen watched her closely. "Do not let this lesson go to waste," he said. "You must take control of your fate from here on out if you want to survive, and that will mean controlling the fate of others. Do not fail me."

Through her haze of guilt and horror and fear, Kerraii suddenly realized the worst of it.

Sarnen actually meant his words kindly.

420 Tz. NECROPOLIS

Once was all it had taken.

Even now Kerraii did not relish the memory, knowing how foolish she'd been to have shown such weakness. So she did not hesitate to answer Sarnen's question. *Shall it be swift? Or shall we let the Bloodsucker play?* She accepted the decision as the reward it was meant to be and said immediately, "Let it be swift. It will leave the Bloodsucker fresh for the next time."

Sarnen chuckled, a dry sound that resembled someone choking. "My wise Kerraii. I shall do just that." And he made the smallest of gestures. The Bloodsucker snarled in frustration, but instantly and effortlessly killed its prey.

Kerraii watched dispassionately as the Bloodsucker bent to feed, her mind returning to Sarnen's words as she'd left him to deal with the slaves—and, ultimately, with Skulk. She said, "He is too ambitious. He thinks he has something to prove, as the first human to raise himself so high, and he goes too far to prove it."

"I am well aware of his activities," Sarnen said, but his voice held the mildest of amusement, not disapproval. He did not turn to look at her as he said, "Sit by me."

Kerraii instantly moved to obey, stepping down into the pit seating and folding her long legs into a graceful position from which she could nonetheless respond to an attack from any direction. Not that anyone would dare, here at the top of Sarnen's tower. But when the only method of advancement to a Deathspeaker's seat was to assassinate the current Deathspeaker, one remained prepared. Always.

The Bloodsucker tossed the limp body away in a careless gesture and stalked out the door that opened for him, the hidden door on the opposite side of the pen. Kerraii was well familiar with that door by now.

She'd even used it.

As slaves appeared to remove the body, handling it in such a way that Kerraii knew it would provide food for the voracious leathery-winged fell beasts that served as mounts for banshee and Necromancer alike, she considered Sarnen's words. She thought on his amusement, on his pleased mood of the day, and she thought about Skulk, how indeed he had been unusually bold in both his attempted acquisition of the pit-bait slaves and in his treatment of her. Had he been successful with either, he would have gained favor and status, raising himself with his domination of Sarnen's favorite. But why take such a risk? Now that he'd failed in such an open bid against Kerraii—and, by proxy, Sarnen—Skulk's opportunities and future in Sarnen's Tower would be even more limited.

And suddenly she knew for sure, and the knowledge sang in her body like the thrill of an imminent fight. He, too, had been trying to position himself for the coming days. "The Dark Crusade," she said. "It's time."

Sarnen laughed out loud, unusual enough in itself to tell her she was right. "The Dark Crusade," he agreed from within his cowl. Kerraii had seen him without it, but she couldn't recall anyone else doing so for years. At least not anyone else who had more than mere moments of life re-

maining. He said with satisfaction, "The rebels and their
black powder have taken the Atlantean Empire by surprise.
Even the Wylden Elementalists are rousing to the fight. But
between them they've left the Land disheveled and open to
change. She nearly begs for someone to take up the task of
putting things to order. The humans of the Divide have already proven how amenable they are to our rule, and how
easy they are to use. The rest of the Land will follow suit.
Yes, it is time."

Kerraii pulled a small blade from her boot, examining it
idly. This blade had ended many a life, had been in the blood
pit and done its work on uncounted personal missions for
Sarnen. But it had never been in battle. Not true battle, with
the fierce unearthly howl of the banshees demoralizing the
enemy, Screeching Terrors thick in the air, enraged Seething Knights throwing themselves into the worst of the fighting. Necromancers would stand to the side, reanimating the
best of their fighters, bringing back the Zombies as fodder
to tire and horrify the Atlantean guardsmen and the oh-so-
sanctimonious crystal bladesmen of the Elementalists. And
the Nightblades, the Nightblades kept their own loose for-
mation, relying on stealth, speed, and perceptiveness to
eliminate the crucial players on the other side: an unranked
guardsman, fighting valiantly enough to inspire his companions; a warlord, spitting out orders and rallying his troops;
the unsuspecting, holding strategic ground.

The Nightblades could make the difference between battle won and lost. *Kerraii* could make the difference. She ran
her thumb over the back edge of her little blade, caressing it.

"Yes," Sarnen said, answering her question before she
could even speak it. "You will go."

"Where?" she asked instantly, forgetting for the moment
the cool, sardonic persona that suited her best. "When?"

Sarnen gestured at the sand pit, which the slaves had raked
into order before quietly retreating. They had done well, but

beneath the sand blood remained . . . and now that blood came to the surface at Sarnen's command, shaping an astonishingly detailed map of the Land's northeastern territory. "We will strike many places, and soon. The larger picture is not for you to know. *You* will supervise a company of Nightblades to support this objective." He gestured, and the map bubbled, smearing and re-forming to show a close-up of an area that encompassed the Roa Kaiten and the western crescent of the Serpine Mountain ridge, considerably north of Fairhaven. Sculpted clumps of bloody sand rose to show the mountainous features, while a clear stream of bright red represented the river. Fields, docks, buildings, tree clumps . . . each were distinct, globby formations, glistening slightly with a constant, subtle motion.

Kerraii gave the map a discerning look; as a young Wylden Elf she'd known little about the Land outside her own Wylden Plateau, but Sarnen had improved her understanding considerably since then, tutoring her intensely on both the geography and the politics of the Land. "There's a new settlement there," she said, thinking back to the most recent Nightstalker reports. "Not big enough to be called a town, but enough to provide shelter to our troops. They'll be trapped up against the river . . . and they're Atlanteans. They won't get any quick support from the Wylden at Fairhaven." She ran a long finger down the back edge of her little knife. "At the same time, once we establish ourselves there, we will have easy passage across the river to gain further ground."

Sarnen made a noise of satisfied affirmation. "I am pleased to offer you this opportunity, Kerraii. As usual, I know you will represent my interests to your fullest abilities."

"It is my honor," Kerraii said, and meant it. To take a company of Nightblades into such a crucial skirmish! Sarnen had made no effort to emphasize its importance, but he expected her to perceive such things on her own . . . and then to accomplish them.

She made a habit of success.

The blood of the map sank slowly back into the sand, leaving Kerraii to contemplate the battle and the rewards of victory. Sarnen, watching her, gave a slow and subtle smile, an expression manifested as a grimace on his immortal features. He reached for her knife, gently reversing it in her grip, positioning the sharp edge of the blade under her thumb.

She knew what he wanted. After so many years, she no longer even hesitated. She ran her thumb down the blade, feeling the slick bite of it through her skin. By the time she turned her hand over, blood had already gathered at the lips of the cut.

She held her hand out to Sarnen, and he took it.

CHAPTER 3

420 Tz

WIND blew steadily in Necropolis, shifting only with the seasons; it brought with it a permanent, chill dampness that pervaded the towers and tunnels, lifting only on those mid-summer days when the sky turned hot and sullen and still, leaving the Elves cranky and the humans gasping for breath. But those days came rarely enough, and the denizens of Necropolis took the cold wind for granted, along with the overcast sky, damp air, and rust.

Three days after her assignment to take the Roa Kaiten settlement and another day before she'd lead her company out of Necropolis, Kerraii stood on the sunlit edge of a blood pit. Here she came when she could, taking advantage of an aspect of the blood pits few people seemed to notice. Down in the pit and buffered from the wind, she could soak up what little sun broke through the clouds and reflected off the sand. Even in early summer, she found the tunnels chilling; here she could throw off her cloak and tip back her head— never as unaware of her surroundings as she might look, but as relaxed as it was possible to be in any public area of Necropolis. In the early morning, she had only the slaves for company; they groomed the sand with a pleasantly rhythmic sound, apparently oblivious to the anticipation swelling within the city. Vast wood and stone benches circled the

arena, rising far above her . . . also oblivious. This was far
from the largest blood pit arena in Necropolis, yet it held
thousands of people.

In spite of her relaxed posture, she was well aware when
Rangle entered the pit, and followed the crunch of his hesi-
tant step in the sand as he approached her. He no longer had
any significant say in her activities; her training and schooling were long done, and he considered her one of his biggest
successes. He certainly assumed that she knew of his approach, that her acute sense of smell and discerning hearing
would allow her to identify him, for he spoke without waiting for her to look at him, and he did it from within easy
range of her sword with the quiet assurance that she would
not turn on him—as she would on any fool who dared to approach her so closely unknown.

He said, "All of inner Necropolis prepares for the Dark
Crusade, and yet here you are."

A criticism, or a query? "Yet here I am," she said. "I have
been told my objective; I have gathered my company. I have
seen to their billeting and their food." An army wins and
loses battles on its stomach; her Nightblades would be well
fed. Necropolis could afford them the food, given that a huge
percentage of its forces required no food at all: Skeletons,
Zombies, Dark Spirits. She turned her face away from the
sun, giving him a lazy-lidded look. "Let others worry about
their *own* roles in the Crusade. Sarnen knows upon whom he
can depend."

"Sarnen needs no help in that matter, else he would not
be one of the few surviving original Deathspeakers," Rangle
agreed. Like Sarnen, his lifespan had been stretched with
early techniques; he, too, had witnessed the construction of
Necropolis after Tezla's death. As such the sun was not kind
to him; it mercilessly revealed his tight, dry skin and every
flaw therein. Rangle wore the changes like a man proud of
his battle scars, and did not flinch from the sun. He looked

at Kerraii, a piercing look that alerted her. "But you . . . do *you* know on whom you depend?"

"Myself," she said drolly. Out in the pit, the first wave of fighters stumbled into loose formations to spar. They were new, forced to use the slot of pit time before distribution of morning rations—which meant that most of them would in fact miss those rations. A good system, it weeded out the sickly right at the start. A corner of her mouth twitched, part approval, part amusement, as one of the fighters took advantage of his sparring partner's wandering attention and dealt him a sword blow to the midsection that had likely nicked gut—making it fatal in the long run, though perhaps not before much suffering. The injured fighter wore a look of astonishment and betrayal, as though just because they were warming up, he should not have been subject to such a blow. That it was not *fair*.

There was no such thing as *fair* in the pit. Only survival and the reward for cruelty.

Kerraii looked at him and gestured out at the ring. "And that. I can depend on that." *Cruelty. Betrayal.*

"You may be certain of it," Rangle said. "And do not make the mistake of thinking that because your Nightblades are a separate unit, they are independent of the other troops marching to Roa Kaiten. There will be companies involved who are not of Sarnen's Order of Girgul. Uhlrik, Aulrud . . . perhaps Vladd. They, too, will be part of this particular campaign."

This time Kerraii looked more sharply at him. She understood what he meant, there was always underlying competition between the orders, especially those of the original Deathspeakers. If any one of the other company commanders saw a way to earn an advantage over another—over *her*—while still fulfilling their roles in this campaign, they would take it.

"Skulk," Rangle said casually, flicking what looked like a

bit of dried flesh from the velvet of his cuff, "will be directing a company of Zombies."

Displeasing to learn he was assigned to the same objective as she, but not astonishing. "He is of value to Sarnen, who knows best how to use him."

"Not Sarnen," Rangle said, smiling ever so slightly and not the least bit pleasantly. "Skulk rides with Spider. He seems to have shifted his alliances."

Kerraii spat into the sand. "He embarrassed himself with his own clumsy manipulations and now he runs to align with someone who won't know the details."

"He is in error if he believes so," Rangle said mildly. "Spider may not be as old as Sarnen, but he's thorough. No doubt he has burdened Skulk with the need to prove himself in some substantial way."

No doubt.

She gave him a slanted look, still half-lidded. Her dangerous expression, the one that warned any wise man back. Rangle made no move; he knew that look was not aimed at him. She said, "I have no wish to be a pawn in Spider's games and Skulk's foolishness. I'll take your warning."

"But not with gratitude," Rangle said dryly. In the pit, the sounds of combat intensified; above them, spectators began to trickle in.

"You're not doing it for my sake," Kerraii said, and knew that for the absolute truth. Rangle worked for Sarnen, always. As did she. "I'll save my gratitude for someone who truly earns it."

"Then you'll have quite a supply of it in waiting when you die," Rangle said without rancor, still that trace of a sardonic mood about his dark red lips, so startling in a face as pale as his.

"Yes," she said. "I expect I will." And at that she turned to go, for her sunshine had moved on and the pit soaked up blood instead of warmth.

"Give my regards to Sarnen," Rangle said, staying to watch the fights from this privileged vantage point.

"I'm sure he'll receive them with delight," Kerraii told him darkly. Rangle had never been entirely convinced that Sarnen's long-term cultivation of Kerraii was a good thing. Habits, he had been heard to say, led one to predictability and weaknesses. So even a thing as straightforward as this warning she would not take for granted.

But now she knew. One way or the other, she was not simply leaving this particular field of combat for another. She was combining the two, with Skulk under immense pressure to prove himself, mostly likely at someone else's expense. And come the morning, one way or the other, the Dark Crusade would begin.

In a light early morning fog, Kerraii led her company across the Prophet's Bridge linking Necropolis with the mainland. The massive structure spread wide enough for fifteen to walk abreast, arching slightly over a sturdy base that sank beneath the waves. Daylight shone through deliberate gaps in the base; small waves lapped against the stone. Because Kerraii led a company of silent Nightblades, she could still hear the constant kiss of water against the bridge—unlike those among the Seething Knights ahead of them or Skulk's Zombies bringing up their rear. Vampire Lords led the other companies, with Necromancers working alongside to control their supernatural troops as necessary.

Zombies moved below them as well, affecting repairs to the bridge. It had been Zombie made from the start, by a horde of newly created undead carting fitted stone blocks through the water with no need to breathe: solid rough granite for the base, with a deeply polished, deep gray granite forming the great walkway and its low, stout side rails. Intensely green verdite marble ran through the granite in straight-line patterns, leading the eye onward. The results were magnificent and imposing, a fitting introduction to Necropolis. Kerraii turned that she might see the city from the perspective of someone approaching it for the first time—the central Prophet's Tower rising high above all else, the twelve Order Towers ringing it, the faint tracery of sky bridges between them. The Temple of the Blood Goddess rose nearly as high, but not quite, and it never would; unlike the towers, the temple nearly blended in to the jumble of massive buildings that comprised the city, while the familiar outline of blood pit stadiums drew Kerraii's eye. *We will bring you a victory,* she promised the city fiercely. *Ground gained . . . and power.*

For more than a hundred years those aligned with the necromantic arts had been crowded into this little corner of the Land, up against the vast Ailon Mountains and closely hemmed by Cainus Mons and the Serpines. All that time, the Necromancers had perfected their skills and prepared for the day when they could enlarge their hold on the Land. And during that time, resentment of their limited place in the Land had festered, built by ambition and need. And now Necropolis would take what it wanted, and those who scorned the Sect arts would understand their error. The Black Powder Rebels, as insignificant as they might be on their own, had started the ripple of warlord warfare that made this campaign possible.

That backward glimpse of Necropolis stayed with Kerraii over the next days, as she led her company through the Vale of Dawn. The tireless Zombies traveled ahead of them and the Seething Knights followed them, and behind the knights and the camp followers and supply wagons came the Necromancers, controlling their dark spirit and Mage Spawn charges—and keeping them from mingling with the Elves and humans. The Necromancers were used to those startling beings, but many of the others doubted the Necromancers' abilities to control the creatures.

Kerraii didn't concern herself with them. She concentrated on establishing her leadership and learning the strengths of her women. She'd fought each Nightblade in the blood pits at one point or another; some she'd fought more than once, and these she knew well enough. As for the others, she set up sparring practices during evening camp, throwing them together one after another, studying them and their moves, and inevitably taking them on. They were a striking group, all of them. Like Kerraii, they were dark of hair and eye, long of limb, unerringly graceful, light-footed, and keen of senses. Collected in a single group with their black strap harnesses over sleek bodies, black leather boots with reinforced metal shins and knee plates, and shoulder plates of metal with a skull in deep relief, they drew the gaze of every man in the combined forces.

One such man from the support wagons approached them those first evenings on the road, when the long summer evening tipped into dusk and the Serpine foothills were thick with the smoke of cook fires. He seemed fresh from the Vurgra Divide, not familiar with or accustomed to such proximity to Nightblades—and in some foolish way he'd arrived at the conclusion that the minimally clad Nightblades were meant for his lusty entertainment as well as for targeted stealth work. Illona, an older Nightblade whose quick dagger play was much admired, was the one to find him lurking in the darkness, waiting for the right moment to accost one of them. She propelled him in from the edge of their tidy little camp, her smallest knife drawing a trickle of blood from just behind his ear as she drawled, "Just *look* what I found."

"He brought our evening rations," Kilte said, the most robust of them. "Don't hurt him; I want to eat tomorrow, too."

"He brought more than that." Illona dragged the man to the fire they shared. He stood frozen, hunched away from her knife, only his eyes betraying his trepidation. "He brought a longing for company."

"Let me guess," Kerraii said, putting her empty plate aside. A pity, too, since the meal, a blood stew thick with fresh elk meat, smelled just about ready. She stalked up to the man, walking around him as the Nightblades gave a most predatory groupwide grin. She ran a hand down the leather strapping of her harness, following the section that connected her bodice and loin pieces and then indicating the straps circling her thighs. "No one told you that these harnesses don't come off unless *we* say they come off?"

The man gave a half-hearted smile, looked around, and decided to keep his silence. Kerraii leaned in close. She swiped her finger along the knife cut on the back of his neck with a gentle, knowing touch, making him shiver in spite of himself. She held the finger out so he could see the dark shine of his own blood, and then she deliberately licked it off.

He shivered again, in an entirely different way. The other Nightblades cheered Kerraii on as the man finally managed to speak. "I've made a terrible mistake—"

"You have, haven't you?" Kerraii said. "And here I was wondering about the evening's entertainment." She looked at the company—only twenty of them, but twenty was more than enough for a small battle like the one to which they marched at Roa Kaiten. "Pity there's not more to go around." She gestured at him. "You may play, 'blades. But don't harm him. We *do* want to eat tomorrow."

The company gave a collective shout of approval; Kerraii drifted back to her camp stool to retrieve her plate, feeling no real interest in their sport much as she gave them the impression otherwise. Attending stomach before amusement was the thinking of a survivor, and Kerraii was ever a survivor. Many of the others seemed to feel the same, though they watched with an intense gleam in their eyes as their fellow Nightblades surrounded the man, jostling him, tasting his blood, oh-so-skillfully removing his clothing by the simple expediency of slicing it clear of all belts, buttons, and lacings. One by one they tossed the items in different directions to disappear in the stubby brush that filled this area of the rocky foothill terrain, tsking when he happened to take a slight cut in the process. *He* may have thought the cuts to be accidental, for they amounted to barely enough to bleed, but Kerraii knew that her Nightblades were pushing the limits of her orders, waiting for her reaction.

She gave them none. She let them disrobe the man and send him on his way, humiliated and well-educated, and she enjoyed their high spirits as they sat down to eat. But they'd indeed pushed too hard, and the next day she would work them long in sparring, hard enough so that they would wonder, and the smart women among them would figure it out. Seeing who those women were would simply be another step in her process of evaluating them for use in battle.

For Kerraii was Sarnen's pupil, and she knew the subtle ways of handling those in her power.

412 Tz. IMMEDIATELY AFTER CAPTURE

Night fell as Kerraii first arrived in Necropolis, shoved along and jostled and surrounded by the Zombies who had been her keepers from the start, sequestering her from the other captives, quashing her attempts to reach them with her futile cries. She had no idea what had become of her family and friends, whether they traveled nearby or not at all. One evening she heard a tremendous commotion, and she secretly nursed the hope that some of the prisoners had escaped; she never heard anything to confirm or crush those hopes, but she held on to them nonetheless.

The Seething Knights and single Nightstalker who had staged the raid on her village pushed onward, as they had most nights, with no care for the darkness that made Kerraii trip and stumble. *Dark Elves,* they were called, and with reason—their masters rewarded them with vision that equaled any night predator's. Her own eyes had adjusted well enough that she would find the cloud-dimmed glow of the moon over the water as they approached Necropolis, and the looming silhouette of the city itself. But when she would have hesitated, the Zombies pushed her right onto the hard, mildly arching surface of the bridge between the shore and the city's island. And so she made her way, escorted by stinking Zombies on either side and perceiving very little of the city's sinister majesty. After the longest of times—longer than she thought any bridge could run over water—they descended to the rocky shoreline of the island.

There the group paused. Upon a few muttered orders in the Atlantean language Kerraii did not know, the Zombies and most of the Seething Knights left them. A familiar grip settled on her arm just above the elbow: the Nightstalker, he who had first spotted her out in the woods and had clamped a similar grip on her when she would have helped her family.

This time, she didn't fight him. She was in a strange city in the pitch-black night, exhausted by forced travel, poor rations, and constant fear. Better to rest, assess the situation, and gather herself for escape. Surely, if she were persistent enough, she could escape.

I will *escape.*

The Nightstalker dragged her along the road and then off of it, down steps that seemed to lead to nowhere, then through a door set into the ground and into an underground passage. Kerraii's usually excellent sense of direction abandoned her; she instantly lost track of their route, and stumbled to her knees when they reached a set of stairs leading upward. The Nightstalker hauled her back upright in a most detached way; as ever, she had the sense that she was nothing to him personally.

At the top of the stairs he effortlessly found and opened another door. Light flooded in, blinding her; hands she couldn't see pulled her forward. Blinking back involuntary tears from the light, she resisted for the first time in days; the Nightstalker leaned in close from behind and murmured into her ear, "Let them attend you. If you are of no use to me, I will kill you even now. Especially now."

Kerraii froze. She did not doubt him for an instant.

To those who held her, the Nightstalker spoke in the language of the Sect Elves—a language similar to Kerraii's own, and one she'd listened to every evening since her capture. He said, "This is the one about whom I sent my message. Prepare her for an audience. If it goes well, I will remember you."

Even Kerraii, unfamiliar with this place, the way he put his words together, or the people, could hear the implicit threat. *If things do not go well, I will also remember you.* She shuddered—for these people, for herself, for the unknown that lay ahead of her. By now her eyes showed her bits of color, and she realized that she saw no more color than that simply because there was little color to see. The room around her was hung in velvet curtains of deepest, barely perceptible blue, with trimmings the color of old bone. The two Elf women who received her wore skimpy gray garments with tight half bodices and gauzy skirts; they regarded the Nightstalker with cowed expressions and an obvious desire to please. The brightest spot of color came from the mirrored dressing table in one corner of the room, where a few red candles sat next to a hammered tin bowl and pitcher. The walls there were uncurtained, and lined by open trunks of clothing. Two torches placed in that corner lit the room, streaking the exposed stone.

Prepare her for an audience.

They were going to dress her for someone. Someone important.

"I am going to feed," the Nightstalker said, ever brusque. "Send someone for me when she is ready."

Feed? Not eat? And was that awe in the women's eyes when he spoke, or fear? Or maybe a little of both . . .

The Nightstalker left them, using a second door through which Kerraii glimpsed a lighted corridor. Not everyone traveled in the dark, then. The two Seething Knights who had accompanied them left by the same door, but Kerraii could see them settle in to guard the room as the door closed on the corridor and whatever lay beyond.

As soon as they were alone, the women dropped their cowed manner and started work with fervent efficiency. They pushed Kerraii down in the room's lone chair, a hard-seated structure made from . . . was it wood carved to look like bone, or actual *bone*?

She didn't have time for a second look. One woman splashed briefly in the tin bowl, then attacked Kerraii's limbs with a soapy cloth while the second woman tugged at Kerraii's clothing. Kerraii instantly tugged back, both on her finely woven but travel-worn tunic and on her manhandled limbs. Just as instantly, one of the women slapped her, a ringing slap that jarred Kerraii's teeth and made her vision go red and black before it returned.

The woman hissed, "He *will* kill you. Or *worse*."

"Not to mention what he'll do to us," added the other woman, still plying her soapy cloth and now working her way up Kerraii's leg. "We know how to pinch you so it doesn't show, and those Seething Knights know even more. So by the Blood Goddess, do not fight us."

Rest. Assess. And persist in survival while working toward escape.

Kerraii let them tend her. Like a child, she sat for them. They did not try to wash her hair; they had not the facilities or the time. Instead they rubbed it with a subtly perfumed oil and pulled it tightly back, fastening it at the crown of her head to fall unimpeded down her back. They clothed her in an outfit similar to their own, in black. With quick, practiced hands they smudged cosmetics on her face, eyes and lips, and it was only as an afterthought that they turned her to the mirror.

She had never been overly familiar with her reflection; the Wylden Elves kept only a few simple mirrors on hand, polished brass for use on feast and festivity days. What she saw now shocked her with its contrast to how any Wylden Elf should look: muted clothing of the finest weave and embroidery or the softest deerskin, loosely captured hair, lively eyes, and a gentle expression. Nothing of that looked back at her. Instead she saw a scantily clad young woman with haunted eyes accentuated by smoky rims, stern, slick hair that exposed every refined, elegant line of her pale face, and startling rouged lips.

But the women looked satisfied. More than satisfied . . . relieved. One of them cracked the door and spoke to the guard in Atlantean, which Kerraii recognized but didn't understand.

When the Nightstalker returned, he looked her over with critical eyes, then strode over to the small rack of straps and accessories. He returned with a supple black leather belt and cinched it around the bare skin of Kerraii's waist with a touch that felt far too familiar. She didn't understand why he left it slightly loose, until he rested his hand at the small of her back and gave the belt a tug.

It was her leash.

Numbed all over again by this reminder of her captivity after such personal attention, she allowed him to guide her out of the room and into the corridor, where he dismissed the knights. He alone took her on the winding path upward, twisting through the passageways of the high tower until they spilled out into a receiving chamber of some sort. It, too, was hung with velvet curtains, these of a red so dark and deep it looked black except where directly struck by torchlight. Also lining the chamber along the walls to either side were Elf women dressed in nothing but black leather strap harnesses. Oh, they had reinforced knee-high boots and metal vambraces, not to mention stout shoulder guards. But other than that . . .

Other than that, they looked remarkably like her, as if they'd been chosen for it. As if *she'd* been chosen for it.

Kerraii tore her gaze away from them, and it immediately lighted on the figures at the end of the room. A man sat broad-shouldered under his cloak and cowl, his face nothing but a glimmer of shape and shadow. On a low stool by his side—or more accurately, at his feet—a woman lounged. Her clinging velvet dress matched the wall curtains, but her expression was one that Kerraii could hardly fathom. *Satisfaction?* She had the slightest of smiles, and Kerraii could all but hear her purr; the malice in that expression startled Kerraii. She stiffened, fighting an unbearable instinct to run. It only made the woman smile more widely. Her lips had been rouged redder than Kerraii's, and she idly licked the tip of one finger.

A third figure, a man in black tunic and trousers, stood beside the thronelike chair, wood embedded with whole bones. He held the fourth and final occupant of the room, a young woman who seemed to be ill or at least fainting; she arched gracefully back over the man's supporting arm, her hair hanging long to touch the floor and her clothes identical to the grey garb of the women who had dressed Kerraii. The man, too, seemed to be wearing makeup. Kerraii was all but sure his strong widow's peak had been enhanced with blacking, and his lips were as red as the lounging woman's. Unlike the woman's, his expression held a touch of annoyance. A man interrupted . . .

By the Land.

Their lips weren't rouged. They were tinted with blood.

Necropolis. Vampires. She'd heard of it. And now she'd seen it.

And she wanted to run; with all her being she wanted to run . . .

The enthroned man spoke, and his voice struck Kerraii's ears as grating and strained, like a whisper that could never grow to a shout. "What have you brought me?"

He spoke in the Sect tongue and Kerraii, struggling, caught enough of the words to follow him.

The Nightstalker bowed slightly. He approached the group in a respectful manner, none of the confident strides with which he'd brought her this far—and then, by roughly bumping her behind the knee at the same time he jerked on the belt, took her down to her knees in front of the man. "This is she about whom I sent you the message," he said. "I found her in the Wylden raid, and I thought she would please you."

Kerraii had never wanted to please anyone less in her life. *I should be home. I never even finished the door tabard.* She didn't even know if her sister was still alive . . . "Please," she said, hoping he would understand her Wylden words, "what about the others? What about my family?"

The man stood, throwing off his cowl. Kerraii recoiled, and then instantly steeled herself to hide the reaction. She didn't know who he was or even *what* he was, but she couldn't afford to anger him. Not if he could tell her about her family. So she looked up at his aging ageless face and stretched, leathery skin, at Elvish features once obviously handsome but now a parody of themselves. She hid her horror and her fear, and tried to present herself as dignified and respectful.

He stared at her for a long, long moment, a terrible moment in which she could not have read his expression even had he not been so adept at schooling it, not with his features so changed by whatever dark magics had touched him.

And then he smiled slightly, his lips thinning without opening. He looked over her head to nod to the Nightstalker.

"She has potential," he said. He stepped forward, and the Nightstalker's hand clamped down on the tender spot where Kerraii's neck joined her shoulder, warning her to behave. The man walked around Kerraii, assessing her. He ran a finger down her arm, prodding slightly to check her muscle tone. He ran that same finger along her jaw, stopping just under her pointed Wylden chin to tip her head up and examine her features. He looked into her eyes at length.

Furious and offended, Kerraii forgot to be afraid. But she didn't forget the deference the Nightstalker had shown this man, and she didn't forget that her fate rested in his hands. She fought to keep her feelings from her face . . . and though for the most part knew success, felt a sudden betraying quiver in her lip and chin, and knew her eyes seethed with resentment.

He dropped her chin, turning away from them. The Nightstalker's fingers dug into her skin, and she had the sudden feeling that he was prepared to slay her on the spot did she not meet this man's expectations.

But without even looking, the man said, "Do not bruise her, Histe. I want her to start training as soon as possible."

Instantly, the grip eased. Beyond the man, those lounging by his chair looked disappointed; the man who still held the woman—fainted or dead—nuzzled her neck slightly. The woman on the stool stretched like a knowing cat.

Kerraii's new patron turned to face her again. He must be one of the powerful Necromancers, to have undergone such changes. She'd heard enough throughout her childhood to know that the people of Necropolis vied with each other to earn the bestowal of vampirism by one of the Necromancers. The Necromancers themselves drank blood only out of habit or pleasure. Necromancers had their own hard-earned, hard-kept secret spells for immortality.

But just *who* this particular powerful Necromancer was

she had no idea. And she doubted it would mean anything to her if she were told.

He didn't bother, at least not at first. "You have fight and anger in you. That is good. And you have the wits to suppress them when they will do you harm. For that, you might even survive here. You will join those in training to be a Nightblade—" And here he gestured at the female guards lined up against the velvet wall hangings. One or two of them gave her a haughty look, as if Kerraii had offended them simply by presuming she could earn a spot among them. "—and you will also have special training sessions to acquaint you with my ways. You will be schooled in the details of the Land. You will learn to serve me in all ways; you will learn to make my desires into your desires."

Kerraii took a deep, shaky breath. *I'll do what I have to.*

"My name," said the man, narrowing his eyes a little, watching for her reaction, "is Deathspeaker Sarnen."

But she didn't react, not at first. After so many days of fear and fatigue, she couldn't quite take in the fact that she knelt before one of the twelve Deathspeakers, the most powerful men in Necropolis. And then the import of it struck her, and her eyes widened slightly. For that moment she simply stopped breathing altogether. *How will I ever escape him?*

But she wouldn't have to. She wouldn't always be with him, under his gaze and supervision. There would be times when she was forgotten by this powerful man.

Surely there would be times in which she could plan and carry out her escape.

There will have to be.

He smiled at her without humor, but with far too much understanding; for a wild moment, she wondered if he could read her mind. But she'd never heard of it . . .

"Your family," he said suddenly, "is perfectly safe. Upon receiving Histe's message I made sure of it. And they will stay safe. Over time I will show you tokens to reassure you."

Relief flooded through her—but only for an instant. Without thinking, she whispered, "But why? Why would you—"

"I'd like you to enjoy your life here," he said. "I want your entire attention on learning your new duties and excelling in them. I don't want you distracted by fears for your family."

She couldn't respond. *They're safe.* Except for Oaklen . . . but his death had occurred before Sarnen intervened. She opened her mouth, found herself trembling again. "Thank you."

"You may thank me with your attentiveness and your loyalty," he said, and that seemed to be the end of his interest in her for the moment, for he turned away abruptly enough to make his cloak swirl, replacing the cowl over his head with a practiced gesture. "Histe, you may install her in the section with the other recent arrivals. And then you and I will talk. I presume that's what you want."

"Yes, my lord," the Nightstalker said, inclining his head slightly. "Thank you, my lord." He hauled Kerraii to her feet, and she left the room on wobbly legs that had cramped from being sat on after so many days of hard travel. She followed him blindly, trying to absorb her change in fortune. In the end she focused on the most important thing: *My family is safe.* The rest would come later.

But Kerraii was Sarnen's pupil, and it had not taken too terribly long to understand that her family was safe *if*: *if* she gave her utmost effort to her training, *if* she excelled.

If she pleased Sarnen.

CHAPTER 4

420 Tz

ILLONA and Kilte and Silona understood Kerraii's lesson first. They responded with loyalty, an appreciation of Kerraii's subtlety and methods. A handful of the others were less responsive but adequate. Three of Kerraii's Nightblades showed their true mettle with resentment, and she made sure to pair them with her strongest fighters during any exercises she put them to on the march to the settlement. By the time they reached their final camp, only one Nightblade proved so intractable that Kerraii did not trust the woman to direct her individual efforts for the company's good.

In a way she could not blame the woman, a Sect Elf named Yevena. Kerraii had chosen Yevena for her blood pit successes, but in fact Yevena had spent too much time in those very pits and could think only in terms of individual victories.

Kerraii had been better trained. She knew all her victories belonged to Sarnen.

She set Yevena to the task of guarding the base camp upon their arrival near the Roa Kaiten. Although they maintained their distance from the other members of the warband—no one wanted to stumble onto a fell beast unaware—by necessity they camped close enough to make easy communication possible, and there was always the chance a local could stumble on to them. Kerraii emphasized the importance of Yevena's task and the individual glory of success, and then she sent her other Nightblades out to scout—not just the terrain and the activity within the settlement but also the behavior of the other companies. Kerraii, too, went to examine their surroundings. The Vampire Lord Reever, Order of Aulrud and commander of the campaign, had called a meeting of the company commanders, but they all knew what would come next: a day of preparations and plans to decimate the settlement's occupants, and then, before dawn of the next day, attack.

Not that the strategies of the attack would come as any great surprise. The banshees would sweep through the early morning settlement, stunning the occupants. Her Nightblades would take care of the out guards, as well as any key figures in the resistance to follow. The Seething Knights would follow the banshees, killing what they could, while the Zombies tromped in on their heels, crushing the life out of the wounded and gathering up prisoners. Should anyone attempt to flee or gain ground on the Necropolis base and its commanders, the Nightstalkers would be there to prevent them.

Kerraii found the terrain far too reminiscent of that of her own abandoned childhood, those useless days before she'd found true purpose and learned how to apply herself to worthy goals: improving her situation, earning personal power, survival, and victory—all while pleasing Sarnen, because pleasing Sarnen meant accomplishing all of those things at once. She felt no kinship with the villagers.

But some buried part of her mind still remembered how she'd enjoyed the Wylden woods. As she eased through these woods—more oak than on the Wylden Plateau, more pine, fewer leaves underfoot and more needles—to the crest of the small hill that overlooked the settlement, truly alone for the first time since she'd joined Necropolis, Kerraii found

herself growing annoyed. Her pleasant anticipation of the
following days changed to an inconvenient swirl of memory,
both tactile and emotional—memories she thought long
gone and with which she wanted nothing to do.

She needed something to fight.

Below her, the trees gave way to the scrubby kind of
growth that occupies the edges of any lightly and newly
cleared field, as the woods fought to reclaim their space. The
fields themselves were still rough, the plow rows struggling
rather than marching in straight lines, but the early summer
growth looked green and healthy. Beyond that sprawled the
settlement—equally rough, with crude, low wood buildings
of Atlantean craftsmanship—and beyond that the long ribbon of Roa Kaiten, reflecting silver in the sunlight.

She saw a flash of movement at the juncture of the woods
and field, a clumsy, graceless movement. *Zombie.*

But no, that made no sense, and she'd only had a glimpse.
Much more reasonable to expect a settler up here, tending
the field. There was no reason for Skulk to have sent any
Zombies into that area; it would risk the entire objective.
Zombies were blundering and obvious and even the most
naive settler would understand the implications of one's
presence.

Except she couldn't convince herself that her first impression was wrong, that her finely honed instincts could
mistake one for the other, no matter how briefly she'd seen
the creature—or how much she was looking for action.

Silently, she moved off her hill, slipping down through
the woods toward the field. She heard the thing; then she
smelled it. Most definitely a Zombie.

It shouldn't be here. She'd learn just why it was, but damage control came first. She circled slightly, naturally silent;
she kept her sword at hand but low. When she appeared in
front of it, it startled, and in spite of herself she found a wry
amusement in the sight of a startled Zombie, especially one

that had been returned to life as the damaged and phlegmatic creature before her. Cannon fodder. She kept her voice pitched low and said, "Return to camp immediately."

It hesitated for a long, long moment, thinking thickly, if at all. In body it was strong, hugely muscled and hulking, as were most of the delayed revivals. Skilled Necromancers assured it, to produce cannon fodder that could at least fight— or, in their spare moments, join in the repairs to the Prophet's Bridge. But their thought processes . . . little to none. So Kerraii didn't bother to explain why its presence here was a problem. Deceptively at ease, she waited for it to weigh her command against whatever it had been told previously.

With exaggerated effort, it frowned, its ill-made features no longer quite able to form accurate expressions. "Against orders," it said finally.

"I understand," she told it, and she did. There was no point in further attempts to convince it.

So she killed it. Her sword flashed, and in its wake the Zombie's head hung crookedly on its shoulders; it staggered and Kerraii struck again, ducking a wild ham-sized fist on the way in, nimbly skipping out of reach as the Zombie's head rolled aside and the body, not quite yet aware it was on its own, lurched forward. Like a falling tree it toppled, crashing to the ground.

She regarded it for a moment, then muttered out loud, "I said I needed a *fight*." This hardly qualified.

But it had been better than nothing. She felt more focused again, her thoughts ordered and aligned as they should be. She gave the greenish grey head a precise kick, rolling it up against the giant body. But for all its proximity to the field, she did nothing more than cover the bulk in a layer of leaves and needles. Zombies were undead, held together with magic until they should happen to take some mortal blow. Unless they were immediately revived, the magic slipped

away—and the flesh did too. There was little chance it would
be discovered, and Kerraii had more important things to do.

It seemed she and the others needed to have a little talk
with Skulk.

The Vampire Lords, several Necromancers, Skulk, and
Reever all gathered in the neutral area between their camps.
They'd be cold camps this evening, with the food little more
than dried meat and berries—although the Nightstalkers had
already caught a few rabbits and would likely eat them raw.
But there'd be no wood smoke, no faint glow of fire in the
night, nothing to alert the settlers. They'd take no chances.

Or at least, they'd take no *more* chances. Kerraii threw the
Zombie's boiled leather pot helm at Skulk's feet, provoking
immediate interest from the others. "You have endangered
our victory," she said to him.

"And *you* are a self-important child who will pay for forgetting her place," he snarled back.

"Very good." She nodded approvingly, one casual hand
on her hip . . . not coincidentally near the small dagger
sheathed in her harness. "Attack me and draw attention from
the real matter at hand."

"What is this?" Vampire Lord Strang demanded. As the
commander of the Nightstalkers, he among all of them
would understand without being told that Kerraii had been
scouting in territory where the Zombie had no place.

Kerraii took her gaze from Skulk only long enough to
meet Reever's implacably demanding look. He was listening, but she'd have to convince him, and she had no theory
to back her words. Under other circumstances, her behavior
would merit severe censure. "I found it down near the settlement fields," she said. "It wore the sash of Skulk's command. I ordered it to return to camp with me and it refused;
it was already acting on orders to be there, and it remained
loyal to those."

"You killed it, of course," said Strang, with full grasp of the most immediate priority.

"Of course," she agreed.

"For that you are commended," Reever said. "But I am not convinced you have justified your attitude here, for all that you are Sarnen's chosen."

"Aren't you?" She glanced at him, and back down at the Zombie's helmet. "It was acting on orders. Who knows how long it had been tromping around down there; who knows how many people had a chance to see it? Even now, there's a significant chance they're arming themselves against the possibility of more Zombies in the area. Perhaps they've even guessed there's more to it than that."

Strang nodded, and said, "Much of our strategy is based on taking them by surprise."

Reever brought up a leech light—so named because it clung to its conjurer like a leech, and drew its energy by leeching from those around it. It shone with a light no unenhanced Elf or human could see.

The others eased slightly away from it, a subtle and tacit group decision. Reever made a *tsking* noise, running his fingers along the gleaming pommel of the eerie bone knife at his side. "It is assigned to me, or are you implying I have not the power to spare?" No one responded, but they all resumed their earlier positions—all but Kerraii, who shifted as though she was in the process of joining them and then settled right back into her new position, not doubting in the least that the Necromancer had the power to spare but doubting very much that he'd bother to use it. No one seemed to notice; they were all too busy trying to look unconcerned as Reever transferred his gaze to Skulk, an inquiry clear enough for all that it was silent.

Skulk shook his head. "It's true. A Zombie went missing shortly after we arrived. But he had no orders to walk near the settler's fields."

"He told me otherwise." Kerraii crossed her arms before her and arched a sleek eyebrow at him.

His answering expression of annoyance was clear enough in the growing darkness; her night vision perceived only shades of blue grey, but no less acutely. "Are you suggesting that I'm lying?"

She gave the slightest of shrugs. "Are you suggesting that the Zombie had enough wits to lie?"

None of them believed *that,* it was obvious. So she and Skulk watched each other in a moment of stalemate, and then Reever said brusquely, "There is reason here to be concerned, but not enough information to draw conclusions. Tomorrow we will set 'stalkers and 'blades to watch the town while we finalize our strategy and prepare a holding area for our prisoners." He let his gaze linger on Skulk again. "If there is evidence of the settlement preparing for us, I will find it necessary to reexamine this question."

Skulk narrowed his eyes. "And if there's no evidence at all?"

"Then perhaps I will find it necessary to make special note of Kerraii's indiscretion," Reever said. "But I will not act on it. Any potential disciplinary action is Sarnen's to take."

Skulk glared across the circle of company leaders, pinning her with his cold gaze. Unaffected—Kerraii knew what she'd seen, she knew what she'd heard—she gave him the slightest of cool smiles. As in the low chamber when they'd faced off over the slaves, he spun on his heel and stalked away from her. The others, glancing to see that Reever did indeed consider this particular discussion over, took to the darkness with more decorum and less noise.

Strang leaned toward Kerraii as he passed her, hesitating to speak even as he watched the others go with a close eye. "Tsk," he said. "Not nice to annoy the ambitious Death Merchant."

Kerraii's smile grew more genuine. "No, it isn't, is it? I so thoroughly regret my behavior." She didn't; they both knew it. "It's unfortunate he keeps putting himself in my way."

He smiled, a ruthless expression, and they shared that moment of disregard for those who tell other people what to do in battle or even in the pits without actually having done it themselves. But he added, "If you are wrong, it will mean trouble for you. But if you're right, it will mean trouble for us all."

"I'm not wrong," she said, not bothering to put any force behind the words. Shouting was louder, but no more convincing; either he'd believe her based on what he knew of her, what he knew of Skulk, and what he'd seen here, or he wouldn't. "Eventually, we'll learn what happened, and why. The appropriate question right now is how *much* trouble will it cause for us?"

But the next day the Necropolis scouts saw nothing alarming. Kerraii herself lingered long near the settlement, easing in as closely as she could get while the settlers traveled in and out of the busiest market area before her, unaware of her scrutiny. Up close, the settlement was no more impressive than it had been from the hill. The buildings were if anything cruder than she expected, the product of hasty workmanship and an obvious air of *build fast now, replace at leisure later.*

Not that they'd ever get the chance.

From the roadside brush in which she lingered, Kerraii had an excellent view of the main market area, a wide dirt arena encircled by flimsy stalls and tents that could easily be crushed or flung out of the way. A good job for Zombies. In the center of the arena, split-wood corrals held livestock. The livestock would feed the invaders, and the corrals . . .

The corrals would serve to hold the prisoners Reever wanted to preserve.

At the far end of the market stood the tallest building in town—two stories of it, and it still looked long and squat to Kerraii's eye. A public boarding house to judge by those going in and out, especially considering those who went in and reemerged in different clothing or with a change of possessions. The place might be a pocket of resistance; most of the occupants seemed to move with much assurance and perhaps even a little arrogance.

In fact, the settlement as a whole boasted a variety of fit, capable-looking occupants, a fact which initially surprised her—but then again, one wouldn't expect to find weaklings in the blood pit, either, and this business of carving new homes from unoccupied territory was not for the faint of heart or constitution.

The others made the same observations, and when they met that evening they agreed to herd the salvageable prisoners toward the main market area near the end of town, where the Zombies would guard them while ferreting out any settlers hiding in the market stalls and tents by the simple technique of destroying those potential hiding places. Otherwise, all was as she surmised—the banshees on their fell beasts would sweep through the town in the early morning hours, softening it for swift subjugation by the knights and Zombies. All that was left were her own final assignments within her company.

She hesitated warily as the command meeting broke up; she'd expected Skulk to make a hard point about the settlement's apparent ignorance of their presence. But as she made her way back to the Nightblades, preparing to feed their fighting spirit with news of the bounty and the fresh meat that would be theirs by this time the next day, she realized she was not alone. Someone with more stealth than any average human in the dark and in the woods approached her, angling in from the side—but no human, Death Merchant or not, could out-stalk a Nightblade.

Kerraii eased into the woods, drew her sword, and waited, very much at ease. And soon enough, Skulk made his appearance. He stopped not far from where she'd been, shrouded in darkness but not hidden there, and though his bone helm obscured a great deal of his face, she could see him frown, puzzled by her absence.

After a very long moment, she stepped out in front of him, startling him and in turn earning the full brunt of his anger. "I could kill you for that," he said. "I could strike you down with Dark Spirits . . . or just simply drain you of blood and life."

"Probably," she said. "But could you do it *before* I dismember you?" She gave her chin an idle tap with one long finger, pretending thoughtfulness. "Of course, I'm sure your friends would put you back together again. I'm just not sure if you'd ever quite work the same."

"There was no evidence my Zombie had been seen," he hissed at her, as if that had been the conversation all along.

"That doesn't mean you didn't send it down there," she said, still unable to fathom *why,* but knowing what she'd seen. "As for evidence . . . tomorrow will tell."

He smiled suddenly at her, taking her by surprise for the first time in their recent spate of encounters. "I'll give you that," he said, bowing slightly. "Indeed. Tomorrow will tell."

CHAPTER 5

420 Tz, ALONG THE ROA KAITEN

LIKE all Nightblades, Kerraii had had hours of exposure to the shocking blast of banshee wailing, in training and even in combat. More than one of the blood pits featured mass melees with random banshee strikes; the patrons of the pits enjoyed the unpredictability of just which Nightblade would be distracted enough to die the most horribly.

Like all Nightblades, she hated the wailing anyway. She hated crouching in the darkness, waiting for the unearthly screams to shatter the air, for the skeletal fell beasts to swoop down with their keening riders, thunderclaps of sound from their wings punctuating the wails.

The banshees always rode as though they were the ones possessed, not possessing; they rode as though the opportunity to wail provided them with a release so necessary and satisfying as to be an addiction. Kerraii's perfect night vision picked them out against the sky, their heads flung back with the effort and their eyes eerily wide open, reflecting their deep, inexplicable pleasure.

This predawn morning was no different. Kerraii and her Nightblades, positioned around the perimeter of the town, waited to target the crucial factors in the settlement's resistance—assuming the banshee blasts didn't incapacitate the occupants right from the start. Kerraii herself occupied nearly the same position she'd held during her reconnaissance; she felt the presence of the Seething Knights on the hill behind her, tapping the uniquely stored angers that fueled them through their own fighting. Behind them were the Zombies. Only the Nightstalkers themselves knew where the Nightstalkers waited. Not a huge contingent of fighters overall, but plenty for an ambush of this modest settlement. Kerraii would be surprised if the fighting lasted beyond midday.

If only it would get started in the first place . . .

Gauze-winged insects hovered near her in their unsteady flight, almost as if deliberately tempting her to bat at them, giving herself away. A faint light appeared in the eastern sky. The merest whisper of dry, leathery wings against air warned Kerraii; she steeled herself for the pain of the banshee wail reverberating in her ears, head, and soul. Her heart started to pound, and though she could for that moment hear it in her ears, she knew it would only be a moment and then she would hear nothing but the powerful wailing, feel the literal shock wave of noise. The unprotected humans would have no chance. They would stiffen and writhe and even die. They would hardly be able to fight.

Except—

Kerraii froze in disbelief. A faint haze of magic rose from the settlement. Not a small magic, not a feeble, wishful thing without substance, but robust magic, magic that didn't falter as the banshees flung themselves through the air and opened up their howls—magic that literally leapt to meet the attack, blasting the fell beasts out of the sky. The banshees faltered, unprepared for such a fierce assault. Their cries died away to whispers, and even though one of them took up the cry anew, a leaping blast of magic immediately struck her down. For all their fierce joy in their power, the banshees were unaccustomed to this kind of resistance.

A Technomancer. They somehow have a Technomancer.

It meant a longer fight. A bloodier one. The Seething

Knights would be pleased, and so would the Nightstalkers—
it was a chance to vent their fury, and indulge in rampant
vampirism. Kerraii tensed as the thwarted banshees faded
away, waiting for some sign of activity within the town. The
Seething Knights didn't wait at all. They flung themselves
down the hill with lung-rattling battle cries, an unmistakable
clash of armor and sword and pounding feet. They built
momentum charging down the slope and they swept past
Kerraii into the town, all but pulling her into their battle
fury. She had to force herself down, force her thoughts to the
cool and calm place from which she fought her best.

And because she waited—because she held to her assignment—she saw how, as the knights poured into town,
the town poured Atlantean forces back out at them. The
building doors opened, the merchant stall covers ripped
away, and Altem guardsmen rushed to meet the Seething
Knights in a clash of blade and blood, a visceral connection
of forces that made the ground tremble beneath Kerraii's
feet. The mage blasts continued, targeting not only the warriors but the Necromancers hidden up on the hillside.

Chaos bloomed before her. She fought the impulse to join
it. *Follow the plan. They need you as a* Nightblade, *not just
as another sword—now more than ever.* The signs of magic
faded as the sounds of battle swelled—the cries, the moans,
the fierce shouts of attack. Skulk sent the Zombies in early,
sacrificing them to give the knights as much of an edge as
possible.

Had the settlement been lucky, or had they been prepared? And if they'd been prepared, how—?

Not even Skulk's stray Zombie could have given them
time for *this*. Not with no sign of such preparation the day
before. No suspicious trickle of Atlantean troops, no sign of
Atlantean military at all. They had to have been there before
the Necropolis troops ever made camp in the woods above

town. They'd known the Dark Elves were coming. They'd *known*.

From a building at Kerraii's edge of town emerged an Amotep gunner with his Magestone-powered lightning gun. With practiced precision, he aimed for the small group of Seething Knights who pressed an equal number of Atlanteans up against the rubble of battle-dismantled merchant stalls; the gunner blasted away with a giant burp of sound followed by the distinct *ker-ack!* of the lightning. The Seething Knights tumbled through the air as if they were dolls, slamming against buildings, becoming impaled on rubble, scorched and singed and damaged. The stench of burnt air filled the market area so completely Kerraii could smell it from the gunner himself.

Mine. This *one's mine.*

Indeed, he nearly invited her sword, so unheeding was he of his back, expecting the two Utem guardsmen flanking him to provide him with safety.

But the Utem guardsmen squinted into the early-morning darkness, blinking against the blast from the lightning gun, and Kerraii did not. She could see at night; she could see during the day . . . she could do both at the same time if she had to. Sword in one hand, knife in the other, she crept up to the building from which they'd emerged, dipped her head around the edge to confirm their position, and moved out into the open with swift grace just as the gunner released another volley, this one not quite as successful but still damaging.

The soldiers were distracted by the rush of Zombies coming in from the side; they didn't even know she was there, not even when she was close enough to smell their old sweat and rancid armor padding, to see the flush of red at the back of the gunner's neck above his high-collared protection. "Turn around, boys," she said, giving them just enough warning so they'd know terror before they died. She punched the pointed, triangular blade of her knife into one Utem neck right where the most blood flowed, and channeled the effort of removing it into a sweeping turn that slipped behind the other guardsman's shield and sliced through his leather baldric, leaving him doubled over a fatal wound.

The gunner whirled to face Kerraii, prepared to impale her with the next crack of lightning, or perhaps merely with the jagged defensive blades jutting out from the end of the gun. He thumbed the control jewels, refocusing—

Her sword sliced through his stiff gauntlet, taking those fingers right off. "Nice of you to let me in so close," she said, as blood spurted and he jerked his hand back, crying out in disbelief. Not pain; not yet. And mercifully, *never*—for she closed in, drawing the blade across his throat in a high guard position, whirling away as he fell, dying, to check her back. *Clear.*

She withdrew, easing back to the nearest building and the vague shadows of dawn. The chunky, debarked wood of the building pressed into her back as she reassessed the market area, looking for her next target. What she saw made her eyes narrow, and seeded the first doubt in her soul. More guardsmen, both Altem and Utem, poured into the limited space. Worse yet, crossbowmen were clambering up both wreckage and standing buildings to find the high ground. Another gunner took position on the other side of the market, trying to line up for a clear shot. No Nightstalkers or Nightblades in Kerraii's sight, just a handful of Zombies trying to bludgeon their way through. And, most startling, Skulk stood exposed at the edge of the road just outside of the market, his fists clenched at his sides, howling something in what she could only call thwarted fury.

Narrow-eyed, she stared at him, half lip-reading, half picking his words out of the battle din—trying to make them fit what she saw and what she knew. "No-ooo!" he cried, staggering slightly with the force of his own cries. "This isn't how it was supposed to happen!"

From up on the hill, one of the Necromancers revealed his desperation by loosing his pack of Zombie hounds. They charged down into the town, amazingly swift despite their awkward, leaping gait. They were nothing more than a sacrifice—for this was the worst of circumstances for the hounds, who were best at harrying widespread prey. Another Necromancer brought a nearby Seething Knight back to life. Grey magics danced around his body as he climbed to his feet, regaining his weapon. His face pasty, his features mildly thickened, he immediately plowed into the fight. And in the middle of the market area, in the thick of the battle, a tormented soul appeared, a difficult Mage Spawn ally whose appearance meant the Necromancers were reaching for every potential weapon possible. The Atlanteans fell before its cold wrath.

But still the Necropolis forces died faster than the Necromancers could bring them back, and still the Technomancer lurked untouched, entirely free to wreak further havoc.

No. This isn't how it was supposed to happen. But Skulk's howling desperation was a much more personal reaction than that of a battle commander surprised by an opponent. Kerraii glanced away from him to take measure of the battle . . . and counted the fight essentially lost. Poised between scant opportunities to help her forces and the unique opening to question Skulk, she shifted away from the building and into the brush by the side of the road, stalking one of her own.

Skulk's shouting continued unabated. "You can't possibly have gathered all these troops in a matter of days! This isn't right!"

His tone was that of a petulant child discovering that the world doesn't play by his rules. And Kerraii began to understand. Skulk spoke of *days;* their forces had been here but a

day and a half. In a sudden flash of insight she realized
that while he'd denied sending the wayward Zombie out to
walk the fields, he hadn't denied sending it out altogether.
Zombies . . . slow, steady, never needing to sleep, to eat . . .

He sent it long before I ever saw it. It had arrived before
the Necropolis troops, and was meant to be seen—*why*? And
whatever Skulk's purpose, it had gone awry. Somehow this
small settlement had already known of their approach. The
Zombie had merely confirmed it, allowing the settlers to
turn the tables, grabbing the element of surprise.

She emerged from the covering brush to slink around
Skulk like a cat on the prowl, until the tip of her smallest
knife, deceptively innocuous, lifted the point of his chin. He
ranted right up to that last moment, entirely unaware of her
presence, and then her knife cut him off. Somehow even the
battle cries seemed distant. It was just the two of them, facing off over the tip of Kerraii's blade.

Her dark velvet voice barely covered the hard steel of her
anger. "No," she said, pushing close, using her Elvish height
to intimidate him. "It's not right. Nothing here is right.
Where did these Atlantean troops come from? How long
have they had a mage?" Her lips were just inches from his,
their noses almost touching. "And just when did you send
the Zombie away from your stable?"

"I—I don't—"

"You *do*," she murmured, circling him without removing
her dagger. Its point dug into the soft skin beneath his chin
and made him pivot to follow her. Above them, a fell beast
flapped in over the town; a lone banshee tried once more to
penetrate the shielded area with her shocking voice. For this
once, Kerraii paid it no attention whatsoever. "You know
exactly what I mean. The Zombie I killed. You may not have
sent it to stomp around above that field, but you *did* send
it out."

"I—" he said, protest and denial in his voice, but fear in

his eyes, pale, weak, human eyes. Kerraii smiled fiercely, with just a glint of glee.

From somewhere within himself, Skulk found the strength to shutter his fear and replace it with haughty offense. "You will pay for this behavior."

"Possibly," she agreed. "Then again, you have to live through this battle for anyone to know I dared to accost you at all. I think the chances of that grow smaller with every passing moment."

"You wouldn't dare," he said, and an ugly sneer crept into his expression, a bluff revealed by his desperate eyes. He looked over her shoulder, hunting one of his Zombies, or one of the Zombie hounds from which he could transfer loyalty.

"They're busy," Kerraii told him. "Would you like to try calling up a dark spirit? I hear that requires intense concentration." Her voice dropped to its most dangerous purr. "I know many ways to break a man's concentration."

Bitter voiced, he said, "It's true what they say about a Nightblade, then. Never let one get close."

"In all ways, it's true," she told him, nudging his chin with the dagger and watching as a single drop of blood ran down the edge of the blade. She let him see her pleasure at that blood, and then she asked sharply, "What *did you do*?"

"Nothing of any great consequence," he said hoarsely. "Deathspeaker Spider required me to prove myself in this battle, to place the credit firmly with the Order of Uhlrik." He gave a little laugh, cutting himself further with no apparent concern. "With *Zombies*? Zombies are our work-horses, not our heroes." Standard battle tactics—send the Zombies in to round up the prisoners, to overwhelm the opponent with numbers once the front lines have broken. "Zombies exist to die without actually costing us anything." A Zombie hound howled fierce sorrow as if in agreement— and its cry choked off in the middle, making Skulk's point.

Kerraii gave him a cool scowl, although she felt not nearly so calm on the inside, not as she realized the extent of his treachery. Whether he'd meant it or not . . . "So you did what? Created circumstances in which the Zombies could play a bigger role than expected? Sent your dullest Zombie out ahead to reach the settlement long before we did? Let the settlers get a good eyeful of him, maybe make a few extra arrows?"

"It should have made no difference!" he cried. "A little extra fighting, nothing more! Our victory would have been less assured, but still certain—I was prepared! The Zombies' entrance would have been the turning point of the battle! Instead I had to send them in early. I have no idea where these mages came from. My loose Zombie should have made no difference, not in the end!"

She balled the front of his cloak in her fist and swung him around to face the settlement, watching his surprise as he felt her strength. "Look!" she cried, and shook him in her anger. Bodies littered the market area: Necropolis fighters the Necromancers simply couldn't revive fast enough. The hounds lay in pieces, cloven by swords, blown up by the lightning gun at close range. The Seething Knights slumped over each other like crossbow-bolt pincushions, their partial armor no impediment to the Utem weapons. Zombies struggled to function without limbs, determined to follow their recent orders and unable to comply. "*No difference?* You risked us all to impress your Deathspeaker? Didn't you have the guts to simply assassinate someone, like everyone else?"

He jerked away from her—or tried to. His expression grew more desperate, each grimace and fear exaggerated. "I was going by the reconnaissance reports. They mentioned no mages! How was I supposed to know?"

"It wouldn't have mattered if you hadn't acted so foolishly," Kerraii muttered, but like Skulk, she swung her gaze out over the carnage of the battle, feeling the despair of it.

The dark spirit had succumbed, its essence shattered by the repeated hits of a lightning gun. The Nightblade who'd tried to stop the gunner lay dead at his feet, impaled by five arrows. *Silona.* "At least one of the mages must have been here when your Zombie showed up. The Atlanteans had the time to hide their readiness from us, maybe even to gather more troops." She turned to him, anger flaring again. "Imagine how they laughed at us, knowing we thought this settlement easy to conquer, that our victory was assured!"

"Survival is victory," he snarled. "No one but you knows why they were prepared for us. It will be easy to blame it on a Nightblade mole who's no longer around to defend herself."

"Except I'm still here," she said, softly and oh-so-dangerously.

A new rumble of noise came from the town; Kerraii didn't take her attention from Skulk, barely glancing at the town and even then relying on her peripheral vision. The Necromancers had banded together for a mass raising, to judge by the stirrings in the formerly still bodies scattered throughout the market area, the gray, leaden haze wreathing the battlefield. No doubt they'd pulled everyone down from the encampment, from grave robber to Reever himself, and they'd drawn death magic through every corpse within their magical grasp. A wave of unexpected hope strengthened her resolve to not only live through this, but to bring Skulk to justice before his peers. They might slyly admire his ambition, but they'd be ruthless enough when it came to punishing his failure.

"Oh yes," she said, smiling darkly at Skulk. "I'm still here."

It was at that very moment that power slammed into her body with the force of two giant hands clapping against her. Dazed, she staggered, losing her grip on Skulk. Skulk leapt away, much more able to absorb the blow than she. *Techno-mancer . . . magic blast . . .* Kerraii staggered a step, badly dazed, and though he could have easily escaped, his freedom assured, Skulk lingered, eyeing her. *Not one to pass up an opportunity,* she realized—in this case, the opportunity to kill her. He held a bone knife—a powerful thing beyond Skulk's means, a stolen blade. She'd seen it in Reever's hands. The man must be dead, blasted by Technomancers, for Skulk to have his weapon. And even in her hazy thoughts Kerraii knew it would be tipped with magic, that any injury it caused would fester and slowly, painfully drain the life from her.

A magic blast rocked the other end of the market area and Kerraii met Skulk's gaze with the simultaneous, unspoken realization. *There's more than one mage.* Skulk hesitated, lowering the bone knife, calculating the odds—and then he turned to run.

Kerraii wasn't about to let him get away. She started after him, still unsteady but swifter than he could ever be.

A second blast of pure magical power rocked the area. It knocked Kerraii right off her feet—

And then it spun her down into darkness.

CHAPTER 6

420 Tz, ROA KAITEN SETTLEMENT

KERRAII awoke to the sound of groans and moans and muttered oaths all around her.

None of them had the sound of Necropolis. The oaths were Atlantean, spoken with the clear, broad Atlantean accent. Sect Elves using the common tongue—and Kerraii had always applied the term *common* in the least complimentary way—invariably put a little twist on the end of the words, hardening the consonants along the way. Kerraii's Wylden origins always betrayed her in the way she softened Sect words, and put a slight lilt into the Atlantean language.

Here, she heard a few murmurs that might have been Wylden. *Crystal bladesmen.* She'd seen several among the Atlantean Imperial forces, apparently willing to fight against a common enemy even with no love lost between the Elemental League and the Empire. They might even have a Mending Priestess here, or a Centaur Medic.

As if she'd let either healer touch her under any circumstances.

Fortunately, although her ability to assess her situation was limited as long as she lay motionless and feigning unconsciousness, she could find no ache or pain to indicate she was wounded by anything other than the magic blast and its lingering effects. She might well have overindulged in blood wine, with this headache and ringing ears. She had the sense her limbs weren't quite ready to obey her, not even to crawl out of this ditch.

Several people approached, their footsteps careless and loud, their conversation likewise. "Ran like Mage Spawn cur," said a gravel-voiced man, coming within Kerraii's earshot. "Right down to the last Necromancer!"

"Can you blame them?" This man spoke more smoothly, with a smug overtone. "Did you see their faces when they realized we had more than one mage working with us? They never had a chance."

"Not after that Zombie came bumbling around and warned us they'd arrived," the first agreed. "Obliging of them to lose track of it like that. What good's all their stealth they're so proud of if they send out calling cards?"

"Our brass golem's not sneaky, but it gets the job done all right," the second said. "And it doesn't go wandering around to warn the enemy, either."

The gravel-voiced man made a grumbling noise. "Wish we hadn't been set to doing perimeter work. Looked like good spoils in there. Half the Zombies are fresh enough to make their stuff worth taking."

"Just be glad you're not helping the medic sort the dead from those that can be fixed."

The other snorted; he was close enough for Kerraii to hear it clearly. "Most of *theirs* are dead, too. I saw a Nightblade get away, and maybe a few others. The rest of 'em were mostly undead, anyway, and you know the magic blasts take them down pretty hard."

A moment of silence followed, in which Kerraii did her best to sort out the sounds of the market area. The metal noise she heard, faint but distinct—most likely their brass golem, helping to cart the dead away. And still the moaning of the wounded, the sharp words of command.

None of it had the flavor of familiarity. If these men were

right, she was nearly alone in her survival. Other than those who had run, of course. *Like Skulk.* Skulk, whose foolish conniving had turned this unexpectedly mismatched battle into a massacre. *And no one would know.*

Unless she continued to survive, and *made* it known. Somehow.

"Say there," said the gravel-voiced man, surprise in his words.

He's seen me.

But she remained "unconscious," knowing her legs wouldn't carry her with any speed just yet, hoping if they thought her dead or still blasted senseless, they'd leave her long enough that she could indeed slink away . . . she had only to gain the roadside brush, and they'd have little chance of finding her.

But they were far too interested in her.

"Nightblade," said the gravel-voiced one. "Ever seen one this close before?"

"Once or twice," the other responded. He had a hint of something—confidence, perhaps—in his voice that made Kerraii think he ranked the first man. "Never fought one."

Obviously. You're still alive.

"They say they even fight in the pits. Hard to believe they're so deadly," said the first, his leather and metal complaining as he crouched, his voice growing loud enough to be annoying. "And look at this. This hardly counts as armor!"

"They're deadly enough," the second man said, his voice dry. "And that strapping is stronger than you think. Not to mention lightweight and nearly noiseless. You think they could sneak around so well wearing the same armor we carry?"

One of them plucked the sword away from Kerraii's hand, tossing it some distance away. By the Prophet's Bones, they weren't going to take any chances.

It doesn't matter. If I can gain the brush—

"Probably not," the first man said, responding to the other's question. "But what good is it if it comes off as easily as this?" And he made as if to illustrate his words, tugging on the wide strap that ran over her hip.

Idiot.

Kerraii remained limp, letting herself move with the tug as the man tried to get his gloved fingers beneath the strap and couldn't. He made a surprised noise, and she surmised from the sound and motion as he inadvertently jostled her that he was removing his leather gauntlet. But his bare fingers had no better luck, and he switched to the upper strap that circled her thigh, then the one that ran between her chest piece and pelvic strapping, and then carelessly flipped her over to try the straps across her back and even the high throat collar. Tugging, poking, prodding—she didn't so much as grit her teeth. *If I can gain the brush . . .*

"By Tezla!" said the guardsman. "I don't think it comes off!"

Of course not. Only if I want it to. Or if Sarnen wanted it to. But unless she escaped, he'd never make that choice again.

"Of course it comes off," the second man said. "Try a knife."

Kerraii knew the answer to that. She took a few clumsy scratches, but the harness remained untouched.

"Move out of the way," the second man said, shoving the first back. Kerraii took the moment to crack her eyes, discovering she'd been right; the second man was a commanding Altem, and the first wore the stiff crest of hair that marked him as a lower-ranked Utem guardsman. And the first one had a *manaclevt* blade in his hand, Magestone-powered to vibrate at high speed with cruel efficiency. "This'll do the trick."

It wouldn't. But Kerraii might take more than a scratch or

two along the way. That her limbs still didn't quite feel connected became irrelevant; it was time to move and move *fast—*

She tucked in around herself, twisted to change direction, and launched herself at the Altem, coming in under the blade and closing her long-fingered hand around the man's leather gauntlet, triggering the sword with her finger on top of his; she felt its slight quiver as she jerked it down to slash across his thigh. The Altem roared in anger and pain, bending over the wound; the Utem gaped at her, standing off balance where his commander had just shoved him. She made an instant assessment to abort the attempt at his sword even as she slammed her knee guard up to meet the Altem's face, and went for the Altem's lightning pistol instead.

But the Utem wasn't as stunned as she'd thought, nor as slow. He made up in brute strength what he lacked in finesse . . . and he had backup. He'd barely clamped his hammy hands around her upper arms when the struggle caught the attention of another Utem; Kerraii saw him coming from the corner of her eye, and knew she had to get away *now*. She jerked one arm free and lowered that shoulder, ramming the spike from her shoulder guard into the Utem's torso. She felt the satisfaction of his surprised grunt as the spike sunk home, and pulled back to wrench herself entirely free of him, ready to *run*.

Hands grasped at her. Slick hands, bloody hands, gloved hands . . . too many hands. She staggered under the clutch and pull, and then suddenly she was on her knees, a sword at her throat. Even then she would have fought, had not one of those hands buried itself in the long tail of her hair, yanking backward with perfect timing to stop her from surging right back to her feet. Another sword joined the first, and another, and then her throat was ringed with sword points, and even the harness collar couldn't protect her from all of them.

Quietly, gracefully, she sank back on her heels, resting

her hands on her thighs. She tipped her head back in submission, closing her eyes. Either it would be enough . . .

Or it wouldn't.

Captured again.

At least this time she'd made the choice to be in the field of battle.

Not really. She hadn't made her own choices about her life since that day at her village eight years earlier; she'd simply picked as best she could from the limited possibilities before her. She'd found ways to survive and even thrive in the world to which she'd been introduced.

All right, then. At least this time she was a warrior, trained and strong. Not baffled, terrified, or exhausted. Maybe just a little hungry after a day of fasting in her chains.

Kerraii sat straight-backed and cross-legged, not looking at the raw rabbit haunch on the battered tin camp plate a sneering Utem had placed beside her only moments earlier. "No point in cooking it," the man had said. "We know you Dark Elves like blood."

Perhaps some of them did. The ones Necropolis bred and born, or those who had been lured into the Sect by the seductive promises of longer lives and personal power—those fighting for the reward of bestowed vampirism. Kerraii stared coolly at the manacled hands resting gracefully in her lap and pretended she couldn't smell the raw rabbit meant for her evening meal. If they persisted in feeding her raw meat, she'd eat it before she allowed herself to weaken from lack of food. But she'd been given water, and for now water was enough.

"Hey," said the prisoner closest to her, a Seething Knight with flies coating the gory remains of his eye. The injury had yet gone untreated, but the other eye was bright enough. "You ever going to eat that?"

He was like Kerraii: one of very few Sect survivors.

Those who did their fighting from afar or from the air had fled. Those on the edges of the fighting, those who were able to break and run after the first magic blast, they, too, were gone. That left only a handful of those wounded lightly enough to live, and they'd been manacled, assigned guards, and mostly forgotten. Theirs was not a pleasant location, and the guards changed frequently. On the one side were those warriors from either side who were wounded so badly they weren't likely to survive. Arrows inflicted quick death on rotting flesh; gut wounds made their own unique stench. And then there were those who'd simply bled too much, whose lives slipped away in spite of the efforts of both Mending Priestess and Centaur Medic. As with any battle, the healers were forced to harsh choices, and used their energies on those most likely to survive.

Kerraii shut her ears to their feeble cries and gut-wrenching moans. She'd heard worse, and she'd heard it often.

On the other side of the prisoners was a sight even less pleasant, a smell even more penetrating. The dead, gathered for disposal. Although the season had not yet reached the high heat of summer, many of the Necropolis casualties had quickly entered a state of confused decomposition. The newly made Zombies had not been Zombies long enough to crumble neatly away, yet once they'd become undead, they were in an altered state of existence. Their bodies, changed by magic, could no longer follow the natural course of decomposition. After a day in the sun, the young Zombies' flesh melted off their bones, turning the piled bodies into a stack of dripping skeletons within a soupy pile of putrescence.

It created a smell Kerraii could not begin to pretend away.

She glanced at the Seething Knight. Like the rest of his kind, in battle he would churn his own anger and fury into a pitch of emotion that turned him into a killing machine. Like the rest of his kind, he thrived on it. But for now he merely

looked hungry. She nudged the plate his way and turned her
attention to the small group of Atlanteans who were making
a tour of the market area.

The market itself had been destroyed, as had several
buildings near the thick of the fighting, where defending fire
from a lightning gunner had run amuck. She'd gotten a
glimpse of that, of the power crackling out of control as the
gunner went down under a pack of Seething Knights. But
the people could easily rebuild; the settlement had taken no
major losses on this day the Necropolis commanders had expected to be theirs. And it *would* have been—if not for
Skulk's foolishness, in spite of the inexplicably prepared settlement.

The members of the small group gestured at one another,
gestured at the settlement, and then gestured widely toward
the northeast in a way that could only be referencing Necropolis. They wore scowls, and typical Atlantean righteousness.
Kerraii gave an inward snarl, an ingrained response of resentment and hatred—but she didn't let her reaction interfere with
eavesdropping as they drew closer. One thing she had learned
most thoroughly in Necropolis: Knowledge was power. She
might be a prisoner, she might be on her way to mines or
slavery or execution, but she might also learn something she
could turn to her advantage. This month, next month, or a
season from now.

The Atlanteans seemed not to have learned this lesson at
all—or else they considered her so insignificant that they
didn't mind offering her a piece of their power. They made no
effort to quell their conversation as they came closer, circling
the area to come up on the dead in their separate locations—
the respectful rows of Imperial heroes, the careless pile of
Seething Knights, Nightstalkers, and even Kerraii's Nightblades, along with the chaos of bones, goo, and dust made
from Zombies new and old. She watched their faces, the
quick cycle from regret to satisfaction and finally to disgust.

By then she could separate them into individuals. Several Altems, a warlord, *five* Technomancers . . . one of them even had three Magestone cabochons set in his forehead, a sign of potent power; three others, men and women both, had two. Just one man, a slight human, had only a single stone.

How had this settlement gathered so much force so quickly? Even had one of those mages been here all along, the odds against getting so many to this remote area so quickly . . . Kerraii gave a small mental shake of her head. Skulk was right. It shouldn't have happened this way, even with his foolishness in play.

The group eased over to eye the prisoners. Kerraii stayed as she was—coolly distant, not acknowledging their presence by so much as looking at them. Maybe they thought she wouldn't know their Imperial tongue. Maybe they didn't care.

"Did you see the looks on their faces when they realized we had mages here?" the Altem said, and she couldn't blame him for the cruel satisfaction in his voice. Had the situation been reversed, she might well have felt the same, although she was rarely so blatant in expression, so unguarded.

"They had no idea. The opening salvo of their Dark Crusade may have cost us lives and territory elsewhere, but in this our man has served us well."

What does that mean?

The most powerful mage tapped his staff against the ground and said, "We had more than good intelligence on our side. It was most thoughtful of them to lose track of that mindless undead creature—as well as a good object lesson about the failings of their techniques and so-called spiritual pursuits. With that warning of their arrival, we were able to conceal ourselves entirely."

Our man. Good intelligence. Kerraii's cool facade cracked for the briefest of moments; she felt the anger flicker through her, and felt it flash over her features before she schooled herself to conceal it.

An Atlantean agent in Necropolis. Maybe even someone she knew. Not someone she trusted, for she trusted no one, but possibly someone she'd cooperated with, worked with. Someone who even now might have access to Sarnen.

In that moment her ingrained responses flared, triggering the need to find this traitor, to protect her master. Protecting Sarnen meant protecting her family, a fact she'd lived with so long that they'd become one and the same thing in her mind.

"Ah," said one of the weaker mages, a woman. "We upset the Nightblade." She raised her voice slightly. "You didn't know, did you? You think yourself so impregnable on your island, think your society so obscure and elite that none of us could secretly acquire a position of influence. And now that you do know, you'll never have a chance to warn your masters."

"We are her masters now," the Altem said.

This time Kerraii looked at them directly. "I have but one master," she said, deliberately distancing herself from any potential association with the elite of the city's meritocracy. If they thought her insignificant, they would not guard their tongues nearly so well. And if they thought her insignificant, they would not guard *her* nearly so well, either. "I am my *own* master. You cannot say the same."

None of them seemed greatly affected by her words. The Altem said, "Nor will you, after some time in the mines. Every Atlantean will be your master then."

She gave them a sharp look despite herself. The Magestone mines. Did he know for sure, or was he merely baiting her?

She could survive a mine. After the blood pits, she could even thrive in a mine, at least for a while.

And she could escape from a mine.

But first Kerraii had to reach the mine . . . and that meant marching.

The prisoners and guards didn't create a large traveling party: a handful of Utems and one Altem, Kerraii, and one injured and permanently lamed Seething Knight, stripped of his gear. There were also a few prisoners who had been awaiting transport at the settlement before the battle: two male Dwarves and a puny, older human woman who didn't look capable of hard labor of any sort. "I'm a cook," she told Kerraii, getting chummy when Kerraii would have preferred none of it. But since they were chained together, she could hardly escape the woman. "Not only that, but I'm a good one. Thrifty. I may be a little weak right now—that damp little hole of a prison they put me in didn't do me any good—but they need me badly enough to let me recover. My name is Hepetah."

Her proximity and chatter was enough to inspire escape in the most literal sense. Kerraii had not been so close to the signs of human age before; in Necropolis no human lived that long, and the Sect Elves either turned vampiric or necromantic—or they failed to achieve these goals and died. There were plenty of humans in the Vurgra Divide, none of whom she'd bothered with on a personal level. Now Kerraii found Hepetah's wrinkles disquieting, and was not at all convinced that the woman would indeed get any stronger. She slowed Kerraii down, making even the simplest of activities a true chore; she drove Kerraii to distraction with inconsequential words.

But no matter the inspiration, Kerraii had no intention of trying to escape just yet.

Escaping prisoners would be shot on sight, targeted by lightning pistols. Escaping prisoners who thought better of it and gave up would also be shot on sight, simply because they could no longer be trusted. Their labor in the mines

wasn't worth the precedent their survival would set, and
would reveal a small speck of mercy within the Imperial
guards that might inspire others to risk running. And meanwhile, there was nowhere to run *to*. Kerraii stared down the
road stretching out before them. Narrow, dusty, and surrounded by low hills with little in the way of tall vegetation,
it went to nowhere and it came from nowhere. They'd been
through one small town already and were headed for another, beyond which lay the Magestone processing facilities
associated with the small mine for which they were headed.
The mine was so small that it sported no town; it had only
its own enclosed facilities and the careless name of the
Mana Cut.

No, she would wait until they reached the mine, and beyond. She would learn the lay of the land, learn from the others in which direction the best safety lay. If the slaves were
anything like Hepetah, they would gush the information just
for an excuse to talk. And if not . . .

She wasn't concerned about convincing them.

"There." One of the Utem guards gave Kerraii a seriously
self-satisfied grin, pointing off to a distant hill, one of the
many among the hummocks that rose and fell in this area of
high plains grasses and occasional groupings of bent,
windswept trees. "Manacut." He turned it into one word, as
so many people seemed to do. Even from here she could see
the bright scar of exposed rock along the hillside, and she
winced. To so harm the land, scarring and damaging her to
steal their Magestone . . . It was an old thought from old
thought patterns, and on the heels of it came surprise that
those patterns still ran deep within her after so many years
of the Necropolis way: *use up and destroy*.

The guard gladly misread her wince, gave her a small
prod on the shoulder. He made it look almost companion-
able, but it wasn't. Not in the least. She had no doubt he

was working up to testing her harness; they all seemed to feel the need to take a turn at it, as if what the rest of them had failed to do would suddenly become possible. She'd known what he had in mind the moment he'd separated her from Hepetah. "Won't be an easy life, not for the likes of you."

She didn't hurt him. She could have, as little as he realized it; the same magic that kept her harness and armor close to her body meant they had not been able to strip her of several slim blades secreted about her person—and that they didn't even know about them.

Not that she'd need blades to harm this oaf. He'd days ago relaxed his guard around her in ways that not even the lowest of Utems would assume had he known who she was. Who she *really* was.

Not just a Nightblade, but Sarnen's Nightblade. Not just a Sect Elf, but one who traveled the hallways of Sarnen's own quarters with impunity. One who knew all the secret passages, and in which of the dark warrens of Necropolis any particular Death Merchant or Necromancer might be. One who knew the names of the most powerful, their habits and their weaknesses. One who thrived among them, fighting hard enough and well enough and clever enough to earn the position for which Sarnen had chosen her.

It meant she could have killed the guard in an instant. And it also meant she could not kill him at all, for she shunned any hint of behavior that might draw attention her way until escape was certain. Bad enough that these men found her so fascinating, that they loudly speculated among themselves about the various types of training a Nightblade might receive and how they could take advantage of it. Should they even begin to guess that she was Sarnen's chosen, the rude speculation would turn to more expert and focused questioning. They would question her harshly and

endlessly, until they were convinced they'd wrung every bit
of useful information from her damaged body.

And if she talked . . .

412 Tz. SARNEN'S TOWER

My family is safe. It was all that mattered. Kerraii forgot
to watch the turns and twists the Nightstalker, Histe, took as
he led her away from Sarnen's chambers to a room much
closer to the base of the tower. A long interior room, with no
windows and little candlelight, nearly dark to her eyes after
the torch-lit hallways.

Histe shoved her inside and closed the door behind her,
locking it audibly.

A row of narrow beds ran down one wall; opposite each
bed, and looking oddly out of place, stood a dressing table
with a small mirror. The mirrors caught the candles, refract-
ing sharp pinpoints of light that somehow didn't seem to il-
luminate the room.

Most of the beds held bodies: womanly shapes under thin
covers, none of which stirred although none of them displayed the relaxed fluidity of sleep, either. In the corner of
the room opposite the door, something moved; Kerraii
jerked to face it, her exhaustion replaced by heart-pounding
wariness as she struggled to see in the near-darkness.

Low and scratchy, a woman's voice came from the corner.
"This is your new home, until you either prove yourself worthy of better or fail to survive. There are rules. You will learn
them quickly. The foremost rule is that you must obey my
every word."

Kerraii's eyes had adjusted enough—barely—to see that
the woman sat in an oasis of comfort in this stark room. Her
plush and cushioned chair had a footstool; a sideboard held
food and drink, and plenty of it. A small creature sat on the
arm of the chair, and the woman idly stroked it as she spoke.

Kerraii could make out the details of none of it; the woman was nothing more than a slight shape buried in shadows who rattled softly each time she shifted.

The creature reached out to catch her arm with its paw, claws catching audibly in the fabric of her sleeve. The woman disentangled herself with no apparent distraction. She said, "I am not your friend. Do not make that mistake. I have my own interests, and my duties here advance those interests. Because I receive credit for each of you who survives this introductory period, in that way our interests are the same. So you will do well to listen to me." She paused, and her teeth gleamed dully in a faint smile. "If you choose not, I have other incentives. As you will see, it is up to you."

Kerraii had no impulse to disobey. Overcome by the weariness of the trip and the fears that hung over her, she wanted nothing more than to find an empty bed and sink into it.

"Tonight you may sleep," the woman said, startling Kerraii.

No. She is not reading my mind. She has simply been through this many times before.

"Other nights, you will be kept busy learning the more subtle arts of survival." This, too, the woman said with a smile, one Kerraii couldn't quite interpret. Knowing? Darkly humorous? She wasn't certain, but it gave her a little spark of trepidation. "Tomorrow, you will carefully observe the other women, and learn what is expected of you. You will notice we have provided you with ways to make yourself attractive. Observe how best to employ these tools. At the moment you are little more than a slave, but unlike a slave, you have the chance to improve your status here. If you're wise, you'll do everything possible to take advantage of that chance." She hesitated for the first time, and Kerraii could see a canny expression come over her sharp features. "I have word that you've caught Sarnen's eye. *If* you're wise, you'll work with me to enhance both our interests. But if you work against me and ill-favor falls on me because of it, I have many ways to make your life a more miserable failure than you can imagine." She smiled unpleasantly. "My name is Slawinda, and you will never forget me."

Kerraii found her gaze suddenly trapped by the woman's direct stare; she stiffened. She tried to tear her gaze away and couldn't, and she felt a strange urge to fall to her knees and babble reassurances to this woman who threatened her.

It made her angry. She'd been torn from her beloved home, from her family, from her very way of life, and now this woman threatened her for her own selfish interests? Ohh yes, it made her angry. She did not fall to her knees. She glared.

After a moment, the woman gave a faint smile. "Well, then. Perhaps you're strong enough to suit Sarnen after all."

Kerraii said nothing. Closed in this room with her new guardian, the burn of Sarnen's gaze still upon her flesh and the feel of Histe's fierce grip stinging her arm, there seemed nothing to say. She was here. She would find a way to survive, whatever it took, and one day she would find a way to regain control of her life. Until then, the things she wanted to say to this woman would only anger her, and hurt Kerraii's chances.

It was, she supposed, her first lesson. It was a start. To-morrow there would be more lessons, and no doubt more difficult ones. She reached for thoughts of her family and used them to buffer her battered sense of self. As long as she knew they were safe, she could endure what she must.

And then she'd return to them.

420 Tz, THE ROAD TO MANA CUT

. . . If Kerraii talked, then her family would no longer be safe.

She held few things sacred in this life any longer, but the

habit of protecting her family—of *depending* on the knowledge of their safety—was too ingrained to abandon. Like an addiction, she leaned on it, turning to the knowledge when she felt weakness or despair . . . and soon she learned to turn to it before she felt so much as a glimmering of those distracting emotions, and thus avoided them altogether.

It doesn't matter, as long as . . .

So she turned to the Utem guard who placed his hand high upon her shoulder, on the bare skin between her neck and her shoulder guard, and she smiled. She knew from the way he faltered that he'd seen the darkness behind that smile, that her total lack of fear startled him and made him uncertain. "We'll reach Manacut tomorrow?" she asked him, slurring the name of the mine as he did and in that way allowing his influence over her to defuse any anger that might build. Subtle, but that was the heart of success in Necropolis. Beneath all the blatant scheming and assassinations and collusion were the subtle signs and interactions. The unspoken things.

"Yes," he said harshly, withdrawing his hand. "And then you'll find out just how kind we've been to you."

She cast him a slanting glance and said nothing. Their kindness had more to do with her harness than anything else . . . at least at first. Now, she noticed, her implacable confidence had begun to affect them. Hepetah had seen it too, had cackled quietly over the soldiers' increasing wariness of Kerraii.

Even that was too much attention. Once in the mine, she needed to find a better way to blend in. Her half-truth tale to Hepetah, that she was Wylden born and Wylden by nature, would not stand up under scrutiny. Necropolis captive, now captured by Atlantis, but still a Wylden village girl in her heart . . . *How tragic. How . . . transparent.* But so far it was all she had.

The Utem took her back to Hepetah and fastened them together, stomping off to find his supper. Kerraii's was waiting for her—a cold gruel for which she was grateful, and grateful, too, to the old woman for saving it. No one bred in Necropolis would have. Or perhaps the Atlantean was not so different after all. She'd become well aware that an association with Kerraii was to her advantage.

"Always nice to have a private moment to take care of business," Hepetah said brightly in greeting from the bit of smooth ground she'd claimed as a seat. "Did you see the mine?"

"It is an abomination," Kerraii said, though she kept her voice low. She sat next to the old woman and took the bowl of gruel. "It rakes the skin off the land, and its spoils give the Empire false power."

Hepetah's gap-toothed smile faded away. "Those are not safe words to say around here."

"Of course not." Kerraii used two fingers to scoop gruel into her mouth, thinking of Sarnen's table with its fine, deeply dyed linens and highly crafted silver and place settings. A long life had given him an appreciation of quality, and the means by which to acquire it. Kerraii had been one of those quality items . . . but she had also shared in his bounty. "But better here than there. We will reach it tomorrow."

The old woman showed fear for the first time. "I hope . . ." she said, staring off in the direction of the mine as her words trailed away. After a moment she picked them up again, her voice still quavering. "I hope I'm not so old I can't survive there . . ."

Kerraii licked one long finger clean and said in her most offhand voice, "You have skills they require. You'll be fine." And then, almost against her will, "You're with me. No one will harm you there."

Relief washed across the wrinkled old face even as something tightened inside Kerraii. Offering protection . . . offering to stand up for this old human woman . . . it was no way to remain inconspicuous. No way to protect herself or her family.

She'd have to do better.

CHAPTER 7

420 Tz, MANA CUT MINE

ON first approach, the mine and its facilities did not impress Kerraii. Even the hum of newly exposed Magestone in her body came weakly, and no one else gave any indication of feeling it at all. Of course, they were human, aside from the injured Seething Knight. They probably wouldn't feel Magestone even if they rolled in it.

"*This* is supposed to hold me?" she muttered, staring up at the high log walls with their pointed tops. She'd spotted no out guards as they came up upon the damaged hillside, prisoners walking single file on a narrow path with high grasses all around them. The Altem led the way, the rest of the guards brought up the rear, and the prisoners were left to their own thoughts in the middle.

Perhaps Manacut was meant to have out-guards. Perhaps the success of the Dark Crusade had siphoned off every available man to defend the Empire's interests. Kerraii smiled at the thought, a secretive and satisfied expression.

Hepetah gave her manacle a little jerk, throwing her slightly off balance. Single file as they were, Hepetah walked behind with one arm extended and Kerraii led the way with her manacled arm held back. It was an awkward, untenable position, and the deliberate jerk got Kerraii's attention instantly. She turned on Hepetah and hissed, "By the Land, if you—"

"Be quiet," Hepetah hissed back. "And do not smile like that where they can see you. No prisoner smiles like that, and they will wonder what you're up to."

Kerraii scowled at her, but could not deny the soundness of the thought. She turned back around to continue her assessment of the fortlike mine exterior, ever climbing, and this time kept her face expressionless.

Hepetah said slyly, "That was a Wylden curse, if these old ears heard right. I didn't believe you before, but perhaps—"

This time Kerraii gave the manacles a jerk, and heard Hepetah stumble forward behind her. After a long, sullen silence, Hepetah added, "I know why you had that look. You think these logs are the only thing between you and freedom. This is a *mine,* missy. It's what they do to you inside—what the *Magestone* does to you—that keeps you here, not their feeble walls. The only slaves they don't work to exhaustion are those like me, the ones who are already weak. From us, they try to eke out a few more years of usefulness with other labors."

"These walls will not keep me in," Kerraii said in a low voice. "Not once I am ready to go." She swung away from the view of the mines to look out over the hilly plains they'd traversed to get here. From this high point the land spread out before her; any escape would have to be made at night, for there was not enough cover to risk a daylight run. She was perfectly capable of remaining unseen in the tall grasses, but if they had hounds or even Mage Spawn were-creatures, they could track her faster than she could run.

Or if they didn't have dogs, and the guards here were anything like those bringing the prisoners to the mine, they might well simply trip over her or step on her in their attempts to quarter the area and find her. Bad luck for anyone who did, but the alarm would be raised all the same.

No, she'd go at night. She took a moment to mark the position of the tree clumps. She'd go at night and she'd go from copse to copse, traveling swiftly and silently and out of reach before they even knew of her escape.

But not until she'd been here long enough for them to grow complacent.

The limping Seething Knight before her stopped, and Kerraii looked up to see the wall of logs directly before her; the Altem gave an incomprehensible shout that must have meant something to someone, for there was a spate of fumbling from the other side, and then a section of the wall swung inward, revealing itself to be the entrance.

The Atlanteans hustled their prisoners into the mine compound and then dispersed, leaving them before a single Dwarf. Kerraii eyed him. He seemed to be too well dressed and too well fed to be a slave, but he carried himself with a petty arrogance, not with the quiet dignity of someone with true power. Someone in collusion, then. A slave who had worked himself into a better position. No doubt the humans were grateful to have a Dwarf in charge here so they could rotate their own people as often as possible, protecting them from the harmful Magestone emissions. Dwarves took no ill from Magestone and its magic, but they could take no benefit from it, either.

Kerraii marked him as someone to beware of. Dwarves as a race were known to be as resentful of the Atlanteans as any, thanks to their long history of enslavement in the mines. That this one had less care for the plight of his fellow Dwarves and more for his own skin meant he might be more easily influenced in other matters as well.

He waited until he had their attention. His dark red beard hung before his body in thick, stiff plaits, and he'd gathered his bushy hair behind his head. His trousers and tunic were rough but clean, and his belt was studded with a small, raw Magestone—an expensive reminder to the rest of them that he was immune to its dangers. He had a metal-tipped walking stick with a heavily gnarled, highly polished top, although he showed no signs of a limp or fatigue. Kerraii wondered if there might not be dried blood caught in the creases of that gnarled ball.

"My name is Jarl Gunndar," he said abruptly, and his voice was as gnarled as the walking stick.

Jarl. She thought not. It was an honor the Dwarves accorded their own.

He used the walking stick as a pointer, indicating the building on their right. Like the rest of the compound, it was made from rough logs, and Kerraii had the notion that perhaps these plains had not always been *quite* so bare of trees. Just like the humans, to take and take with no concern about replenishing the source. Unlike the other buildings, all of which were low and squat and of squared, ugly lines, this one was built on a high platform—just high enough for an occupant to see over the wall. Beside it stood a slight, one-stone mage, looking not entirely pleased to be there. "These are my quarters and my office. You will never approach them unless accompanied by a guard."

He swung his stick toward the building directly behind him, pointing accurately without so much as a glance over his shoulder. "This is a common area. You will take your meals here, bathe here, receive your orders here, tend your wounds here."

The stick moved to the next building. "Your quarters. Floor mats are provided. The building is split in half. You figure out which side you want."

And the next building, the farthest away, was snugged up against the bottom of the hill, in the juncture of the log wall and the hill. "Magestone is stored there. Once a month mages will arrive to take an accounting and transport it down the hill. I make sure they're never disappointed. So will you."

He said nothing about the long, shallow, crudely built

building with many doors tucked behind the quarters, but Kerraii's nose had already informed her of its purpose.

The Dwarf focused his attention on them as individuals, assessing them. Hepetah he quite evidently expected, for he jabbed the stick in her direction without hesitation. "You. Into the kitchen, put yourself to use."

Hepetah glanced at Kerraii, to whom she was still shackled; Gunndar made an impatient gesture at one of the guards. The man hastened to unlock the shackles, making no attempt to spare their raw and chafed wrists. He moved among the others, releasing them all, and the Jarl's stick swiftly sorted them with one-word grunts of assessment. "Mine. Compound maintenance. Mine. Mine. Mine." He gave Kerraii a slow, long look and said, "Mine."

She inclined her head slightly, as if accepting a gift.

He gave a surprised little frown, then brought himself back to the procedure at hand. "It's too late today to head up to the benches. Tomorrow you'll go up with the others, and you'll learn fast. We'll have no one here taking up space without earning it. We recite Manacut rules over each meal; you'll learn those fast, too. For now, go familiarize yourselves with the compound's layout."

Kerraii waited until some of the humans had made a tentative move in the direction of the quarters, then followed them, overtaking them in a few confident strides. On second thought, she held herself back, pacing herself to their slow gait. Once inside the building she would assess the situation at her own practiced speed, but while the Jarl was watching . . .

Then she'd do her best to seem ordinary, even though she was far from it. Even in Necropolis, she was not *ordinary*. Her training for the past eight years had seen to that.

A human male reached the first door, glanced in, and gave a slight shake of his head. He was the one who should have been their leader—the least damaged of all the humans, the strongest. But he'd never taken any steps to fill that role; instead he often glanced Kerraii's way when it seemed there might be a decision pending. He was Prieskan and went by the name Jobe Trademaker; Kerraii could only guess he'd made one deal too many, and with the wrong person at that.

She entered the building. The early evening gloom barely triggered her enhanced vision, although the low ceiling created in her a persistent impulse to duck. Another few inches and her head would be scraping the log support beams, a feature that only made the interior seem even smaller than it was. Sleep mats made a neat row of rectangles that filled the end of the building; unused mats, rolled and tied, sat in a pile in the corner. The room held a single freestanding stove for winter, currently disconnected from its chimney and shoved up against the wall. Beside it sat a rough, wood, stone-topped stared with a bowl and pitcher on top and drawers lining the front.

Kerraii scooped up a mat and went to the drawers, quickly examining the contents of each. First aid, a few common herbs, supplies of the sort needed by a room full of women, a few hard soaps, a well-used brush that would likely give her lice. A sturdy woven basket sat on the floor beside it, filled with neatly folded clothing. Nothing fancy, nothing more than the worn slaves' castaways she'd first worn upon her arrival at Necropolis.

Otherwise it was simply a rectangular room with no windows and a second, narrow door along the back wall that no doubt exited close to the outhouse row she'd seen.

It would do.

While the other two newly arrived woman stared dully at their new home, acquiring rolled mats with reluctance and placing them in the lineup only to promptly collapse upon them, Kerraii helped herself to the clothing that would most cover her. A dull brown home-weave shirt with small cap sleeves; when she held it up to herself it fell short of her navel, leaving her waist and part of her harness exposed. A nominal skirt of the same material, too short for practical use but saved by the split that turned it into a short pair of pants. A very, very short pair of pants.

They would do, too.

With quick, practiced movements, Kerraii pulled off her shoulder and knee guards. She held them for a moment of thought, searching the building for some safe place in which to secure them. Nothing but square corners and unadorned ceilings. Without wasting any more time, she turned and popped them into the stove. If the two women were paying any attention, they hid it well; they slumped on their mats, quite probably already asleep.

There the armor could stay until Kerraii was ready to leave, long before the stove came into use for winter.

With little wasted time or motion, she shrugged into the clothing she'd chosen. In the next building, the men moved around somewhat more noisily than she or her two fellow slaves, conversing loudly enough to be heard if not understood. Their tone was clear enough: some despair, some defiance, some ill-chosen derision—possibly aimed at the Jarl. Something about the length of his stick.

Kerraii used her time more wisely . . . but then she had something to hide. She pulled the sueded leather strapping from her tightly bound hair, scrubbing her fingers through it to eliminate its sleek, smooth fall. After that she braided it securely, wrapping the end of the braid around the base to form a club of hair, its length completely camouflaged. Harness covered, armor safely tucked away, hair restyled: the sight of her would no longer instantly conjure up the image of a Nightblade. She ought to remove her boots as well, but in this terrain she could not afford to do so. She could not run on sore feet.

She froze in the act of finishing off the sueded leather hair strap, listening intently to the swell of noise from behind the quarters. A glance out the open door confirmed what she suspected—twilight was upon them and the miners must be returning. Returning, and discovering the newcomers. Feeling them out . . . or testing them out. Facing the miners was not a prospect that concerned Kerraii; she would deal with it, as she dealt with everything—as long as the process didn't draw too much attention her way.

The doors to the long outhouse slammed in quick syncopation; no one came in the little back door meant for that purpose. No doubt letting the odor into their quarters wasn't worth the mild convenience of it. Kerraii untied her mat, flipped it open, and by the time the first women entered the building, sat upon it to meet them with composure.

They stumbled through the door with exhaustion written in every line of their bodies, every dragging step. They were dirty and bruised, and one woman's unhealthy yellow complexion spoke of the Magestone's slow poison. Most of them were human, but three Dwarves walked among them— strong, healthy women who looked little the worse for wear, other than the dirt and their ragged clothes. One of them said, "I told you I saw a new batch coming in." Then, to Kerraii, the only one paying any attention to them, she said, "Not many of you, were there?"

"No," Kerraii said, brushing away the light touch of a night insect. "Not many."

"And what'd *you* do to earn your place here?" another of the Dwarves said. "I'm Grelva, by the way. And you won't get any grief from us. Only you new folks are any company, the rest are too tired." Her glance rested briefly on her human comrades, all of whom had collapsed on their mats to rub their tired feet and arms. She twitched a black braid— one of many—over her shoulder, and added, "Manacut is small, but they're working us hard. It's a tough mine. You don't get here without earning it."

Kerraii stopped the cold note she'd been about to infuse

into her words. This was not Necropolis; she had no status here. She could not use familiar ways to handle such intrusive questions; she'd have to adapt. She said simply, "My name is Willeta. I was in the wrong place at the wrong time."

Eventually they might learn the details. The Seething Knight was not likely to be nearly as discreet as she. But the longer it took, the better. In the meantime, her sister's classically Wylden name would misdirect them.

Grelva let out a snort of a laugh. "Weren't we all," she said, but she didn't push. "They'll bang the dinner bar soon," she said, addressing her words to the other two newcomers as well as Kerraii. "If you want to run out back, do it. Gunndar doesn't treat stragglers kindly."

With twin groans, the other two women climbed to their feet. Several of the others went to the basin, pouring water to splash on their arms and faces.

"We all do our share to keep that full," said the third Dwarf, the shortest of them. She came to stand by Kerraii, who was still seated, and only topped Kerraii's head by a few inches. "My name is Feywold. We," and she indicated the other two Dwarf women, "were here before any of these women and I guess we'll be here when they all go—or until the ley lines move and make the mine a bust. We know how to make things easiest for all of us, and how to stay out of Gunndar's way. You'll listen to us, if you want to fit in here." She nodded at the third woman and said, "This is Inger."

"It's not exactly like home," said Grelva, and she snorted another laugh at the thought, "but it can be far, far worse."

"As long as I'm here, I'll make every effort to fit in," Kerraii said truthfully. *As long as I'm here.* She was more than glad to let these three take the leadership roles—and the attention it would remove from her.

The three exchanged a satisfied look. "I like your attitude," said Feywold. Her hair was as blonde as Grelva's was black, but contained in the same arrangement of braids.

Were it not for their hair—the third woman's was a dull brown—Kerraii would have had difficulty sorting them out. She was unused to Dwarvish features—full, lively, rounded features with plump lips and deep-set eyes—and could see only the sameness of them. She wondered how she looked to them—she was everything long and slender, from top to bottom. Her own features were fine-cut and angled, with the bone close to the surface. Even her eyes were angled.

At a sudden thought, she said, "Have there been many of my kind here?"

"Not many," Grelva said succinctly. "Though from the rumors I hear, there'll soon be more. More of the Black Powder folks, as well."

The Dark Crusade. Word was spreading. And the Black Powder Rebels . . . they'd be fools if they didn't take advantage of the distraction to press their cause.

From outside came the sound of raised voices, a man laughing, a woman protesting in fear. Inger rolled her eyes. "Men," she said. "Some of them don't make it as easy for newcomers as we do."

Kerraii came to her feet, well able to surmise what was going on outside. And then she heard Hepetah's voice, fearful and quavery, and stiffened with anger. A quiet voice in her head spoke reminders to her. *Be unremarkable. Go unnoticed. Escape.* Except she was already in the doorway, looking out on a twilit yard that was plenty bright to her eyes.

Not all the men were involved. Most of them didn't even care; they were as tired as the women, and wanted to get ready for their meal. The few male Dwarves turned away with gestures of dismissive disgust, not wanting anything to do with the fuss yet not willing to risk themselves. But two of the humans had come across the new women returning from the crude facilities, and Hepetah had come into the middle of it, on her way from the kitchen to the quarters.

Kerraii sized the humans up in an instant. They were big men, hearty enough that the mine work didn't tear them down as it did most of the others, hearty enough that they probably acquired more than their share of whatever food was available.

Hearty enough that they weren't used to opposition.

Kerraii thought perhaps they should learn what opposition felt like.

Grelva put a hand on Kerraii's arm, seeing the intent in Kerraii's unconsciously straightened posture and narrowed eyes. "You don't want to do that," she said quietly. "They won't treat the women too badly, or they'd get in trouble with Gunndar. If you get hurt for starting something, it'll go badly with you."

"Looks like *something* is already started," Kerraii said, struggling with the protective instincts that had reemerged during her journey with Hepetah. The old woman now scolded the men terribly—and then landed on the hard dusty ground when they shoved her aside. Kerraii's eyes narrowed even further. If anyone knew what it was like to have a single, decisive moment in her life when someone else's protection would have changed everything . . .

I do.

She strolled out into the common area. To her surprise, Grelva eased in behind her. Not crowding, but close enough to let the men know she was part of this if she had to be. *Gutsy little woman.*

The swirl of activity and noise stopped; the men looked at Kerraii and looked at each other and grinned. They each held one of the women, one-handed grips with fingers digging into flesh. The women, exhausted and terrified, had clearly put up a fight nonetheless; their already worn clothing showed the signs of it, and one man's face bore the red imprint of a hand.

"Boys," Kerraii said, her voice soft and low but with

enough of an edge to show her disdain, "I think you've had enough fun here." She reached down, helping Hepetah to her feet. "And hasn't anyone ever told you it's not smart to make an enemy of the cook?"

The reactions of the men lingering in their own doorway told her that one had hit home—but only with the ones who were thinking sensibly to start with. Those men gave each other nudges and knowing smiles, though they were distracted as the Seething Knight—Kerraii had never bothered to learn his name and didn't care if she ever did—limped up to the doorway behind them.

He looked out on the scene in the common area, saw Kerraii standing there, and smiled a dark and knowing smile. This, she could tell, he would enjoy. The nearest thing he would get to watching blood pit action, no doubt.

Not even close.

The men didn't seem to share the assessment; they seemed to think themselves quite impressive. One sneered at her and said, "Dunno. Looks like maybe the fun is just starting."

"By *my* definition of fun, yes." She took up enough of a stance that they recognized her intent to see this through. It was as much warning as she'd give them.

They thought to scare her off. "You don't want to get hurt," the first man said, holding his captive at arm's length. "You don't want to mess up that pretty face."

And the second man laughed. "You have no idea what you're getting into."

She smiled at him, a full smile. A true smile. A dangerous smile. "Funny," she said. "I was about to say the same to you."

412 Tz. TRAINING PIT

Kerraii had no idea what she was getting into.

She knew it, and the fact terrified her.

The blood pit stretched out before her, the sands hot and

bright. Too bright, to her newly enhanced night vision—a gift from Sarnen, and one that most Sect Elves had to earn through deed and blood pit success. "You'll earn it quickly," he'd said, as if reassuring her, "one way or the other."

She hadn't found it reassuring at all.

And now she squinted out into the afternoon sands, knowing the night vision would be as much a hindrance as a help until the spell fully integrated with her body, and that no one would make allowances for the handicap even on this, her first day in the pits.

She didn't want to fight. She didn't want to kill. And yet . . .

Do what you must to survive.

She'd been in the dark city just shy of a week. The light, well-balanced sword still felt strange to her hand, and the swordplay drills had not yet taken hold in her body. Yet here she stood, hovering in the entrance to the blood pit, waiting her turn. A line of Nightblades-in-training—her companions from Slawinda's crowded room within Sarnen's tower—pressed in behind her, leading back into the dark tunnel that circled the blood pit. Even though this was one of the smaller pits near the island's rocky shoreline, it had still been built with all the amenities . . . rooms beneath the soaring stadium seating for preparing and recovering from the fight, rooms for celebration after that. Death Merchants and Necromancers feted their Nightblade and Seething Knight champions here in ostentatious and indulgent displays that were as much a part of the power-jostling as anything in Necropolis. Those rooms were as richly appointed as any Deathspeaker's tower.

And then there were the other rooms. The rooms where the dead were stacked, for disposal or for reincarnation in Zombie form. Perfect fodder on which the Necromancers could learn and perfect their arts.

Slawinda made sure they knew that any young woman to

die today would be taken to just such a room and used for practice by the greenest of Necromancers. If they were lucky, the students would fail to revive them at all. If luck went against them, then they'd come back as the crudest of Zombies, slated for brute labor and battle with only a hazy memory of what they'd once been, and a constant itch of yearning for the same.

Kerraii knew she was swift and graceful and strong. She knew she'd be paired with one of the very Zombie fighters Slawinda threatened as their fate. Necropolis was a merciless battleground of kill or be killed, but through the Dark Prophet, Tezla counseled the Deathspeakers against wasting their new acquisitions, and the Deathspeakers trained those new acquisitions accordingly—pushing them hard enough that the timid would indeed succumb, but not so hard as to waste those with potential.

Still, she was terrified. Because Slawinda had whispered into her ear, as she came to take the place of the next woman into the pit, Slawinda had confirmed the truth Kerraii had suspected within days of her arrival. *Your family is safe* only *so long as you please Sarnen.* She'd given Kerraii just enough time to understand, then she'd added, *And I am the one who reports your accomplishments to Sarnen, so see that you make me look good today.*

Her eyes hurt. Her legs trembled. Her arms felt leaden, and the sword was suddenly a dead chunk of heavy metal in her hand. Out in the pit, a young woman—one come to this training by choice and through family connections—had failed to dispatch the Zombie before her stamina failed her, and now she flailed her sword before her in an attempt to stave off its attacks.

The Zombies were slow and stupid, but they were persistent. This one battered its way through the exhausted Elf's guard and dealt her a deep slash across the leg; the Elf shrieked in pain and then—in utter desperation—somehow managed to run the Zombie through entirely. Her blade grated to a stop; as the Zombie looked down in a vapid kind of astonishment, the young woman fought to pull it free—and failed. When the Zombie toppled, it took the sword and the woman with it, falling atop her and trapping her.

Slawinda made a disgusted noise. She poked Kerraii. "*You,*" she said sharply, "will do better than that. Now go!"

Startled, Kerraii made a less than graceful entrance to the sound of laughter. As few spectators as there were, there were still enough to notice and comment on the new fighters. One in particular, down in the bottom row, seemed to enjoy her clumsiness. As slaves removed the Zombie from the pit and dragged the young Elf away, she marked the observer as human and wondered about his presence here.

But not for long. The sand called to her, beating against her bare legs with reflected heat. Soon she would acquire a Nightblade harness; after that she'd have the opportunity to earn the spells that would enhance it and make it unique to her. Until then she fought like the others—in a sleeveless, metal-studded gambeson that stank of the previous occupants' fears worn over her short, flimsy skirt, and low boots that kept her ankles from knuckling over in the sand. Except, unlike the others, she was blinded by the sand. She squinted over the expanse of the ring, uncertain if the wavering view came from the heat, tears, or the troublesome new spell.

From across the pit, her Zombie opponent trudged toward her, showing no enthusiasm but with the dogged obedience of its kind. Tentatively, she went to meet it. She expected it to hesitate when they closed to sparring distance—most of them had—but this one slashed at her without any such interruption, a stroke she barely parried—and because her parry was late, rather than block the clumsy blow with finesse, she needed strength. Off balance, she struggled to right herself for the next exchange, desperately trying to watch the center of the Zombie's chest, to gauge its—*his*—

next move. But her watering eyes saw only a blur, and the Zombie's next stroke caught her equally behind the action.

The human laughed again, a cruel sound. Kerraii would have ignored him but for Slawinda's warnings. If this man saw her as something to laugh at, surely Sarnen would not be pleased. Not pleased at all. And she remembered what had happened to the woman who'd fought before her, how quickly she'd worn down in this heat. Sweat prickled at Kerraii's back and sides; fear prickled down her spine. She didn't really want to kill this creature—

Do what you must.

And suddenly she saw a glimpse of the same reluctance on the Zombie's face. Whoever it was—whoever it had *been*—it did not like its task. But orders were orders; it had even less choice than she. No choice at all. One of them would kill the other.

Determined to grab the initiative, Kerraii blinked to clear her vision, slipped her light blade inside the Zombie's guard, and slashed its arm. It roared with surprise . . . and still the human laughed. *Why—?*

And then she saw why. A second Zombie had entered the pit and was doggedly making for the confrontation. Kerraii whirled back to the dark blot of an archway within which Slawinda stood, waiting for her to protest, to stop this unfair fight. But Slawinda said nothing, and the second Zombie closed in on her even as the first one batted at her with its crude sword. Kerraii understood, then, that there was no such thing as *unfair* here, that Slawinda would not risk her own interests by protecting Kerraii, no matter the error that had allowed the second Zombie to take to the sands. That Kerraii could only look to herself.

Panic gripped her chest, making it impossible to exhale the breath she'd just taken. *Two Zombies.* And she couldn't see. Not well enough.

And if she could see . . . ?

A sudden surge of anger took her. If she could see, she'd cut these Zombies into little pieces and stuff them down the throat of the one who'd opened the door for the second. *If she could see . . .*

Then do something about it.

To the derisive reaction of the sparse and scattered crowd, Kerraii skipped back out of range, quicker than both Zombies, quicker than most anything. She yanked her skirt down tight and drew her sword along the taut material, slicing off a long, wide ribbon. With a calculating glance at the advancing Zombies, she jabbed her sword into the sand and quickly tied the material around her eyes, yanking it tight as she knotted it. Flimsy enough to see through, it nevertheless blocked the worst of the sun glare on her sensitive eyes.

She finished as they came upon her, and she yanked the sword from the sand, using the momentum to pivot in a quick circle and come back around outside the nearest Zombie's guard.

She cut his arm off.

Now she could see. Now she was mad.

She killed the second Zombie while the first was staring stupidly at the stump of its forearm, and then she killed that one, too.

And she began to understand what she had gotten into.

420 Tz, MANA CUT MINE

"Gunndar won't stop us," said the first man. He had dark hair and lots of it . . . not just on his head, but coarsely sprinkled down his arms, and fluffing out at the neck of his rough tunic. He more than made up for the other man's paucity of hair, the remaining fuzz of which looked like it had probably been light red. Magestone at work, that baldness. It followed no natural pattern. Soon this man would feel the other effects, and then he would no longer be quite so much of a bully. But until then . . .

"Not unless we make you unfit for work," the balding man added, running a hand over his peach fuzz head in an anticipatory gesture. "But we know better, so we won't, and he'll leave us alone. You should have stayed out of this. No one's going to save you."

Kerraii gave him a disdainfully amused little snort. "What makes you think I need to be saved?"

They exchanged a single glance and simultaneously released the two women, shoving them away to sprawl in the dirt. Feywold and Inger rushed in to help them up and pull them out of the way, all the while casting baleful glares at the rest of the men, especially the Dwarves who had done nothing. Kerraii gave a little smile, thinking that those Dwarves were probably going to be mighty lonely over the next week or so. She waited, unconcerned, while the two men reached for her, hesitating only at the last moment when they realized she was not flinching, cringing away, or even apparently going to react at all. For the first moment they doubted their own course of action.

Too late.

But she remembered what they had said. There would not be a problem so long as she did not render them unfit for work. She grasped a reaching arm, twisted *just so,* a two-handed move that took no strength yet would have broken both bones of his arm had she wanted it to. As he squawked in pained astonishment and went down to his knees, she pivoted behind and planted her boot hard in the middle of his back, knocking the wind from his lungs and leaving him whooping, facedown in the dirt.

The hairy fellow was not so much the fool he'd seemed; instead of roaring with anger and rushing her, he hesitated. Kerraii was in no mood to let him go unscathed, he with his arrogant, bully threats. Another step, a pivot, her chambered leg releasing its kick at just the right moment. She hit him behind the knees with a roundhouse blow that took him down, moving with her momentum in a smooth arc around behind him and then bringing the back edge of her arm across his throat just hard enough to make him gag and choke and wheeze.

The men fell and moaned and twitched; Kerraii brought her effortless dance to a halt right where she'd started. She put a thoughtful hand at her waist, standing hipshot. "Hmm," she said to Grelva. "He was right. Gunndar didn't even try to stop me."

"Not even if he'd had the time," Grelva agreed, her eyes still wide even as she strove for a casual tone of voice. She leaned a little closer to Kerraii. "But you can be sure he saw it all."

"He'll have no trouble from me." Kerraii glanced up at the tower dwelling. Not a great beginning to her plan to remain inconspicuous. "None that I *start*," she amended. She nudged the bald man with her toe. "You listening to me?"

Quickly, in a reaction tinged with comical panic, he nodded. *Yesyesyes.*

"Leave the women alone—unless, of course, they don't want to be left alone. Do you understand, or should I look for shorter words to use?"

"No, no," the man said. "We understand. Don't we, Aderic?"

The hairy man only grunted, but his assent was clear enough.

Kerraii gave them a small, amused smile. "And remember what I said about the cook. I'm not really going to hurt you. I don't want Gunndar to hold a grudge against me. Bruises, fleeting if excruciating pain, nothing serious." Not unless she thought she had to, and even then she'd wait until the moment of her escape. The men needed to have other consequences in mind, consequences having nothing to do with Kerraii. "But the cook . . . don't make her mad."

Off to the side Hepetah scowled, made mighty throat-clearing noises, and spat quite meaningfully—and accurately—between the two men.

Their simultaneously surprised and dismayed expressions told Kerraii they'd understood completely.

She smiled complacently and said, "Hepetah, do I smell food waiting?"

CHAPTER 8

420 Tz. Mana Cut mine

THE brief fight didn't end the small troubles and intimidations for the new arrivals, but Kerraii pretended not to see those. They gave the men—and some of the women—an outlet for their frustrations and aggressions.

And I'll be Land-damned if I'm going to hold everyone's hand. Let them deal with the small things on their own.

The first day after her arrival, Gunndar spent a long moment standing before Kerraii during the routine morning lineup, in which he daily took the time to strut before them with his pet one-stone mage, remind them of his importance, and then send them off to their labor. He tapped the ball of his walking stick against his palm in a thoughtful way, regarding her with narrowed eyes . . . and then he moved on. Kerraii didn't bother to sigh with relief.

Nor did she react to the guards during the following days, when they found excuses to push and nudge and yell at her. Their crude intrusions were barely worth noticing after the much more skillful machinations of Necropolis. She had her goals set. She'd do what she had to, and then she'd escape. And when that happened . . . *Then look out, you fools.* But for now she was merely an Elf of indeterminate origins, dressed in rags, her harness hidden from the world. No doubt Gunndar had seen it when she arrived. Her family's safety relied not on the plausibility of her cover story so much as making sure she gave him no reason to question it before she could escape.

It took only a day to understand the rhythms of working on the strip mine benches. With a plain but decent breakfast in their bellies, the slaves trudged up the switchback pathways to the top bench of the strip mine, forced to do the labor that magic-driven machinery, disrupted by the thick Magestone radiation, could not. They were working the hill back by an arm's length each pass, and unless they found a major cluster, they'd chop the hill back in a strip, then take their picks and shovels and mason's hammers down the switchback to the next lower bench, repeating that exhausting pattern all way down to the bottom.

And then they would no doubt start at the top again, repeating the cycle over and over until the ley lines that generated the Magestone moved or the hill gave out. Or until the slaves gave out . . . but that didn't seem likely. Already there were rumors of new prisoners on the way. Kerraii wondered if Necropolis had its own share of new slaves . . . and new Zombie troops.

But she didn't wonder out loud. She did her share of honest work and she spent most of her time listening in the process.

It turned out that the Dwarves liked to gossip. They didn't go for idle gossip. They prided themselves on spreading accurate details of the Empire's progress and defeats. Not necessarily fresh news, but always reliable news.

"Snow, Karrudan's assassin, stole a shipment of Magestone on the way to Caero," they'd whisper, carefully loading the egg-shaped Magestone into the padded cart that carried the deposits down the switchbacks to the storage building. Not that Kerraii had ever seen a Magestone break, but Gunndar was determined not to waste a single one—not when the processed crystals were needed for all the

Atlantean Technomantic devices, from lightning guns to golems to even the floating cities. Later, as the Dwarves bent close with their mason's hammers to chip the Magestone free from the matrix of hard rock around it, they'd murmur, "Blackwyn freed a batch of slaves near Enos Joppa. Maybe he'll come here . . ."

She heard much about that Blackwyn, a warlord who'd somehow captured the attention of the people. He seemed unique among the Black Powder Rebels—less inclined toward showy violence and more inclined to thoughtful, long-term goals—but he caused his own share of trouble. Kerraii found herself thinking that he fit more into the Necropolis way of doing things than any other, with his patience and more subtle approach. The Atlanteans liked to roll over their opponents with a blast of showy force, while the Wylden Elementalists used more righteous but equally violent tactics. In Necropolis, one did best by keeping the long view in mind, working quietly toward each goal, and attacking with efficient violence when the time was right.

All the same, she grew impatient with hearing Blackwyn's name spoken so reverently. "He might be the one," Inger would say to Feywold, and Feywold would nod most seriously. The Mageprince, they meant. The fabled hero who would one day unite this chaotic and warring land.

Kerraii depended on no fabled hero. She would take care of herself.

After Kerraii had been there for a week of mind- and body-numbing labor, one of the human men died and the big balding fellow started to show signs of weakness. Another arrived to replace the dead man, an Atlantean ex-gunner already battle torn and scarred. And the day after that, Kerraii was chipping free a Magestone egg the size of a troll's head—the largest she'd seen here—when Inger crouched by Grelva, wiping grimy sweat from her brow and upper lip but with the satisfied expression that came with good gossip. "Necropolis attacked the new Roa Kaiten settlement north of Fairhaven, two weeks since."

"Those people were fools to settle so far north—and yet not far enough north to have the protection of the mountains." Grelva stopped work long enough for a wistful look at the thought of the mountains.

Inger nudged her, glancing back at the bored guard . . . one of the cookie-cutter Utem guards. The merest hint of slacking would bring him running to apply his short whip or his boot, just because it was something to do. Grelva quickly reapplied herself to a flaw in the rock that looked like it might lead to newly formed Magestone. Inger jammed the end of her pick into that flaw and pried at it, grunting with effort. "Well," she said between attempts to flake away the rock, "they're still there."

"The settlers?" Grelva asked in surprise. Rock chips flew, stinging Kerraii's thigh.

"The settlers," Inger said. "The Empire might not have known the extent of this new Dark Crusade, but they knew about *that* attack. Our new Atlantean gunner says there was a spy in Necropolis, so they had mages waiting and they not only fought off banshees and fell beasts, but they killed *every one* of those dark Elves."

Kerraii pried the Magestone loose with a grunt of effort. Then she looked down on the Dwarves, hefting the Magestone, expression thoughtful. The Dwarves had speculated about her, she knew. And now, to judge by the sly, clever look Inger gave her, they seemed to think they had it figured out. "*Every* one," Inger repeated, and then added in the lowest possible murmur, "Funny thing is I was checking the stove for rat nests the other day . . ."

Kerraii's fingers tightened around the Magestone. She said nothing.

Grelva said earnestly, just as low, "We don't care, not now. Not *here*. If you want to be Wylden, that's fine. You know how we feel, we're in it together. We have to be, to survive. But what *news* have you? He said the Atlanteans killed *everyone*—"

They knew. Not all, but enough to spurn her if she should confirm it. From what she could gather, Gunndar himself took in his slaves with no concern for anything but the work they might do. Certainly he'd seen her Nightblade harness upon arrival, but he believed her name was Willeta. Now consistently dressed in rags with her sleek black hair in a rough braid, she would do nothing to attract Gunndar's thoughts back to her original attire—even though, as a simple Nightblade, she was likely to be safe regardless.

Willeta the former Nightblade was of no exceptional note; Kerraii, *Sarnen's* former chosen, was a different matter. *That* detail the Dwarf women would not learn, whatever else might come of this conversation.

We don't care, Grelva had said. If it were true, Kerraii could only strengthen their alliance by sharing, by providing the news they cherished. If it were not true . . . it was already too late. Deliberately, Kerraii said, "No. The Atlanteans did not kill every single one of the enemy."

Perking up, Inger said, "The new man—"

"Is wrong."

Inger's expression grew Dwarf-stubborn, but good-naturedly so. She gloried in a good debate. "He says he was there. Fighting for the Atlanteans. But he stepped on the wrong toes afterward, so they sent him here."

"Then he lies," Kerraii said, knowing the Dwarves would consider this even worse than an honest error.

They absorbed her laconic reaction for a moment, working at the rock, showing no reaction to the confirmation that she'd been at the fight, that she was other than she now seemed. If she acted like one of them, then she *was* one of them. Under those terms, Kerraii had earned her place that first day, when she'd protected Hepetah and the others.

As if there'd been no interruption, Inger said, "Tell us more of what you know, then."

Carefully, Kerraii set the big Magestone at her feet and applied her pick to the bench face. She was supposed to take the Magestone immediately to one of the carts sitting midway along the bench, but as long as she was working, the guard would leave her alone. Besides, when she went to the cart she intended to keep right on going; the new arrival worked on the other side of it and she had words for him now. Taking a mighty *thwak!* at the rock and dirt before her, she said easily, "Most of the company leaders made it to safety." She didn't know for sure how many, but she hadn't seen them at the settlement afterward or with the dead. "A few of the warriors." Yevena hadn't been among the dead or wounded; neither had Kilte. "The ambush was thorough, but you can rest assured the survivors returned to Necropolis. The spy is no doubt dead by now."

"You can't *know* that," Inger said, puffing slightly as she continued to work the promising crack of rock.

"No," Kerraii said. "But I believe it. That there were survivors, however, is a certainty."

Grelva glanced up beyond the cart, where the lamed Seething Knight worked. He'd been stripped of his armor, but retained the black tunic and trousers he'd been wearing beneath. Unlike Kerraii, he had no reason to hide what he was: *Roa Kaiten survivor*. And fortunately for Kerraii, it amused him to keep her identity a secret, if he even knew her true name. No doubt he was waiting for—and looking forward to—the day one of the guards went too far in prodding and provoking her, and the resulting entertainment.

He'd be waiting a long time. Kerraii had no intention of jeopardizing her escape over what amounted to minor annoyances. Bad enough the Dwarves' discovery of her armor had backed her into the chance she'd just taken.

To Grelva she said, "Yes. He was there."

"And you," Grelva prompted.

Kerraii didn't answer, not willing to say it out loud.

"I don't see why we should believe you over someone who admits he was there." Inger frowned at her, putting her hands on her hips—though only long enough for the frown; then she cast a quick look at the guard and got back to work.

Grelva flipped a braid of barely contained curly hair over her shoulder and gave her friend a *tsk*. "Our tall friend has made life easier here for a time. Have you not noticed the way the others cling to her shadow, feeling safer there?"

Kerraii certainly had.

"Leave her be," Grelva continued. "Mayhap if you press the ex-gunner, you will get more truth from him."

"As it happens, I'm headed that way myself." Kerraii shouldered her pick and scooped up the newly mined Magestone, tucking it along the inside of her crooked elbow as she headed for the cart. Behind her, Grelva made a noise—warning or protest, but broke off when she realized it would only alert the guard. Kerraii strode past where the human women worked, trying to block the guard from seeing that one of them had weakened so badly that she could hardly lift her pickax. She approached the cart with her Magestone bounty and, as gently as you please, placed it in among the other, smaller stones. *The Empire must be desperate, to keep us at work for such small reward.* They could not have known about the extent of the Dark Crusade . . . and that meant the Black Powder Rebels were already pushing the Empire hard. The Atlantean masters and warlords could not afford to pass over even a nugget of Magestone.

The men watched her approach with something akin to trepidation, and turned back to work with relief when she eased in beside the ex-lightning gunner and put herself back to work. He gave her a wary look; he either recognized what she was, or he'd been warned what she could do. For his own part he moved slowly, his arms and hands stricken with a strange palsy. Kerraii recognized it right away. Remembered it. "You must have been near a magic blast, but not actually in the thick of the battle, or you'd be dead," she observed, digging her pick into the rock-studded dirt near his head.

Very near to his head.

"Around the edges," he said, definitely wary now. He had none of his Amotep armor left to him, and his side-shaved haircut was filling in with bristle.

"And were you running away?" she asked, soft words with bite.

He jerked around to glare at her.

Kerraii landed another blow close to his head; dirt sprayed, peppering them both. "A gunner belongs in the thick of it," she observed. "And quite obviously you have displeased your masters."

"I was going after one of those Dark Elf dogs," the man said sullenly, using his small mason's hammer to pry free the most modest of Magestone eggs.

"I guess they thought that wasn't your job," Kerraii said. She waved at the touch of an unseen insect. "Nor is it your job to spread false information about that fight, no matter how much it makes you feel better. There were Sect survivors and you know it."

The man grunted. "And what do you care?"

"Aside from the fact that if your quarters mate the Dark Elf dog hears you, he's likely to make your shockwave palsy feel like a welcome distraction? I don't." She did. It annoyed her. But it was not in her best interests to mention it. She nodded down along the bench, where Grelva dumped a handful of tiny Magestones into the cart. "But she does. All the Dwarves do. When they pass along news, they want it to be *real*. And I like them, so I'm telling you." She gave him a thoughtful, slant-eyed look. "I don't expect that part to matter to you. But your best chance to last around here is if the knight doesn't hear what you've said."

The man made a hawking noise in his throat, made as if to spit at her feet, and changed his mind, aiming instead in the other direction. "And I suppose you chat with him all the time."

"Often enough," she agreed, and smiled. Indirect threats were a Necropolis specialty. "Enough to know he won't take kindly to your lies about his battle."

"Dark Elves," the man said, making the words sound like a curse. "We've held you off for years."

"You mistake me," Kerraii said. "I am Wylden."

He gave her a sharp look, raking her from top to bottom with his gaze and then doing it again, looking unconvinced all the while. But he didn't argue. He said, "Then you know what I'm talking about. Within the past five years we've liberated dozens of remote Wylden villages. I've helped liberate at least five of 'em myself."

Wylden villages? Freed? My village? My family? Startled, shaken to the core, Kerraii drew on every bit of her Necropolis experience to hide her turmoil from him. *If it's true . . . if they're free . . . if I can find them . . .*

Trembling inside, on the outside she merely arched an eloquent brow and said, "Liberated? Or just occupied by new intruders?"

He snarled at her with his expression. "You've got a bad attitude."

"Yes," she said, and thunked the pick into the wall of dirt so solidly that he couldn't hold back his wince.

Kerraii had wanted to ask the gunner about her own village, had wanted to ask him so badly she literally bit her tongue until the sharp taste of blood filled her mouth.

Sarnen would have liked that.

But she didn't trust the gunner, and she wanted no more conversation with him. She could not give him the opportunity to pierce a story almost as thin as the ragged clothing that covered her battle harness. Fortunately, the gunner seemed fully immersed in his own misery, and unlikely to pursue any suspicions he might already have. Or maybe, like her, he realized it made little difference to Gunndar.

She left him, dumping a handful of small Magestone eggs into the cart on her way by, and averting her gaze from the guard's. She was having a much harder time than she'd anticipated, keeping herself inconspicious. From protecting the women—and they definitely clung to her shadow when the slaves mingled in the common area before and after meals and work—to controlling her own fierce spark of anger.

On the other hand, a Wylden Elementalist forced to mine Magestone has plenty of incentive to anger.

But she needed to quit thinking like a Nightblade and keep her mind settled in her Wylden persona.

Oddly, it bothered her that she could not slide right back into her childhood ways. For years she'd accepted her new life, done what she had to . . . and now she was suddenly not entirely certain of her role, not certain who she should be to continue to thrive . . . or who she *wanted* to be.

But she was entirely certain of one thing. She needed to know more about the gunner's claims. She needed to know if Necropolis had lost its hold on the Wylden villages to the Atlanteans . . . and if one of them had been her own, if, for five years and more, the occasional appearance of belongings from her family's home in Sarnen's quarters meant nothing more than his foresight at the time of her kidnapping. Had he merely gathered those items at the time to dole them out over the years as a way of convincing her he still had her family's fate in his hands?

It had worked.

Not only had it worked, it had worked well. Kerraii had never even entertained a moment's doubt that her continuing success ensured her family's safety. Her mother, her father,

her sister: keeping them in mind had given her strength. Now she didn't know if they'd been free all along . . . or if the Empire had long ago taken them away to rot in a mine like this one.

She'd have to find her own strength, now.

But first she had to *know*.

The Dwarves were her only chance. She didn't speak to them upon her return to their sides; she didn't trust herself to remain casual, and the guards would take too great an interest in anything that wasn't. They, too, looked for diversions in their dreary days, and distractions from the fact that their relief was long in coming—while radiation from the Magestone mine was killing them. The escalating conflicts in the Land had left the Atlantean Empire short of more than just Magestone.

So she waited. She ran her bitten tongue along the inside edges of her teeth and she worked through the rest of the afternoon, uncovering several large eggs of Magestone deposits with her vigor. The Dwarves eyed her askance, knowing better than anyone the importance of conserving energy in this place where no one had a chance to recover from weakness or sickness. Grelva even hissed a warning at her, though not one Kerraii could heed.

What if they're safe?

What if they've been safe?

She waited through the end of the work day, and then through the spare rations of their evening meal. The guards ate well enough, as did Gunndar . . . but Gunndar saw no point in wasting good food on short-lived slaves. Yet Kerraii was not so distracted that she didn't see the ex-gunner huddled with the hairy fellow she'd taken down on her first day here, nor did she fail to notice that they kept glancing her way as they spoke, almost in spite of themselves.

If my family is safe, Sarnen has no hold on me. If they're safe, I can escape this very night.

Darkness fell; Kerraii found her sleeping mat and sat cross-legged there, alert and gracefully straight-backed even after this day's work. She waited until Grelva moved into the maze of mats across the end of the room and stopped her with little more than the lift of her chin.

"You're acting mighty strange today," Grelva said, looking at her in the dull candlelight. "First you get all huffy because the gunner got his story wrong. And since you came back from talking to him, you've been no sort of company at all."

Kerraii was not used to being considered "company" in the first place. She hesitated, and wasn't used to *that,* either. The importance of the answers she sought overwhelmed her . . . not a feeling she'd allowed herself for a long, long time. Grelva waited, putting a fist on her hip in impatience. Finally Kerraii said, "He mentioned the Wylden villages. The remote villages, the ones Necropolis raided and held starting eight years ago." The massive influx of new Sect Elves, all in preparation for the long-view planning of the Dark Crusade. "He said the Empire had . . . *freed* . . . those villages. Do you know of it?"

Grelva shrugged. "Old news," she said, but then she took a moment, her hand falling from her hip, to give Kerraii a narrow-eyed look. "Not old news to you."

Kerraii took a long, considered breath. *It's true. They're safe from Sarnen.* No longer would she have to make her decisions based on the potential consequences to her aging parents. "I had been told elsewise."

"It's been years," Grelva said. "Not that Necropolis ever did anything but claim the territory, once they'd finished with the initial raids. There was no one left in the villages worth taking, I guess—either too young or too old. Now the Empire occupies them all." She crouched beside Kerraii, deeply intrigued. "What's your story, Willeta?"

Kerraii gave a barely discernable shake of her head. It

was enough; disappointment crossed Grelva's face and she sighed. "Anyway, the Empire doesn't keep a tight hold on them. It's enough that they have the territory; the Elementalists would be spurred to action if they messed with the people overmuch—what's left of 'em, anyway."

"Have they not rebuilt?"

Grelva lifted her hands, an admission that she didn't know. "Some have, I think. The Empire doesn't know it, but most of 'em spend their energy finding quiet little ways to help the Black Powder Rebels."

Surprise rippled through Kerraii; it must have shown on her face.

Grelva nodded vigorously, though she glanced outside and kept her voice low when she spoke again. Around them, most of the other women had already taken to their beds. No one bothered with their murmured conversation; no one bothered with anything but closing her eyes. They'd be back at the mines before the sun lit the face of the heavily scarred hillside, an unsatisfactory breakfast in their bellies and picks in their calloused, blistered, and bleeding hands. They cared little if Grelva and Kerraii gave up precious moments of sleep. Grelva said, "Makes sense to me. The Elementalists didn't protect them. The Dark Sect stole their children and their lives. The Empire struts around pretending to own them. Who does that leave? Why not fight for the cause of freedom?"

Kerraii felt a perverse pride in knowing her people were choosing their own path . . . much like she now had the chance to choose hers.

"Who do you fight for?" Grelva asked, thinking herself canny.

"Myself," Kerraii said, but her tone was gentler than it might have been even a few weeks earlier. "My thanks, Grelva. Don't let me keep you from your sleep any longer."

"Hmph," Grelva said, but without the emphasis it might have held. "One of these days you'll tell your story."

Kerraii's smile held no humor. "Perhaps one day you'll hear it."

That pretty much depended on how things went from here.

CHAPTER 9

420 Tz. Mana Cut mine

KERRAII waited until night fell solidly over the compound; even the guards quit their games of chance and settled in to the light dozing that was their norm. With the soft snores of exhausted women around her Kerraii eased to her feet and found her way to the door—secure in the knowledge that while no one else in this room could see without fumbling to light a candle, she had Sarnen's gift of night vision to show her the way.

That it was a gift he might someday rue came to her in a sudden thought that beckoned her to dwell upon it. She forced herself to concentrate.

She cracked the door and left it that way. If anyone was alert they might notice it, but odds were they'd barely glance inside if they chose to close it. Meanwhile Kerraii would know who was paying attention—and therefore to whom *she'd* need to pay attention.

Retrieving her armor from the stove was a harder chore, and slower. After each inevitable *ting* of metal again metal, she waited, both patient and impatient, checking to see if anyone had woken or noticed her. It gave her time to review her observations of the previous nights . . . how the guards were tired and dozed, how there weren't many of them on post at night anyway. How they counted on the slaves' exhaustion to act as a deterrent to trouble—that, and their big, stout wall. Guards took posts at the bottom of Gunndar's tower, by the awkward compound entrance, and by the Magestone storage shed—the one that snugged up against the fence and the hill.

That last would create the hardest part of this night, for she intended to climb the shed and spring from the roof to the top of the inconveniently pointed log fence. She would head out into the hostile, unknown land with nothing more than the small knives in her boots and harness, and a piece of coarse bread stolen from their evening meal. She still wasn't sure whether she'd eat it or use it for snare bait. And since she wouldn't be building any fires for a while, maybe she'd finally acquire a taste for blood.

At last armored up, she stuffed her thin rags through the sword belt slung across her shoulder. The harness would keep her warmer than anyone guessed with no need of the rags, but she wanted to keep her options open. She intended to avoid people entirely until she reached more neutral terri- tory—perhaps even her own village—but she might well run into a situation where being able to cover her harness came in handy.

She took one last look at the heavily sleeping women and headed for the door, freezing in place as Grelva stirred. *Don't look, Grelva. Don't look.*

Grelva looked.

Ready to spring, Kerraii waited—for while she didn't think Grelva would call the guards, any attempt to dissuade Kerraii from leaving would be just as damaging. Intense midnight conversations didn't go unnoticed.

Grelva quietly put her head back down on the pillow of her arm.

Kerraii let out a deep breath, gave the slightest nods just in case Grelva could see her, and eased out the door. She felt an odd reticence in leaving the Dwarves behind. They were forced company, but they were decent company nonetheless, and if Kerraii were someone else and somewhere else, she might have called them friends. She wished she could say good-bye to Hepetah.

Good-bye, friends.

She moved only a few steps, and immediately came to rest in the moonshadow of the building. In this light the humans could see little, but movement—any movement— would attract their attention, give them a reason to move closer. So she pressed up against the building and breathed long, shallow breaths until she'd spotted each of the guards. There was one, sitting on his butt and leaning up against a support post for Gunndar's high-set quarters and look-out. Two more were over by the entrance, half draped over the big post that barred it. A third was tucked up inside the doorway of the Magestone shed with only his legs sticking out, no doubt ruing every moment he spent near the dangerous emissions.

She headed for number three. Slipping through the darkest shadows, silent and graceful and barely cutting the wind, she was a dark blade in the night. She came up to the shed from the side, flowed along the side of the building, and peered around to see that he had not so much as twitched his legs from their original position. She gave a satisfied smile, but didn't expose the whiteness of her teeth in doing it. Not even that much of a risk until she was free.

By the time the guard opened his eyes, Kerraii sat straddling his lap, a small knife digging into the soft flesh at his throat and another aimed directly at his groin. He started, his mouth dropping and his eyes widening, and drew breath to make some sound, some objection. "Shhhh," Kerraii said, velvet-voiced. The dangerous voice. She prodded him slightly with the lower knife and kept her voice to the merest of murmurs, leaning in to speak directly in his ear. Goosebumps prickled his neck. "You don't want to lose anything," she told him, in tones that might have been seduction but with meaning that definitely wasn't.

He shook his head, somewhat frantically; his eyes had widened even further.

"Ah-ah," she said, pressing a little with both knives. "Moving can get you into trouble, too."

Frantic now, he nodded.

Scared to stupidity.

"I need some manacles," she said. "They're for you. So I don't have to kill you. I don't suppose you have any?"

His still-wide eyes darted down to his side.

"It means I have to move one of these knives, of course," she said, her voice a silken whisper. "Do you have a preference?"

His gaze instantly darted downward again.

"I thought as much." She removed the knife at his throat and, keeping her gaze on his, felt around for the manacles. It wasn't a process he seemed comfortable with, but the pressure of the remaining knife kept his squirming to a minimum. One-handed, she found them, removed them from his belt, and clicked a cuff into place around his wrist. The second cuff went around his ankle, and with him thus secured she could move more swiftly, stuffing his own sock in his mouth and cutting off a strip of his tunic to tie it in place. She patted his cheek gently and said, "I'm leaving now. You won't hear me go. You won't know when it's safe. But," and she leaned closer, speaking in his ear again, watching the short hairs on the back of his neck stand on end, "if I hear you moving, I'll come back and kill you. There will be no second chance."

And she was a fool; she should kill him right now. But she feared the other women would pay for her escape, and adding a dead guard to the mix could only make things worse. Much worse.

In Necropolis, it wouldn't have mattered. She wouldn't have cared. Here . . . she did.

With a few steps of a running start, she leapt at the side of the shed, grabbing the exterior structural beams along the roof line and swinging herself up to the crude thatching. As quick as that she was back on her feet, running along the back edge of the roof where the peak would hide her from almost anyone's view. At the far end she angled back up to the high point of the roof and without hesitation, flung herself at the thick pointed posts of the wall. Hands sore from the work of the day cried out in silent protest at the rough wood; her skin tore in places but her grip held, and with the precision of strength, she hooked a foot up between two of the points.

The captured guard made not a peep.

Kerraii hesitated just an instant, preparing herself for what came next: the long fall down the other side. She'd have to land well and immediately sprint down the winding trail for the closest stand of trees, sprint with stealth, her best speed, while hugging cover and shadows. She'd have to land silently . . . no thudding, no grunting, no sounds of relief.

Ready.

Over she went. The landing—not quite silent, but nearly—jarred her. She took it in a crouch and before her vision had cleared from the shock, she reoriented toward the narrow path and pushed off for speed.

She collided with something. Hard. She hit with the clash of metal against metal, and though she rocked the object— *hard muscle, the smell of sweat, the onions from the last meal*—ultimately it stood fast.

She gave her head a quick shake, cleared it. *Utem guardsman.* Unbearably smug guardsman. *Waiting . . . ?*

Kerraii didn't try to make sense of it. She drove one of her small blades deep into the inside of his thigh, below his sectioned, leather skirt. She aimed for the big blood vessel

that ran there and from the spurt of blood knew she'd hit it.
Her equilibrium restored, she dodged around his falling
body, ready to make an outright run for it. The Utem cried
out, a sound alarming in its intent. He cried not for help, but
as a command, a signal.

He is not alone. She ran jaggedly, erratically; the bolt
from a lightning gun barely missed her, making the skin of
her hip tingle. It hit the ground not far in front of her and she
quit dodging to run flat out, taking herself out of range.

Power slammed into her; she stumbled, hit the spikes of
her knee protection, and tumbled along the trail. *The mine
mage.* He wasn't strong, he wasn't terribly skilled . . . and
the Magestone radiation interfered with his magic. Even
though he'd hit her dead-on, she scrambled back to her feet.
If she'd had her sword she would have charged back to take
them all on, mage included, but her sword was long lost. So
she aimed herself back down the trail and ran.

She'd only taken a few steps when it hit her again.
Weaker, this time, but so was she, and she went down just as
fast.

This time she didn't have the chance to get up. This time
they hauled her up and dragged her back toward the mine.
She flipped her feet out before her and dug her boot heels
into the ground, pushing off against the resistance to flip up
in the Utems' grip, twisting free.

The men broke left and right, getting themselves clear,
and the mage blasted her one last time.

Kerraii woke not quite certain where she was or who she
was, her inner sense of self askew beyond immediate repair.

She knew only that things were no longer the same.

Slowly it came back to her, even as she began to identify
the sharp pains in her shoulders and arms, the aches in her
body. She hung her by manacled wrists, her escape attempt
failed. And yet, in the greatest of ironies—

I'm free.

Free from weighing every decision against her family's welfare. Free to take her own risks, deal with her own failures. Responsible only for herself.

Hanging there, her head still too heavy to lift and her eyelids refusing to open anyway, Kerraii gave the smallest of satisfied smiles.

A familiar voice came to her ear, both scolding and worried. Grelva. "I don't know what you think you have to smile about," she said. "You foolish woman!"

What was Grelva doing here? Surely they hadn't targeted her for punishment—

Kerraii forced her eyes open. Only halfway open, but enough to see that Grelva stood before her unchained. Relief.

Maybe she'd never quite be responsible *only* for herself, at that.

"What did you think you were doing?" Grelva crossed her mine-muscled arms over her stomach and glared. "Didn't you know when you had it good?"

Kerraii found her voice to be thick and unwilling. "I guess . . . I missed the clues."

"The good food? The cheerful company? An appreciative supervisor?" Grelva said, and made a face. "Maybe not. But better than *this*."

Kerraii blinked a few times, managing to get her eyes fully open. She should have known. She hung from a support timber of Gunndar's tower, sagging against the manacles; her feet dragged and her knees almost touched the ground. If she could stand, she could remove the weight from her shoulders.

A few futile efforts convinced her that no matter how her shoulders screamed for relief, her feet weren't yet ready to take up the job. "Puny mage," she muttered. "Took him *three* blasts."

"I wouldn't worry about that," Grelva said. "Worry about what they'll do *now.*" She glanced around in a furtive way, then eased closer. "We found you like this when we came out in the morning," she said. "Most of the others are finishing their evening meal. I managed to sneak out a little food . . ."

Kerraii's stomach pinched ominously at the thought, but there was no telling when she'd be fed again. Grunting with the effort, she finally got her feet beneath her and ever so cautiously stood—though not all the way. Just as the support timber kept her from sitting all the way, it kept her from straightening entirely. Pain shrieked through her arms and shoulders as she moved abused muscles and tendons; she wiggled her fingers, trying to bring down the swelling now that she'd removed the pressure from the manacles. Deep grooves remained in her wrists.

Grelva tsked, and carefully placed a meat roll in those fingers. "Feywold's going to try to bring something, too."

"Thank you," Kerraii said, and meant it. She bent to tear a bite from the roll, knowing Grelva would go without in order to provide this food. Kerraii would not let it go to waste, no matter what her stomach thought about it all. "You didn't have to do this."

"I don't suppose you had to help those women the first day you were here, either," Grelva said. "That turned out well for all of us. The men got more polite all around, and now one look from Hepetah quells the worst of their intentions. Doing things when you don't *have* to is when they make the most difference, don't you think?"

"I don't know," Kerraii said, more honestly than was her wont. She took a second bite before it was really wise, just to get as much in her stomach as possible in case Gunndar showed up and snatched the food away. "I suppose I should remember. But I don't." Recent years had been entirely too full of survival, Necropolis-style. "There must be guards. Where are they?"

Grelva snorted. "Not worried about you anymore. They figure you'll be lucky to come around before morning after three hits, but I figured there's more to you than that." She narrowed her gaze, recrossed her arms. "Lots more. You aren't exactly Wylden."

"Once," Kerraii said simply.

"*You* were in one of those villages," Grelva said, obviously having come to this certain conclusion in the hours during which Kerraii was unconscious. "Something I said when we were talking ... that's when you decided to go. And *you* were in that battle. The one the gunner told wrong."

"I was there," Kerraii told her. "I was to the side, dealing with a traitor. No doubt that's why I'm still alive." She glanced at the manacles. "For now."

"Tell me, then," Grelva said. "Tell me how it really went. And why it went so wrong for your side. I admit I don't understand the Dark Sect, but surely they expected to *win* when they went after that settlement."

"I assure you, they did." Kerraii felt her expression darken as she thought of Skulk and his foolish treachery. He hadn't scouted the situation, hadn't sent out his own spies to define the exact parameters of his playing field. The entire Necropolis force had paid for it. And one day Skulk would pay for it, too.

But right now, she would repay Grelva for giving up this food. As darkness fell, she sketched the quick details of the battle, though some wary impulse made her blur the details of Skulk's foolishness. In a strange way, that felt like Sect business, business Kerraii herself would follow up on if she ever got the chance.

Grelva didn't seem to mind, if she even realized there were pieces missing at all. "*Real* news," she said with satisfaction.

But then she jerked her head up, emitting an un-Grelva-like squeak as she scurried off into the darkness.

Kerraii took a quick bite to finish the meat roll, swallowing too quickly. Her stomach roiled; she willed it to be still. She heard the footsteps behind her, now—the easily identifiable scuff of Gunndar's graceless feet on the ground, and the tread of another with him. No guards, she thought; she heard no creak of armor and leather, only the gentle swish of material and the crackle of the torch. *The mage,* she realized. For protection . . . or because Gunndar thought it would intimidate Kerraii, make her more biddable?

Offhand, Kerraii couldn't think of a good reason to ever be biddable again. Not even falsely biddable with rebellion lurking in her heart. She eased down into a casual crouch, letting her arms rest easily along the timber.

"Did you really think," Gunndar said while still behind her, rolling his tongue thickly around some last bit of food in his mouth, "we weren't aware of what you were?"

Kerraii didn't bother to look over her shoulder at him. Her voice was flat and disinterested. "I thought you might not care."

"We knew," he said, stating the obvious as he moved around to face her; he jammed a torch into the holder provided near the tower ladder. With his other hand he nibbled the last of the flesh off a drumstick; one of the guards must have had luck hunting today. No doubt he thought the sight of food would torture her. Thanks to Grelva, she could pay it no attention. "Why do you think we never asked questions of you after that first day in the common area? Or did you think all new slaves came in here and waded through two of the yard toughs? We were waiting for you, *Kerraii.* We knew you'd make a break. After all, Sarnen's very own personal Nightblade . . . who would expect less?"

She glanced at him, realizing the worst had happened. They'd known exactly who she was all the time. *Stupid,*

stupid, stupid. She should have planned more carefully, should have taken something other than the most obvious route over the wall. Now, looking at Gunndar, she saw that he was far too smug to have missed the implications of her identity. She would be questioned now. Heavily.

The prospect bothered her less than it once had. She cared little what she revealed about Sarnen, and she no longer feared what would happen to her family when she did. "Who told you?" she asked, but it was idle curiosity as much as anything.

"Another Nightblade," the magus answered, speaking for the first time. He drew a magelight into being, augmenting the torch; he winced slightly in the process, making Kerraii wonder just how much her capture had taken from him. "Before she died. She pointed you out."

Kerraii gave him a sharp look. The slight, one-stone mage.

"I was at Roa Kaiten," he said with the slightest of nods, looking far too serene in his scholarly robes. "I was reassigned here. I reached the mine shortly before you did."

No doubt using some perversion of Technomagic. A flying mechanical dragonfly, maybe. The mage wasn't strong enough to transport himself, nor the situation dire enough to use enough magic to have it done.

On the other hand, a simple saddle horse would have done the trick.

She frowned, and looked around the mine compound, indicating it with her gaze rather than her confined hands. "Why bring me here at all? Since you *knew.*"

Gunndar snorted, and his face had the look of someone who's been proven right. "The Altem thought you might be less discreet here than if they dumped you straight into a prison. You think we don't know the gossip that goes on in a place like this? There are always those willing to pass it along to me when I ask. They figured to give you some time to settle in, and they wouldn't have to waste that time in prison softening you up." His satisfaction came through in an outright smirk. "I told 'em they were wasting effort, but I can always use a good strong back here, so it made no difference to me."

She should have known it. She should have known it was too easy—Gunndar hadn't asked any questions, hadn't taken her to task for causing trouble in the yard. That she had actually been *responding* to trouble in the yard should have made no difference to those such as he, who enjoyed every opportunity to display their authority.

If she'd come ripping out of the quarters at top speed, killed the guard on the way by, and vaulted over the fence with no attempt at anything more than her normal stealth, she might have made it. If she'd sprinted from beginning to end, they wouldn't have been able to catch up with her.

I underestimated them. Too many years in Necropolis, listening to the spiteful put-downs common among the Sect Elves, not to mention the jokes—*how do Utems kill a Feral Bloodsucker? Throw themselves down its gullet until it bursts*—and here she'd just jumped down to where they'd been waiting for her, with barely any more thought than the Utems in the joke. "You've been watching me."

"Watching you?" Gunndar grinned. He tossed the denuded bones of his meal against the log wall behind the tower; the greasy object bounced off with a thunk and landed in the weedy grass there. "We did better than just watch you. We found a Faerie sprite who would do the trick, all for the pleasure of making life more difficult for you. Well, that and a few honey sweets."

Kerraii could not hide her startlement. All those unseen insects . . . not insects at all. The Wylden in her felt instant hurt that a sprite would wish her any harm—and the strong, solid layering of Sect Elf ways responded with instant disdain. Of course a sprite would watch her just for the pleasure of crying alarm when she went for the fence. Necromancy offended the sprites beyond bearing, and any in the Dark Sect were targets of sprite ire when the opportunity presented itself. "Of course, a sprite. Certainly you could not have done the job on your own."

Gunndar's smugness vanished. He scowled at her, wiping his fowl-greasy lips and beard across the back of his forearm. With no more warning than that scowl, he lifted his walking stick, slid his grip down to the bottom, and swung the heavy, gnarled head at Kerraii's shoulder.

Quick as he was, Kerraii was quicker—standing, bringing her leg up in a lightning-swift block. Kicking him might anger him beyond rational thought; she didn't do it. She met the stick right where it came out of his grip and used the angle of the kick to torque it out of his grasp.

One of the guards came rushing across the yard to retrieve the stick and present it to Gunndar, who very much looked like he might just give it another try. As Kerraii watched him—dispassionate, ready for whatever came next—Gunndar hefted the stick, eyeing her from a fury-reddened face.

The magus spoke suddenly, making his presence known. "Leave her," he said. "They will want a clean slate."

"*They,*" Kerraii repeated flatly, with far less interest than she felt inside.

The magus might have shrugged. "You've tried to escape. You came close. We won't risk it happening again, and there is nothing to gain by keeping you here now that you know we have you named. Tomorrow you'll leave by cage cart."

"Bound for where?" she said, putting enough of her subtle command manner into it that the man responded without thinking.

"For Caero," he said. "For the prisons. You still hold

information between those pointy ears of yours, and Atlantis needs it."

"Atlantis," said Kerraii, who rather liked the sweep of her pointy ears, "will be sorely disappointed."

Gunndar scowled again, and snarled a word at her in the Dwarvish language that needed no translation. He added, "What happens to you after you leave my keeping is not my problem. For now, I will have your knives."

She just looked at him. Not a blank look, not a stubborn one . . . just a long, steady regard.

"Come now, come now—you think Garet Armorborne was too frightened to remember you threatened him with a set of nasty little knives?"

"It wouldn't surprise me." Privately, Kerraii didn't think the man would stand up straight for a week. No doubt his first new purchase would be a nice steel codpiece.

"They'll be hidden in your harness. I can't take them, but you can give them. And give them you'd best, for no matter the magus's words, I am within authority to mar a clean slate for the purpose of retrieving known weapons."

No point in arguing further; she knew he'd back up his words and a look at the magus's distantly concerned face confirmed it. She propped a foot up on the timber, stretching to bend over the leg so she could retrieve the boot knife. She caught a glimpse of the magus, finding his expression entirely altered: riveted on her, on the length of exposed leg, and the skimpiness of her harness as she bent at the hips.

She'd heard that of the Empire's men, that they all secretly wanted to be with a Nightblade, that they all wondered what part of the wild rumors were true and what . . . wasn't. She smiled, but kept it to herself. They might think they were disarming her, but they weren't. She had many tools at her disposal, the rumors among them.

Using two careful fingers, she held the little knife out to

Gunndar. The second knife she retrieved so swiftly that neither of them saw where it came from, as she intended. No need for all her secrets to get out.

She didn't tell them about the third, tiny blade at her hip, or the knife in the second boot. She didn't think they needed to know. Neither would free her from the cage cart, but if she was to end up in a Caero prison, she would need all the advantages she could get.

Gunndar gave an exaggerated bow, the tips of his stiff beard braids sweeping the ground. Kerraii managed to stop herself from snapping her foot up to meet his chin.

Barely.

The women huddled in the doorway to their quarters, barely daring to peep out as two guards took up the shafts of the two-wheeled cage cart. Kerraii, crouched to absorb the bumpy ride, looked back at them, acknowledging them with nothing but her gaze. Another part of her life left behind. A short, ugly part of it, to be sure, but one of these days . . .

She'd make her own decisions.

Next time, maybe. Next turning point. She'd almost done it this time, and next time she would be more careful.

One of the burdened guards cursed; Kerraii made a grab for the bars as he regained his balance, lurching the narrow cart dangerously close to the edge of the trail. Neither guard looked quite steady enough for this task; Kerraii knew this assignment was a mercy for them, getting them away from the raw Magestone before it was too late.

Kerraii herself found it an unexpected relief to get away from the feel of the Magestone grumbling in her blood. At least the dangers she faced within the Caero prison system were predictable. Tangible. Something she could fight and resist.

The second man stumbled, throwing her against the bars

on the other side of the cage. She hissed her displeasure, and was pleased to see him flinch. That was good. These guards, whether they knew it or not, were going to help her adapt her subtle Dark Sect ways to deal with these anything-*but*-subtle humans.

CHAPTER 10

ENTERING Caero.

The worst part of the journey.

Kerraii saw the great pyramids of the merchant's city long before her new escort drew to a stop at the port gates. At first she thought they were foothills of some sort, but as her lurching, wearisome cage cart closed in on Caero, the symmetrical lines of the pyramids behind the city resolved and separated into individual structures. Eventually she discerned the lower, blockier structures between them, and careful eavesdropping revealed that they were not, as she'd thought, buildings for government officials similar to the Deathspeaker towers, but temples. Temples built by rich, ancient families for the worship of their ancestral lines—although she gathered at least one of these temples had been donated for a show of devotion to Tezla, who also commanded the newest temples within the city walls.

In Kerraii's world, no one did anything for nothing. She could not help but wonder how that particular family had been so out of favor, and what they had won—or been forced to lose—when they gave up their temple. She wondered, too, if the Empire was truly dismantling the smaller pyramids to put the stone to use in its own structures. The city certainly needed repair; from here it was easy to see the great blackened areas of fire damage from the Atlantean attack a year earlier. Sarnen had chuckled over the Atlanteans' foolishness for some time.

She might have asked the guards her questions, but these men had replaced those from the mine, and never directly acknowledged her. These were stronger, fitter, Caero-based guards who considered this a homecoming; they used a donkey between the shafts of the cart instead of pulling it themselves. They were fascinated by her, and so disdained her in order to avoid admitting their interest. As they settled in for their last night on the road, one of them slipped her a bowl of gruel through the food slot in the cart's bars and gave her a sidelong glance, as they all did, and thought himself unnoticed.

The last night on the road. Until now, Kerraii had given them their games of eyeing her while pretending she didn't exist. Now she gave him a slow wink, a little curl at the corner of her mouth. He kept an admirably stony face—and immediately tripped over some nonexistent impediment in his path. Satisfied, she scooped the gruel into her mouth with two fingers, and considered the various ways she could devastate these men if she were clean, bathed, and groomed for court. Her sword was not the only weapon at her disposal, and from their behavior, they well knew it.

What they did not realize was how she ached from her confinement and travel in this little wheeled cell, but she would never have them know it. Let them think she was impervious, that she had not been humiliated by the cart's rude facilities—a simple hole in the corner—and that her continuing feral grace as she prowled the cart came at no cost to her. Let them go home to their families and their fellow Caeronn citizens and talk about the strength of a Nightblade, at her combination of pale beauty and dark danger. Let *these* men—possibly the last to see her with even this much freedom—never forget her.

She finished her meal quickly, and sat back to relish the

luxury of *not* jarring and bumping over roads she would have considered well-maintained had she been on foot. She crossed her legs and leaned her bruised back against the bars, considering the city as the sun sank behind the tallest of the pyramids, spearing gold rays of light from the pyramid's apex and painting the city with rich ruddy light and deep shadow, glinting briefly off the wide, deep Roa Vizorr between their rough little camp and the city. Well might the merchants consider it a treasure, this place where everyone was welcome but troublemakers. Even though Caero remained loyal to the Empire, any and all races journeyed here seeking fortune and trade.

Kerraii resolved to take a good look on the way in, very much doubting she'd glimpse any of that fortune herself once she hit a prison cell.

She had not counted on what it would be like to face a city of gawkers from within her cage.

In the morning, the guards shoved dried meat and water at her, pulling themselves together with anticipation. The other occupants of this informal overnighting area did likewise, making hasty breakfasts or skipping food altogether. A savvy confectioneer had set up a stall just off the road, and did brisk business with the comfits and cheeses she displayed. Kerraii found herself staring at the stall, her thoughts suddenly and abruptly drawn to that day in the woods when she'd eaten her last honey flake-layer comfit, back when she'd been naive and fully Wylden. Did the woman have—?

Of course not. Kerraii resolutely tore herself away from the sight and put her back to it, aware that she might well never taste such a thing again.

No. You'll deal with this, you'll do what you have to in order to get through it, and then you'll eat whatever you want.

And if at the moment she felt a nudge of despair, there was no use dwelling on it. She clenched her fists—first one, then the other—hidden in her lap. And when she looked up, her face was clear of any emotion other than mild interest in the city they approached.

They fell into line behind a row of similar donkey carts, although Kerraii's cage was the only such prison within sight; the other carts held burlap bags, boxes, leather satchels, woven baskets, piled furs . . . goods and containers. Kerraii had an extended chance to view the city and its contrasting areas of ruin and beauty, for they made progress only by inches. She pulled her knees to her chest and folded her hands around them, resting her chin atop. Caero sprawled out below the small hill they now crept down, an ancient place constructed by the Kos with the extensive use of slaves and engineering arts now mainly lost. With the dazzling white pyramids towering behind the collection of temples and homes, and the broad streets and open places crowded by merchant stalls, the city was a mix of huge monotonal red sandstone structures, smaller, brighter, and newer limestone buildings, the charred lower quarter, and the bright clutter of merchant chaos—rugs and silks and weaving, leathers and furs.

Kerraii found it beautiful and beguiling, and at once a confusing muddle. She looked instead to the city walls, tall stone walls built on the backs of the merchants; she'd heard about the taxes levied on visiting merchants here. Now she saw part of what those monies went for. The city pushed up hard against the water, its horseshoe shape brought up short. The banks of the tremendously broad river were lined with angled docks, and just behind the docks were rows of warehouses, constructed by slaves out of laboriously formed bricks—a fact made obvious by the presence of a mud-splattered crew on their side of the river, mixing clay and straw and shoving the result into brick molds.

Kerraii wondered at those open docks, so obviously vulnerable. But as her cart lurched forward another foot, she saw the flicker of Technomancer magic in play, blue and red shimmers rippling away from a dock preparing to receive the next approaching boat, and nearby, a sizable box levitating from a docked ship to the shore.

Perhaps not so vulnerable after all. And perhaps the very reason these people stood here in line for the bridge instead of ferrying their own flatboats across the sluggish—but protected—waters.

As far as she could tell, the bridge was an extension of Caero itself; the elaborate and symbolic arches serving as a gate on this side reinforced her conclusion. While people seemed to move freely enough across the bridge as they left the city, those in this entry line went through inspection, tariffs, and questioning.

Tax the goods on the way in, leaving the burden of sales on the merchants. Clever system. Almost worthy of Necropolis, in a crass, commercial way.

She contemplated the gate, the ornate column work and stylized figures, and then the practical, no-frills bridge beyond it.

No question about it: Necropolis knew how to make a better first impression, though she had to grant the pyramids their due. Even from here they projected an aura of ancient power and splendor.

"Purpose of visit?" intoned a bored voice, and Kerraii brought her focus back close again, realizing that extra gate officials had begun to work the line, seeking to speed it along. This one was a plump, soft-looking man with a single narrow braid of beard down the center of his chin and carefully pleated white linen tunic-skirt folded around his body. Neat and competent-looking, right down to his carefully shaved head.

One of the guards said, "We're coming home, under assignment." He jerked a thumb back to Kerraii. "It's not her home, but I assure you she'll never be leaving it."

This amused the man. "Two citizens, one permanent prisoner. No sales goods to declare?"

Both men shook their heads, although Kerraii knew for a fact that the bundles atop her cage cart held furs from various predators found only in the northeastern mountains. The official wrote out a gate card for each, and suggested they not hold up the line. He might have passed Kerraii without looking, except Kerraii gave a languid stretch. As he glanced at her, she rolled her eyes upward, giving him a secret little smile.

The official didn't so much as blink an acknowledgment. But he reached up to tap the bundles, marking them with chalk. He went entirely unseen by her guards, who seemed preoccupied with examining their papers.

They were taken utterly by surprise when the next official pulled them out of line and searched their goods, confiscating the furs as undeclared. Kerraii watched through a half-lidded doze. *Treat me like clotted blood,* she thought at them with a velvet inner voice, *and pay the price.*

Within the city, Kerraii had little time for a resurgence of her despair. She quickly learned to meet curiosity with her coldest stare, at which men looked away and mothers grabbed their children, bustling and huffing to hide their fears. The children either burst into tears—or looked back with increased interest even as the women towed them off. Of everyone here—and it seemed everyone *was* here—Kerraii thought she would be able to talk to those particular children.

As it was she spoke to no one. Her escorts were grouchy after the loss of their furs, and they carelessly jerked the donkey through the busy streets and then entire sections of the city. Amidst the more imposing temples, the market area was a forest floor with the sun shining through in patches, warming and inspiring activity. The people reminded Kerraii of bustling ants and colorful insects, with the occasional jewel of a snake or a quick darting weasel, all going about their life with little regard to what happened in the upper strata of the environment—not the temples, the government structures, or the pyramids beyond. Kerraii became one of the ants, her cart bobbling in the streaming life around her.

They moved from a collection of flower and seed sellers to harvested produce to freshly slaughtered carcasses—there, Kerraii's expert nose caught the taint of spoilage beneath any number of strong spices meant to hide it. In the clothing and yard goods section, a young woman dressed in crude slave leathers and carrying a basket crammed with goods stared openly at Kerraii. Her face held not so much curiosity as a fear that meant her future was no more assured than Kerraii's. Kerraii could have given her the same cold stare she gave everyone, but she thought of the women in the mine, and of Grelva, Feywold, and Inger, especially—the ones who would never sicken from Magestone poisoning, who merely endured in the best way they could. Endured, as she now would, wondering when some man or woman of power would make yet another blithe decision about her fate.

Maybe there was time for despair after all. Maybe it was just exactly what she saw reflected in the face of the slave who watched her little cage cart bump past.

Run away. Break free. Escape. Steal clothing, bundle her armor in a satchel, find a weapon. Kerraii could disappear in this city with its multitudes of peoples and traditions. She could turn Wylden for a while—in that she could convince anyone but her own people—and head south, south and then east, back to her own home.

Or to what had *been* her home until she'd spent eight years learning how to live in ways that would appall her people.

Never mind what they would think of you. Run away. Do

it now, before that building gets any closer. Before it sucks you in and swallows you whole.

That building up ahead, the imposing thing of brick on top of massive sandstone slabs with the cogged wheel of the Atlantean seal chiseled into its impressive frontage, the one with Altem guards flanking the entrance, as spotlessly turned out and disciplined in their sharp military stance as Kerraii had ever seen, their helms shining and their *mana-clevt* swords at the ready.

The prison. Their court of judgment.

It might be better than the blood pits . . .

And it might not.

A startling wind of panic rushed through Kerraii, raising the hair on her arms, prickling right down the center of her spine. She tested the cage door, the bars made of poor iron, thick but rusting. The lock crude.

She could get out. She could have gotten out long earlier, had she not considered herself too weak from the magic blasts to waste the effort. She had a stiff pick secured in the greaves of her boot—a slender, needle-sharp tool that could kill as easily as it gave her access to those parts of Necropolis others foolishly thought beyond her reach. She removed it, hesitating, and then berated herself for her foolishness. No one would come riding to her rescue—not the Night-blades she commanded, not the Necromancers who had fled the battle. Not even Sarnen. To all of them, she was naught but a liability—and if she saw a familiar face here, she would do better to hide than to smile.

She glanced up, saw the slave still watching her—and then saw the woman quickly glance away. Not out of fear or awkwardness, but with the sudden understanding that Kerraii was about to act, and that the woman needed to be able to say in all honesty that she'd seen nothing. The woman ducked her head, shifted her basket to the other arm, and swiftly walked away.

But not all were so inclined. As Kerraii plied the lock with her pick, a soft-looking woman escorted by two men who wore as much makeup as she did looked over and pointed. Squeaked. The squeak seemed to be the only alarm she could raise, and Kerraii would have struck her down then and there if it hadn't already been too late. The men saw her, then several merchants, and then a dirty little urchin skipping up to follow the cart's slow progress. And then the lock made a distinctive click, rusty innards creaking, and Kerraii pushed the door open; only then did her heart dare to beat a little faster with hope.

"Get her!" someone said, although not someone brave enough to act on his own words.

He didn't need to. Another of the splendidly polished Altems appeared from behind a stall of silks and lace, reaching for her as she crouched in the doorway.

She kicked out at him—

And astonished herself by falling on her bottom at the edge of the cart. Too long crammed in the small space, too long without nourishing food, too soon after being struck by not one but three magic blasts.

The Altem grabbed her leg, jerked her back as the cart jerked forward; she landed hard on the ground, with no chance to roll, no way to absorb the shock that knocked a grunt from her lungs. But long-trained reflexes still worked; as he reached for her again, she twisted around to jam the pick into the vulnerable spot inside his elbow. The Altem bellowed, as much in anger as in pain, slapping at the wound. Too late; by then she'd whipped her hand back, climbed to wobbly knees, and targeted the thin open strip between his helm and his chest protection, a hidden spot that only showed itself if one knew where to look.

Kerraii knew. She drove the little spike home, yanked it out, and drove it in again, the side of her fist thumping against his armor with the force of it. The second blow hit home; an arc of blood spurted through the air, pulsing wildly with the man's heart.

Too bad she'd never wanted even the faintest touch of vampirism laid upon her; Sarnen would have done it had she asked, and now she'd have been able to drink from this fountain, replenishing herself, regaining her strength. Instead she left the man cursing, tearing at his own armor in an attempt to staunch the blood, and wobbled to her feet, assessing a hostile crowd. The people seemed to melt away before her black-eyed gaze. A quick whirling survey—not up to her usual agility, but these people would hardly perceive that with so much fear in their eyes—showed her that even her erstwhile escorts hesitated to approach.

But the cart shuddered slightly; a startling visage appeared above what remained of the escorts' goods. Dark hair stood up like a stiff fan around the man's head, and he held a battle staff in one hand. He had not bothered to draw his sword, and Kerraii almost immediately saw why. The man did a flip off the edge of the unsteady cart and came to land on his feet directly before her, a fanatical light in his eyes. Unlike the Altem, his light armor protected only his shoulders and upper torso; a studded breechcloth was his only other protection.

He didn't draw the sword because he didn't need it. Like herself, the man was skilled in hand-to-hand combat as well as edged weapons, and Kerraii did the only thing she could. She lunged at him, grabbing hold of the battle staff before he could wield it. She made no attempt to take it from him; she used it as an anchor for the swift knee she jabbed at him, aiming the knee guard spike at that soft spot just above the breechcloth.

He twisted aside with no visible effort, using the staff as a fulcrum just as she had. She'd never seen his like in person, but she knew him—an elite Surok apprentice. Under normal circumstances she'd take him on without hesitation or fear, but now . . .

Now she knew who would win this battle, if she didn't break off and end it. Especially since the apprentices tended to travel in the company of a mage, whose spells they could support even as they guarded the magus's back—and when it came down to it, the apprentices could conjure their own magical attacks. *No more magic blasts for me . . .*

It didn't take a magic blast. It took only the two Altems from the prison doorway, stomping up behind her to each take an arm, yanking her back and out of the fight so quickly she felt the astonishment on her own face, saw it echoed in the Surok apprentice's. They picked her up and flung her into the cart as if she were no more than a light husk of herself, and slammed the door closed so quickly she had to snatch her foot out of the way. One of them jabbed imperiously at the prison and her escorts hastened to respond; the cart lurched forward. Behind them, someone called for a medic. If they acted quickly, the wounded man might survive.

The Altems walked behind the cart every step of the way, impersonal and imposing behind their armor. Kerraii, flat on the cart's nasty floor, *felt* like only a light husk of herself. Stunned, weakened, and defeated, she closed her eyes to the sight of those who'd suddenly become brave enough to surround the cart again, and let the Atlanteans take her where they would.

At first the cell was a relief. It didn't lurch and jostle her. It didn't leave her exposed to curious and leering gazes. The food was just as bad—worse, in fact—and she still used a hole in the corner to relieve herself, but she had gotten some privacy. And though the small room cramped her, at least she could stand up straight. She could stretch and pace and keep her blood and muscles moving.

At first.

But after several days during which no one spoke to her and no one even acknowledged her, she began to wonder when the questioning would start. After that she wondered if this was part of the Atlanteans' tactics: leaving her with plenty of time to imagine the worst.

She could imagine plenty. And she had no illusions about her ability to resist questioning. Even with the best of incentives, no one could hold out forever—and she no longer had much incentive at all. Her loyalty to Sarnen had been generated by two basic realities: the first was that it was in her best interests to please him, the second, and more important, was that it had been in her family's best interests. Many Sect Elves in her position would harbor hopes of returning to Necropolis, hoping for the rewards due a faithful one . . . but Kerraii had seen too much. She knew she would never be trusted again. She might not be killed outright, but before long she would be discarded and forgotten, left to haunt the dark corners of Necropolis.

There were a lot of dark corners in Necropolis.

Those who sought the extended life spans and increased power Necromancy offered usually closed their eyes to those dark corners . . . or arrogantly believed that they themselves would never end up lurking there. But all it took was the wrong word at the wrong time, embarrassing someone in power without concurrently delighting someone else who might offer protection . . .

Kerraii would never return. *Could* never return, even if she wanted to.

She no longer wanted to.

It was what she knew, but she could learn. She'd already proven that to herself. And discovered as well that plenty of the young Kerraii—complete with the tenets and desires she'd held in her Wylden village—still lurked beneath the mannerisms and skills of her hardened Nightblade exterior.

So she had no intention of enduring anything to protect

Sarnen or Necropolis, except that she had no desire to *help* the Empire, either. And she knew they'd question her hard no matter what she told them, just to ascertain the truth of it.

In the end she ruefully decided that if leaving her here to stew about the impending questioning was part of their tactics, they were successful tactics indeed.

As it turned out, they were merely saving her as a treat for Jeet Nujarek.

CHAPTER 11

EVEN in Necropolis, the name Jeet Nujarek, overseer of Prieska, was known. He had a reputation for cruelty and political manipulation that garnered amused respect from the Deathspeakers. Respect, because few humans outside Necropolis—and few *inside* Necropolis, for that matter— mastered the long view. They thought in the short term, and often sacrificed their ultimate goals because something tempting was in their grasp *now*. To all appearances, Jeet usually had the long view in mind, and that commanded a certain respect.

But also amusement, because he wielded his influence with a heavy hand, miscalculating the benefits of doing so and forgetting to provide enough reward as a counterbalance. The Deathspeakers and skilled Necromancers offered extended life, vampirism, enhanced eyesight, and excessive pleasures; they were never short of sycophants and volunteers. Jeet Nujarek dangled power and advancement before many while awarding it to only a few.

Still, in his crude way, he made progress, consolidating power. And since he had only a short human life over which he needed to sustain his successes, perhaps it was progress enough.

Kerraii was stretching one long leg up against the damp

stone of the underground cell when she heard multiple foot-steps outside her cell door. It had not been that long since the last meal, so she brought her leg back down and stood quietly against the wall directly opposite the door, her hands relaxed by her sides. *Now* was not a moment to run, and until the moment came, she wanted to give the guards no reason to remain alert around her. She'd tried to escape; she'd failed. Until she tried again, she was what she was . . . a prisoner.

A guard peered through the small square opening in the door, his eye roaming almost comically until he found her. When he opened the door he turned out to be not even a Utem, but some Atlantean underling with no armor and nothing but a personal knife. Kerraii arched an eyebrow at him, and he gave her a nervous look—right before he looked over his shoulder and moved out of the way.

Ah. All was explained. The other footsteps belonged to an elite Surok apprentice. Not the same one who'd braced her in the marketplace, but nonetheless a formidable-looking man. Amused, Kerraii waited for his instructions. Obviously they thought Surok apprentices to be her match, not taking into account how her cramped accommodations and days of travel had hindered her in the previous encounter. She itched to take this man on if only to expose their foolish assumption.

Something of it must have shown in her eyes; the man gave her a hard look. He, too, had a staff, as well as his blade. And there, down the corridor, a shadow. A robed magus, targeting her for a magic blast . . . in case. Kerraii forced herself to give a little nod to the apprentice, enough of an acknowledgment between warriors to indicate she would behave.

For now.

"Come with me," he said. He wasn't worried; no doubt the magus would keep her targeted until they reached their destination.

She moved slowly away from the wall, giving the Atlantean

peon the time to scurry out of her reach. She was hungry and her ribs were beginning to show, but she still moved with the lithe assurance of a Nightblade. She still commanded her space.

Even on her way to what could only be an unpleasant encounter. Finally, the questioning.

She walked ahead of the Surokian, but not so far ahead that he couldn't reach her should he feel so inspired—simply because he was less likely to feel so inspired as long as he *could* reach her. She kept her pace moderate, comfortable for him, choking her normal stride considerably.

She did not want to allow the touch of his hands, so she made sure he had no reason to touch her. With a Utem, it wouldn't have worked. But the Surok apprentices were trained for more subtlety, and a clean style. He wouldn't handle her unless she gave him an excuse to do so.

With the nervous servant nervously skipping on ahead of them to lead the way, Kerraii traveled the maze of prison hallways, instantly memorizing them. Although they encountered no stairs, there was enough upward slope in some of those hallways that Kerraii wasn't surprised when the first window appeared, and she wasn't surprised when the room they finally entered also had a window.

She was quite certain the city view wasn't for her benefit.

The chair in the center of the room, however—that was entirely for her: the one with arm straps and leg straps and a strange tilt to the seat guaranteed to keep any prisoner constantly tensed to avoid putting pressure on the fifth strap, a flat, slip collar. The one that would go around her throat.

The Surokian indicated the chair with a gesture he might have used to allow a highly placed government official to take the most comfortable seat in the room. With the same aplomb, Kerraii sat. She felt magic in this room, and swept her gaze around—taking in the narrow but heavy table next to the truly comfortable chair across from her, the bars across the window, the poorly scrubbed blood spatters on the thickly plastered walls—until she found the faintest of shimmers across the inner wall she faced.

A door, there. Or a window. Without a doubt, someone was watching her. As the Surok apprentice fastened the leather cuffs tightly around Kerraii's wrists, she watched the shimmer. Guessed the average height of a human male, and aimed her gaze there, even as the apprentice brought the leather collar around her throat.

She'd worn worse.

He fastened it only loosely. A token, until someone else chose to make it more functional. More persuasive.

As he stepped away from the chair to take up a position beside her, the wall flushed a faint red and a door-sized section of it disappeared.

A man strode through the opening. He held himself like he owned the prison—no, like he owned *all* of Caero—but the apprentice kept his gaze on the second man. Whereas the first man wore a deep violet cloak shot through with subtle gold-threaded designs, the second, bald man wore what Kerraii had seen on other wealthy Caeronn citizens—a pleated linen toga, secured at the waist. This man's belt shone like liquid gold, and a closer look revealed it to be made of gold wrought in a fine link of mesh. Wealthy, indeed. And at his heels came a third man, a three-stone magus.

The first man gave Kerraii a smug and anticipatory smile from behind the tattoos of blue flame that licked up the sides of his neck and face; the second gave the Surokian the merest of nods, at which the apprentice stepped back slightly from Kerraii's chair.

The second man rules this place, Kerraii decided. The Grand Magistrate of Caero, to judge by his watchdog mage, courtesy of the Empire. And the first was a man of power. A guest of some sort. A guest who wore his power like an ostentatious second skin, for all he lacked obvious finery. It was there if she looked for it, in the details of his cloak and fine boots, leather gloves of the finest doeskin, dyed black, with the back of each finger reinforced with carefully crafted metal sections. No doubt his sheathed sword was as finely made.

Her gaze flicked from one man to the other, assessing. The second man was in charge here, but for the moment he'd handed his authority over to the other. Had the other truly possessed that authority on his own—a higher ranking man from outside the city-state of Caero—the Surokian wouldn't have turned so obviously to the commander to whom he was accustomed.

"You don't know me," the first man stated, watching Kerraii carefully.

To judge by the way the notion displeased him, it was in her best interests to say she did—but she'd only be caught in the lie a moment later. Kerraii gave him the slightest wry twist of her mouth, a barely perceptible shrug. Part admission, part apology—and part turning the question back on him with an unspoken *should I?*

"You are unusually honored," the Grand Magistrate said. "Emperor Tahmaset personally sent Jeet Nujarek to interrogate the fabled Nightblade of Sarnen. If you cooperate, I think you'll find your fate not so grim as you have no doubt assumed."

Jeet Nujarek. Kerraii took a second look at him, unconvinced that he would be of any benefit to her. Convinced, in fact, that his presence here complicated her situation significantly. For Nujarek . . . wanted something. She swept her gaze over his narrow-set eyes and broad face, wary of the expression she saw there. Expectation. Of what, she didn't know—only that the set of his mouth indicated he was quite used to getting what he expected. Not quite pursed, his lips were nonetheless set together in haughty disdain.

Jeet Nujarek was in control. And the way he maintained

that control was to make sure everyone knew he had it. His every gesture spoke it, his expression, the lift of his chin and ill-defined jawline.

Kerraii found herself patently unimpressed. Ignoring the uncomfortable tilt of the chair, she crossed one long leg over the other and spoke to him in a lazy, unconcerned tone. "Would you like me to cooperate immediately? Or should I offer up a token resistance to make my capitulation seem more realistic?"

"I prefer to avoid damaging you," Nujarek said, matching her tone—or trying to. A faint irritation seeped through; Kerraii instantly got the impression that immediate capitulation would have been fine had she offered it with words of flattery and perhaps even a little begging, but . . . "But, you understand, we must be certain you tell us the truth. The *complete* truth."

"Only to be expected," she said. "Especially since I know far less than I imagine you think I do."

Nujarek laughed, a cruel sound despite his genuine amusement. "Deathspeaker Sarnen's chosen Nightblade. For years he's cultivated you, taught you, *trusted* you . . ."

417 Tz. NECROPOLIS BLOOD PIT

KERRAII bent to work with thoughtful concentration, replaying those last moments of her opponent's life in the blood pit. She was pleased with the flashy nature of the blow that had killed him, and pleased as well that it had nonetheless been a quick death. The crowds liked agony, liked to read entrails spilled in the sand, liked to see blood spilled in inkblot shapes across the ground.

Kerraii preferred to be clean and quick. A Nightblade who could manage clean and quick kills under blood pit melee conditions was well-prepared for planned excursions, for those moments in the dark when circumstances required her to be there and gone before anyone noticed, leaving mysterious death behind. So Kerraii wasn't a favorite in the pits—except for those who bet her to win.

And for Sarnen, who used *clean and quick* for his own purposes.

So Kerraii was satisfied enough, as she cleaned the blood from her blade, inspecting the long, slender sword for nicks, then sharpened the sword-catchers that spiked out from the guards. Hers had been a duel match, and the poor fool had had no chance. Yet another one of those young Seething Knights out to gain enough favor to earn vampirism traits from his Necromancer patrons and seeing Sarnen's Nightblade as a quick leap to notoriety.

For most of them, it had been a quick leap to Zombie servitude. For Kerraii . . .

Simply moments in which she finished what they had started, leaving her to the small victor's room of her choice. She could have chosen something ostentatious, but she chose a modestly furnished room with a tray of nourishing delicacies and the supplies with which to attend to her equipment, to keep her armor spotless and rust-free, her blades sharp, her leather supple. Others depended on sycophants to do this work for them, but when Kerraii left this room she would be prepared for anything.

Even the sight of an exalted Deathspeaker, here in the back rooms of a blood pit.

Sarnen stood in the doorway.

"My Lord," she said, straightening respectfully as she sheathed her sword.

"One of these days, Kerraii, you'll learn to add a little flourish to the moment," he said, but he did not sound displeased.

"If you would prefer," she told him, meaning it.

He chuckled, a dry, harsh sound. "I prefer you just as you

are," he said. "You above all do not play games with me. You do as I please and you cut to the heart of whatever matter you face. No, it is *they,*" and he made a vague gesture to indicate the seating literally over their heads, his sleeve billowing with the movement, "who appreciate the flourish. In that way, I suppose, it would serve us well. But I happen to believe there is value in such consistent, swift demonstrations of the consequences of folly."

"As do I," she said.

"Five years," he said.

She didn't understand the comment, so she waited.

"Walk with me," he said.

Of course, she did.

He guided her out of the pit stadium to the magnificence of the Prophet's Bridge . . . and across it. They walked in silence, and in a chill spring air that made Kerraii glad she'd slipped her cloak over her battle harness. Although she still did not understand the purpose of his visit, his conversation, or the walk to the mainland, she said nothing. He would speak when he was ready and until then questions would do nothing but display her lack of patience.

Once upon land again they passed the lightly manned guardhouse made of the same stone and in the same style as the bridge, and then Sarnen turned back to face the city. Even from here the Prophet's tower rose toward the sky with dark purpose, surrounded by the slightly shorter Death-speaker Ring. Even from here they whispered of power.

"Five years," Sarnen said again. "The length of your stay with us here in Necropolis. Did you not mark it?"

In fact, she had not. Long ago she had quit keeping conscious track of the days and years, back when it had become a mark of her failure to escape.

"Here." Sarnen gestured at the rugged terrain beyond the rocky shore, the mountains that separated them from much of the Land. They rose strong and forbidding, as if something sharp had tried to escape from the earth, failed, and never given up trying. Kerraii looked at them, looked then back at the city. She took in the details of the moment—the sharp, biting odor of the shore algae, the equally sharp cry of black-headed, dirty-winged waterbirds, the soft lap of waves against the rock. Come the afternoon warmth, the wind would howl off the lake and get tangled in the mountains, creating a confusing gust of unpredictable winds. The birds would ride high in the sky, the waves would go unheard, and the wind would invade every crevice it could find. "There is your so-called *freedom*. It's yours, if you want it."

She arched an eyebrow at him, hearing and not quite understanding.

"Yes," he said, smiling in a way that exposed his long yellowing teeth. "There is no trick here. You may leave if you want. If the mountains do not take you on the way through, you are free. You may go back to the life you knew."

For that moment, she let herself believe him. *Go back?* To what?

To a family who could never comprehend who she'd become and what she'd done to get there. To a village that would not be able to accept her. To an Elementalist culture that would revile her.

Suddenly she understood. She'd stopped marking time not because it reminded her of failure, but because she was no longer focused on escape. This was what she was, who she was. She had a place here in a way she no longer had a place outside the Sect. The realization cut her deeply, making her ache in a way she'd thought long forgotten. Regret. Sorrow. Grief. Acceptance.

There was nothing she could do to change where she was, who she was. Not anymore. And no one but the Dark Elves would embrace her now.

Looking at Sarnen, she shook her head.

"But you thought about it," he said.

"Of course," she replied. "What would be the worth of my answer if I hadn't?"

He gave the slightest of humorless smiles. "Not much worth at all," he said. "But you would be surprised how many give it anyway, seeking only to please. This is why I keep you with me, my Kerraii. Why, though you rarely draw the roar of the crowds with your swift blood pit victories, and why, though many others in my service are reluctant to trust you, I keep you with me. I know the depth of you. And though you play our games of power as well as any, there is a directness in you that serves me."

Kerraii did not mention that most of his trust in her was built upon the fate of her family, but she didn't need to. They both knew it. No doubt Sarnen also knew that if ever the day came that she turned against him, he would see it coming the moment her decision was made.

Besides, Sarnen was fond of making meaningful speeches to captive audiences.

Kerraii stood on the shore, looking back toward . . . home. Not the home she wanted, but the home she had. The home she'd earned, by facing every challenge Necropolis and Sarnen's enemies—and Sarnen himself—had thrown at her. The first fitful breezes of the afternoon played with her long fall of black hair pulled back in the sleek Nightblade style, twitching and pulling at it like so many mischievous— or hateful—sprites.

But the sparse vegetation around them remained still: the burr-filled water thistles were motionless, the dry husks of last year's grasses were silent.

"My lord," she said, a hand going to her sword hilt—even though in this city, among those who played out their bid for power at this highest of levels, a sword was often of little help at all.

"Yes," Sarnen murmured, an acknowledgment rather than

a question. He knew what she was seeing, that she spoke warning.

Darkness gathered in the air before them, wispy pieces of black fog joining to form a whole. The malevolence of it permeated the air, reaching for Kerraii.

She drew her sword, snarling at it. Angry spirits drawn by Necromancy were all but impervious to her mundane weapon, but she'd taken them apart before and she'd do it again. Even though Sarnen was perfectly capable of handling far more than a single summoned spirit, she stepped into place between him and the advancing spirit, bringing her sword up to guard position. She was Sarnen's Nightblade; it was what she did.

Except suddenly the spirit was not alone. Even as Sarnen gave a negligent wave to dispel it, others coalesced along the shore where the waves lapped at the gritty rock, appearing to draw substance from the juncture of earth and water. One, three, eight . . . too many to count. Mingling, joining, drifting apart, they took form, and their discontented mutters merged to create a seamless, hissing threat. Long-dead beings now fueled by their own hatred and aimed by whichever Necromancer stood behind this attack, they advanced in a sinister line, their eyes nothing but dull pools of darkness.

"Who?" Kerraii asked him in the shorthand of their long acquaintance, scowling at the spirits. Even this many, Sarnen could take—just as he could detect who had launched this attack. A Deathspeaker grew adept at such things out of necessity. *Who is behind this?*

Sarnen made an impatient hissing noise of his own. "Many," he said, and gestured a command that scattered the foe.

Instantly they re-formed, startling an oath from Kerraii, and silent, stiff surprise from Sarnen.

Surprise from Sarnen. *Not good.*

In that instant, she realized what the foe had done, that

whoever had launched this attack had planned it well, drawing on the furious spirits of those lost in battle. In a *single* battle. *A battle lost by magic in one fell swoop.* They wore eerie remnants of their armor, brandished aged weapons. Very real weapons.

Not even a Deathspeaker could fight an army. Not alone.

Against these numbers not even determination would prevail, but Kerraii stepped up to slice a path through the unresisting forms of three spirits one after another, taking the initiative of that one swift attack before they set upon her, forcing her into swift, defensive parries as they drove her back, driving Sarnen back behind her. At his command, the spirits dispersed, earning Kerraii an instant of respite. Briefly, they stood side by side, glancing to assess each other's status.

Sarnen brandished a short wand, one Kerraii rarely saw. Made of petrified human bone, sliced and stacked and perfectly aligned, gleaming with its own slick sheen . . . and the rising glow of Sarnen's magic. A single spell channeled through that wand dissolved the entire front line of attacking spirits into nothingness, a gap instantly filled by those spirits pressing in from behind. And again, and then the spirits were closing ground and Sarnen aimed the wand at Kerraii.

Startled, she stood her ground, hiding her flinch and knowing all too well the power in that wand, the things he could do to her, altering her for his own defense, forever changing what had already been changed so much.

But only her sword showed any response, shivering in her hand with a vibration that made its cold way down the bones of her arm, chilling her to the core. A glow swept out along the sword, a swift crackle of force; in spite of her resolve, Kerraii's eyes widened slightly.

Sarnen dispersed another row of spirits, those that were almost upon them. "Take your sword to them!"

Kerraii did as commanded without hesitation. The sword

bit into the spirit before her as though it was comprised of flesh, and a wicked grin slid onto her face. The sword, light and alive with power, disarmed the next spirit, beheaded the one after that. And the spirits, who had no remaining guile or skill nor anything but anger to drive them, fell before her more swiftly than any corporeal foe ever had, screaming their fury as they dispersed at the end of her sword. By the time they reached the ground they had disappeared; no ungainly pile of bodies remained to trip her or distract her. She moved back into position before Sarnen, protecting him as he unleashed a purer power on the ranks of spirits rising at the edge of the lake. And then she fought the ones who came behind, and those after that . . .

. . . Until her sword cleaved the last advancing spirit, and the gibbering shrieks died down to a single forlorn and fading wail. Kerraii turned in a slow circle, disbelieving the spirits were gone. That she survived. That Sarnen survived. She stopped when she faced Sarnen, and he gave her the slightest nod of acknowledgment, the faintest tightening of his lips over his teeth in a smile.

Her sword made a sound like a skim of ice shattering into a thousand pieces, and fell to the ground in sharp shards that quickly sank into the dirt as though it were water. She stared at the hilt a moment, then flung it far out into the lake.

"We will get you a new sword," Sarnen said easily. The look he gave the city was not so easy, nor anywhere near forgiving. Somewhere in those dark tunnels and twisting corridors, his enemies waited for news of their victory, never imagining that between them, Sarnen and Kerraii would defeat an army of angry spirits. Sarnen turned back to her, one sparse, painted eyebrow raised. "An excellent sword, one worthy of your skills and the trust I place in you." He gave the city a meaningful glance. "You'll need it."

. . .

420 Tz. CAERONN INTERROGATION

But even Sarnen's trust in Kerraii went only as far as he could monitor her, hold her family over her, use her. He might give himself over to her keeping, but he had no cause to explain to her his strategies, his plans, his hidden defenses . . . and he didn't.

Although Nujarek had no reason to believe her when she said so.

Kerraii let her foot bob up and down slightly, a casual gesture. A relaxed one. Necropolis had taught her one thing: she could endure. And in knowing that the moment for endurance was upon her, she lost the tension that had haunted her past few days. Now it would start. And then it would be over, one way or another. "If you're hoping I have some little treasure bit of information, the key to Sarnen or even Necropolis itself, you're about to know disappointment."

"Nonsense," Nujarek said. He eyed her, revealing a gleam of greed. "You cannot possibly disappoint me."

"Then no doubt I'll surprise you as well," she told him. The restraints kept her wrists clamped tightly to the chair; she managed a negligent wave of her fingers anyway. "Ask your questions. I'll answer you, you won't believe me, and then . . . you'll apply some means of persuasion. I'll give you the same answers, for as long as you care to play the game."

Nujarek drew himself up slightly. "I do not *play games*. As you're about to find out."

She smiled at him. "Everyone plays games," she said, her voice close to gentle. As if she were speaking to a child, or a man entirely out of his league. Nujarek understood the insult; he scowled at her and threw himself across the room in a spate of powerful pacing. Wordlessly taunting her with his ability to do so while she sat bound and fettered in a chair that ceaselessly tried to eject her. At his nod, the Surok apprentice stepped forward and tightened the collar around her neck, just enough to serve as a reminder.

"Good," she said in approval, as if such mild tactics could possibly be effective. It made her wonder if he'd been instructed to keep her whole . . . at least for now. "No point in wasting time."

Nujarek scowled. "What is Sarnen up to?" he asked. "What's the meaning behind this Dark Crusade of yours?"

"That should be obvious." She glanced at the Caero leader, as if confirming the question. Another little insult to Nujarek. "Necropolis is no longer satisfied with such a small part of the Land. Tezla's will demands that they reclaim former glory."

He turned to her with a little sneer. "For a Sect Elf in a Nightblade's gear, you speak as though you are no longer one of them."

"Things change," she said simply.

He dove at the next question. "Where will they strike next?"

The slip collar tightened; Kerraii fought off a faint, primordial surge of panic at the need to struggle for breath. With effort, she schooled her expression to stoic calm. "I don't even know where they struck last, or where else they struck on the day I was captured. Would you like to know the women I commanded? I can tell you all their names. I can tell you the name of the idiot human who caused our defeat that day. I can tell you how many Zombies we started with, though I'm sure that number grew during the battle."

Nujarek gave an impatient gesture. "Those things mean nothing to us. They are many weeks past. We do not need to know the names of your dead Nightblades."

Kerraii said nothing, dropping her head to look up at him from beneath a lowered brow. Foolish man. Did he assume Skulk had died with the rest of them? She had offered him a true advantage, hidden in its casual delivery. Skulk was no doubt desperate to offset his losses of that day, and would be happy to deal with Nujarek just to find a way to betray him—even as Nujarek did the same to Skulk.

"The armies," Nujarek said suddenly. "What forces does Necropolis amass against us? What strategy of battle?"

She took a deep, difficult breath. "Their strategy . . . is to kill as many of you as possible and use your own dead against you. But surely you knew that. Everyone knows that."

He crossed his arms, looking down at her from above, those narrow eyes striking in their violet hue. They belonged in another face, a face with pleasing features and a mouth that smiled instead of this sulky, haughty mix of feature and expression. "A Zombie would be of more use than you."

"Perhaps you aren't asking the right questions." And then, as Nujarek drew breath for what looked to be a shout—an order, an attempt to intimidate her . . . she wasn't sure, but she forestalled it. "Or perhaps I'm simply of less use than a Zombie."

The Grand Magistrate spoke. "It may be that it was an error to delay her in the mine," he said, sitting on the edge of the small desk, trying to look bored but instead simply looking mildly anxious in spite of his quiet authority here. No doubt the mage had something to do with that. He might act as an advisor, but he also served as a political spy. Someone else had expected results from this interrogation, that was certain—someone this man would report to, and not someone Nujarek had to face. "Whatever information she had is indeed outdated."

Kerraii said, "Sarnen has no doubt changed his plans, ordered the access to his rooms altered, and chosen a handful of Nightblades to attend him in my place until his new chosen is selected and trained. I never knew the overall battle plans. My place is by his side, not on the field."

Nujarek whirled around, clamping his cold hands over

her restrained wrists and leaning over so closely that the blue tattoos on his cheek seemed to writhe strangely in her vision. "*But you were*," he said. "In the field. Why was that?"

She looked straight into his eyes, unaffected by the posturing and the effort to intimidate her. "Because it was to his advantage to have me there." Black eyes stared into violet, calm and remote eyes stared into a gaze so fervent it had a manic glint.

"How?" he hissed, as if this were a thing of utmost importance.

"I followed orders. I represented his interests. I had no need of *whys*." She sighed. "You surprise me. This *is* boring." *Get it over with, one way or the other* . . . even if she had to goad him into it.

It didn't surprise her when Nujarek shot a hot-blooded look of command at the Surok apprentice behind her, or when the apprentice snatched her hair near her head, winding it around his fingers to jerk her head back. *By the Land, why do they always go for the hair?* But she knew why. To startle her. To frighten her. To intimidate her by so completely controlling her with leverage and pain.

But she was none of those. She wasn't even angry. She merely endured what had been inevitable all along. Nujarek, still leaning over her, watched her with an eager gaze that told her worse would come, far worse than a simple strap around her throat. She could barely see the Grand Magistrate; the man's expression spoke more of regret and resignation than anticipation.

He knows I speak the truth. Unfortunate that he'd somehow lost control of this interrogation.

Nujarek shook his head with a patently false regret. "We could have done this the easy way."

Even in that tight grip, she managed to shake her head. Her voice came out strained but calm, with no reflection of her slamming heartbeat as she struggled for air. "There's never an easy way."

His face flickered with anger at her resistance. Not to the questions—that resistance was so expected that he couldn't even take note of its absence. It was her refusal to be intimidated that angered him so. Nujarek was a man who liked to control . . . and Kerraii could not be so easily controlled. She might die here, she might end up screaming and pleading and begging, but she would not succumb to simple emotional mind games.

Nujarek gripped her jaw with thick fingers, squeezing tightly. Painfully. "Baruti," he said, "we're wasting time. Bring in your torturer. I hear he's quite good."

"He is," the man said calmly. "But I don't waste his talents. After all the delay, this woman has nothing to tell you that can't wait. A few more weeks in an isolated cell will weaken her body and her will, and we can easily learn what little she knows."

Nujarek's grip tightened, squeezing so hard Kerraii thought he might actually break her jaw. She closed her eyes, her breathing a mere rasp. If he looked he would see her pulse leaping in her throat, but he was caught up in his own drama now. Resistance from both sides. He said, "She's been living with Sarnen for years. She *must* have information for us."

"Sarnen's favorite color?" Baruti said dryly. "On which side of the bed he prefers to sleep? We don't have anyone in place right now to take advantage of those details. She's right. The moment she was lost, he changed everything that might be of use to us. Those in the field made a serious error when they didn't interrogate her immediately upon her capture. No Deathspeaker lives long without taking those kinds of precautions, and Sarnen is among the oldest of such unnatural creatures. As for those things that might be useful in the long term, they'll still be useful several weeks from now.

And my experience assures me they'll be a lot easier to extract by then."

"We have no reason to spare her," Nujarek growled.

"Only that she is strong enough now to resist us to the point of damage. Just look at her, Lord Nujarek. You're not far from breaking her jaw, after which it will be much more difficult to pry loose answers of any sort."

Abruptly, Nujarek released her. Kerraii's face throbbed as blood flowed back to the pressure points of his grip. He said reluctantly, "It's true my usual dealings are with higher strategies. You have greater experience in this realm of grime and prisoners."

Kerraii didn't need to open her eyes to recognize Nujarek's face-saving opportunity. Nor did Baruti, for the man immediately picked up on the opening, ignoring the insult that had been embedded within it. "You are quite right, Overseer Nujarek. And in a trade city such as Caero, we are adept at discovering the best result for the lowest price. When dealing with information that is no longer time-critical, our patient approach delivers results for less effort." He nodded at the Surokian, a gesture Kerraii saw through slitted and watering eyes at the very bottom of her vision.

But Nujarek held up a quick hand, staving off Kerraii's release from the cruel grip wound in her hair. Again he leaned over her, his two hard, broad hands closing over her wrists just above the tight cuffs that restrained her. He put his mouth, semipursed in petulance, close to her ear and said, "I have the influence to change your fate. You have other secrets I would learn. Skills only a Nightblade knows . . ."

That she did. But she trusted him only in so far as she believed with utter certainty that he would fail to keep any such bargain once he had what he wanted. She made no attempt to lower her voice, or to hide the purr of contempt in it. "Even a Nightblade has her standards, Nujarek. The only skills you'll ever learn from me involve the many various painful ways I can kill you."

He jerked away from her as if branded, and instantly backhanded her with all the strength behind that meaty fist. Kerraii's mind exploded into darkness and whirls; angry shouting reached her in only the vaguest way, growing clearer as she regained enough of her senses to push herself back up in the chair and release the dangerous pressure of the collar at her neck. Baruti and Nujarek railed at one another, the first demanding restraint of the second until Baruti gave Nujarek into the honorable—and inexorable— escort of the Surokian, with the mage in attendance to soothe him.

Silence fell over the little room, and Kerraii sat with her eyes closed, assessing the damage—nothing broken, but lips and cheek and eye fast swelling into proportions that already felt grotesque. She considered the fact that she might perhaps be alone, and wondered how quickly she could get out of the restraints.

But she was not alone. In her daze, she'd lost track of Baruti. *Careless error*. She couldn't afford to make those. He spoke into the silence. "You're either most stupid . . . or terribly clever."

She opened her eyes—no, only one eye, the one that wasn't swelling shut—to regard him, to find honesty and perhaps even a touch of admiration in his calm expression. Whatever shouting had transpired, Nujarek had not overly upset him. "Clever, I think," he said. "He wants you killed. I won't do it, of course—not yet. Knew that, did you, from the mild nature of our little information-extraction area? So he demands you be thrown into the deepest, darkest corner I can find and lost for a very long time. It doesn't seem to have occurred to him that this will only delay further questioning—and that it places you entirely out of his reach."

"A man may have desires," Kerraii said, her speech slightly slurred through puffy lips, "but he errs to let them rule him." And in spite of the pain, she smiled.

CHAPTER 12

420 Tz. CAERONN PRISON

GRAND Magistrate Baruti or his people would get back to her, but Kerraii had some time. She was no fragile creature to founder and fail simply because her circumstances were dire. Eventually her body would weaken from the poor food and prison parasites, but until then she would watch and learn and take any opportunities she saw. Baruti and Nujarek might well be aware of her night vision, but without experiencing it themselves, they had no notion of its clarity—of just how far she could see, and how well, in how much darkness.

Much better, she knew, than they imagined.

The first day after the Surokian escorted her to her new cell—a tiny thing far underground where the damp darkness seemed to suck the very light from the torches and even from the single magelight she'd seen in use—Kerraii rested. She pressed her aching face to the damp, cool stone of the cell wall, ignoring the uneven coating of slime. She contemplated the odds that Nujarek would return, bellowing for her, against the odds that he'd already left the city, leaving his embarrassment behind with the assurance she'd never see the light of day again.

As she likely wouldn't, if she didn't do something about it before she lost her strength.

The second day she commenced stretching and strengthening

exercises, hampered by the low ceiling and tight walls; if she stretched her arms their widest, her fingers touched the opposing walls of her cell. All the walls were made of the same enslimed stone, and the door rang dully under her tapping fingers with the unyielding sound of solid iron. At the bottom of the door she found a slit for food; in the top third, a small shuttered hole controlled entirely from the outside. She examined every corner, every line of stone and mortar, using both touch and sight. A small grille in the corner covered the waste hole; her jailors wasted no effort on such things as bedding, not even moldy old straw.

The harness—still clinging stubbornly to her body unless it was her willing hand on strap and buckle—kept her warmer than they had any reason to suspect in this imagination-starved Technomagical society.

In the following days she determined the ebb and flow of the prison rhythms—this day-driven society did their torturing in the early morning, losing the advantage of the deep night fears and fatigue that weakened most prisoners. Food came twice a day, the same weak rice and potato gruel, along with the only light to reach these obsidian depths, used partly to determine which of the cells needed body-removal duty. Always she was ready; never did she have opportunity to act. No one came to question her. No one responded to her experimental cries of distress—except for the man two cells down who railed angrily at the disturbance. A few days later she tried again with cries that indicated anything but distress. Any number of prisoners whooped approval, but if anyone else heard she saw no sign of it.

No one so much as touched the lock and latch to her door.

She considered using her remaining knife to pry at the single small spot of crumbling mortar, but opted to save the blade; if the tactic got her anywhere, it would only be into the next cell. She'd learned to pick locks early and well with fingers grown up to nurturing fragile seedlings and completing complex weavings, but it was a useless skill when the lock itself remained entirely out of reach.

Nothing in the daily routine of this dismal place offered her a chance for escape.

Fine. She could endure. She'd become expert at it. Sooner or later, something *not routine* would occur. The *not routine* always happened . . . the unanticipated. These Atlanteans thrived on their schedules, their comforting reliance on their false Tezla, and on their Emperor's rules. Kerraii had learned to thrive on the unpredictable. When it came, the Atlanteans would scramble to cope . . . and by the time they did, she'd be gone.

Passing days only renewed her confidence. For although the extensive prison complex had been quiet and half-filled upon her arrival, the renewed warfare throughout the factions quickly filled the empty cells. The sporadic moaning became a constant background noise echoing down the lightless corridor; the more extreme cries from the lower questioning chambers rang out through the day. Kerraii missed a few meals, but begrudged them not. The more pressed they were, the more undermanned, the more likely one of the Atlanteans would make the mistake that offered Kerraii her freedom.

She was ready the morning she heard their clumsy footsteps along the hall . . . several of them, scuffling along with one who stumbled more than the others. *Now. Now I'll take my leave of this place.*

She flexed one hand as though it already held her stubby leaf-edged knife. Through the food slot at the bottom of the door, she watched the torchlight turn from mere shadowed edges to true light. Mere ignorant soldiers would expect her to be blinded by that after so many days in darkness. No matter their common knowledge of the Dark Elves' night vision; they didn't truly seem to understand the differences between that night vision and their own. Kerraii saw the cell in its entirety, with the acuity of the eagles these Caeronn seemed to hold in such high regard. She saw every nook, every cranny, unobscured by shadow. In this total darkness she saw not in color, but in a cool blue wash of shades. Adding torch- or sunlight, no matter how abrupt or bright, would do nothing but introduce the missing colors.

The entourage came to a shuffling stop before her cell, complete with muttering and a short conversation of partial sentences and monosyllabic responses. Kerraii's hand hovered over the knife, still hidden in her boot; she eased into the corner beside the door and crouched down, ready to explode into action.

Magelight flared into existence inside the cell—magelight, the one thing that *would* confound her vision in the transition between dark and bright. Kerraii hissed a curse, throwing her forearm up over her eyes. *Not so ignorant after all.* Blinking, her eyes watering, she resolved to launch herself at the open door. *I won't pass up this chance.*

But it was no chance at all. The lock creaked, the hinges groaned—and as Kerraii exploded into motion, she crashed headlong into the body they threw at her, colliding so solidly with it that she sprawled back on the hard stone, striking her head against the opposite wall in this tiny space. Even dazed, she rebounded instantly, her body moving with long-ingrained training—only to collide once more with what could only be a new cellmate. Still blinded and dazed, she nonetheless automatically collected information about this potential new problem. *Woman. Shorter than me, but not by much. Muscled but slim. Probably human.* The faintest tang of blood reached her, along with fear sweat and human body gone unwashed. *Roughed up, but not badly wounded.*

And even then Kerraii shoved the newcomer away and leapt for the door. The latch clicked home as she reached it, thumping against the metal with the speed and force behind her charge. A bark of harshly amused laughter rang out from the other side, and then the torchlight diminished and her world shrank back into darkness.

Kerraii snarled and slapped the door in utter frustration, turning away to lean her back against it and consider her new circumstances. Her vision recovered slowly from the assault of the magelight, but not so slowly that she couldn't already spot the woman against the wall on the other side of the cell—not very far away at all. The woman stood with her back to the wall, hands pressed back against it at the level of her hips, steadying herself. Maybe even holding herself up. Her hair was a dark shade, curly, and straggling almost entirely out of the ties that bound it; her eye color was impossible to tell. Deep blue or brown or green, they all looked the same to night vision. She wore basic homespun over a generous figure, several layers of it, in fact. A practical, country look, and not a uniform; Kerraii suspected she was a Black Powder Rebel.

The woman cocked her head at that angle many humans adopted when they found themselves in the dark in unfamiliar territory. Her hands lightly explored the wall behind her.

Kerraii glared at her. *Had you not been in the way . . .*

That wasn't entirely fair. The guards had been ready for her; they'd even had a magelight. They'd used this woman as a weapon to prevent any escape attempt. But Kerraii didn't particularly care about fair. She only cared that this woman had gotten in her way, and she glowered.

The woman was oblivious, lost in her own darkness and her own thoughts. She gave a short, surprising laugh, startling away Kerraii's glower, and said in the Atlantean tongue, "They thought it was funny, putting me in here. With you. Why was that?"

"I don't know," Kerraii said in a low voice. She eased to the other corner of the cell, as soundless as ever, and added from there, "What do *you* think?"

The woman's head jerked as she reoriented on Kerraii's

voice. She said matter-of-factly, "I think there aren't many people who can move like that. They probably expect you to make short work of me."

Kerraii spoke in neutral tones, from the third corner. "I'm not used to sharing this cell. You and your blind human eyes . . . have you yet figured out it's a snug fit for the two of us?"

"It seemed evident," the woman said dryly. "If you *are* going to try to kill me, could we do that now? Otherwise, I'd like to sit down."

"Sit," Kerraii said, just as dryly as the human. "It does not do to give them what they expect or want."

The woman slid to the floor, a careful descent; she crossed her legs once she reached bottom. "Now that's a philosophy I can embrace." She kneaded her leg above the knee, most likely forgetting that Kerraii could see the gesture— along with the torn cloth of her loose-fitting trousers. "My name is Rikka."

Kerraii did not respond in kind. She didn't put it beyond the Atlanteans to play games with her by planting a cellmate who would, in commiseration, gain what Nujarek had not managed to intimidate out of her. Or what the Atlanteans *thought* she was still hiding.

Nothing left to hide . . . except those few little details that would gain them access to Sarnen's chambers.

But *those* details Kerraii was saving for herself.

On the other hand . . .

They already knew who she was.

So she said, "Kerraii," and left it at that. And then, eyeing the woman's clothing again, said, "I smell the stench of black powder."

Rikka snorted. "Anyone who's been in a skirmish these days ends up smelling like black powder. I could be a leech medic for all you know."

Kerraii considered her a moment. *No. Too hard. Too pre-*

pared for this place. And mostly not affected enough by the cries of those around us. If anything stirred a leech medic, it was the sound of those in pain. Kerraii had seen them at work after the Roa Kaiten battle, seen their tears and frustration for those they couldn't save. "I don't think so," she said out loud.

The other woman gave another little laugh, a hard little laugh. "I forget just how well you see under these conditions," she said. "I can't even find the hand in front of my face." And, unthinking, she held a hand up and stared blankly in its direction, close enough for Kerraii to have examined the lines of her palm had she been in Rikka's place, though Rikka clearly saw it not at all.

But then Rikka looked straight at her. "What does it matter who or what I am?"

"It changes nothing," Kerraii said, crouching against the wall. "But it would be convenient to know how to annoy you, if I choose. Or how to avoid annoying you."

"Or how to goad me into some sort of thoughtless physical reaction so you'd have an opportunity to kill me."

Kerraii smiled, knowing the other woman couldn't see her and so letting the humorless amusement through to her voice as well. "I need no untoward opportunity to kill you. You are the one who keeps mentioning the possibility, not I."

Rikka hesitated at that, drawing her knees up and tucking her arms around them to regard the dark spot—to her eyes—that held Kerraii.

Kerraii saw no fear on Rikka's face, which pleased her. Sharing this cell with a twittering mouse would be severely annoying. With a casual mercy she would not have shown in Necropolis, she said, "Should you perish, the Atlanteans will only replace you with someone else. And since the Emperor does his best to obliterate or dominate anything not Atlantean, that *someone else* could turn out to be much more inconvenient than you. An orc, perhaps. That would make breathing most difficult in this small space."

The corner of Rikka's mouth twitched; she fought it, but gave up and allowed herself a brief grin. "I wouldn't have expected you to have a sense of humor."

"Well," Kerraii said, relaxing against the chill nastiness of the bricks, "no doubt I'm severely out of practice. We in the Sect spend all our time drinking blood and torturing small animals, paying any price for a few more years of life—as I'm sure you know. Just as I know you rebels are so idealistic that you're easily manipulated by any warlord—Blackwyn, for instance—who can convince you his goals are for the spurious cause of freedom."

Rikka stiffened. "Not Blackwyn."

Kerraii refrained from mentioning that Rikka had only proved her point, reacting with instant idealistic loyalty to the vaguest slight on the warlord's name. She found herself curious—enough to avoid the easy score. "How not Blackwyn?" she asked.

But Rikka rested the side of her face on her drawn-up knees, looking away from Kerraii. "I'm tired," she said. "Find a small animal to torture."

But Kerraii could not help but consider the difference between her forced—and easily severed—loyalties to Sarnen, and Rikka's strong personal reaction in Blackwyn's defense.

The cell, once too small for Kerraii, quickly became intolerable for the two women, no matter how they tried to work around it.

"Some fat Caeronn merchant might be happy to inhabit a space so small," Rikka grumbled, doing arm-presses against one wall as Kerraii did the same against the opposite wall, syncing her movements so she moved forward as Rikka straightened her arms, avoiding a collision. "They never move, anyway—if you don't count having yourself carted around in a litter."

"Why go anywhere when you can put your thoughts down and send them through mage writ to whomever you might choose?" It was an exaggeration; mage writ was too expensive for casual use by even a successful Caeronn citizen. Kerraii knew for herself how dearly the Magestone was wrought, and teleporting mage-writ messages burned out a small stone for good. But Rikka only grunted agreement, although Kerraii knew the Black Powder Rebels—even Blackwyn—were happy and willing to use any Technomancer who allied themselves to their rallying cry of freedom for all.

But since that first query, she no longer asked Rikka directly about the warlord. The woman considered Kerraii as loyal to the Sect as she herself was to her own cause, and no amount of *telling* or *asking* would change that. Only *showing*. So Kerraii said, "My own people are happy enough to run through the woods on their own two feet, visiting neighbors in person."

"What are you talking about?" Rikka said, breathless as her exertions caught up with her. "Even I know Necropolis is a place of cold buildings and dark places."

Kerraii deliberately altered the rhythm of her arm-presses so she bumped against Rikka's back; there wasn't enough room in the space for both women to straighten their arms at once, and Rikka took up the challenge, pushing against Kerraii in her effort to be the one who took the space. Kerraii only held her own, letting Rikka expend her effort. "Necropolis also has a habit of replenishing itself from unwilling sources."

Rikka trembled with the effort to straighten her arms. She'd arrived already weakened, and had not taken to prison life as patiently as Kerraii. "Don't tell me you're *Wylden*."

Kerraii said nothing. She waited a moment, and then

easily straightened her arms, pushing Rikka abruptly enough that the rebel woman stumbled forward.

"You *are*," Rikka said, rubbing her upper arm with a dirty hand. Her dark hair hung lankly around her shoulders, more than ready for a bath. And Kerraii still said nothing, but went back to a series of arm-presses as though the brief battle for space—and the conversation—had never happened.

"Don't move," Kerraii murmured.

"Why—"

Kerraii hissed her quiet, adding a nudge, her foot into Rikka's side—for they'd both been asleep and had quickly become accustomed to the bumping and occasional overlapping required in the small cell. Rikka stifled a protest, but otherwise held her silence, stiffening slightly as she listened for clues.

Kerraii kept her attention trained on the small food slot at the bottom of the door. She'd seen a whiskered little nose poke through just a moment earlier, and now she eased herself into position, hunkered down with hand hovering to—

—*snatch!*

The rat twisted wildly, a nice plump thing squeaking in fear and trying to sink its teeth into Kerraii's hand.

She bashed its head against the wall and held the rat out for Rikka, taking her cellmate's hand to press the warm, twitching body into Rikka's grip. Rikka gasped in surprise and revulsion and instantly dropped the creature.

"It's meat," Kerraii said. "It no doubt ate better than we do."

"*Eat* it?" Rikka said. "*You* eat it. You're the one who—" She cut herself off, aware as she hadn't been only days earlier that perhaps her assumptions were not all true.

"Tortures small animals and drinks their blood?" Kerraii arched an eyebrow Rikka couldn't see. "I'm afraid I never acquired a taste for it, though some do. You need the strength more than I. Eat it." She picked the rat up, retrieving her little knife to slice it open and peel back its skin.

Rikka frowned at the noises she heard, trying to understand them, and then frowned again when Kerraii returned the rat to her, pushing it at her with a brief but insistent motion. "But—" she said, and then, "You have a *knife*!"

"I have a sharp edge." Kerraii lifted the blade briefly, eyeing the cool gleam of silver in her monochrome vision. "*Knife* is too grandiose a term for something so small. But I intend for it to serve me well when the right moment comes."

It was a risk. Rikka could endear herself to their captors by crying out an alarm and alerting them to the small weapon. They might not be able to remove Kerraii's harness or find the knife within it, but they could make her life miserable in the trying.

A calculated risk. Rikka had every reason to believe she wouldn't live past the first cry. And she had reason to leave her cellmate armed. For if Kerraii's chance came, so might Rikka's.

"Eat." Kerraii wiped the blade on the side of her boot and returned it to its hidden sheath. "I've done what I had to in order to survive, to keep my family safe. I've done worse than eating a nice raw juicy rat. I wouldn't hesitate to eat it now."

Rikka whispered, "Then why give it to me?"

"You need it." Not that her own strength wasn't slowly waning, making each exercise session just a little harder with each passing day. "Isn't it what your vaunted Blackwyn would do? Freedom for all? You cannot gain freedom if you can't pick yourself up off this cell floor and run for it when the time comes."

Slowly, Rikka held her hand out for the rat. Kerraii pretended she didn't see the trembling.

· · ·

"The time *will* come." Rikka kneaded a cramp in her leg, leaning forward in such a way that they became accidental confidants.

Kerraii had no need to ask what Rikka meant.

"Blackwyn takes care of his own," Rikka said. "He keeps our families safe . . . and . . . my son." She hesitated a moment there, her voice full of longing, and then spoke more brusquely when she continued. "He never wastes lives if he can complete a mission without bloodshed. He never sends us out into situations where the cost is more than the gain, even when *he's* not the one paying the cost."

"He sent you out to be captured."

Rikka turned on her with a fierce scowl, with aim that had become fairly accurate after all this time with Kerraii in the darkness. "We weren't out on a mission at all. We were ambushed by orcs, who traded us in the Caero market for cheap baubles that made their beady little eyes gleam. Blackwyn would never—*Blaize* would never—"

Ah. Blaize. A new name from Rikka's life. An important one, to judge by the raw emotion in Rikka's voice.

Rikka took a deep and obvious breath. "Blackwyn lives his own words. His drive to free the oppressed comes from his heart, but he's not about to sacrifice more of us along the way. He's the only one who proves his words with his actions; so many others are in the fight for what they think they can get out of it, and even most of the Black Powder Rebels can forget to weigh cost against gain. They waste too many lives."

Kerraii didn't press her. If nothing else, Rikka had certainly bought into Blackwyn's image.

Many people bought into Blackwyn's image, it seemed. Especially those who were caught between the struggles of the various factions. The ones who needed help.

And where will I go when I get out of here? Where will I call home, and what will be my cause?

The distant sound of a key scraping in an old and rusty lock reached Kerraii's ears; she glanced away from Rikka, who seemed to be waiting for an argument, and eyed the door. She rose to it, as ready as ever for her chance at freedom. "Food's coming."

Rikka hid her eyes behind her hands, having come to terms with the fact that the transitory torchlight offered more pain than reassurance; only after Kerraii gave her the word would she uncover her eyes and grope for the food the keeper shoved under the door.

But today the keeper took longer than usual to move down the long row of cells; as he grew closer, Kerraii realized he had something to mutter at each door.

He'd never spoken to any of them before; he'd never done anything to indicate his awareness of the cell occupants at all. Her only clue to his identity had been his heavy tread and the occasional grunt of effort as he straightened. She gathered he was not a lightweight man.

Rikka frowned behind her hands. "Where is he—"

"Shh," Kerraii said sharply, up against the door. "Listen."

Two cells away, then one, and still she could not catch his words, although the hissing slide of the wooden food tray under each door came clearly enough, along with the squeaky wheels of his serving trolley as he dragged it down the corridor. She moved alongside the door, pressed up against it as though this, somehow, might be their chance to escape. The keeper bent down, then hesitated before shoving the food tray through. With malicious pleasure, he said, "Baruti is tired of feeding you. We've won a big battle south of the Fist and we're cleaning house. You'll all be dead within days." And he shoved the food tray through.

But he hadn't counted on Kerraii's vision—fully functional even in this strong torchlight—or her quickness. Or even that after all these days of imprisonment, her temper would snap at such wanton taunting. He shoved a little too hard in his cruel glee, with a little too much follow-through. His hand flickered through the opening, ever so briefly.

Long enough for Kerraii.

Her hand shot out, snatching him by the wrist. She yanked hard—*once, twice*—slamming him into the solid metal door. Then she released him, listening to the satisfying thump of his body hitting the floor. The torch went out. He moaned, cursing her; Rikka's hands dropped from her face as she listened, both astonished and appreciative. Kerraii muttered, *"fool,"* at him, and pulled their meal out of his reach. *Keep your baiting to yourself.*

After a moment he collected himself, climbed to his feet with much groaning and shuffling, and made his fumbling way back down the corridor—presumably to fetch another torch.

Rikka took the bowl Kerraii pressed into her hand, sipping cautiously from it. "They could come after you for that."

No doubt. It had not been wise. But she said, "They're going to execute us soon anyway. They won't expend the extra effort."

Rikka shook her head with some assurance. "They won't have the chance to execute us," she said. "Blackwyn will hear. And the Black Powder Rebels have too many people in these dungeons. They'll come for us."

Kerraii grinned wickedly into the darkness. "They won't have the chance to execute me, that's for certain."

She wasn't sure how Rikka took her words. But when they came for her, Kerraii intended to fight for her freedom, even to the death. What did she have to lose?

CHAPTER 13

420 Tz, CAERONN PRISON

RIKKA and Kerraii received no more meals. No one along their row of tiny cells received food after the meal during which the keeper spread the news of the death sentences.

"Makes sense," Kerraii said over the growl of her stomach. "Why waste the food when they no longer have hopes of extracting information or work from us? Better to devote their energies to the new crop of prisoners."

Rikka gave her a strange look, pale and thin in Kerraii's dark-vision. "It doesn't *make sense* to anyone with the slightest compassion."

"What have these people done to give you the impression they had compassion?" Kerraii knew she looked as bad or worse than Rikka; she'd been a mine slave and then a prisoner, and her ribs rose distinctly under her fingers. No doubt she was far from the sleek, strong creature who had last graced Sarnen's sight.

You made me strong, Sarnen. If I get the chance, I'll make you sorry for that.

Rikka winced, a self-deprecating expression. "I thought . . ."

"You thought it was my own way of thinking. Don't trouble yourself. Were I in Necropolis, it might well be." Kerraii, too, could be hard on herself. She stretched against the wall,

187

one leg forward, one back, and detected a troublesome quiver in her thigh.

"You should rest," Rikka said, identifying the activity with her head cocked to the sound of it. "No food. Save your strength."

"What strength I have will be of no good if I'm too stiff to move when I need to," Kerraii said—although, like Rikka, she'd dropped the hard exercises as soon as she realized they'd go hungry. The muscle she had left would carry her through these next few days, and these next few days were all that mattered.

Rikka scrunched up her nose. "I suppose you're right," she said, and climbed to her feet. "At least this way I can be sure you won't step on me."

Kerraii smiled briefly into the darkness. It was a tease, and it spoke well of the woman's spirit. Still . . .

She'd do just enough to keep herself from stiffening up, and then she'd rest and do it again. And again. For however long it took.

A distant shout echoed down the corridor. A shout, and a wave of reaction up and down the cells.

Rikka tensed. "This could be it." Shouts of protest, shouts of those being led off to die.

But Kerraii cocked her head, listening intently. If there was one thing she knew, it was the sound of despair, and that cry had not held despair. That cry held . . .

Hope.

"This is it," she said, as another shout reached them from beyond the door to this hall, followed by the crash of a door flung open hard, the clash of weapons. "But not execution."

"Rescue," Rikka breathed.

"Don't go taking it for granted," Kerraii said sharply. "One way or the other, we'll have to fight our way out." And she eased her knife free, taking up position beside the door.

Rikka moved in beside her, crowded along the adjoining wall in the tight space.

The fighting grew closer; the cursing more audible. And then there was a sudden lull, and clear—if winded—voices from the other side of the door.

"They've pulled back." A man's voice, sounding sure of himself. A commander, Kerraii decided. "They'll try to block us on the way out."

"Our exit points *are* limited," came the wry rejoinder, and Rikka gave the slightest gasp, a sound of utter relief.

"Blaize," she murmured to Kerraii. "It's Blaize!"

"Mmm," Kerraii said, completely noncommittal. Blaize was not here for *her*.

The first voice responded with a cheery confidence. "That means our own forces know exactly where to squeeze from the other side." Keys jangled, and then the door opened with its usual squeal of protest. Dim light swept down the corridor and in through the food slot; Rikka blinked quickly, trying to keep her eyes from squeezing shut against it.

Someone bellowed, "Anyone here want their freedom?" and a great shout went up.

Kerraii could barely hear the commander's directions. Only by listening intently did she catch the gist of them. *Free them all!* No doubt he counted on finding the prisoners so frantic for freedom that those from opposing factions wouldn't take each other on.

She hoped he was right. She didn't want to do battle with Rikka's people, not when she didn't know which one was the Blaize who meant so much to her cellmate.

The light grew brighter—too bright, a mixture of mage-light and torches. *So it's true. Some of the magi work with the Rebellion.* Rikka, though she stood tense and ready, her features tightening into a more angular version of her relaxed self, threw an arm up before her eyes. "I can't—"

"If they're your people, you don't need to." Kerraii could

not say the same for herself. She shifted the grip on her small knife as running footsteps hit the corridor, hesitating only to throw open each cell door along the way—although not without making noises of disgust and dismay at what they found inside. Kerraii reminded Rikka, "The prison guards have retreated to block our escape. You'll have until then to adjust to the light."

A call rang down the corridor. *"Rikka!"*

"In here!" Rikka cried, close enough to Kerraii's ear to make her wince. "I'm in here! But the light . . . I can't . . . "

The door was flung open, revealing for the first time the deep red color of Rikka's hair. Kerraii found herself confronted with a human—a tall, lean man with intense brown eyes and an equally intense expression on his olive-complected features. *Handsome*, she thought absently, as Rikka cried out with the pain of the bright light and Kerraii herself crouched, battle-ready even with the tremble in that one leg.

The sight of her warrior stance stopped the man short . . . respectful. At the same time Kerraii got the impression it was all he could do to keep from leaping over her to reach Rikka, even though the three of them would never fit in this space. They eyed each other, he with his short sword and buckler, she with the stubby knife that barely protruded from her grip. She saw on his face the moment he realized she was overmatched, and she said, in a very low-key way, "It's not the length that matters. It's what you do with it."

His startled reaction bought her a moment. She had to find a way to make things clear: She would <u>not</u> fight them unless she had to; neither would she simply go from being one kind of prisoner to another. She'd leave this cell on her own terms, and if someone had to get hurt before they understood that, so be it.

"Blaize?" Rikka said, both hands pressed to her eyes.

"Rikka! What did they do to you?" He was fierce enough

it almost made Kerraii laugh. Fierce and young and sounding so certain he could and would do whatever it took to track down the ones he thought had hurt Rikka.

"I'm fine—"

"She's fine," Kerraii said at the same time. "She hasn't seen light since she got here. For mercy's sake, wrap something around her eyes."

"Bandages," Blaize said, barely taking his eyes off Rikka to look down the corridor and bellow, *"Bandages!"* When he faced the cell again, he said, "We brought leech medics. A single layer of bandages should help cut the light—"

"And I'll still be able to see somewhat," she agreed. "Blaize, Kennet—?"

"He's well," Blaize said, but brought his attention back to Kerraii. "Bruna has him. What about your friend here?"

Kerraii gave him a cold look. *"Friend* is not a word I hand out freely. Say rather I will fight beside you if it means getting out of here . . . and I will fight against you if you get in my way."

The leech medic ran up, a small woman who looked incongruous against the backdrop of warriors moving in the aisle behind her. She shook loose a length of bandage from the roll she held, already cut to size. "None of them can face the light just yet," she said, panting. "Was there anything else? Wounded?"

Blaize gave a short, sharp shake of his head, dividing his attention between Rikka and Kerraii. His gaze went remarkably hard when it landed on Kerraii. "Let's concentrate on getting out of here," he said. "After that . . ."

"After that, we may well just see how much size matters, after all," she said, eyes half-lidded, voice velvet enough to fool most of the men she'd faced into mistaking the ferocity of her intent. But by then she intended, also, to have acquired a sword. Long, short, narrow, sweeping . . . she didn't care. A sword.

"So we may," he said, and stepped aside so she could leave the cell and enter the chaos of the corridor—rebels running from cell to cell, the leech medic dispensing bandages, another medic shepherding weakened prisoners toward the exit. A Nightstalker in the ragged leftovers of his costume crawled along the juncture of wall and floor, too weak to get to his feet. Several Dwarves stumbled forward, leaning on each other, squinting, with tears rolling down their cheeks. A Wylden Elf, still nearly blinded, gave Kerraii a look of great betrayal and moved on.

Kerraii stood beside the open cell door as Blaize rushed into the cell, taking Rikka's face between his hands to give her a good, hard look—*Yes, boy,* Kerraii thought impatiently, *she's all there*—and forced himself to keep moving, wrapping the bandage around her head and then slipping her, if Kerraii wasn't mistaken, a brace of quality knives.

Then another man caught her attention, moving against the tide of escapees. Helmeted, lean, but with enough upper body mass that it couldn't all be his armor. He had a fuser rifle in one hand and was checking the powder load of a pistol; satisfied, he shoved the pistol into his wide belt just about the time he looked up to see her.

Once more, she readied for conflict, taking a balanced stance—a minor shift of weight that told this experienced warrior all he needed to know.

But rather than stepping up to meet her, he eased his weight back and opened his arms slightly. "You want out of here?"

"I've seen enough of the place," Kerraii said, deceptively cool. Given some sleep, some food . . . she might take this man. As it was . . . She lifted an eyebrow at him. "You?"

He gave her a hard little grin. "Looking for all the able-bodied fighters we can get. After we're out of here? We'll see."

After we're out of here you won't *see. Me. Not if I don't choose it to be so.* But she gave a short nod.

He made a polite gesture indicating she should precede him down the corridor and up the slant that led to the first, wide-open door. She didn't bother to give him the look that said she didn't like it, didn't like having him at her back at all; she had no choice. Refusal at this point would put her right back in the opposite camp.

The new corridor led to an open room—high ceilings, stairs leading up to two separate exits, second-story guard balconies jutting out over the area below. A holding and sorting area; Kerraii remembered it from her journey into the bowels of this place, although at the time her vision had been blurry and her head ringing. She moved swiftly, mindful of the all-too-competent man at her back. Fuser rifle and pistol. He'd never let her get close enough to use her little knife if they came to oppose one another.

For now they'd hardly have the time for such enmity. The guard balconies were hung with wounded and dead Atlanteans, and a stout little brass golem struggled to free itself from one such tangle. More soldiers filled the exits, while hovering magelight revealed the existence of mages behind the foot soldiers.

There they all waited. Blocking the doorways, blocking the corridors beyond. Waiting and ready.

Even to Kerraii, it looked grim. But the rebel who'd followed her didn't seem concerned. He waved them all forward, and prisoners and rebels filled the holding area as he shouted orders over his shoulder. Noisy, chaotic . . . it was worse than a blood pit, in its way. Rikka entered the room, shepherding those who were weaker than she, whose eyes were not adjusting as quickly to the light. She planted them in a corner directly under a balcony and took up a protective stance before them; when Blaize hesitated beside her, she nodded him on.

Blaize joined up with Kerraii's self-appointed overseer, and a line of rebels straggled out beside him—a Dwarf with one of the black-powder fuser weapons, another with an ax and a manic gleam in his eye; a bladesman from the Elemental league who had somehow thrown his lot in with this rescue. Beside him stood an Amazon, a sturdy, exotic woman with barely constrained wild hair and a wickedly fast blade. The others . . .

Just . . . people. People fighting for a cause.

At the moment, she was part of that cause, no matter her reasons for joining it. A skinny Nightblade with all of her skills and some of her strength and every bit of determination she'd ever had.

She gave her commander a slow smile, lifting her brow in invitation. "Shall we?"

The man settled his unique skirted helmet more firmly on his head and thrust his fuser rifle over his head, shouting a rally cry: "Blackwyn!"

The others raised their weapons in reply—rifles, crossbows, staves, swords, even candlesticks, and the room echoed with their roar. "Blackwyn!"

The rebels rushed the stairs. The guardsmen on the stairs—a combination of Utem, Altem, and even a few who must have been hastily pulled from Baruti's private retinue with their pleated linen finery beneath token armor and padding—tried to hold fast, but several young Caeronn enthusiasts broke forward.

They met midstair. The ax-laden Dwarf let out a mighty howl and tumbled the first wave off the freestanding stone stairway even as several fuser pistols ignited, filling the air with their peculiar thunder and the stinking aftermath.

Kerraii did not join the howling charge. She did not trust her legs to the stairs. She shot a glance at Rikka. The woman stood ready before her charges, balanced to use the knives she held, the slightest of snarls on her face. Not in need of help. But Kerraii's chance came soon enough, as the soldiers and their damaging mana-enhanced swords pushed through the thin rebel front line. *Better than lightning gunners.* She snatched up recently abandoned chains and crept along the walls, unusually aware of the colors she hadn't seen for so long, unusually aware of how red the blood turned the stone, and startled by how strange it seemed.

But not so distracted that she didn't duck the short sword thrust her way, spinning around to fling her chain around the soldier's neck, knowing just the angle to set her arms and *jerk* . . .

She snatched the soldier's blade as it settled atop his still-spasming body, glancing up just in time to dive and roll; a *manaclevt* blade slashed the air where she'd been, jamming into the stone only inches from Kerraii's eyes. She was in no position to retreat, sprawled against the wall in a most vulnerable way, the sword and the gauntleted hand that wielded it filling her vision.

The fingers wrapped around the hilt suddenly flexed and jerked, releasing their hold. Kerraii looked up to find a knife sticking out of the man's eye, and glanced back to Rikka to find a satisfied look on the woman's face. Kerraii lifted her chin in thanks—the only kind of *thanks* there was time for in a battle—and reached out to yank the knife free, steel grating against bone until the tip appeared from the jelly of the man's eyeball. She quickly swiped the knife clean on the Utem's thigh, then returned the knife to Rikka in an easy underhand toss.

Atop the stairs, the rebel commander stood briefly outlined within the doorway, sighting down his long rifle. The squeeze of the trigger wasn't visible from Kerraii's position, but the results were impressive; the fuser round took a Utem right through his protective gear and emerged from the man's back to bury itself in the stone wall not far from Kerraii's position. The rebel commander instantly reloaded, shoving a new round into the breech and flicking it closed with an expert thumb. Raising the rifle, he shouted, "Push on! Our reinforcements are at their backs!"

Kerraii pulled the *manaclevt* sword free and scanned the room for remaining enemy; she found only a small pile of wounded and two men who wisely had tossed their blade weapons aside when confronted by the Dwarvish fuser. Rikka hurried to help secure the surrendered, and Kerraii ran lightly up the steps to join forces with the commander.

"Snow," he said as she reached him. She slanted a gaze at him, and he added, "My name. Snow," as they jogged down the corridor. The Atlanteans ran before them, seeking the next staging area—although Snow seemed to believe they'd find it already occupied by rebel forces.

Ah. Exchanging names, were they? "Kerraii," she said. She tested the balance of her newly acquired blade and thought it clunky but serviceable. Snow gestured at the button at the back of the mana vial. "There's the trigger to energize the blade," he said, not the least bit winded as they jogged down the corridor. Deep-set windows lined the wall—*must be getting closer to the public areas*—and wall hangings depicting the family symbols of the different influential Caeronn merchants hung between them. He glanced at her, his expression asking a question. "In case you haven't used one before."

"I haven't. But such weapons defile the Land; I will not push that trigger." Much more winded than he, legs definitely getting shaky, she managed yet to flash him a darkly confident smile. "I will not need to."

He shook his head. "One moment you sound Wylden, and the next you match that outfit you wear."

"All that matters to you is how I fight."

"You're about to get the chance to show me." He glanced over his shoulder to make sure the others were following; Kerraii did likewise and found Rikka pushing the rescued prisoners along, her bandage pulled off her eyes to lie loosely around her neck. Abruptly, he slowed the pace; an instant later Kerraii heard the sound of fighting. A fuser discharge echoed down their corridor. "Just around this corner," he said. "More Black Powder Rebels will be closing in from the other side."

"You've got more—?" But she stopped herself, simply because the answer was obvious. Snow had planned this rescue just as carefully as it needed to be done. *Snow.* It hit her then, as it had not hit her when he gave her his name so casually. A man named Snow had killed the Prophet-Magus Karrudan, striking the rebellion's first blow—and opening the way for Necropolis to start its Dark Crusade. "*Snow,*" she said, giving the name enough meaning to turn it into a question.

"Yes," he said simply. He pulled his pistol from his belt— but not before hesitating to scrutinize her, raking her up and down and not just to count her ribs. It was an assessment she wasn't expecting. He added abruptly, "Ready? Let's go."

Kerraii's weeks of slavery and imprisonment had caught up with her, turning her legs watery and her grip on the sword uncertain. But she growled, "*Ready,*" and followed him into battle.

The corridor intersection filled with mayhem. A berserker Dwarf took his ax to a brass golem; the golem fought doggedly to flatten the Dwarf. The mage stayed out of reach, occasionally finding an opening to neatly target one of the rebels for a blast of magic. Fuser discharge and fuser stink filled the small area; Kerraii became one of those who smoothly moved in when the riflemen stepped back to reload, covering Snow when he needed it and getting out of his way when he didn't. She cut down a guardsman, and another, and used her tiny little knife to slash the throat of the one man who pushed too close to Snow during reload. He gaped at her in astonishment, unable to figure out before he died just how she'd cut him. Her vision grayed and she fought through it, knowing she could.

For now.

"'Ware! Golem from behind!"

Kerraii recognized Rikka's voice; so did Snow. The golem's clanking was unmistakable. Magestone, harnessed for Atlantean domination, powered the golem down the corridor. It bashed indiscriminately through the rebels and prisoners alike, with clear intent to run the gauntlet right through the trapped rebels.

"Best option . . . *run*," Snow muttered. Amidst the chaos he put his rifle to his shoulder and took aim calmly; when he squeezed the trigger he sent a round through the guardsman directly in front of the barely visible mage—and instantly pulled out his pistol to drill the mage.

It seemed everyone stopped to watch as the man crumpled slowly to the stone floor—rebel, guardsmen, the Caeronn men at arms—even the battered golem seemed to hesitate.

From beyond the Atlanteans, a deep voice bellowed out: "For Blackwyn!"

Troll?

Kerraii blinked, breathing evenly and deeply to work through a wave of weakness. Troll. Probably one of their brawlers. A devastating opponent in these close quarters.

Except this one wasn't her opponent. This one was on her side.

As she struggled to shift her worldview to a position where any troll could be fighting on her side, the men of the Empire's forces looked at one another and came to an instant, tacit decision. They fell back. Dragging their wounded, leaving the confused golem, splitting off into stairwells and hallways that afforded them retreat and cover, they ran.

The rebels raised their weapons and their voices, surging forward to meet their reinforcements. Caught up with them, Kerraii flowed along with the movement, keeping always within reach of Snow. *He* knew she was with the rebels. This new group would see her only as a Dark Elf.

And indeed, the troll's joyful greeting to Snow turned into a snarl of warning, and Snow threw up a hand, a commanding gesture that stopped the troll's impending charge short. "Hold, Kal'din! She is with us today. She watched my back well."

Kal'din made an unconvinced growling noise, standing his ground amidst the swirl of greetings and cries of relief around them. Someone bumped Kerraii hard, an intrusion she wouldn't have tolerated in Necropolis, nor been expected to. But now she just stood in her most relaxed posture, the borrowed sword at her side and one leg twitching with imminent betrayal. *I don't want to fight you.*

Snow made a sharp gesture. "Later, Kal'din. After we're free of this place. Are the wagons waiting?"

Kal'din lowered his great horned head, his craggy features acknowledging the orders. Kerraii counted herself lucky; as an Elementalist, Kal'din likely felt far more intractable than he looked when it came to her fate. He said, "Wagons and horses, well-guarded and ready to go. The priest holds them for us. Anyone who wonders what an Elementalist priest needs with a whole caravan of wagons will soon regret it."

Snow lifted his voice in a shout of command. "To the wagons!"

And so they ran. Kerraii caught glimpses of unsuspecting Caeronn servants and staff rushing out of the way or pressed up against the walls. Statuary on pedestals toppled with the rebels' passage, and a wall hanging hung crookedly along the wall, inadvertently caught and torn by someone's weapon. Rikka and Blaize ushered the newly freed prisoners along at the tail end of the group; like Kerraii, they ran on determination alone.

At last they spilled out into a courtyard behind the prison, a long, narrow hitching area for securing wagons and horses with what could only be a livery stable on the far end of it. An Elementalist priest stood in the bed of a wagon, barely breaking his vigilant guard to acknowledge their arrival. "Prisoners into wagons!" Kal'din ordered, his enormous arms waving them on as he himself turned back to guard the exit from which they'd poured. Drivers leapt to their posts, and a handful of the others made quick girth checks and mounted up the individual horses.

"The rest of you, disperse!" Snow cried, and suddenly they had half the number of Rebels they'd started with.

Black Powder Rebels here within Caero, Kerraii realized with some amusement. *Going back to their lives as if this had never happened.*

As Rikka joined a batch of prisoners in one of the bigger wagons, a simple box conveyance meant more for transporting goods than people, Snow caught Kerraii's arm and indicated one of the horses, a short but substantial sand-colored creature with a stiff bristle of mane and dark points. "Mount up," he told her, voice raised against the sound of horses snorting and calling to each other, excited by the sudden activity—all but this one, which turned to give her a placid look.

She stared at him as stupidly as she'd allowed herself since her capture by Sarnen's forces. "I don't ride."

"You do now. You're sure not getting in one of those wagons, not with a bunch of loyal Black Powder Rebels."

"I can take care of myself." She eyed the wagon and then the hitching area, considering her chances in Caero on her own.

Except that this Blackwyn sounds . . . intriguing.

Not only intriguing, but open-minded. His rebels had

freed *all* the prisoners. His trusted man, Snow, had accepted her at his back. Of all the places in the Land, Blackwyn's camp might welcome her.

Might.

"It's not you I'm worried about," he said, heedless of her inner dialogue. "In case it's not obvious, I'm not offering you a choice. I don't want you in with the others and I'm not about to turn you loose. Kal'din will be happy to see to you if it comes to that."

And so he would. Fuzzy grey veils crowded Kerraii's vision, making up her mind for her. She would be vulnerable here alone, and she had no wish to deal with the troll just now. *And then, too, Blackwyn . . .*

The whisper of possibility called to her. *Home?* Or just a cause she could call her own?

She heeded it. She had that much freedom, at least.

But . . .

She gave the indicated beast a wary gaze. It stood cockhipped and unconcerned about the activity around it. "Truly, I don't ride."

Snow gave a great big grin, one that Kerraii didn't appreciate in the least. "We'll see how fast you learn, then!"

Kerraii remembered little of that escape. Snow all but flung her into the saddle as Kal'din held the prison door against the rallying Atlantean forces, then jumped into the small wagon reserved for his use and which he drove like a giant chariot. They galloped out of the hitching area with the guardsmen spilling out from their exit and rounding the ends of the building; a gunner took hasty aim at them and blasted out several chunks of ground from the hitching area.

The stout little horse—Friz, she mentally named him almost as soon as she got a look at his stiff, chunky mane from the saddle—was fat and round beneath her, and the stirrups of the fleece-padded saddle turned out to be too short for her; she soon lost them. The stirrups bounced wildly, battering her high boots and their greaves.

"Relax!" Blaize called to her from his wagon at one point. "It'll be easier if you relax!"

Relax? With this creature bounding along beneath her, entirely out of her control? She'd grabbed the saddle, grabbed at his bristle of a mane, grabbed at—and mostly lost—the leather reins. She could not help but think how Skulk would laugh to see her now, as she charged through the streets with the rumble of wagon wheels, a symphony of clattering hooves, and grim intent.

They had yet to make the city gates.

But the thought of Skulk had energized her, reminded her of her training. Not for riding, but for combat. *Center yourself. Move with the energy of the fight.*

She put herself in that centered place within, and suddenly caught the rhythm of the horse's movement. His ears, which had been ignoring her, flicked back to indicate he'd given her his attention, as though she were suddenly worth bothering with.

Tentatively, she gave him a pat.

It was then that the entire group slowed down and the horse abruptly changed to a jarring, bouncy movement that sent Kerraii clutching for the saddle again.

Ahead, the gates loomed. Not the gates to the bridge, but those leading west and out toward Khamsin. She'd thought they'd have to stop and fight their way through, but Snow had not come to this rescue unprepared; several of the weary-looking women waiting in line to leave the city suddenly shed their cloaks, put the gate guards to knifepoint, and then jumped aboard the wagons as they rumbled by.

Friz broke into the easier gait after that. Kerraii found herself with time to become accustomed to it.

Plenty of time.

CHAPTER 14

THE first day, Kerraii stepped off the stout little horse and collapsed into a thin, weary heap on the ground, as if her legs had no working muscles at all.

No one seemed surprised. Snow lifted her to her feet and walked her over to the tents someone had already erected, advised her to keep moving, and left her with a modest plate of flatbread soaking in an all-bean soup.

Kerraii ate the soup and fell fast asleep, much to her detriment when the time did come to move. In the morning she climbed back into the saddle by dint of will alone. Snow walked by with his own handsome mount in tow and hesitated, as though he might offer to give her a boost.

He wisely thought better of it.

But by then word was spreading that she had played a part in their rescue, that she had even watched Snow's back. She traveled more easily after that. The good food—nutritious if not copious—gave her some strength back, though she had weight and muscle to gain before her harness fit naturally again. She had time to relax and learn to sit the various gaits the horse offered, and she learned to take care of it after a day's ride and to saddle it in the morning. She observed that Friz's stiff mane was really a thick line of black hair between two lines of sand-colored hair, and she learned to pay close attention to the swivel of his small, furry ears. She especially learned to pay attention to his mouth, as he sucked on lead ropes, reins—and, most distastefully, her hair.

The day Snow and his rebels discovered that she'd named the creature Friz was one that required great restraint and a display of dignity on her part.

Friz himself cared little for the amused reaction that swept the group. He merely ignored her heels thumping at his sides and stopped to snack on the leaves of some plant Kerraii couldn't identify.

That alone told her she was traveling to areas of the Land in which she'd never been, for she knew all the plants east of the Roa Gaitor. These lightly wooded foothills held more pines, cedars, and junipers than leafy trees, and the hardwoods that did grow here were stingy with their leaves: oaks with tight bunches of leaves held close, small, strange bushes with tiny butterfly-shaped leaves. Instead of chittering chipmunks and flitting birds, this land came rife with sunning lizards, long-legged running birds, and a large number of raucous ravens.

At first they traveled roads and paths that were barely there, always checking their back trail. Snow was busy on his mount—something taller and more appropriate than Friz—and spent plenty of time circling around behind them, checking for signs of pursuit. "They must be busy with the other prisoners," he said to Rikka and Blaize, not caring that Kerraii was close enough to overhear. "There were many who were too proud or stubborn to come with us." And he might have glanced over at Kerraii, but kept the gesture so subtle she couldn't tell for sure.

She'd noticed almost instantly that the three had a history of some sort. Occasionally they even mentioned "Sarah," who could only be Sarah Ythlim, the founder of the Black Powder Rebels. Now she watched the three having a quiet discussion over a small campfire. She'd unsaddled Friz and fed him, pitched the little lean-to tent she'd been assigned—in lieu of joining the large group tents where she was not yet welcome—and sat chewing on the hot haunch bone of a giant-eared rabbit she'd killed that day simply by slinging a large stone at its head; she threw with unerring accuracy. The rest of the rabbit she'd given to one of the rebels acting as cook for the evening; no point in letting it go to waste, and there were others as thin as she.

Rikka was recovering nicely from her much briefer imprisonment; hers had been a torture of the mind more than of the body, for this fierce-willed woman had not learned how to live while caged, let alone blind. Kerraii had been living in a cage of one sort or another since her capture eight years ago, and being behind stone and iron had only made it that more obvious. But the length of time without nourishment or true activity gave her other things to recover from, slower things.

As Rikka recovered, Blaize looked more relaxed. He was a quiet sort anyway, but only as Rikka started to smile again did any amusement cross his face. And Snow . . . Snow looked like he'd been in control the whole time. He watched their backs, he quietly ordered their retreat, he forbade the others to harm Kerraii. Too bad he couldn't order them to *include* her.

She had the feeling that if he did, they'd try their hardest to find a way. They looked up to him, all of them. The ones who'd been rescued, the ones who'd been along on the rescue. Surely Kal'din would have held back his enmity with Kerraii for no one else here—and, in fact, since the troll was the *only* one to take Snow's orders regarding Kerraii to heart, he was now one of the few who ever volunteered conversation with her. Otherwise she got by with responses of grunts and nods.

The Wylden Elves followed their leaders out of love and

support of family. Those in Necropolis responded to their leaders out of greed and fear. But Blackwyn . . . here was a man who could command the instant respect of a troll, who chose to follow him instead of leading his own war band.

Kerraii took careful note of the fact, pondering it even as she heard Kal'din coming up behind her with what passed as stealth for a warrior troll. He stopped just behind her, a great looming shadow in the darkness. She asked him, "Hasn't anyone ever told you only fools creep up on a Nightblade?" But she said it with no rancor in her voice, and no warning. They'd settled into that kind of relationship, one more comfortable with gibes than heartfelt remarks.

"You have no weapon," he pointed out, rather with the tone of voice he might have used with a child.

Gently, she poked him with the broken thigh bone from her meal of crispy rabbit. He made a noise of exaggerated pain and moved his shin out of range. She said, "A Nightblade is never without a weapon. Would you care to guess how many others I'm carrying at this very moment?"

"Not tonight," he said congenially, and helped himself to a piece of hardscrabble ground beside her. "You look thoughtful. Wishing you'd stayed in Caero? Taken your chances and returned to your own people?"

"I have no people," Kerraii said, not as bitterly as she might have. "I am Wylden, too touched by Necropolis to return home, and Necropolis has no use for me now. I have no future there." She stopped, giving the small fire a baleful look. "Too bad Nujarek couldn't understand the concept."

"Would you want one?" Kal'din prodded the fire with a stick, sending up sparks and making the flames leap. He took no apparent offense when Kerraii relieved him of the stick and banked the fire back down again.

"It's helpful if we don't give off *too* many 'catch me' signals to anyone who might be out there." She broke the stick in half and tossed both halves into the fire. "Would I want one what?"

He shifted his massive legs to put one foot on either side of the now-discreet fire. "A future. *There*. If you had a choice, would you go back?"

Kerraii felt as though she were in front of Sarnen all over again, on the shore of Black Lake. Sarnen who trusted her above all others, Sarnen who gave her status in Necropolis, with the personal power and comforts that came along with it. Not that she hadn't had to fight to earn that status, to prove herself, not that she hadn't continued to prove herself right up to the day she was captured. Sarnen, who had once asked her nearly the same question. Would she go, or would she stay?

At the time, she'd had nowhere to go.

Now . . .

She thought she might.

As several of the rebels recovered from their brief imprisonment, the group left one of the wagons behind and let the travelers move on foot, north and west and toward the mountains with which Kerraii was familiar by reputation alone. The rebels holed up there, gravitating toward their preferred warlords just as much of this group clung to Blackwyn. But none of them had made a name like Blackwyn's.

She made good use of the travel time—and the conversations around her. Unable to anticipate the stealthy nature of a Nightblade, the travelers spoke freely in her presence and never knew it. Like Rikka, these people responded to Blackwyn on a personal level; they trusted him. They spoke of their relief at knowing their families were safe with him, and at knowing they could return to finish their healing and recovery, and then rejoin the fight.

As opposed to being deemed no longer trustworthy and discarded.

Even so, as they finally arrived at a foothills location thickly surrounded by scaly-barked pines and stunted oaks, she was startled at the sights that greeted her: everyday sights, like laundry hung between the trees, the sound of a horse being shod, a small schooling group tackling each other with wooden and padded weapons . . .

And children. *Laughing.* Running from tree to tree, standing at the threshold of log-sided tent structures, dashing up to meet some of the returning prisoners with shrieks of glee.

Kerraii had a sudden, poignant flash of memory: her brother at that age, luring Kerraii to forget her dignity and join in a game of touch-and-go or climb-high. He always won—he was smaller, lighter, and always made it to the top of the tree, laughing in triumph as he swayed above her. And then they'd linger, looking down on their world from above. Admiring it. Learning it. Sharing it.

Kerraii blinked, drawing herself back from what had been to the reality of what would never again be. And then, shaken, back to what now lay spread out before her.

The sights were not all so domestic. One tent structure held the sounds of people in pain, and the unique stink of death. Some of these people's wounds had been caused by Necropolis arrows, tainted with magical corruption. Off to itself, guarded at the back by the massive stone of the rising slope, stood a fully enclosed log and plank building. Those gathered around it had serious expressions as they clustered for discussion; each of them looked fit and trained; each of them bore arms. Swords, fuser rifles, knives, axes . . . Some of them bore wounds, as well—bandaged arms, hands, heads . . . Enough to show they'd been in action, not enough to keep them from going back to it.

For some reason it made her throat tighten all over again.

The people, believing in something, working together—it made her think of . . .

Home.

But this was not her home, no more than any other place was. So as the rest of the arriving rebels dispersed and Snow came to Kerraii's side, she slipped in place her all-purpose mask and said, "And is the great Blackwyn here to greet us?"

The idea amused Snow. "No," he said. "Blackwyn rarely spends time here. He doesn't want to make this place a target."

"I should think you do that well enough all on your own." Kerraii nodded at the wagons in which most of them had arrived. At her back, Friz nuzzled her hair, never having been quite convinced that it wasn't edible. A woman from the camp came up to Kerraii, clearly expecting to take the horse; Kerraii narrowed her eyes and made no move to relinquish the reins.

Snow smiled in understanding. "We need him here for other things, other missions," he said of the horse.

Abruptly, Kerraii passed the reins over. "It doesn't matter. I don't like horses anyway." But she trained a scowl on the younger woman who now held the obliging Friz; indeed, his mobile black lips were gently frisking her for any sign of food. "Just see you don't give him to anyone who'll ride him into an ambush." Then she glared at Snow, just on general principles.

He let it pass. "Were you expecting to see Blackwyn?"

"I have some questions for him." She idly tapped the hilt of her sword. "Starting with whether I can trade this thing in for a *real* sword."

"That we can handle ourselves," he said, congenially enough. He'd taken his helmet off upon arrival and scrubbed his black hair into complete disarray; he suddenly looked far too young to have fired the shot that killed Karrudan. "As for anything else, I'll let him know you want to talk."

From the way he said it, Kerraii gave a glance around the camp and suddenly wondered just how many of these people had seen the man whose orders and tenets they followed.

If Snow followed her thoughts, he didn't show it. "Let me show you where you can stay," he said. "For now."

"And after that. . . ?"

He didn't shrug it off. He looked straight at her and he said, "We'll see."

We'll see. For days, *we'll see.*

Kerraii stalked the camp, aware always of the eyes trained upon her—some out of curiosity, some out of wariness. She never detected any specific single person set to watch her, and after a day she realized there was simply no need. These people were too alert, too aware. If they somehow managed to provide their children with the safety and rambunctious play that youngsters needed, they also never forgot they lived in a rebel leader's encampment. Not everyone had their family here; Rikka's son lived at the edge of Khamsin with the Dwarf woman Bruna. No doubt other families were equally splintered.

The one person who surely was not here was Blackwyn.

War bands came through the camp; their leaders, like Snow, disappeared further into the mountains and reappeared without drawing any questions. She realized soon enough that Blackwyn seldom if ever came to this camp.

It ran smoothly enough without him. Kerraii acquired the sword she wanted, a quick, slender blade with which she practiced until it was familiar in her hand, feeling summer sweat trickling down sides once more growing sleek. She set aside her battle harness, tired of watching men trip over their own feet and somehow not feeling worthy of it as long as she did little other than pitch in with camp chores. She visited Friz, who always immediately tried to suck her long fall of hair into his mouth. She acquired information, hovering near conversations unnoticed—at least until someone realized they'd lost track of the Dark Elf again and set a rebel specifically to locate her.

Blackwyn had set a raid on a Magestone storage facility. Blackwyn had talked another warlord out of an attack guaranteed to rack up casualties, arguing that the small mining-slave town would be more vulnerable to liberation after Necropolis worked through their first wave of attacks, against Atlantis drawing more manpower from the guards. Blackwyn had declared that all his fighters should add another close-range weapon to their arsenal, increasing their chances of survival should a battle close unexpectedly.

Blackwyn. Kerraii was plenty and enough tired of hearing about Blackwyn.

Except that she still wanted to talk to him. Wanted to be convinced . . .

Wanted *him* to be convinced.

For if she decided to stay here, she had to be sure. And Blackwyn had to be sure, or she'd never be anything but a token, unused member of this war band.

She'd strike out on her own before she let that happen.

She was close to doing just that.

And on a hot midday when Kerraii was pushing herself through another set of sword-pattern exercises—unopposed because there were none who ever offered to oppose her— Snow came to her. He came without his helmet or armor, which at first disappointed Kerraii, until she recalled that he preferred his fuser weapons or hand-to-hand fighting. She let her sword drop to her side and gave him an appraising glance; perhaps he'd join her for bare-handed combat.

But she realized then that his black hair was in disarray and his plain, once-white shirt was stained with sweat and dirt; he dropped to sit on one of the stumps at the edge of the practice yard, weariness pervading his movement.

"Blackwyn works you hard," she observed.

"I make my own choices."

She took up her exercises again. "Of course."

He slapped at one of the little biting flies that seemed so prevalent in this area. "You wanted to talk to him."

Kerraii almost dropped her stance, giving away her eagerness. But her control prevailed, and she merely said, "And has he chosen to appear?"

"He will not."

This time she straightened, catching his eye to drill him with the depth of her annoyance. She faced life-changing decisions and *he* played games with her. "You knew all along."

He dipped his head. "I know his ways. But I had my reasons for waiting."

"Of course," she said, holding the sword in the most casual of stances, a position from which she could easily kill him. She wouldn't, and they both knew it—even were she still thinking purely like a Sect Elf. It was an act with little gain but fleeting satisfaction, and much in the way of consequence. "You wanted to *watch* me. To see if I went around kicking small animals. Or, better, drinking their warm blood."

Snow winced . . . but not at her anger. At the image she'd painted for him. "Not exactly," he said. "But close enough."

Paradoxically, she suddenly liked him much better. It would have been easier on all counts for him to lie. She sheathed the sword in a quick, easy move and crossed her arms to regard him hipshot. "And now?"

"Now you can talk to me. I'll take your words to Blackwyn." He watched her dissatisfaction for a moment and added, "That's the way it goes here. If it doesn't suit you, you're free to go."

"I may yet." She tapped her fingers against her upper arm, both thoughtful and impatient. She hadn't really prepared herself for this moment. "We need to earn each other's trust. I have a way to accomplish that."

"What makes you think Blackwyn needs to earn *your* trust?" Snow asked, amused.

Kerraii said flatly, "Because he needs me. I'm good. I'm more than good. One to one, I can take anyone in this camp."

Snow raised an eyebrow.

"Not Kal'din," Kerraii admitted, "but the others. And I can pass unnoticed where your people would be detected. I can see without light. And I know the way Necropolis fights, and the way it thinks. That could come in very handy in the days to come."

"Yes," Snow agreed. "That's why I brought you back. Although if Rikka hadn't spoken for you, you'd still be back in Caero trying to slink your way out."

She gave him an impatient look.

He waved it away with a lazy gesture. "All right, you'd be out by now. But on your way to where?"

"Irrelevant, since I'm already here." She cocked her head at him, waiting for him to refute it. Or to try.

He didn't. He swatted another fly and scratched his cheek, leaving a smudge of dirt. Kerraii bit the inside corner of her mouth, stifling a smile. If it weren't for the slight bloom of stubble across his jaw, the smudge would make him look far too young to be sitting here having this conversation with a Nightblade who'd had enough experience in her short life to make her feel far too old. She said, "Tell him about my village. Tell him my people were raided by Sarnen's warriors, and that whole families were killed and torn apart, some left behind and some enslaved in Necropolis. Tell him that the Atlanteans took over where the Dark Sect left off, and that they deserve freedom as much as anyone here. Tell him I can lead a small group of fighters to liberate the village—and if he doesn't want me to lead, I can guide whoever does. Tell him those things, and then tell me what he says."

Snow gave her the smallest of smiles. "There are plenty of causes to fight for on local turf."

"That would be the easy thing," Kerraii said.

"What will you do if he says no?"

She hadn't thought about it. But she opened her mouth and said, "I'll do it myself. And you'll be without me."

That felt right. It felt *right*.

Snow got to his feet, dusting off his pants. "I'll let you know."

It wasn't much better than "we'll see," and Kerraii had already run out of patience for that one. Her course decided one way or the other, she set about preparing herself. She oiled the harness leather, not willing to trust its integrity entirely to the spells bound within it. She polished the armor of her knee and shoulder guards. She checked the soles of her boots and decided they were sound enough. She spent some time considering Friz—stealing him would be as easy as a few treats in the dark—and ultimately decided she had neither the resources nor the expertise to keep even a sturdy pony going on long roads. She'd resole her boots as needed.

She gathered, too, the few articles of clothing she'd acquired since arriving here. A comfortable tunic, pants that were too short, a belt along with her own trim baldric; none of these would give away her origins. She even had a few blankets and a thin nightshirt. She'd need coin, but she had no qualms about acquiring it from a well-to-do Atlantean, perhaps someone who'd earned his wealth on the backs of enslaved miners.

She folded the blankets flat on the dirt floor of the little house she'd been using, a shack set off to the side where no one seemed to have any casual reason to stray. Carefully smoothing her few extra items on the blankets, she rolled the whole thing up into a sturdy package. When she heard Snow approaching—and it was ever only Snow who actually approached her—she could have met him at the habitually open door; she could have hidden her handiwork.

She stayed where she was.

"You wasted no time," he said.

"I don't," she told him. "Waste time. Not when I know what I want."

"Something you have in common with Blackwyn." Snow leaned his rugged shoulders against the door frame of the little house and crossed his arms. "Although possibly he thinks things through a little more thoroughly."

Kerraii shrugged. "He has to. He's making decisions for many people. I'm making a decision for myself." She bound the rolled blankets with a rope woven of old rags and sat back on her heels to regard him. "Was that your way of saying he wants time to think about it?"

Snow gave a single shake of his head, and a pleased grin. "No. He'll do it. He thinks it's a good statement. And, as you say, a way to earn trust."

"To prove myself," she said dryly, but was suddenly aware that she *did* want to earn Blackwyn's trust, and badly. She'd earned Sarnen's trust because it was the best way to survive. She wanted Blackwyn's trust because it would give to her a new start to her life. It would allow her to choose what *she* wanted to fight for, and put her in the best position to do it.

Snow shrugged. "He never said as much. He's a fair man, Kerraii."

"So I've heard."

"And now you'll find out for yourself." He nodded at her bedroll. "No need for that."

She narrowed her eyes slightly, quite aware that he had further information that would make traveling without even meager supplies make sense and that he was stringing her along.

Snow made an amused noise of defeat. "You're a tough one. Just come on out when you're ready. We've got a mage waiting."

Kerraii hesitated. *Teleportation.* It was unfamiliar magic; not common Sect magic. Not common Elemental or Technomancer magic, for that matter. She'd heard of it, but knew it required the use of ancient devices—*found* devices, which the mages didn't truly understand. *Talk about* trust. To be booted from one place to another by someone she didn't know using a device not of his own making? Slowly, she said, "No mage can teleport the number of warriors we need."

Snow pushed off the door frame, having grown more serious, hiding more of what he was really feeling. "We'll meet them there. Your choice, now," he said, and left her there.

Another test. She'd have to give herself unto this mage—unto Blackwyn's orders—if she wanted to accomplish this mission. If she wanted to stay here.

She closed the door to the little house, but only long enough to strip off the tunic and pants. Then she walked out into the camp in full battle harness, the sword at her side.

CHAPTER 15

BEHIND the training grounds, beyond the carefully marked firing range with its pockmarked cloth targets pinned to wood backings, an aged, red-skinned troll wizard waited. Kerraii found him there with Snow, and Snow alone.

She stood just at the perimeter of the firing range, in the shadows of a giant pine. Last chance to think about this. She'd be trusting the mage with her life; she'd be trusting Snow with her life.

Hadn't he already trusted her with his?

The wizard held a gnarled staff—nearly as gnarled as the thick spikes jutting out from behind his ears. A wizard with enough years to have experience, then. She wondered if he had the strength.

Snow thought so.

Kerraii strolled into the small clearing as though she'd never had any doubts at all.

"Kerraii," Snow said, as if *he'd* never had any doubts. "This is Maren'kar."

Kerraii gave him a quick nod—but a respectful one. If the troll was surprised to see a Nightblade in Blackwyn's service, he gave no sign of it. Then again, there were representatives from many factions here in the camp.

Anyone could fight for freedom, it seemed.

"If you're ready . . . ?" the wizard asked.

Snow shifted inside his armor; he had his helmet tucked under his arm, and a full pouch of what could only be coins or jewels at his belt. Kerraii put a hand on her sword hilt and nodded.

"Closer, then, closer!" the wizard said with some irritation, gesturing Kerraii in to stand by Snow's side. She complied without comment, moving in until her shoulder guards touched Snow's—at which point the wizard ceased his prompting gestures. "Fine, then, good," he said, and put the staff aside, much to Kerraii's surprise. *But if that's not the device he uses—*

She had no more time to ponder it. Maren'kar took them each by the hand and an instant later, a prickly tingle ran through Kerraii's body, a flush of magic that enveloped her and . . .

. . . took her back home.

No, not quite home. Not within sight of the village where she'd spent her youth, but close enough so the trees and plants around her cried out of home. Kerraii gasped, and Maren'kar gave her a look of concern. "This form of travel can be unnerving, especially the first time," he said, not quite releasing her hand.

Let them think it was the teleportation. Let them think the magic had taken her unaware. Let them think anything but that the sudden sight of her childhood home had hit her harder than any blow taken in battle. Let them think . . .

Kerraii took a deep breath and disengaged her hand from the troll's immense but gentle grip. "Startling," she agreed, but kept her voice steady, riding the edge of boredom as it did any time she had the need to show she was particularly unaffected.

Even when she wasn't.

Snow gave the wizard a shallow but sincere bow of respect. "Check back late tomorrow," he said. "I hope to be well done before then."

"I will indeed," Maren'kar said. "Blackwyn is particularly concerned with the outcome, I hear."

"When is he not?" Snow said simply, stepping back far enough so he wouldn't accidentally be in the circumference of Maren'kar's magic. Belatedly, Kerraii did the same, watching with interest as a silvery nimbus engulfed Maren'kar, intensified enough so that she had to turn her face away from it, and then faded. By the time she could look at it directly, the wizard had disappeared.

"No less unsettling from this side of it," she decided. She took a closer look at their surroundings, finding no clue as to their actual location. Only major landmarks would mean anything after eight years—almost nine, now. The woods grew and transformed, closing off some paths, allowing others, giving way to lightning strikes and springing back to life after treefall. These particular woods told her nothing— except that someone other than her own people had been at work here, sloppily harvesting trees with no thought to replacing them and no thought as to which were the best trees to take. Raggedly cut stumps littered the forest beside great gashes in the earth where the logs had been dragged away.

Atlanteans.

Dark Elves would not bother. They threw themselves into their art, using life to create perverted life—or power, or longevity. Atlantis *consumed*. They consumed the Land to find Magestone, they consumed it to build and expand their empire. They blithely cut their way through whatever stood in their way, reckoning it as part of the process.

As did the Black Powder Rebels, when it came down to it.

Except Blackwyn. Of course.

They stood in a small clearing beside a narrow, barely

discernible path—a path Snow took to immediately. "Enemy territory," he said. "Let's not linger."

She followed him onto the path. "You have another place to be, then?"

"A meeting place, yes. A tavern to visit."

"There are no taverns here." Surprise made her release the words, though she knew Snow would not have said so unless it were true.

"It's been a while." He cast a meaningful look back at her. "When Atlantis took over the territory, they brought some comforts with them."

Kerraii could not help but make a face. "There are other changes, then."

"Probably not as many as you fear. This is a quiet place. Atlantis does not waste manpower here."

She caught a branch that would have whipped back in her face, holding it gently aside until she passed. "So we go to an Atlantean tavern . . ."

" . . . where the Wylden tap keeper is one of ours," Snow said. "Atlantis has not nearly the hold they think in this area. They take quiescence for acquiescence."

"Always a mistake," Kerraii said, her voice droll. She knew her people. Although others often mistook their life-and-Land-nurturing ways as gentleness and even meekness of soul spirit, the fierce Wylden soul fueled the Elemental League.

The Elemental League should have been here . . . should have been here long ago, in fact. But much of their fight had turned outward in recent years.

Snow led the way, along the twisting path and down through a creek bed; Kerraii gave that stream a long and narrow-eyed look. Snow told her, "Don't worry about it. Things *have* changed. There'll be people to take us to the right spot. From what I understand, your village is now a base of logging operations, so the Atlantean presence is sig-

nificant. You can tell us what to expect when we get there—
and it'll be your task to eliminate their perimeter guards.
Until then . . ." He paused, peering through the woods. "This
is it. The tavern's half a mile further on. Best you stay out
here until I make contact. We're trying to stay unnoticed,
and in that tavern . . ."

". . . The Atlanteans will attack first and ask questions
later."

"Likely."

She didn't like it. This was *her* rescue, *her* people,
damn it.

Too bad his reasoning was so sound.

She found a mossy stump by the stream and crouched beside it. "I'm waiting," she said. "Just you don't take too
long."

He would. He'd have no choice. He had to get there; then
he'd need to take in at least a mug or two of whatever ale the
place served; flitting in and out would only serve to make
people wonder why. And they really didn't want anyone asking that question just now.

She watched his broad shoulders retreating through the
woods and sighed an uncharacteristic sigh, lowering herself
to sit cross-legged beside the stump. Until now, this mission
had moved along at a brisk enough pace. While she was still
in Blackwyn's camp, she'd had plenty to focus on—gathering gear, the logistics of travel—and after that there'd been
no pause in which to think.

What did she have to do now *but* think?

Think about how she was home, but could never really
come home. Her people might judge her for the life she'd
lived these past years, they might not. Kerraii herself knew
she'd done what she had to, and in the end it had brought her
here. But she also knew she couldn't stay—*wouldn't* stay.
For those things she had done, for good or for bad or for

even a little of both—had turned her into something other than Wylden.

If not as much Dark Sect as Sarnen thinks.

Still. There was only so much sitting and thinking one person could do, especially when it included thoughts of what had been, what should have been, and what could have been instead, and how those two worlds were about to collide right before her eyes.

Snow's rebels would have a fix on the lay of the land, but not as a Nightblade could acquire it. *Reacquire* it.

Kerraii left a small, deliberate pile of stones where she'd been sitting. With luck she'd be back before Snow, but just in case . . . *Yes, I was here; yes, I should be here; yes, I'm coming back.*

Kerraii headed downstream, hunting familiarity. After a quarter mile of picking her way through the streambed, small things plucked at her memory—the unusual shape of a tree trunk, a tangle of dark roots trailing into the water, the bend of the stream . . . and then she came upon a fallen tree running from bank to bank. Barely clearing the shallow water, its trunk sagged with time. Moss dripped off the sides and the wood had turned dark and slick and punk . . .

But she knew it. She knew exactly where she was, and exactly where to go.

She leaped lightly over the stream and headed into the woods. Here, a patch of bee mint she'd planted with her own hands. Here, a tree in which she'd spent much of her time in her early teens, hiding from the very same younger brother whose death now clung indelibly to her memory. Here, she'd picked goldenseal, leaving two of three plants so the patch would flourish . . . and it had.

The very plant she'd been picking when she'd caught a glimpse of what she now knew had been a Nightstalker, when she'd first heard the screams.

But no one was screaming now. Now there was a sullen,

quiet feeling to the woods. She crouched by the goldenseal a moment, surveying the area. The undergrowth was sparser; it looked carelessly trampled. A small patch of nearby trees had been harvested—all desirable ironwood, and not a single one of them left to reseed the area. Instead it grew thick with sumac, a short-lived, opportunistic shrub of a tree that infected entire hillsides with its weak wood.

Atlantis was here, all right.

Assuming there to be village out guards, Kerraii eased toward . . . *home* . . . following shadows and avoiding exposure. A few swift moments later, she slipped past an Atlantean lounging against a tree trunk. The man was fully armed, but also fully occupied with cracking open the sack of butternuts he'd somehow acquired. Kerraii was willing to bet he hadn't gathered them himself.

Around her, the woods showed clear and growing signs of depredation. Along with the distant sounds of logging— bellowed orders, a falling tree, a raucous sawing noise too consistently vicious to be anything other than the sound of a Blade Golem—the sun filtered through a thinned forest canopy with startling brightness. Majestic trees stretched across the ground like fallen giants awaiting dismemberment. Sick realization slid into Kerraii's stomach and stayed there. While she'd been oblivious in Necropolis, the Atlanteans had scarred her home like a disease moving across the woods.

I'm here now. And I'm going to stop this.

Ten minutes later, she slipped by a guard busy polishing his leather. Assiduous, but not in regards to his actual duties.

Then again, why *should* they be alert? They were watching the edges of a village that gave them no trouble, a village they found convenient to use as a meeting place and a stopover point, and the best place from which to conduct their lumbering activities.

Then at last she saw the village itself, and she gave a

soundless gasp. She hadn't known what to expect, but this was not it.

The remains of the community longhouse still stood, as sturdy as ever . . . as beautiful as ever. Smooth "found" wood took advantage of every sinuous natural curve, combined and constructed to last an Elvish lifetime. But obscuring her view of half the longhouse were chunky human-made dwellings, blots on the Land. Although not much different from the little house in Blackwyn's camp where she'd spent her time, here they were abhorrent and entirely out of place. The humans were careless about where they dumped their wash water, creating mudholes by their doors instead of dumping the water in a different place each time. And the *smell* . . . an ill-maintained toilet house was tucked away somewhere close, one that obviously failed to use the composting system of a Wylden facility.

For a moment Kerraii despaired. If her people had let *this* happen to their village, she wasn't sure there was anything here left to save. Liberation would do them little good if their spirits had been entirely broken and their ways subsumed by the Empire.

And then she settled into another vantage point, and spotted the end of the longhouse that had been destroyed in the raid. She could still see those Zombies clambering through the wreckage, tossing aside weavings and carvings and family treasures whose worth had gone unrecognized. Ironically enough, it was also in this very wreckage that she saw the distinct signs of Wylden spirit. The decimated longhouse section had been cleared of obvious debris, and now a living monument twined around the remains, deftly cultivated to create subtly pleasing patterns. The Atlanteans might not even realize what they were looking at, but Kerraii knew. It was an act of defiance, crafted here right under the watchful eyes of the occupation. A young, slow-growing ironwood, symbolizing Wylden endurance. Tall, fragrant herbs of healing guarding the old foundation. Vines twined among the fallen timbers, binding them together so completely that even a Zombie would fail to tear them apart.

She gave a small, hard smile. She'd seen what she needed to see.

She circled the village, taking note of the Atlanteans, of how casually they ordered the Wylden around. She found signs of habitual guard points—usually up against one of the trees, with the ground packed to bare dirt beside it. She found a few paths, also beaten down to bare dirt. She found signs of Wylden movement, as well—subtle disturbances of undergrowth and ground cover from which the forest would recover in days.

She marked it all, committing it to memory, and left as unnoticed as she'd arrived—not even the Wylden were looking for someone of a Nightblade's skills in these woods, and they failed to see her as thoroughly as the Atlanteans. More confident of her bearings, she moved swiftly through the trees and reached her small pile of smooth streambed rocks just as she heard the first sounds of Snow's return. She reclaimed her seat, and by the time he arrived—with several others in tow—she was composed and unruffled, offering no clue that she'd even moved at all.

Snow smelled of ale and the smoky tavern, and so did the two with him. She eyed them, noting their age—one a little too old to be fighting, one a little too young to be any good at it—and general disrepair. She watched them until they got their first good look at her and stopped short, the young one with jaw literally dropping, the older with pinched-mouth disapproval. Then she turned to Snow and arched a cool eyebrow.

"Derwood and his son Clayn," Snow told her. "This is Kerraii."

"She looks fresh out of the dark city," Derwood said bluntly, offering a display of tobacco-stained teeth.

"Fresh," Kerraii repeated. "Not a word that comes to my mind."

"Blackwyn sent her," Snow reminded the man. "And I trust her to watch my back."

"It's *my* back I'm worried about," the man grumbled, while Clayn managed to get his mouth closed, finally hearing the displeasure in his father's voice.

"Consider it covered," Kerraii told him.

"Kerraii's participation is nonnegotiable," Snow said shortly. "This is her village. She knows it better than any of us."

Derwood held Snow's gaze long enough to express his dissatisfaction, then dropped heavily to his knees, clearing away old leaves and choosing a sharp-ended rock as an inscriber. He quickly sketched the village layout, accurately placing the buildings. He dropped pebbles into place to represent the guard postings. "The village is just under a mile away. The remaining Wylden are in this area," he said, indicating the curve of the longhouse and the ground it encompassed. "They'll know we're coming; someone's passing the word right now."

"Good," Snow said. "And the guardsmen?"

"There are three spots to look for them—"

"Four," Kerraii said, without challenge but also without apology.

"Four," Snow said, accepting the correction so casually that Derwood's scowl had nowhere to go.

"Don't worry about them," Kerraii said. "I'll go in ahead. They won't be a problem."

Derwood stared at her, then looked at Snow. Not a stupid man, he was already learning to double-check Snow's reaction before he threw intemperate responses at Kerraii—even if his resentment remained clear on his age-weathered features.

In this case, Snow merely nodded. He did so thoughtfully,

and Kerraii saw a hesitation there that Derwood didn't seem to notice; she had a feeling they'd exchange words on the subject later. She didn't concern herself with Snow's doubts—the stealthy business of taking care of sentries literally defined a Nightblade's strengths. She moved the conversation along, pointed at the rough blots that indicated the intruder housing within the village grounds. "The Atlanteans in the village . . . we'll want to subdue them without allowing them to take Wylden children hostage. And we need to take down their support system—their buildings, their loggers, everything. If they try to come back in, they'll be starting from scratch."

"And they'll have us to deal with this time," Clayn said, rather boastfully.

Snow hid a small smile, then raised his head to agree. "Making it clear that rebels support the village is important," he said. "But keep in mind that ultimately the Wylden are Elementalists. We need to support them without possessing them. We'll avoid future trouble that way, and possibly even earn a few friends among the Elementalists."

Kerraii gave him a quick, startled look, one he met with quiet understanding. "That's Blackwyn's way, Kerraii. His philosophies aren't just words he follows when it's convenient."

Not as composed as she might wish, Kerraii said, "We'll see."

Derwood gave her a hard look. "We've plenty of other things to do in this area, important things for the rebellion. We aren't interested in bullying any Wylden village."

Kerraii watched Snow; he knew what she'd meant. *We'll see how Blackwyn stands up to his reputation.* His understanding was the important thing, and she didn't bother to correct Derwood. The man's mind was made up to dislike her, and she could only change that through her actions, not her words. Much like Blackwyn would convince Kerraii through action and not words, nor the words of his followers.

She used a stick to smear out the guard points. "No longer in play," she said. "How many warriors are working with us? Do you have an estimate of the number of Atlanteans who stick to the village in the morning?"

"There should be six locals, plus us," Snow said, "against approximately twice as many in the village. With those odds, we can't afford to make mistakes. Unfortunately, many of the strong Wylden have been put to work hauling logs, but I think we can count on help from the others."

Kerraii wasn't so sure of that. But she hoped. She hoped she'd read them right in that subversive longhouse memorial right there under the Empire's nose. Her hope lived as a strange flutter in her chest, a feeling so alien that she was momentarily overwhelmed by it— and by the realization of how many years it had been since she'd even felt it. "Nice odds," she said eventually, when it became obvious they were waiting for her to say something. *Nice odds.*

But she meant it.

"We'll meet here tomorrow," Snow said. "Dawn. But we're going to go in slowly—give them a chance to send their men out to work. Aside from surprise, our biggest advantage is that after so many years of entrenchment here, the Empire feels secure enough to leave this village under light guard. Kerraii will deal with the sentries, and then we need to move in on the Atlantean section of the village before they have any idea we're there."

Shades of the Roa Kaiten battle. Unless they caught the Atlanteans unprepared, the odds were . . .

Grim.

Then again, that's what being a rebel was all about: fighting grim odds—and winning.

"Will you brief your people?" Snow asked Derwood. "I

need to be able to rely on them to act independently. Kerraii and I will be there to handle the surprises."

"You can count on us," Clayn said, standing a little straighter.

"I prefer to *be* the surprise," Kerraii said to Snow in mock disapproval, words she infused with true humor.

Snow blinked, then gave another of those barely there smiles of his. "Trust me," he said. "You are. And you will be."

They parted ways with Derwood still not quite certain of her and Clayn completely smitten. Snow's satisfied expression came as some reassurance, but as they moved out in the direction from which they'd come, Kerraii still found herself uneasy. Depending on ragged-looking rebels? What if the entire force was made of Derwoods and Clayns, warriors too old and too young? Of course, they'd done well enough at the Caeronn prison . . .

Still . . .

"And where is it, exactly, that we're going?" Kerraii asked, looking at the unrevealing expanse of Snow's back under his armor as they backtracked to their arrival spot. "Considering we traveled with no supplies and I notice the coins you brought seem to have disappeared?"

"They're exactly where they belong—with the local Black Powder Rebels," Snow said. "As for us, I thought we'd hang upside down from the trees until dawn."

He said it with such natural ease that it took a moment for her eyes to narrow; she broke a spongy shelf fungus from the northern side of a tree as she passed it and bounced it off the middle of his back.

Amusement made his eyes lighter in expression than usual. He let her come up beside him and then pointed ahead. "There's a small cave system a couple of miles from here. More like a shelf of rock overhang, but we've enhanced it; it's fully stocked. We always put up there when we're here; it keeps suspicion from falling on our people."

Kerraii gave a slight nod. She could have said it was clever, but he knew that.

Then again, when they finally arrived, he could have warned her about the welcome mat—a distinct pile of bobcat leavings at the entrance to which he guided her.

"I think your cave is already occupied," she said, looking at the pile. A shame; the overhang ran deep, and her enhanced eyes told her that the dark pocket at the back ran even deeper. Trees embraced and shaded the entrance, while shrubs and tenacious plants covered the unusual outcrop of rock until it flattened at the top and made way for more trees.

This time he out-and-out grinned. "That's our own doing. Keeps the Empire's people from suspecting how we use the cave. I thought you'd appreciate that."

She gave him a cross look, but restrained herself from any further reaction. If she again reached for the nearest soft thing and threw at it him, this time he *really* wasn't going to like it.

CHAPTER 16

420 Tz, THE WYLDEN FOREST

THE cave stayed cool in spite of the warm, humid night that settled in around them; few of the biting insects ventured all the way to the back. Straw-filled pallets made their beds and soft, expertly tanned furs their blankets. Along with the earth-cairns of potatoes, canned apples, and a wax-sealed cache of dried meat that hissed with released air when they opened it, the accommodations were what Kerraii could only call luxurious.

Not as indulgent as the blood pit victory rooms, but for field quarters on the eve of a skirmish . . . far more than she'd expected. Better than an inn, where she'd have to deal with the other occupants. Here there was only Snow, and he was preoccupied with cleaning his fuser weapons, applying smelly cloths and oil in the dull magelight. Kerraii ate with gusto and prepared to sleep likewise.

Snow shook his head with something akin to wonder as he watched her eat her fill and then reach for one of the furs. "You certainly do everything with *intent*," he observed.

"Is there any other way?" She flipped a blanket made of rabbit hides around her shoulders and drawn-up knees and let it puddle around her ankles. "Assuming you want to accomplish something."

"Sometimes," Snow said. "Sometimes things just *are*, and you live within them, for good or for bad."

"If it's for bad, you try to change it," she told him. "And if it's for good . . ."

The truth was she couldn't remember those days—when things just were what they were. She didn't think she'd ever have them again. But, in the morning, she'd help bring them back to the village.

In the morning . . .

Kerraii put things back the way she'd found them as best she could, and watched with a narrowed eye as Snow re-sealed the meat container and snuffed the magelight. "Tech-nomagic," she said thoughtfully, settling a kneeguard into place and strapping it on.

"Yes," Snow said. "We don't spurn useful tools out of ide-alism. If you stay with Blackwyn, you'll be working with Technomancers as well as those in the Elemental League and even other strays from Necropolis. Maybe we'll even find another Nightblade somewhere. But in the meantime, we have plenty of disenchanted rebels from Atlantean terri-tories. They come to us with what skills they've learned, and we accept them. That policy should speak to you, I would think."

"Perhaps." She helped herself to several lengths of the stout, fine-gauge rope she'd found in a storage chest. "We have a certain amount of crossover in Necropolis as well. But in the end those people are often . . . absorbed. I get the impression things are different here."

Snow nodded. "It works well for us. Let's meet up with the others, and we'll go put it to the test."

This time Kerraii led the way, moving soundlessly on the barely discernable path back to their arrival spot, and then, beyond, to the creek. And as they closed on the meeting spot, she faded back into the woods and let Snow go on alone—

or let it look like he went on alone. Then, when it became clear that all the rebels were there—that they'd hidden no one in the woods to betray them—she let herself be seen. Even Derwood looked a little startled and impressed, and they headed for the village with the rebels suddenly more confident in Kerraii's ability to deal with the sentries.

After half a mile of traversing the woods with them, she had their stealth habits assessed well enough to stop them with the first guard post not quite within sight. "Wait here," she said. "I'll be back when it's safe to circle the village."

"And if you fail?" Derwood said. "If you're caught?"

She bit back the droll reassurance that it wouldn't happen. He didn't trust her; he didn't have any reason to trust her. Answering him would be quicker than resenting him. "Then I'll create enough noise to draw the rest of them. I'll be your distraction. Don't fail to take advantage of it."

It satisfied him. He turned back to exchange a few words with his men; Kerraii met Snow's gaze and received a little nod. She moved off into the woods . . . quietly. A moment later she heard Derwood speaking to her; he hadn't heard her go. The surprise in his trailing-off voice satisfied her; perhaps now they'd wait with more confidence.

She turned her attention to the nearest guard, slowly circling his position to come in behind the tree he leaned against. She froze, close to the ground, when he straightened to do a little token circuit of inspection, taking the worn path she'd seen earlier. After a short patrol, he returned, settling in.

In truth, she didn't blame him for his boredom, or blame the commander of this village for stinting on guards. This village had been subdued by one faction or another since her own capture. Rebel activity in the area was light, and the village had no particular value to anyone else. On the other hand . . .

If you're going to post guards, she thought at the man as

he returned to his tree, *do it right*. Otherwise, the *guards* are targets.

She crept up behind the tree, breathing shallowly, so close to the guard she could have shaved the back of his hairy Utem neck with her knife. Finally he shifted, giving her room to snake her arm around his throat, one hand clamped over his mouth. He flopped around, clutching at her arms—but with no blood flowing to his brain, he quickly sagged.

By the time he came to, she'd tied him securely to the tree and used a strip of his own tunic to gag him. He spat unintelligible curses at her anyway.

Kerraii put a finger to her lips, startling him into silence with the graceful gesture. "Shh," she murmured. "Or I'll have to stuff your mouth with your underdrawers." She regarded him thoughtfully as he took that in and added, "And if you're not wearing any, I'll use poison ivy."

He gave her an aghast look, and a fervent shake of his head.

"Good," she said, leaning close to speak quietly into her ear. "I'm leaving now. I'm not alone. If you kick up a fuss once I leave, my partner will see to you." She cocked her head, looking back in the direction from which she'd come. In spite of her words, the rebels were not quite *waiting*; they made just enough noise to give themselves away, if someone happened to be listening during the lulls in the Blade Golems' work. "You hear?" she said. "He's not as forgiving as I am. He'll just plain kill you."

The Utem seemed to think some response was required; he nodded. Then he decided that was the wrong answer and shook his head. Kerraii put her finger to her lips again and this reassured him; he decided rapid nodding was definitely in order.

As far as she knew, he was still nodding when she reached the second guard, handling him likewise. The third

guard was more trouble; he was too mad to be scared or even
to think straight, and she had to slam his head against his
tree several times to knock some sense into him.

Were she with Necropolis troops, she simply would have
killed him. A Nightstalker might even have taken nourishment from them, satisfying his vampiric nature. But she was
with the Black Powder Rebellion this time out—*Blackwyn's*
rebels—and she had seen that Blackwyn preferred less loss
of life. And on an operation such as this, the fewer losses the
Empire took, the less likely anyone would initiate a counter-
attack.

So she slammed his head against the tree once more for
good measure, determined the fourth guard station to be un-
manned, and returned to the rebels. The group had advanced
slightly and then held their ground, although their impatience was palpable; even Snow looked relieved to see her.
"Trouble?" he asked.

"Not by my definition. Are you ready?"

"More than ready!" Clayn said, just a little too loudly; all
the rest of them frowned at him, so Kerraii did not have to.

"I'm going to move in close," she said. "If they get suspicious before you're ready, I'll create a diversion. But then
you'll have to *move*."

"What kind of diversion?" Derwood asked.

Of course he would want to know. As if it mattered, as
long as she gave them the time they needed. But she said, "I
think simply walking into the village will work nicely."

Snow nodded in appreciation. "Good," he said. "Low-key
is best. I want this over before they truly figure out what's
happening." But they all heard his unspoken words: *if possible.*

Kerraii slipped back into the woods. Behind her she
heard Derwood's query to her, and then his quiet if heartfelt
curse. "She's done it again!"

Snow's deeper voice said with satisfaction, "That's

exactly what's going to get us through this operation with low casualties on both sides, if we do our part."

After circling the village once, Kerraii settled in near the damaged end of the longhouse and its memorial. She had plenty of time to watch; the rebels were quiet, but not as swift in their stealthiness as she. In the background, the Blade Golems kept up a steady rhythm; a tree fell. Kerraii found half the remaining Atlanteans asleep—no doubt they worked night shifts—and fully visible through the open doors of their crude buildings. Some wore their hair in the upright strip of an Utem guard, and some looked like laborers. A soldier sat on a bench beside his housing and polished his armor, remonstrating the friend who was fussing irritably with the settings of a lightning gun. Kerraii didn't have to hear them to know the words: *Be careful with that thing.*

No one had said anything about a lightning gunner. Snow wanted low casualties, but they didn't have the odds to take chances. If he didn't eliminate this one, Kerraii would.

No, she'd be good. She'd go for the gun, not the gunner. Failing that, she'd take him out. Assuming he didn't get the thing working again just as she reached him, of course . . .

They had other weapons. Logging tools they might not consider weapons, but which could easily be used as such. No doubt they had swords in their cabins, and all of the men wore blades of one sort or another.

Waiting . . .

Insects harassed her; sweat trickled down her temples. She ignored the discomforts.

One of the Atlanteans hung near a door of the longhouse, flirting with a Wylden girl. Or probably he thought he was flirting; in truth he was harassing her, for her wish to be away from him was clear to anyone with eyes to see it. Kerraii reassessed her primary target. At the moment, the gun wasn't working, but this girl was a potential hostage in serious danger.

Unless Snow took down the flirting soldier.

I can't count on that.

She couldn't even count on them making it to the village undetected.

The rest of the Wylden population was harder to spot. An old man sitting in the sun by a door, sorting herbs. An old woman painstakingly pursuing her weaving at a little out-doors station, taking advantage of the light. A few young children, visible as they darted beyond doorways open to let the hot breezes of summer circulate through the longhouse.

The longhouse had been built with longevity in mind. Longevity and beauty and every effort to celebrate the gifts of the Land by incorporating natural elements into its struc-ture. It had been built with an eye toward the practical. It had *not* been built to act as a defensive point or protection against such things as rampaging Zombies and lightning guns.

So the doors stood open to keep the interior tolerable, and the children ran back and forth, and an increasingly desper-ate young woman had been cornered near the section that was her home.

Then one of the rebels stumbled badly, crashing into the brush beyond the village. Kerraii spat a silent oath as the soldiers instantly came alert; one of them hastily woke his sleeping friends. There'd be no *distracting* them away from that. The gunner gave his weapon a good smack and reacted with a surprised but pleased expression; the thing was obvi-ously working again in spite of the less-than-expert repair. The soldiers ran into the woods to investigate, ready and eager for action.

So much for that all-important element of surprise . . . but Kerraii had already learned not to count on such things.

Even with the alarm, the flirting soldier didn't move away from the girl; he merely looked over his shoulder, a gleam in his eye, as though he intended to get away with something now that his comrades weren't available to restrain him.

Kerraii walked briskly out of the woods and into the village, ignoring the empty human housing and heading for the longhouse. "Excuse me," she said to the girl, as though she didn't have one of her small knives in her hand and as though she couldn't kill this man even if she hadn't. "I'm looking for my family." She switched to the Wylden tongue, words for the girl's ears. "He's a pig," she said, checking to see if the man understood. When he didn't instantly protest, she added more meaningfully, "The help you've been waiting for has arrived."

The soldier opened his mouth to protest, eyeing her harness with wary astonishment. Kerraii smoothly switched back to his own language. "Eight and a half years ago was the last time I saw them. During the very first raid."

Hesitantly, trying to absorb Kerraii's words without giving them away, the girl said in faltering Atlantean, "What . . . what's your name? My elders might know."

In the background came the sounds of a quick clash, weapon against weapon; someone gave a harsh shout. The Utem next to the girl scowled and glanced at her, already thinking in terms of taking her to help control the Wylden.

The Wylden appeared at their doorways, setting aside their tasks to come out with determined expressions and what table and chore knives could be brought to hand.

And Kerraii smiled her dangerous smile at the Utem and said in an equally dangerous voice, "My parents are Arach Treeweaver and Linwood. My sister is Willeta. My brother was killed on that day; his name was Oaklen. And I am Kerraii, and I was taken to Necropolis where I fought in the blood pits and earned my position as a Deathspeaker's chosen." If the girl looked horrified, so did the soldier—and right now it was the soldier who mattered. His surprise gave way to brutish defiance.

Go on. Do something stupid. Reach for her.

The Utem said, "We're not interested in your problems." And then he reached for the girl.

Kerraii slashed out with the little knife; he must have thought it was an incoming slap and didn't even realize he'd been cut until the blood ran down his cheek; Kerraii yanked the girl aside and took her place, and anger suffused the soldier's face as he reached for his sword. Quicker by far, Kerraii slashed through his sleeve just behind his leather gauntlet; he jerked his hand away from the hilt and backed up a step in confusion; she followed, pressing him up against the house, the sharp edge of the little blade already separating the skin at his neck.

"All it takes is a touch," she said, her face inches from his. "Don't move, or you'll find out what bleeding *really* means."

"You're not—you're not—" he stuttered, his gaze riveted on her mouth, on her lips and teeth. "Don't—"

She laughed. He was afraid she'd drink his blood, right here and now. "Not today," she said. "Today I take your sword and leave you for these good people to restrain."

His eyes widened; he hadn't noticed the Wylden coming up behind her. Elders all, except for the girl she'd just rescued. She reached down without looking and deftly relieved him of his weapon, holding it out with the confidence that someone would take it.

Someone did.

Only then did she step back, glad to see that the elders had come prepared with weapons of home and hearth and flexible, woven-bark ropes; she could save her own rope for later use. In moments, the Utem was trussed, shoved down to sit against the side of the longhouse, so helpless that he'd need assistance even to get to his feet. From the outer edge of the village came the sounds of conflict, and Snow's rifle discharged with a blast that startled them all.

Kerraii nodded toward the sounds of the conflict, itching

to join the battle. She knew it showed on her face, in her tension. "If you want your freedom, the time has come to fight for it."

The woman who'd been weaving narrowed her eyes and said, "Is it true? You're Kerraii, who we lost those years ago?"

Up close, Kerraii recognized her. Dyana, who had been one of her mother's elder advisors. "Yes," she said. "And then again . . . not anymore. But we have no time for reunions, or even for rejections." For she saw that on their faces, too, as she'd once feared.

Once. She didn't fear it now. She was as she was, who she was. She wanted to know of her family, but she didn't need this village's approval . . . even if her foremost goal at the moment was their liberation.

Snow's pistol discharged, a lighter, sharper sound than the rifle. As one, they flinched. Kerraii said just as sharply, "I must go to help them free you. Those who would help, follow me." Without hesitation, she turned from them, launching herself toward the fight . . .

And heard them follow.

Not all of them, but enough.

She joined the fight as a Nightblade should. Quietly. The skirmish continued in full force, with Atlantean laborers running in from the woods at the behest of their overseers, joining the fight with axes and even saws.

Kerraii targeted them. She intercepted them, stepping in from behind with a quickly fashioned loop of the rope, nailing first one, then another, and then a third. With perfect timing and just the right leverage, she noosed them, let them dash past the nearest tree, and then leapt to the other side of the tree to let it take the brunt of her victim's weight and momentum. As each man hit the end of the noose, she darted ahead to sweep his legs out from under him—and then the Wylden moved in with rope restraints. Quiet, intent, and efficient, so Kerraii barely had to hesitate before flipping her noose free.

Three of the Atlantean loggers made a pile, and provided confiscated arms for the Wylden. Snow tossed them a fourth victim, the Utem gunner. He'd lost his lightning gun and bled freely from a wound in his thigh, and he offered only a brief, dazed resistance. Derwood and his son deposited a badly damaged soldier with the prisoners, and by then Kerraii had crept off to gather another logger or two, aware that Snow had shoved his second victim into the gathering and then lifted his rifle, squeezing off a quick shot to save Clayn's neck; the attacking soldier fell, and Clayn turned on him in a flash, disarming him.

Kerraii had a sudden flash of understanding of what it was like to have an expert fuser marksman like Snow on her side. He kept the big picture in mind, picking off the strong, trained Utems and leaving the fight in the hands of the inexperienced laborers and their overseers.

A shout rang out—Kerraii had been spotted, and targeted. She faded back behind cover and pulled herself into the branches of a tree while they beat the ground for her; from there it was easy to see that the reinforcements were trickling off—and that the Wylden loggers had finally broken free to launch themselves into the fray, a turning point in the pitched and furious battle. Snow's rifle blasted through the clearing in a few quick volleys, wounding the remaining soldiers. First one, then another, and even a third laborer broke away, his nerve gone.

Wise choice, she thought at their retreating backs, just before she dropped onto the last fully outfitted Utem still in the fight.

He was the biggest of them, the one they'd rallied around and the one who'd shouted orders at them all. She hit him hard and they went down together, rolling and grappling, and inevitably the Utem came out on top simply by dint of his weight. His weapons lost in the undergrowth, his wits lost to the battle, he knelt over her. He straddled her waist and jammed his hands around her throat, uncaring that the leather band of her harness acted as a protective gorget. Flat on her back, Kerraii crossed her arms just above the wrists, wrapping her fingers around his thick forearms and struggling to keep him from applying his full strength to her throat.

The rest of the fighting eased off as the remaining Atlanteans—none of them soldiers—threw down whatever arms they'd snatched. The wounded from both sides tried desperately to crawl out of danger; everyone else looked to Snow with a wary eye, gauging his mercy.

Snow said casually to Kerraii, "Need help there?"

"No, thank you," Kerraii responded, the smoothness of her natural voice harsh with the Utem's grip. In another instant, frustrated by his inability to strangle her, the Utem raised himself up to his knees. Seeking leverage.

Your mistake.

He might still straddle her, but he no longer sat upon her. Free to move, Kerraii released his arms and clamped her hands behind his calves, jerking herself along the ground until his knees jammed in under her arms. Levering her body up, she wrapped her long legs around his neck from behind and jerked him back and to the side, trapping him in an expert grip long enough to gain one of her knives and aim it directly at that very tender region under the leather loincloth. Close enough to make contact.

He froze. He turned pale.

She smiled.

"Actually," Snow said, "I was talking to your friend there."

"My mistake," Kerraii said. And to the soldier, "Did you need help?"

The man didn't hesitate; he also didn't trust his voice. He nodded. Rapidly.

"Yes, then," Kerraii said to Snow, not taking her eyes off the Utem. "He says he'd like help. I think he may have even said *please*."

Several of the rebels—all of them bleeding—immediately moved in to pull the man to his feet; Kerraii released her grip, palmed her knife back into its hiding spot, and regained her own feet.

"I'm not even going to ask where you just hid that little knife," Snow said, coming up to her side to survey the spoils of their victory while the spoils glared back. To the side, the rebel and Wylden wounded began to gather, tending one another.

"Mmm," Kerraii said, brushing leaf litter from the sweep of her ear. "If you're ever quick enough to see for yourself, you'll find out."

Snow looked at her with the faintest of smiles. She almost took it for an invitation of some kind. Camaraderie.

And maybe it was. For he said, "With luck, we'll see enough action together to give me a fighting chance."

A village, liberated.

A test, passed.

Kerraii waited, impatient beyond impatient and therefore hiding behind stillness.

Dyana shook her head, glancing at the other Wylden for confirmation. They were alone in the village now—free of outsiders—that was, if they didn't count Snow . . . and Kerraii.

For Kerraii was definitely an outsider. She didn't need their bemused and wary expressions to tell her that. Some rejected her outright, but those Wylden had returned to the longhouse, leaving the discussion instead of disrupting it. And Snow stood by the Atlantean housing, patiently waiting for her. The other rebels were escorting the Atlanteans away from this place. Far away from it, where they'd be turned loose without weapon or coin and forced to spend their energies on survival rather than retribution. When the rebels returned, they'd destroy every aspect of the logging operation, right down to the human shacks built within the village.

And Kerraii the outsider waited for answers.

Dyana sat heavily in the time-polished chair by the longhouse memorial. She'd aged in these past years . . . but then, she'd reached that time when Elves did.

Kerraii eyed her warily, not certain if Dyana's expression reflected her feelings about Kerraii, or the news she bore.

A youngster brought another chair, a lighter thing of lashings and bent twigs. Dyana indicated it. "Sit."

She was too antsy to sit, too full of anticipation and trepidation. For the first time in many years, she was vulnerable on a level too deep to cover or protect. But Dyana was an elder, so Kerraii sat.

Dyana gave her a steady look, and along with her sternness Kerraii suddenly recognized the sympathy in her eye.

Just as suddenly, Kerraii was glad to be sitting.

"The time after you were taken was full of turmoil," Dyana said. "That raid wasn't the last. The Dark Elves came back only days later, looking for those who, like you, had been out in the woods at the start of the first raid—those who, *unlike* you, weren't close enough to hear the trouble and come to help."

"My *family*," Kerraii said, unable to keep her voice from going husky with anguish.

"During the second raid, Arach and Linwood . . . they had already lost so much . . ." Dyana closed her eyes, remembering. "They fought back. They were valiant. Their efforts allowed several of our young people to escape. But . . ." Her lips pressed together, thin and old. "I'm sorry. They were killed."

Kerraii had guessed it. She had seen it on Dyana's face, had heard it in all her unspoken words.

It did not stop her breath from catching, or her whole body from suddenly going hollow and trembling. *They were killed.*

Wise Dyana, with her chair.

Moments passed, moments during which no one spoke or moved or intruded upon her silence. She started to breathe again. A thought came to her unbidden . . .

All those years Sarnen had held her hostage with their safety, and they'd been dead from the start. No doubt he'd had the longhouse plundered and then held aside objects to reassure her over the years. It was long-view thinking, the kind of detailed planning at which a Deathspeaker excelled.

But her sister . . . ?

Dyana shook her head again, with obvious regret. "None of us knew what happened to her. So many of us disappeared in that raid. For weeks, survivors straggled back in from the woods. The wounded, the frightened, and those who tried to trail the raiding party on their way back to the dark city. Your sister was never one of them, although we never saw her in Necropolis hands, so we hoped . . ."

All those years . . .

Kerraii listened, numbed by the news. Her parents, dead. *All those years.* Her sister . . . disappeared. *All those years.* Her life in Necropolis, her decision to acquiesce fully, to immerse herself in Nightblade training—it had been based on a lie. *Sarnen.*

Kerraii had thought she'd be free to move forward with her life once she'd been here, seen her people, freed them. She'd thought she'd get her answers here.

Perhaps in a way she had. She'd learned the final truth.

She had one more dark debt to pay before she could move on.

CHAPTER 17

420 Tz. THE WYLDEN FOREST

KERRAII stood with Snow in that spot where Maren'kar had left them. The last of those few rebels who'd accompanied them here were still visible through the woods, retreating back to their apparently small and innocent lives within this area. *Appearances aren't everything.* A lesson Derwood must have learned, to judge by his awkward but sincere thanks to her.

His son, bloodied but victorious, threw one more backward glance over his shoulder, then disappeared into the woods.

Finally alone. Finally a chance to speak to Snow without turning the discussion public.

"I'm not going back to Blackwyn's camp," she said.

She'd caught him flat-footed; she had not imagined that invitation in his manner, nor the acceptance. She'd passed the test, won the prize . . . and now she didn't want it.

Not quite yet. "Listen," she said, before he could say anything. "I have some things I need to do. I want Maren'kar to send me to Necropolis instead of taking me back to Blackwyn's camp. For now."

Snow hunted for words for a moment, and finally said, "Do you think teleportation magic comes cheaply, even to a wizard of Maren'kar's skills?"

"No."

Kerraii let their words stand in silence for a moment, and then she said again, "I have some things I need to do. Call them debts. If I don't reach Necropolis by magic, I'll reach it by foot." She allowed herself a brief, wistful thought of Friz, glad as she was to have her hair safe from his questing lips. "And then I'll return to Khamsin by foot. But while I'm doing all that walking, I won't be fighting for *you*."

"And you think that's a compelling argument?"

"Yes."

"And you want Maren'kar to meet you after you're through, and return you to camp."

He kept his words remarkably even, she thought. She said, "That's up to you."

"It's up to Maren'kar," Snow said, snorting slightly. "He is far from a pawn."

"But he'll respect a request from you," Kerraii countered.

"Yes." Snow watched her for a moment; she returned the gaze. It became an exchange ... weighing each other, weighing odds and determination and cost. He said, "You might not come out of that city again."

"If I don't, and I live, I count on you to find me and kill me. Or whatever I've become."

"I'll do that." But he crossed his arms over his considerable chest and looked at her with a confidence that surprised Kerraii. "I can't imagine it'll be necessary, but I'll do it. As for Maren'kar, he'll be here shortly. I've always found him to be reasonable. Ask him yourself."

Maren'kar heard the request with somber understanding, then looked at Snow, his hands folded within the sleeves of his robe. "You approve of this quest?" he asked, his voice a deep rumble. "It is as good as a death sentence for her, as you must know."

Snow looked at Kerraii. "It was a death sentence when

she fell into Sarnen's hands. It was a death sentence when her forces were ambushed at the frontier. And when she went to the mines as a slave. And when Nujarek had her tossed into that cell."

Mild annoyance crossed the elder troll's features, making them all the more imposingly craggy. "Your point is made."

A similar annoyance washed through Kerraii as she eyed Snow; he seemed unaffected. "You talked to Rikka."

"Of course." He raised an eyebrow at her, the smallest expression. "Wouldn't you have?"

Of course. "I suppose you even think you know why I would return to the dark city."

"Some things," Snow said, "are best left unspoken. But I wish you luck. And to judge by the look on Maren'kar's face, I think you can count on transport back to Blackwyn's camp."

"Harumph," Maren'kar said, clearing his throat in a conspicuous manner. "If you live long enough to return to our rendevous, you'll have earned it." He held out one massive hand for her to take. "There's a spot under the bridge, just where it meets land. That's where we'll arrive; any closer and the Necromancers would detect the teleportation. It's where I'll look for you, one day from now. Is that satisfactory?"

If she hadn't succeeded by then, it was because she'd been caught.

Bracing Sarnen in his own quarters. Not the smartest idea . . .

But if anyone could do it, Kerraii was the one. She knew his habits, all the small things he would never think to change. The prosaic things that a man of great plans, inspirations, and magical talents would not consider weaknesses.

But they were. Even if it took a Wylden Elf of great determination, stealth, and physical skills to see it. And only one of those had any great acquaintance with Sarnen's personal quarters.

She looked at Maren'kar, who still waited for her response, and took his hand. "Quite satisfactory."

Snow said abruptly, "I could come—" but cut his words short. "No. I'd be a liability to you there. Luck, Kerraii. May you pay your debts in full."

And Maren'kar, knowing a farewell when he heard one, took them away.

The ground changed beneath Kerraii's feet; her ears popped. She forced her eyes open to discover them standing under the great bridge with only inches to spare overhead; the stone hung over them like a dark, oppressive sky. "You cut that close. One might think you'd been here before."

Maren'kar's lower tusks curved up over his smile. "One might," he said. "But I cannot stay, not even to see you safely out of this little hiding place. I will return for you on the morrow . . . and hope to find you here."

"Journey well," she told him, and didn't wait to watch him go. Already a Zombie approached, pushing a wheelbarrow full of cut stone. She paid it no attention—the Zombie had its set task and would not deviate—but as the nimbus of Maren'kar's magic behind her swelled and faded, she eased to the edge of the bridge's shadow. Zombies were no problem, but where there were Zombies, there were bridge engineers, supervising.

Ah. There. Alongside the bridge, a human scowled at the schematics he held, struggling to keep the roll of paper from curling up as he read it. Finally he squatted down and weighted it with rocks.

By then Kerraii was past him, moving with stealthy ease and just as glad she hadn't had to kill him.

The land at the foot of the bridge was deceptively barren . . . a Necropolis welcome for newcomers and visitors that pretty much said it all: *you're on your own.* Not far along the cobbled road, tentative establishments appeared, clustering together as though for protection. City guides, amulets of protection, token weapons, small carved skull pendants to wear and display in a show of solidarity. But most of those entering this city knew their way—and for the others, no amount of solidarity would save them from their own naivete.

Beyond that cluster of feeble services and goods, the true market followed the road into Necropolis—until it reached the inner ring of the Deathspeakers' towers. Beyond that, the city took on a cloak of dark mysticism beneath which no ordinary, prosaic transaction intruded.

But before all that—before the shacks, before the merchants, long before the true heart of the city—came the entrances to the tunnels. Everyone knew of them; few dared use them. Unlit, winding, full of traps and pitfalls . . . only the invited few learned those passages well enough to enter on a casual basis.

Kerraii didn't think twice.

She'd walked these underground tunnels upon her initial arrival on the mountain . . . and now she walked them for her final approach. If all went well, she'd take them one last time as she left this place forever.

She passed a witch, who clinked with the bones and amulets tied to her belt and sewn to her skirt; she passed a Necromancer buried in his thoughts, a Grave Digger trailing behind in an obsequious manner. Ironically, only the Grave Digger looked straight at her, paying enough attention that recognition flashed over his features, then doubt. He opened his mouth to speak to his master, glanced at her again as if trying to be sure and subsided into his obsequious posture again. The risk of interrupting the Necromancer was simply too great.

Necropolis's weakness, Kerraii thought. Loyalty through fear was no loyalty at all; obedience through fear squashed initiative. These people had no common goal; they fought fiercely for themselves, and did whatever it took to advance their lot in the Dark Sect. Only coincidentally did that mean working together; more often they were simply individual pieces, working to fulfill the Dark Prophet's strictures in a way designed to bring them personal gain.

True loyalty, she was discovering, came from within.

When she reached the tunnel branching that would take her to Sarnen's tower, she hesitated. Until now she'd had one thought. *Confront Sarnen. Learn her sister's fate.* She'd have to leave the Deathspeaker weakened or compromised—she'd never escape otherwise—but it suddenly occurred to her that she had one more debt to pay.

Skulk.

It was Skulk who had dogged her early years here, from the time he'd sabotaged her first blood pit fight to the constant efforts he'd made to undermine her through humiliation. Skulk who wrongly blamed her for his own failure to thrive, who hated her enough to carry his campaign of insults and injuries through the years.

It was Skulk who had foolishly betrayed them at the battle. *Skulk.*

And it was Skulk who'd taken Reever's powerful bone-handled knife at that battle, a knife so powerful it would weaken even Sarnen, a knife that would irrevocably tie Skulk to any action Kerraii took here today.

She turned away from Sarnen's tower and took the tunnel that would lead her into Spider's lair.

Where Spider and Skulk were newcomers to the power games of the Necropolis meritocracy, Sarnen had been there from the start. Had Skulk truly learned what Sarnen had to teach, he would never have been so foolish as to switch alliances in the first place—from a strong master to a weak one, while branding himself unreliable in the process.

But Kerraii had learned. And so she'd been certain to

acquire the location of Skulk's new quarters before leaving on the failed campaign against the Roa Kaiten settlement.

No doubt he considered her as good as dead, or even dead in truth. No doubt he'd stopped looking for danger from her, if he'd ever been wise enough to keep such a watch in the first place. He'd come back from Roa Kaiten a survivor— and with so few to gainsay him, no doubt he'd successfully disguised his part in the massacre. After all, he'd had the knife. If any of the other survivors *had* been a threat, he was well positioned to eliminate them on the grueling retreat to Necropolis.

She had no trouble gaining entrance to Skulk's rooms. Even Sarnen tended to guard himself by intimidation as much as active prevention, although where Sarnen littered his private chamber with traps—detectable by the triggering objects casually placed about the room—Kerraii stood in the entrance to Skulk's bedchamber and saw nothing.

It was early evening, still the beginning of what had already been a very long day for Kerraii. Early evening saw much in the way of mingling among the Necromancers and Death Merchants. Plotting. Planning. Viewing select fights held in miniature blood pits, lit by magelight into the night. Later in the evening came the more intense ceremonies: bestowal of gifts, drinking of blood, experiments with death magic.

Skulk would be gone for a while. Long enough for her to do a careful search of both chambers in these comfortably appointed and spacious quarters.

But no Nightblade lives long by making assumptions, so Kerraii moved with all the efficient, stealthy speed at her command, listening intently for the signs of encroachment. She confirmed what she'd long known about Skulk—that he had a fondness for Delphane brandy, and kept a luxurious stock of it in a cool cabinet up against the stone wall of his public chamber. *Fool.* It was a perfect way to get to him with

poison, and was protected by no more than an easily picked
lock. She learned he enjoyed furs. All his furniture sported
expertly tanned throws of supple winter skins, bear and fox
and lynx. She discovered he had a notebook hidden in the
cushions of what was obviously his favorite chair, crib notes
for spells he should have memorized long ago. The tooled
leather covers of the bound book showed the signs of much
wear.

She crouched to tuck the book away when she heard the
sound of someone at the heavy wooden door, fumbling with
the heavy thumb latch. Instantly, she dropped into the chair,
arranging herself to look languid and bored.

He might not recognize her right away. She still lacked
her full weight, and it had subtly changed the features of her
face. And she only needed a moment . . .

She forced herself to study her fingernails, and as the
door opened, she glanced up into the surprised eyes of a
young human woman. Too young. She wore not a maidser-
vant's clothes, but what had to be her best finery: pale blue
velvet to bring out her wide, chicory-colored eyes, cut close
and drawn even closer with a leather corset of the same blue.
Her fine blond hair was carefully curled to tumble around
her nearly bare shoulders.

"Come in—or don't," Kerraii told her. The last thing she
needed was for this human child to draw attention with her
lingering.

Visibly awed, the girl slipped inside and closed the door.
In what must have taken all her courage, she said, "Lord
Skulk asked me to wait for him here."

Kerraii didn't bother to rise from the chair, though she
aimed a faint frown at the girl. "You've got the wrong day."

The girl swallowed hard enough for Kerraii to see it, but
said, "We spoke just earlier today. He said tonight. He said
wait in the front room. *Here.*" *Right where you're sitting*, she

meant, and it held as much accusation as anything the girl might dare say to Kerraii.

"He's changed his mind," Kerraii said, as if it were of no consequence.

The girl's lower lip trembled slightly. *Hurt.* Imagine that. Kerraii added, "Never fear, girl, he'll want to see you again." *Except he won't have the chance, if I have anything to say about it.*

But the girl had nerve. And she had a good idea what Skulk's patronage would mean to her family, no doubt. She stuck her soft, still trembling chin in the air and said, "I'll just leave him a token." She plucked a little lady's knife from a strap high on her thigh and cut a long lock of her hair, dropping it to curl around itself on the richly waxed mahogany table by the door. Holding herself proudly, she gave Kerraii one last look—not so much a challenge as a statement—and left.

Kerraii slowly shook her head. "You have no idea what you're doing," she said to the closed door, surprised at the sadness in her voice. *Fortunately, I'm meddling in your business whether you like it or not.* She left Skulk's favorite chair and scooped up the hair, crossing to the small fireplace with every intention of tossing it to burn in the coals.

Except she still had Skulk's bedchamber to search, and although he'd been careless with his belongings so far, she hadn't truly discovered anything valuable or incriminating. And the girl had been instructed to wait in the common room, possibly for her own safety. Kerraii would search the bedchamber for protective talismans, but she'd put this hair to good use as well. So newly cut from the girl's head, it still held her essence and her scent, and would trigger any traps Kerraii missed.

She tied the hair to the end of the fireplace poker and stood in the bedchamber entrance, examining every inch of the room. When she was certain the immediate entry area was safe, she stepped inside the room and looked it over again, using her night vision to see in stark detail in the barely lit area.

There. A finger bone on the floor by the richly carved chest at the foot of the bed, with symbols scratched on its side. And barely visible, a charred rat skull under the little chest of drawers beside the bed.

She found nothing else, nothing other than the usual indications of a Necromancer's lifestyle. Luxury in material, in workmanship, in quantity. Tightly woven silk curtains framed the bed; the scant light gleamed off a dark satin bedspread, a sprawling cover with tiny, detailed embroidery around the edges. A crystal chalice and pitcher sat on the bedside chest; beside them were half-nibbled pastries covered in frosting and sprinkled with death's head seeds. Kerraii snorted inwardly at the sight; only those Necromancers who could not prove their worth with action resorted to the bravado of eating the seeds. Properly prepared, the seeds imparted a pleasurable flush to whoever ate them. Otherwise . . . they killed.

Skulk would never eat them alone. No one did. Without witnesses, the risk was pointless.

Fool.

She decided against a random search of the room. She went straight for the chest of drawers with the blackened rat skull carelessly visible beneath it, and after a thoughtful moment to consider everything she'd ever seen of Sarnen's protections—how they triggered, what they did to the unfortunate who'd triggered them—she allowed the golden hair to brush against the highly polished wood.

She barely dropped the poker in time; only the faintest tingle warned her. The hair turned instantly to ash, filling the room with its stink. The poker itself rolled across the thickly carpeted floor, none the worse for wear. Kerraii returned it to its place by the mantel, giving the smoke time to rise and clear, and when she returned to peer under the chest she felt a thrill of success. The skull, too, had crumbled to ash.

She didn't believe Skulk would double-trap the chest; he hadn't shown himself inclined to that level of caution. Still, she examined the thing from all angles, and then approached it carefully. She pulled a knife to shave the fine hair on her arm, which fell to the surface of the chest—along with some skin—and settled there unharmed. She let her hand hover above it . . . hover closer, and closer, concentrating on her fingertips and alert for any change in sensation.

Nothing.

She brushed her hair from the surface, inspected the top drawer, and eased it open.

The drawer yielded soft scarves and implements with which she didn't waste time. But in the back, under it all, another leather-bound book. Plain to her fingertips, and then to her eyes; unlike the book out in the front room, this one had come at a reasonable price. The rough, thick paper bound within it held tiny notations in a careful hand. She might not have given it a second look if she hadn't realized the pattern of it, that each entry started with a name.

That sometimes the name was hers.

Kerraii: Twice Sarnen canceled policy discussions with the junior members of his tower. Both times he left to supervise Kerraii's training instead. Today I arranged a little extra excitement at her blood pit inauguration. Unfortunately she wasn't killed, but no one suspects me. I count it a success.

The second Zombie. No one had discovered how it had come to be released on her. Even then, Skulk had been working against her, jealous of her successes with Sarnen, learning his skills at her expense.

Kerraii: Faced my enhanced slave in the blood pit today. She prevailed, but no one discovered my interference. I count it a success.

She remembered that, too, the man who'd looked so thin

and yet had been so strong. It had taught her a valuable lesson about underestimating opponents, and she presumed it had been part of the training.

Hers was not the only name in the book, though it was the only one belonging to a Nightblade. Death Merchants were named, as were several humans, a witch or two . . . and Sarnen. Even when Skulk was in Sarnen's tower, he had plotted against the Deathspeaker—with no apparent understanding that he endangered himself unnecessarily with such tactics, rather than targeting Necromancers in other towers of the ring. From what she saw by glancing through the pages of this book, he considered himself bold instead of foolish; innovative instead of unwise. She flipped through the pages, reaching the most recent entries. The words were scribed in a slightly looser hand, a more confident hand. Less secretive, less concerned about discovery.

Kerraii: Thinks she thwarted my efforts to hijack her pathetic batch of slaves, bound for the blood pits. But I cleverly arranged things so I could not lose. I may have lost the slaves, but in her effort to deny them to me, she had them killed—and in doing so killed her own sister. I count it a success.

Kerraii's fingers spasmed against the thick paper, wrinkling it. She forced herself to ease her grip. *My sister.* The slaves, that wretched batch of used-up humans . . . and the single Wylden Elf in the center of them, scarred beyond recognition, speaking for them. Giving them courage. Carrying herself with dignity.

My sister.

Willeta.

I had her killed.

Carefully, deliberately, Kerraii closed the book and put it back in place. No doubt it still held a wealth of information, and plenty of enlightenment about her years in Necropolis. But . . .

She didn't need to know. She'd lived through it, and after this invasion Skulk would understand that although she had long perceived his enmity, she had not failed to retaliate out of fear or inability.

And as for her sister . . .

I would have done it anyway. At the time she'd done it to protect Sarnen's reputation, to prevent Skulk from such a blatant intrusion on Sarnen's authority. Or so she'd told herself. Now . . .

I would have done it anyway. It was the most merciful, the only *merciful fate.*

But Skulk would still pay for it. He would pay for all the little cruelties he'd heaped upon her, all the threats. And he'd pay for his treachery at the settlement battle. That he hadn't meant for it to be such a profound treachery merely made the transgression worse.

In the next drawer, she found the knife she'd come for. Bound in leather, wrapped in silk, placed in the very center of the otherwise empty drawer. A shrine to protect it . . . and to keep it from contaminating those things with which it came in contact. Kerraii untied the leather, unfurled the silk, and let the knife drop onto the bed. It sank down into the pillowy bedcovers. Unmistakably an object of power. A sharpened scapula made up the blade, an upper arm bone the handle. Boiled blood and sinew bound the two together. As a purely physical object, the knife would chip easily, even break. But the symbols carved deeply into the bone showed that its strength lay elsewhere. Those symbols gave the knife its eerie grey cast, an aura of death magic. They gave it its sinister feel; even standing next to the bed, Kerraii felt the knife's . . . thirst. Its hunger for the life force.

This knife could kill even a Deathspeaker.

She hadn't come here to kill Sarnen. She'd come to confront him, to learn about her sister.

I've done that.

Is it enough?

She was no longer certain.

This was her only chance. She was *here*. Here as a free agent, after years of life in Necropolis during which she'd been coerced into submission by lies and treachery. *Stolen years*. Years that had turned her into a Dark Elf without eradicating her Wylden need to fight for the right thing, turning her into someone who fit into neither world.

She didn't hate who she was. This was the Kerraii who had managed to survive those years, and done it when few others would still be alive . . . or sane. She knew her strengths; she did not begrudge them.

But Sarnen . . .

He had stolen from her.

It was time to confront him. To let him know that his conquest of her had ultimately failed. She was free, and she was finding her own way.

Having Skulk's knife simply meant she might actually leave this place alive after all.

CHAPTER 18

420 Tz. NECROPOLIS

KERRAII blew the black ashes of the crumbled rat's skull out of sight beneath the chest of drawers. Skulk might not notice the absence of the skull, but his attention would certainly catch on a pile of ashes he'd never seen before. She made sure there were no stray hairs on the top of the chest, and smoothed the dent of the knife out of the bedcovers.

The knife itself she rewrapped, though she was careful to carry it by the protected hilt. A single Nightblade walking the passages of Necropolis was not likely to attract attention. A Nightblade holding this knife . . . she'd never make it out of Spider's tower. The guards and denizens of the tower might not know the knife was Skulk's, but they'd certainly know a Nightblade shouldn't have it.

She navigated the complex route between the two towers with her head high and her step loose and lithe. Her black eyes, black hair, and refined, angular features had brought her to this place eight years ago, chosen because she fit the look of a Nightblade. Now they protected her, allowing her to blend into Necropolis as though she'd never left.

It hasn't been that long.

Long enough. A short season . . . a life completely changed.

Once in Sarnen's tower, she'd face a much greater chance

of being recognized—but she intended to avoid accidental meetings right from the start. For now, she knew just the right amount of confidence to put into her stride—less than she might have if she weren't trying to blend in, since experience as Sarnen's chosen Nightblade made her accustomed to a certain amount of deference. But she knew where the average Nightblade fit in. She knew the quick assessing glance to give the Nightstalker she passed, and to ignore the slaves altogether. She knew from their appearance and presentation which of the Necromancers had acquired enough power to deserve her subtle but respectful bow, nothing more than the merest nod of her head without breaking stride, and they acknowledged her not at all.

If they'd known what she carried, they would have killed her for it.

In Sarnen's tower, she took an immediate downward turn, spiraling deeper for several abandoned-looking levels, until she paused to draw her sword. She wouldn't be alone long. She came upon an unlit dead-end hallway that few knew about, and the door at the end of it that even fewer knew about: stone set into stone on a revolving axis, with nothing about it to suggest it was a door at all.

Kerraii nudged it gently, knowing just where; it swung open to reveal a scarred passageway. Damage was everywhere—the walls, the floors, the distant steps, even the ceiling. All were missing chunks of rock; all were scored by the strongest of claws. The passage reeked of old blood and beast droppings.

And it wasn't empty.

Kerraii knew it would be guarded. She'd expected it. A Nightstalker held this post under normal circumstances.

Sarnen *had* changed things since her departure.

She'd never expected him to turn a Feral Bloodsucker loose in this passage.

Not even his most highly trained, favorite Bloodsucker.

The creature looked at her, looked straight at her, and of all those beings she'd passed between Spider's tower and this one, the barely tamed Bloodsucker recognized her. He scented her, and his head lifted; he trained his flat black eyes directly on her.

"Let me pass," she ordered him, keeping her voice casual. As though nothing were truly at stake at all.

His wings unfurled with a snap, their leathery folds brushing against the walls; his talons flexed. It was answer enough.

He couldn't maneuver well in this closed space, not in full threat display. The passage left little room for Kerraii to wield her sword freely, but of the two of them she reacted more quickly; she had to. With a hiss of a silent war cry, she leapt at the creature, slashing the tender wing skin under his arm. The Bloodsucker snarled terribly, slinging blood of the darkest red to streak across the walls as he slapped at her with his heavily clawed hand, scraping against the shoulder guard she raised to protect her face and scoring her forehead with hot pain.

The impact sent her staggering back and as she hit the wall she flung her left arm up, raising the vambrace for protection while she scrambled for balance.

Infuriated, the Bloodsucker struck at her, raking along the vambrace and then along her arm, even as she brought the sword up from a low guard and sunk it into his heavily muscled thigh. He struck out at her with the other leg, sweeping it across her harness with a kick that should have opened her belly but instead left no mark, though the power of it sent her back against the wall again, rough stone grinding into her shoulders. "You should know better," she said, her words calm if breathless. "Not with this harness."

He snarled at her and came at her fast and furious, not aiming his blows so much as counting on one of them to get through. Kerraii parried and ducked and slashed and kicked out and in the end slid along the wall to the stairs, slowly going down to her knees. *Not giving up yet*, though her breath came in hard gasps and she bore half a dozen cuts, from scratches to one gaping wound in her sword arm.

The Bloodsucker snatched at the advantage, grabbing the arm to force it out and away from her body, leaving her unguarded. As she kicked out at him, he grabbed the other arm . . . or, rather, he grabbed the leather-wrapped package she bore, closing his talons around the blade end of the knife. He leaned in, his long fangs bared, his snarl full of anticipation, aiming for the soft skin of Kerraii's neck. She kicked him, again and again, landing solid blows on his wounded leg that he ignored, too close to victory to care.

His wings, brushing against her, gave a sudden quiver. His grasp on her sword arm clenched tighter; his entire body gave a strange little jerk, a reverse belch. He hesitated, looking at himself in disbelief, then turned on her with accusation in his gaze.

She'd never seen a bewildered Bloodsucker before. She quit fighting him, understanding it was no longer necessary even if she didn't quite know why. The Bloodsucker gave the odd reverse belch again, releasing her altogether.

Except . . .

The talons curled around the leather-wrapped blade didn't let go. The Bloodsucker whimpered—*whimpered*—and tugged at his own hand. From between his fingers, a dark gray miasma of magic rose, and Kerraii stared, entirely taken by surprise, as the magic swirled out and around the Bloodsucker, surrounding him in a cyclonic mist.

Drop the knife—run!

But she couldn't, no more than the Bloodsucker. And when the air cleared, the Bloodsucker finally fell back—a hard, dried husk of the vital creature it had been. It left its fingers behind, still clenched around the wrapped knife—

though after a heartbeat, they crumbled and fell to the floor, bouncing lightly.

From beneath the leather, the knife continued to glow, pulsing unevenly a few times before it settled into a subtle malicious radiance that made her want to throw the knife far away. There was no way she could control this much power.

She scowled at it. Even after she no longer required its protection, after she was through here, this was a weapon of such power that she could hardly toss it in the nearest trash heap and hope no one found it. Her respect for its original owner, a Necromancer to whom she'd never given much thought, went up several notches. He'd been a man of planning and restraint, to have owned such a thing and yet been capable of thinking in the long view, waiting until he most needed it to reveal its true nature.

Too bad Skulk's bumbling had cut his life short.

Carefully, she climbed to her feet. She'd known the weapon had power; she'd been a fool to think she could control it. *More fool, yet . . . I still need it.*

She couldn't delay. Early evening as it was, as much as Necropolis citizens were out and about and immersed in business heading toward pleasure, surely someone had heard the Bloodsucker's ruckus. Once on her feet, she identified only the arm injury as significant enough to impair her fighting; she would compensate. She closed the still-open door out to the hallway and on second thought carefully set down her weapons to drag the massive Bloodsucker's body over to that door. She jammed it in against the stone with a few well-placed kicks, then took a moment to determine the fastest way to move the body and escape this closed passage. She'd be slowed, but in the meantime, no one could come up behind her.

She retrieved her weapons—picking up the knife with much respect and care, cleaning the sword on the Bloodsucker's stiff corpse—and jogged along the passage, reaching the stairs and taking them two at a time. The passage narrowed, closing in on her. No doubt the Bloodsucker had barely fit at all. She angled her body to prevent the spikes of her shoulder guards from hitting stone, and kept up her pace. Only when she reached the top flight did she hesitate, slowing enough to move forward in total silence. Ahead lay a holding pen, and beyond that the quarters of the witch who oversaw Sarnen's chosen entertainment—for ultimately this passage led to his private, miniature blood pit. Other than Kerraii, only the witch knew of the passage. Those few isolated beings chosen to guard the passage knew only of the entrance, and not where it led. Except the Bloodsucker. The Bloodsucker had fought in this pit. There might be others now.

She'd be on the alert for additional changes.

Without fanfare, the passage opened up into the holding pen; between the pen and the small landing on which she stood thick iron bars blocked the way. She found it empty, and gave the sunken pen a satisfied nod. She'd been prepared to fight her way through whatever creature might wait, but fighting meant noise, and she was glad to avoid it. The empty pen also meant that Sarnen was inclined to experience more personal entertainment this evening, and that suited her plans perfectly.

She sheathed her sword, retrieved her stiff little pick from her boot top, opened the lock to the barred door between her and the pen, and eased into the stinking, gore-encrusted room. Another set of bars blocked the opposite end, along with a door and a lock she picked almost as quickly from the inside.

It was not, after all, the first time she'd done it. She'd once drilled herself on gaining access in this very manner, but for very different purposes: *to save his life, should he ever be beset and all other entries blocked.* She'd done it on her own initiative, reasoning that the fewer people who knew about it, the more effective it would remain. Not even Sarnen had known . . .

At least, she hadn't thought so.

Beyond the pen stood the witch's quarters, and the apparent dead end to the passage.

Halatoa. With her ability to go unseen, she did plenty of Sarnen's eavesdropping . . . and she could be a formidable opponent. She specialized in controlling the dead, not the living, but Kerraii couldn't take any chances. If her luck held, the witch wouldn't even be there.

Peering around the corner of the doorway, she discovered that her luck, such as it was, had not held. Halatoa's wooden door was closed; eerie magelight glowed through the gaps at its poorly fitting edges. Kerraii eased up to the door and heard the rhythmic monotone of Halatoa's chanting. Practicing her skills, no doubt.

Kerraii drew her sword, eased the simple wooden latch free, and pulled the door open just enough to peer inside. She couldn't see the entire room, but she saw the witch herself, sitting cross-legged before a shallow bowl of burning herbs mixed with other, more noxious items. A spare woman of little flesh or muscle, she wore hardly more than the smoke wreathing her body; her dull and listless hair barely reached her shoulders. The smoke seemed drawn to her; only a few tendrils reached out to ride the fresh air currents caused by the newly opened door.

Halatoa didn't notice them, but she sat facing the door, and that left Kerraii few options. *One* option.

Swift effectiveness.

She pulled the door open, took one, two, three long strides, dropped to a crouch before the witch, and had her blade under the woman's chin by the time Halatoa opened her eyes. Halatoa jerked in surprise, and instantly faded into invisibility. A desperate ploy, with Kerraii so close. Kerraii slammed her sword-heavy fist into the witch's face and Halatoa reappeared, dazed and vulnerable. But she saw Kerraii's sword back at her belly quickly enough, and stiffened. She knew the terms of survival.

Kerraii spelled them out for her anyway. "Not a word," she said. "Not a move. Not even a twitch. If the damned incense makes you sneeze, you better do it in a way that keeps me from impaling you on this fine sharp blade."

Kill her. Sarnen's Kerraii would have done it in an instant.

No. That's not who I am anymore. She'd make her own decisions, including this one. *Be merciful.*

Halatoa said nothing. She watched Kerraii with a gaze both knowing and puzzled, understanding her situation but not why Kerraii had put her in it. She started to open her mouth, frowned, and kept silent with effort.

"Go ahead, then," Kerraii told her, taking a quick inventory of the room. Small, crammed to the edges with talismans, parchments, and objects chosen for their power or potential power, it had the untidy look of a workroom in constant use: one project overlapping another, and never any time to sort out the workspace as a whole. "Ask your questions. Or I'll do it for you: Why are you here, Kerraii? How did you get here? What are you going to do?"

"Actually," the witch murmured with quiet care, "I wondered how you'd gotten past Sarnen's pet Bloodsucker."

Kerraii held up the wrapped knife, watching Halatoa closely. Waiting to see what the witch's reaction could tell her.

Halatoa looked at the long bundle, puzzled. But after a moment her eyes widened and she quickly looked away, as if by doing so she could erase the memory of what she'd seen.

Interesting. Kerraii was beginning to wonder how Skulk had managed to avoid killing himself out of pure ineptitude. Halatoa glanced at her again, and this time there was a

difference in her gaze. Resignation, and almost a relief. Kerraii watched it, but didn't let it distract her. "Rope," she said.
"Where in this were-nest is a rope?"

Halatoa said, "You would do me a greater mercy simply
to kill me outright."

"Not my plan." *Not anymore.* Kerraii spotted a coiled
length of . . . something . . . just within reach, and snagged it
with the hilt end of the knife as it protruded from her grip.
Rope, all right. A rope of human hair, with the shriveled little scalps still attached and woven right into the final product. "This will do. Take it. Tie it around your wrist."

With slow, careful moves, Halatoa obeyed.

"Cross your arms."

The witch did as told, and Kerraii set her sword aside—
the blade was a much greater threat anyway, it seemed—and
pulled the rope across Halatoa's back, capturing her other
wrist and pulling so that the witch hugged herself tightly. No
wiggle room there. For good measure Kerraii looped the remaining rope around Halatoa's slight body, tying it off
tightly. "Not a word," she warned, and went looking for a
scarf. She couldn't risk a warning shout . . . or worse, some
kind of spell. In the end she dumped a bundle of bones from
a silk wrapping and tied the wrapping around Halatoa's
mouth as a gag. "Stay quiet," she said, "and you'll stay safe.
It has never been your job to keep this entry guarded. He
knows that."

Halatoa slowly shook her head, and her eyes held no
hope. Kerraii left her that way, scooping up her sword and
leaving the room not as she'd arrived, but through an axis-set
stone door in the wall. Beyond that there was the shortest of
landings, and then another door. Kerraii stood to the side of
the door, as flat against the wall as possible, and on the side
that was barely visible from Sarnen's habitual seat in the
blood pit. If he was there, he'd probably see her anyway. But
if he was elsewhere in the room, or not there at all . . .

She triggered the doorway, holding her breath. Until this moment, she'd moved forward on the strength of her decision and conviction—but now, in the instant of not knowing what lay beyond the door, of *knowing* she had little chance of walking away from this encounter, or escaping Necropolis even if she did, in knowing the enormity of her foolishness . . .

She found herself still holding her breath—as suddenly nervous as a first-timer in the pits, and just as prone to make an error that would result in her death.

I have the knife.

She was only guessing at its power. Sarnen might know it instantly, might have a counteragent to hand. It wasn't too late; she could still turn around and escape this tower with no sign of her passage other than the mysterious husk of a Feral Bloodsucker and a witch who would say nothing simply to protect her own interests . . . and her own life.

I'm doing this. I have to do this. I owe it to my sister. I owe it . . . to myself.

The door opened.

She waited long enough to take a deep breath, and then another. Out of sight. In the silent, palpable tension, something squeaked. Some*one*. With a little breathless gasp of fear, the squeaker rustled with sudden movement, and bare feet padded against the carpet, then slapped against stone.

Mighty Nightblade. She was getting awfully good at chasing off unarmed, untrained bed warmers. This particular bed warmer probably thought Kerraii was the Feral Bloodsucker, breaking through for a snack. If the girl ran true to form, she'd wisely fear for her welfare after leaving Sarnen's needs untended—and if she was smart, she'd disappear into the Vurgra Divide for a while. A good long while.

Or if she had courage, she'd be back with someone both armed and trained.

Just in case the girl had courage, Kerraii waited.

Must have been smart after all. She stepped into the blood pit. As the door closed behind her, she thought she heard sounds from a great distance within the passage behind her. Someone checking on the noise from her fight with the Bloodsucker? Not good. Even if they couldn't get in, not good.

The bed warmer, Kerraii concluded ruefully, was smarter than she was. The bed warmer was doing what she had to for survival. Just as Kerraii had always done. And now she was doing something she *needed* to do instead . . .

She did not pit herself against Sarnen's protections. She did not check the recently vacated bed chamber behind the open door on the other side of the entry room; she did not check the small chamber just beyond the blood pit—the one that gave off a stale, rancid odor, and into which she'd never actually ventured. She'd stood in that doorway a time or two, and counted it close enough. It was a room of death and dark magic and risk; when the door closed, often the screaming could be heard anyway.

Kerraii settled on the polished blackrock blood pit seating, wreathed by shadows and memories, and the screams of pain and fear these chambers had inspired over the years. Some of them had even been hers. But she was safe enough for now. Without the bed warmer to cry alarm, no one would dare enter Sarnen's chambers without him. So she waited. Quietly, composed, her sword sheathed and the bone knife unwrapped; she cut a piece of leather from the wrapping and kept it between her palm and the knife hilt.

Arrogant of Skulk to have put his mark on something so powerful. He would never have tamed this knife, just as Kerraii knew she couldn't control it, either. Not truly. She could *use* it, but that was another thing entirely.

She didn't expect to wait long.

She didn't.

She expected him to come alone, as he usually did when in the mood for something soft and human.

He did.

He strode through his entryway, closing the door with a soft click behind him, only partly visible beyond the half-open curtains that divided the entry from the blood pit. He did a cursory check of his protections from the entry area, and in the process realized his bedroom was empty. Kerraii could see the annoyance in every graceful line of the cowled cloak, and hear it in the barely quickened tempo of Sarnen's steps. The long pause meant he was checking his protections again, making sure the girl hadn't strayed from the safe zone and triggered something. Eventually, he'd reappear to check these more public rooms.

Kerraii breathed lightly, evenly. She concentrated on keeping her heartbeat slow and steady. She sat motionless, awaiting her fate.

He came.

Moving more quickly now, checking protections with a glance, swishing through the divider curtains with assurance . . .

He saw her right away.

He stopped at the top of the blood pit seating opposite her and slowly lowered his cowl, revealing his face freely as he seldom did with others. Those unnaturally harsh features: tight, thin skin, the lips barely adequate to cover yellowed teeth stuck in a vastly receded gumline. *Skeletal*. He let his hands fall to his sides, neatly covered by his long sleeves. "Kerraii."

She gave him the merest of nods. *Yes*.

"I did not expect your return."

"Neither did I," she said, and that was only the truth.

"You were captured."

"I was," she said. "And tortured, of course, but not badly. Ignored, mostly."

"That was their error."

"In the end, yes."

"And now . . . you have returned?" This time his voice rose in a subtle question.

"Not quite."

"I should think not. I taught you better. You can expect no welcome here."

"I didn't come for welcome."

He let the silence lay there for a moment, but in the end he was no less weak with curiosity than the mortal Dark Elves who revered him. "What, then?"

Sitting in the shadows, the deadly knife unobtrusively to hand, she gave him what she'd always given him: the honesty no one else would. "I came to ask you questions, but I've already found the answers. And I came so you would know I'm not rotting in some prison. I'm not dead. I'm *free* . . . and I've learned the truth about my family. I know how you lied to me."

"Dear Kerraii. I gave you hope. I gave you reason to live."

Cold resentment speared through Kerraii's chest. "You stole me from my life, you changed me to suit your needs, and you controlled me with cruelty."

He gave the merest of shrugs, as if those things were of no consequence, and moved to the edge of the blood pit seating—although not without caution. "I gave you status. I drove you to excellence."

Her voice lowered in register, even to the point of threat. "I drove *myself* to excellence. And now I am free of you, and I'll use that excellence to fight you. You and everyone else in this Land who control others for your own convenience." She relaxed slightly, even offered him the smallest of smiles. "Just so you know. The defeats you're about to suffer . . . as many of those as possible will be at my hand."

Annoyance tightened his features even further. He was used to her honesty—but not to the unfettered glimpse of her true feelings. No one spoke to him this way and expected to survive. "Have you a death wish?" he asked her, hissing the words; he suddenly seemed to tower over her, even from across the pit.

"You taught me better than that, too." She stood. "Your enemies gather around you, Sarnen, and now I'm one of them. Only now, you no longer have *me* watching your back."

As quickly as that, he leapt across the space between them. Down the three tiers of seating, across the stained and stinking sands of the pit itself. He did it lightly, as though he weighed no more than a child but had the strength of a dozen men. *Magic.*

With a ferocity she had not seen in him before—not in Sarnen the cold, Sarnen the calculating, Sarnen who channeled his temper into revenge and punishment—he snarled, "What is mine stays mine!"

Startled by his fury, Kerraii jumped to her feet, taller than he by dint of her position on the first step. The knife she kept low, shifting her grip in reassurance. *I have the means to stop him.* "I was never *yours* in the first place."

"Your only freedom comes with death, foolish child! And in death, you truly *will* be mine. *In every way.*" He drew himself up, reaching inside his robe—for what, she didn't know, only that it would mean ready magic, something he had prepared: an amulet, a talisman . . . nothing fancy, not for a magicless Nightblade like herself.

She raised the bone knife. He himself had put her within striking distance, he who should have known better. "Don't!"

He snorted, dismissive even in his anger. "No blade of yours can harm—"

And then he caught sight of it. His eyes widened slightly, an expression Kerraii had never seen on that leathery face before. True surprise. And then, instantly, greed. Want. "Where did you get that?"

"I found it," she said, offhandedly enough to make him give her a quick glance, but his gaze went right back to the knife.

"Give it to me. Give it to me and you may walk away from here as free as you claim to be."

Kerraii gave him only a grim shake of her head. This knife in the hands of one of Necropolis's most powerful Necromancers was not an option.

Not to mention that he'd kill her the moment she relinquished the thing.

"Give it to me! You won't like the consequences if you force me to take it."

"Nor will you. I'm leaving now. And by all means, dredge up a few spirits or Mage Spawn to make my escape exciting. I've already seen what this knife can do. I hope it doesn't take you too long to train a new Bloodsucker."

"You killed—" He cut himself off as the indignation came through in his voice. He'd had that Bloodsucker since before her arrival, and training it had taken years before that. It had known just what he liked to see in the pit; it had learned that fighting its own brutal nature to provide Sarnen with more extended entertainment paid off in the end. It had been pet and more than pet.

She said darkly, "It killed itself, when it comes right down to it." But for all her outer calm, she was coming to realize what a fool she'd been. Sarnen might not be able to hurt her, not with the threat of the knife so close to his chest, but he wasn't about to let her go. And at any moment, someone else might arrive, changing the odds entirely. Normally he'd have ordered that he not be disturbed, but if those below had discovered the blocked doorway, they might report the oddity even if they didn't know just exactly where that passage led, or just how significant the blockage was.

Sarnen might have seen the desperation in her eyes, or his vision might have been blinded altogether by the greed in his own. He made a sudden snatch at the knife; wiser than the Bloodsucker, he went for the handle, clamping his hand over Kerraii's and squeezing. Her fingers ground into the leather covering the bone, crushed against one another, crunching slightly under the strength of his skeletal grip. She gasped, and he only squeezed harder. The protective leather shifted, threatening to put her in direct contact with the powerful object.

Sarnen leaned in close, so close that the scent of hot sand and dried old bird feathers washed over her—the scent of a Deathspeaker, of a man's lifespan spun out in search of immortality at the expense of others. He whispered harshly, "You've forgotten who you're dealing with."

"So," she ground out, making no attempt to fend him off but reaching into her harness with her free hand, "have you!" And she brought one of her small blades down into the back of his hand, grinding between bones, driving it hard enough to prick through to her own flesh.

Sarnen howled—offended, anguished, and not the least defeated. Thick, dark blood trickled from the wound; he snatched at her knife hand with his free hand, jerking her even closer to him. They leaned into each other, Kerraii's breathing jerky with effort and pain, Sarnen's with his fury. And though Kerraii kept her hold on the knife, slowly, slowly he forced it to turn, angling it back toward her. Her wrist strained; her arm trembled. As if sensing prey, the blade leapt to life, pulsing its grey aura, tendrils of magic twining and reaching . . .

Kerraii twisted the small knife in Sarnen's hand, sawing a jagged hole. His surprised cry of pain seemed to startle him as much as her, and she gave the little weapon one more wicked twist, driving it down, unmindful of the blade tip digging into her hand. An involuntary spasm first tightened, then eased his hold.

Instantly, Kerraii jerked her hand back. She didn't try to wrest the knife away; she pulled just hard enough to slide the knife in his grip.

To force the heel of his palm into contact with the blade, even as his fingers still crushed her own around the hilt.

He stiffened instantly with the realization of what she'd done.

"Never," she said, her face up to his, her expression a snarl, "*never* let a Nightblade take the fight close."

The gray tendrils of magic shot out around him, capturing his arm. He jerked at their touch, his body going rigid. Through involuntarily clenched teeth he said, "You'll die with me, Wylden bitch."

Damned if I will. Still tangled in his grip, she struggled for control—except now she wanted nothing more than to free herself, from both the man and the knife. With the lithe flexibility of the Nightblade he'd forced her to be, she brought a leg up, tucked it between them, and unleashed a kick into the pit of his stomach. And again, more solidly, into his breastbone this time, cracking something there, loosening his hold on her, the air driven from his lungs.

And again!

And as the gray miasma engulfed him, Sarnen stumbled back into the pit without her, falling onto the sand to writhe in the grip of fierce, malevolent magic. The power within him fed the knife richly, turning the miasma silvery-bright, forcing it into a pulsing rhythm, one that expanded and brightened and brought with it a low, unearthly howl. Mesmerized, Kerraii realized only just in time that Sarnen's gathered and stolen life forces were too much for even this knife; she flung herself at the closed pit exit and huddled as low as she could, her arms covering her head as the howl built and rose and the pulsating light turned blinding, until with a roar that shook the entire tower, the room flashed beyond sunlight-bright—

And into dark silence.

CHAPTER 19

KERRAII lifted her head with the utmost caution. The blinding light had been too much for both day and night vision; even with her blinking rapidly, the room remained the vaguest blur. *He's dead. He must be dead.*

Could he be dead? She couldn't imagine it; couldn't believe it. He was as close to immortal as a Sect Elf came. One of the original Deathspeakers. The man who had controlled her destiny for so long . . .

She groped for her little knife, discovering it on the floor near where she'd crouched. She'd dropped it to protect her head. Her fingertips found it thick with Sarnen's blood; she blindly wiped it off on her tall boot and sheathed it.

If Sarnen had *not* died, the knife would do her no good now. He would crush her.

Her vision improved a little, enough to crawl to the edge of the pit and survey the results of the deadly conflict. Aches assailed her, her hands throbbed, and her arm bled sluggishly down to her elbow and left bright smears on the pale stone floor bordering the pit seating. *Pull it together. You're not safe yet,* except . . .

Like the Bloodsucker, Sarnen was a stiffened, mummified husk. Bones and tendons showed clearly under the drape

277

of robes over his twisted body. A dry voice in the back of Kerraii's mind could not help but note that with Sarnen, the difference between life and death was not so obvious.

And the bone knife . . . ?

She closed her eyes for a long moment, willing back her clarity of vision as she took a moment to listen. The sounds of someone running up the stairs to Sarnen's floor reached her faintly through the closed door; at any moment someone would be knocking—tentatively at first, if Sarnen had declared himself off-limits for the evening, and then with more vigor. And soon after that, someone would get bold enough to try to force the door.

They wouldn't succeed at first, and that first someone might die in the trying, if Sarnen had protections set. But eventually they'd break through.

Kerraii needed to be gone long before then.

She opened her eyes, sweeping her gaze across the sand. Sarnen's hands were empty; the flat, dull blade was nowhere to be seen. *It has to be here.* She couldn't leave without it. She couldn't leave such a powerful weapon behind. She stumbled down into the pit and fell to her knees, running her hands through the gummy sand, searching with growing desperation and heightened awareness of the threats from without. Only belatedly did she realize the danger she'd put herself in, searching with unprotected hands—she stopped short, her heart racing wildly from effort and fatigue and tension . . . and fear.

Fool. Think! *You'll be the death of yourself before this is over.*

She sat back on her heels, forced herself to take a deep breath—

And saw it.

Or what was left of it.

The inscribed bone hilt, half-buried in the sand, rested just beside her knee. It had no more menace to it; no more power. She let her fingers hover over it, then brushed it with the lightest of touches. It was as dead as Sarnen. They'd killed each other: the knife by siphoning off all of Sarnen's gathered power, and Sarnen by overloading the knife. Time to grab it and—

Or maybe not.

The hilt's inscribed symbols remained intact, including the one near the pommel that identified the object as Skulk's. In this Necropolis society of advancement through assassination and coup, that meant that Skulk, identified as Sarnen's killer, would then succeed him. Deathspeaker Skulk.

Kerraii nearly giggled.

Skulk, the bumbling. Skulk the human, without resources or skills. Skulk without a support network . . .

Skulk the target.

It suddenly seemed better than any justice she could have envisioned.

Kerraii gave the hilt a subtle curl of her lip, an expression that encompassed the dark irony of the fates that hung on this day. Her own, Sarnen's . . . and now Skulk's. Inextricably tied together for years . . . and now split asunder by her own hand. "Good-bye, Sarnen," she told the contorted husk, and got to her feet. An impulse of self-restraint kept her from kicking the body; she left it as it was and headed, none too steadily, for the blood pit exit.

A few more deep breaths, a few more moments; her stride evened out as she got herself moving, ducking through the exit and closing it behind her. Those who came after her would realize soon enough where Sarnen's killer had gone, but it would take them a while to sort out the door's pressure points. And then there was the witch, but even if she described Kerraii as Sarnen's killer, without further evidence they might assume she'd acted at Skulk's behest.

Through the holding pen she went, and into the witch's quarters, fully expecting the woman to snarl demands at her through the gag. But Halatoa lay slumped against the wall, her eyes bulging and open, her face purpled. The hair ropes cut deeply into her flesh, suffocatingly tight. Taken aback, Kerraii could only stare at her. The ropes belonged here. They were the witch's own tool. Only she could have commanded them.

"You killed yourself, then," she told the corpse, rather than face any blame for what had transpired in Sarnen's quarters, even without knowing her intent, or the unexpected turn the encounter had taken. "You should have waited." Skulk would have been glad of the woman's support. Within time Halatoa could have controlled him as she controlled Sarnen's more exotic blood pit combatants—and with Skulk none the wiser.

For a moment Kerraii regretted . . . the woman would still be alive except for her. But Halatoa had chosen her own path, and now there was no one left alive who'd seen Kerraii in this forbidden area. "Stupid," Kerraii said, and added again, "you should have waited." Then she drew her sword again and ran for the passageway, the strength returning to her limbs along with the anticipation of battle. She descended the steps on light feet, jerked the dead Bloodsucker aside enough to slip through the partially rotated door, and gave it just enough of a tap on the way through that the door settled back into place behind her. Down the corridor, smack into a Nightstalker whose divided attention—he seemed focused on something behind him—cost him an eye; they closed so quickly there was no distance to use blades, and Kerraii jammed her guard into his face and left him crumpled on the ground, shrieking as blood ran through the fingers he clutched to his face.

She soon found what had distracted him—she came up behind a small group of warriors headed purposefully upward, making enough of their own noise that they didn't notice her, and then never heard her as she faded back—just far enough back to avoid attention, just close enough to seem like a straggler. Clearly agitated, they shot pieces of conversational speculation at each other as they ran—"Heard there was trouble at the top of the tower," and "Sarnen?" and "Mind your step!"

Soon enough, a full alert would sound.

She trailed them until she had to split off for the tunnel, and it was then that one of them caught a glimpse of her. "Who?" she heard one of them demand of another, and the quick command to follow her. Not all of them; she heard only two sets of footfalls pounding after her, flat-footed running that could not match her swift, light steps.

But she was tired, and tiring. They gained ground on her, and the longer the chase went on, the more convinced they'd be that she ran for a reason, and that they should catch her for that reason. She ran for the long tunnel to the edge of town only because she had nowhere else to go; if she could reach the exit with enough of a lead, it was as good a place as any to make a stand.

Kerraii bounded past a Necromancer, bounced off a witch. Their annoyed cries filled the passageway in her wake but did not slow her, and even through her panting she smiled slightly when the cries finally repeated, more annoyed than ever. She'd gained ground on her pursuers. With luck she'd reach the exit with time to spare. With luck, she might even make it to the bridge, where she could put her back up against something solid and take care of both men before they flagged down help.

With luck . . .

The exit.

Her breathing harsh, almost gasping, she flung herself through the doors and cut her scabbard from her side to jam the latch. It would only slow them a moment, but an extra moment was all she needed.

Curious eyes turned her way as she set her gaze on the bridge, but she ignored them. These were merchants and

servants, exchanging goods and silver and not about to interfere in a Nightblade's business, especially not with darkness fallen and their own night vision nothing more than
normal. Her thighs burned; her calves cramped. She ignored
them, too, and ran for the bridge. *Ah, Maren'kar, I should
have had you wait. I should have had you return tonight.*

But then, who knew she'd kill one of the twelve and be
hard on the run before the night was out?

She heard them behind her. She was slowing, with the
rocky shore still too far away. Torches lit the area, the moon
lit the sky . . . even if some of them hadn't earned their night
vision yet, they'd spot her. She slowed even further, deliberately; if they were going to catch up to her, then she'd take
some small respite before they did. Her body grabbed at the
chance, snatching air and giving her a scant second wind.

Just before they came up on her, she turned to face them,
closing the distance herself. They were Nightstalkers in
training, by appearance, and the chase had worn on them.
Both were right-handed, making her job easier. Kerraii
aimed for the one on her left, coming in fast and using a high
guard that he matched. When she parried his sword to the
outside, making his companion duck away, it left her inside
his entirely open guard. She slammed a quick fist into his
stomach. He bent over the pain, and she lifted her knee,
metal armor and all, sharply into his face.

Bone crunched. Several of them. The man went down in
agony and Kerraii, still moving, swept around with her blade
angled outward, not sure where the second man stood and
clearing everything within her guard. She finished the arc to
find him waiting, breathing as hard as she was and eyeing
her with wary anger. "Friends, were you?" she asked him.
"You'll have to learn his face all over again. Unless I kill
you, of course."

He snarled something and jumped in to bat at her blade,
trying to beat it out of his way. She let her own slender

weapon take the blow, absorbing the energy to circle his blade with her own in a subtle move of no strength and complete finesse, putting her inside his guard. She flicked her saber-edged blade in to slash his chest, then down to cut into his leg. As he fell she leapt away, back on the run—and suddenly became aware of more pursuit: too many to count as she glimpsed them pounding past the last of the merchant stalls. She had to reach the bridge . . .

But knew she couldn't.

Still she ran, sprinting full bore and knowing she wouldn't have the energy left to fight even if she made it. Bloodied sword dripping, she trained her gaze on the ground. She couldn't afford so much as a slip.

She heard the sound of a bowstring, the solid, sharp sound of a crossbow. She made a desperate leap sideways, took a hard slap to the top of her shoulder, and stumbled to her knees. *Not serious.* She knew it; she dismissed the fierce burning—but as fast as she scrambled to her feet, she'd lost too much ground. They'd catch her before she reached the bridge, and there were too many of them to fend off without something to put at her back.

Not to mention that crossbow . . .

Blood splattered down her chest, down her back, warm in the cool, humid night air.

I'm not going to make it.

The night roared around her; it exploded in front of her with a brilliant flash of light. Kerraii flung herself to the ground. *Surrounded.*

Surrounded by what, she didn't know, but she didn't lie there thinking about it. She rolled to the side, instantly adjusting her goals. *The water. It's only a mile to the mainland.*

Not that she knew how to swim.

Another blast, this time followed by a cry of surprise and pain. And as Kerraii hesitated to absorb what she heard, a newly familiar voice hailed her. "Kerraii!" Snow shouted.

Snow. Here.

Maren'kar's deeper, rumbling voice cut through the air. "Come to us, and we'll leave this place!"

Unexpected strength coursed through her body. *Hope.* This time she recognized it, reveling in the thrill it gave her. She launched herself to her feet, and although she'd increased the distance to the bridge by angling off toward the rocky shoreline, her pursuers had lost momentum . . . and certainty. From their approach, they could not see what Kerraii now saw—the troll wizard, deep within the shadows of that space where the bridge met the ground. And Snow, geared for battle, his long rifle at his shoulder and just peeking out from the sheltering bridge.

The crossbow twanged again; Kerraii's back stiffened. But they no longer aimed at her; the bolt bounced off the bridge. In response, Snow took careful aim in the moonlight, and just as Kerraii reached the bridge, the powder rifle discharged in a roil of stinking smoke.

"What if I hadn't come till morning?" Kerraii gasped, grabbing Maren'kar's hand without bothering to sheathe her sword; they gripped each others' hands around the hilt.

Snow slung the rifle across his shoulder, grabbing a pistol in one hand and holding the other back for Maren'kar, still taking aim even as Maren'kar's magic swirled the grit at their feet. "Then it would have been a long, hard night. These rocks aren't the bed I'm hoping for."

"Say good-bye to them, then," Maren'kar instructed.

Kerraii looked at the group of confounded Sect Elves as they stuttered to a stop near the bridge. She looked back at Necropolis itself, and at the skyline of towers, at Sarnen's tower, so familiar she could pick it out from the others from any angle, from behind any growing veil of magic. She looked back at the last eight years of her life. "Good-bye," she whispered, with no regret at all.

CHAPTER 20

FRIZ the horse gave an inquiring sniff at the salve-slathered bandage pasted to Kerraii's shoulder. Instead of shoving his big bony head away as she once might have, she distracted him with a handful of grass, waving away a few persistent flies with her other hand. Shoving him away only made him more persistently curious.

Here in Blackwyn's summer camp, the people remained wary of her. Some of them knew her from before the successes on the Wylden Plateau and in Necropolis, and those folks tended to at least nod in greeting; some of them had been in on her debriefings, and they'd taken to passing a word or two with her. Often they asked about a training technique they'd seen her use, or about the attacks they might face should they ever be up against forces with a Necromancer. Now and then she saw Blaize and Rikka, but as experienced members of the rebellion, those two seldom spent much time in camp. Nor did Snow, although he was the one who treated Kerraii in the most casual manner, which meant he seldom had much to say. But since that was his usual demeanor, she found herself comfortable with it.

She didn't think this place would ever feel like home. It was too alien to her Wylden upbringing, with its brusque, busy approach to life, and at the same time nothing like the dark city that had shaped and hardened her. It might never be home, but she thought perhaps she would acquire a sense of *home* from the people themselves and their companionship on assignments and missions. She hoped.

In the meantime, Friz treated her as he'd always treated her—with easy disrespect as he coveted and nibbled her hair, her fingers, and the hilt of her sword. He hadn't given up trying to get his busy lips around the straps of her harness, either. But he never looked at her from the corner of his eye as though wondering what she was hiding. As far as he was concerned, he knew everything a horse needed to know about her. So here she could relax. Here, and inside the little one-room shack to which she'd returned.

She saw Snow coming down the path from camp; wisely, the animals were stabled and penned below the main camp. She continued feeding Friz the long, thin stems of the succulent grass she'd pulled at the edge of camp, one stem at a time.

"Be faster to give it to him all at once," Snow observed. He was geared up, getting ready to go. Again.

"He thinks he's getting more this way," she told him, and then glanced back with brow arched. "Did you think I was slow to notice how people get uneasy when I spend too much time in my cabin? As though I'm plotting with myself." She laughed at the thought, although it was a dark amusement. "Here I'm out, I'm being seen, and yet it's not obvious there are those who ignore me. Better I feed him stem by stem, don't you think?"

Snow shook his head. "Give them time."

This time she turned to look at him fully. "If I were not, I would already be gone."

He acknowledged this with only a slight tip of his head, and then changed the subject. "I see you're in harness."

During her previous stay, after the prison raid, she'd

adopted more casual attire. Not this time, although she wasn't wearing her knee or shoulder guards. "You have good eyes," she told him, straight-faced, and tickled the end of Friz's creamy muzzle with the last long piece of grass. "The tunic kept rubbing the bandage off. Your healers are good—" *Better than good, but I only needed good and I could have managed without them altogether.* "But this is more comfortable for now."

"I thought it might mean you were feeling up to some action." He tucked his thumbs in his belt and leaned against the sturdy corral post, his ever-present rifle by his side.

She straightened, barely noticing that Friz took advantage and nabbed her last offering. "Is Blackwyn finally ready to put me on the roster?"

Snow looked mildly amused. "You thought he wouldn't?"

Of course she'd thought he might not. She'd proven herself capable, but she'd also gone in and killed a Deathspeaker without clearing it with him. The ramifications from that little development were profound. In truth, Kerraii herself was heir to the Deathspeaker's seat. But she had no intention of claiming the position, or even admitting to her involvement. Only Snow, Maren'kar, and Blackwyn even knew she'd been there.

The initial reports trickling out of Necropolis to detail Skulk's ascension were reward enough for her. Skulk was no more than a small, rudderless craft bobbing around on the high waves of the storm-roused Black Lake, desperately trying not to overturn. The irony of it pleased her, enough so a small smile made its way to her face. Without explaining it, she told Snow, "I made no assumptions."

"We've got a small group of families who need escorting to their new homes in the mountains, goats, chickens, and all. Not a glory assignment."

"Not all the important ones are," Kerraii said evenly.

"True," Snow said. He gestured up at the camp—families, goats, chickens, and all. "How about it? Are you in?"

She glanced at the active area above them, and then higher, to that place that Snow went when he conferred with Blackwyn. "Yes," she said. "I'm in."

Hello, Rebellion. My debts are paid. Now I'm yours.

Dark Debts Scenario
The Village Raid
Necropolis Sect vs. Elemental League

Now that you've read *Mage Knight: Dark Debts,* play out the battle for Kerraii's village with your very own **Mage Knight™** figures, brought to you by WizKids Games!

Mage Knight is a collectable miniatures game in which players take on the role of leaders commanding squads of fearsome warriors to victory! **Mage Knight:** *Unlimited* Starter Sets are available at most game and hobby stores. These Starter Sets contain everything a single player will need to play this scenario: rules, figures, a ruler, and dice.

For more information on the game, and the ever-growing **Mage Knight** world, visit our Web site at www.mageknight.com. If you want to get involved in the **Mage Knight** storyline, know that every month hundreds of stores all over the world participate in the **Mage Knight** Campaign series. Each victory in these Campaigns affects the course of the **Mage Knight** story! Each week's winner receives a special Limited Edition figure and a specially designed pin. Additionally, because WizKids is a strong proponent of sporting play, at the end of each night of Campaign play the participating players in each store vote for the player who was the most fair, helpful, and courteous—and that player gets a special figure and pin as well!

We hope you enjoyed *Mage Knight: Dark Debts,* and we hope that the following scenario intrigues you, whether you are an experienced **Mage Knight** fanatic, or a player who's new to the scene!

Background
In the aftermath of Kerraii's capture, another group of

Necropolis Sect soldiers returns to the Elvish village to capture more prisoners. But this time, the warriors of the Elemental League are ready for them!

Objective

This scenario is intended for two players. The Necropolis Sect player must capture as many enemy figures as he or she can. The Elemental League player must prevent his or her figures from being captured.

Army Size

Two-player game, with 200 points per player. Player 1 represents the Necropolis Sect. Player 2 represents the Elemental League.

Time Limit:

50 minutes

Rules Set:

Mage Knight: *Unlimited*

Preparing the Battlefield

Clear a 3′ x 3′ space for play, and set up terrain as shown on Battlefield Map. Terrain pieces E, F, G, and H are considered blocking terrain. Terrain piece templates can be found on the WizKids Web site. If you don't have access to our Web site, you can use cans of soup, pepper shakers, or any other household object to represent the structures in the Elvish town.

Special Rules

Terrain piece G represents the village longhouse. Each turn that the Necropolis Sect player has a figure he or she controls in contact with the edge of the longhouse, he or she gains an extra 5 victory points. The Necropolis Sect player may gain a maximum of only 5 victory points per turn in this manner, no matter how many figures he or she has in base contact with the longhouse.

Victory Conditions
Use standard **Mage Knight:** *Unlimited* victory conditions, and add the points earned as described under "Special Rules."

Battlefield Map

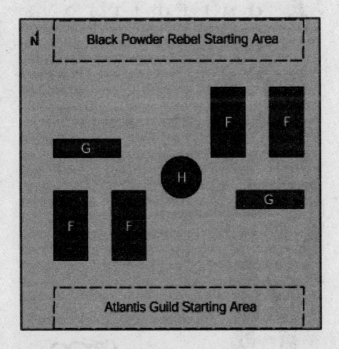

You've read the novel.
Now play the game!

Mage Knight™: *Unlimited* introduces you to the world of collectable miniatures games with fast, easy rules and an intriguing world at war.

www.mageknight.com

Available Now!

THE OFFICAL
COLLECTOR'S GUIDE
— TO —

Volume 1

This perfect book for any **Mage Knight™** fan is a complete, fully illustrated roster of all **Mage Knight**: *Rebellion*, **Mage Knight**: *Lancers*, and **Mage Knight**: *Whirlwind* figures. Plus, you'll find figure listings by collector's number and faction, color photographs of each figure, complete statistics, play tips, short stories, game scenarios, and an introduction by Jordan Weisman, creator of **Mage Knight**.

THE OFFICAL
COLLECTOR'S GUIDE
— TO —

Volume 2

More informtion for the serious **Mage Knight** fan! This book includes complete, full-color photographic listings of all the figures in **Mage Knight**: *Unlimited*, **Mage Knight**: *Sinister*, and **Mage Knight Dungeons**, as well as information on dragons, chariots, tanks, and Limited Edition figures. You'll also enjoy play tips, short stories, game scenarios, and an introduction by Kevin Barrett, the original **Mage Knight** game designer.

www.wizkidsgames.com